What they said about *Malleus Satani -*
The Hammer of Satan:

"Ruthven proves her journalistic expertise with her clear objectivity, her obvious discernment for the truth, and her insistence upon interviewing those at the core of movements themselves."
Lesley Wilkinson
Editor - *Ocular Magazine*

"I found this a thought provoking account which well illustrates the dangers inherent in any religion or social institution which maintains that its way is the only true one and all others are therefore to be condemned."
Editor - *Bulletin of the Welsh Academy.*

"It's an objective, well-researched and well-written book - really smashing a lot of the misconceptions about Satanism from all sides."
Blanche Barton - Church of Satan
Author of *The Secret Life of a Satanist*

"A very interesting book written without the usual diatribe of what we must believe or must do because this is what the media says of us ... It makes a pleasant change to have the subject treated as a serious religion rather than a melodramatic method of selling newspapers."
Dr Meriem Clay-Egerton
Editor - *Phoenix Magazine*

"It was very refreshing to read - for once! - a sympathetic study of the subject, and one which was, not only very well researched, but also managed to avoid ever being dull or academic."

Dr Terry Hale
University of East Anglia

"As well as being very interesting, it was so easy to read. When once I'd started it, I had to finish the book before putting it down. I shall certainly pass the word around that here is a book worth reading ..."

Evan John Jones
Author of *Witchcraft - A Tradition Renewed*

"The purpose of the book is to show that the occult bears little resemblance to its image in literature and the media, and Ms Ruthven succeeds in this admirably, and entertainingly."

Carole Baldock
Assistant Editor - *Singled Out Magazine*

"The author has researched her subject enthusiastically, she is full of information, and gives sharp, incisive judgements wherever necessary to move the story along. For these descriptions alone the book deserves a place in all theological colleges and should be read by every social scientist ... Having thoroughly enjoyed her factual account, there is every likelihood I will be riveted by her fiction."

Trevor Lockwood
Author-Publisher Enterprise

Suzanne Ruthven was born in 1952 in Northampton
and has spent many years investigating the occult.
Those investigations have resulted in the publishing of
Malleus Satani - The Hammer of Satan,
a frank, and at times, startling examination of modern
Witchcraft and Satanism. By discarding standard textbook
references and viewing the Craft from *inside the circle*,
she has produced the definitive work for all those
fascinated by occultism. There are now three more
esoteric reference works in the pipeline, including the
sequel to the *Malleus - What You Call Time -* due for
publication at the end of 1997.

Ruthven grew up in the *Whittlewood* and her first novel
of that name has been based on current research,
attempting to transpose genuine occult lore
into highly readable fiction in the teaching
tradition of Dion Fortune.

Whittlewood

Suzanne Ruthven

ignotus

First published in Great Britain by **ignotus press**
BCM-Writer, London WC1N 3XX

© Suzanne Ruthven 1997

British Library Cataloguing in Publication Data
ISBN: 0-9522689-2-2

Front cover designed by Jim Riley
Printed by A2 Reprographics,
Carmarthen

Printed in Great Britain by **intype**, Wimbledon.
Set in New Baskerville 11pt

Author's Note:

The Whittlewood is the ancient name for the vast royal hunting forest which occupied some 32 square miles, or 20,430 acres of South Northamptonshire from medieval times. Remnants of the old forest can still be traced along the old Roman Watling Street (modern A5) near Towcester. Many historians have claimed that the final battle between Iceni and Roman took place in the area, although to date there is no archaeological evidence to suggest that Boudica or either of her daughters met their deaths in the forest.

The village of Ashmarsh and its stone circle are fictitious
- the magic is not.

The background information relating to the Traditional Craft has been compiled from Evan John Jones' excellent book *Witchcraft - A Tradition Renewed* (published by Robert Hale) and from the surviving material written by the late Robert Cochrane.

.

Dedicated to Fran, Chris and Graham
... true celebrants of the Mysteries

and Hilary ...
childhood companion of the Whittlewood.

Chapter One

Only the very young are impervious to the raw sensuality of an English autumn. Also urbane, successful journalists whose only concept of 'going to the country' was a weekend at a large house in the Home Counties - or a general election. Alexander Martin viewed the countryside with unparalleled distaste. For the past three miles he had negotiated the narrow, twisting lanes in the wake of a lumbering farm vehicle, the driver seemingly unaware of his repeated attempts at overtaking. Finally, exasperated beyond all endurance, he had slammed his foot on the accelerator and risked the hidden dangers cunningly concealed beyond blind corners and tangled hedgerows.

His recently acquired *alter ego*, a normally gleaming vintage Austin Healey 3000, was caked with mud from the damp verges and liberally splattered with cow dung from his abortive attempt at elbowing his way through a herd of bovine complacency. Already perspiring from frustration and flushed with annoyance, he realised he would have to make some immediate effort at restoring his equilibrium; professional egotism would not allow him to arrive sweating and dishevelled for his appointment with, if not actually a 'secret, black and midnight hag', then someone who was rumoured to be a 20th century equivalent.

What on earth had induced him to agree to spending the weekend with a leading expert on the occult, he asked himself for the umpteenth time? Here was a woman who shunned

9

publicity and yet was esteemed in academic circles for her lectures on parapsychology; was retained by a serious national newspaper as a consultant on occult matters; and was even rumoured to have been consulted by the Home Office during a particularly virulent outbreak of *quasi*-Satanism.

She was best known, however, for her highly successful occult novels which had topped the best selling list, with depressing regularity, for the past ten years. She catered for the public's insatiable thirst for matters supernatural and Charlotte Manning had subsequently become a household name. Nevertheless she steadfastly refused to appear on the popular series of television programmes on The Unseen, The Unknown and The Unpredictable.

People of his acquaintance who claimed to know her well, stated she was at best eccentric and one even confided that she was a genuine witch. Photographs of her rarely appeared and those reproduced in the tabloids were extremely unflattering. On the other hand, those who had met her briefly at more private functions had been impressed by her personality and respected her privacy. Her books on the occult were well written and showed a tremendous depth of knowledge in her subject; subsequently over the years she had been hounded unmercifully by the tabloid press and various religious movements, who held her responsible for encouraging weak-minded individuals to follow the "sinister path of black magic and devil worship".

Up on the high road, overlooking the undulating landscape, Alex Martin drew to a halt. Climbing out of the vehicle and leaning against the metallic wing, he lit a cigarette and surveyed the view. Above him, where the land continued to rise, stood a large patch of woodland, a remnant of the ancient Whittlewood, where the monarchs of England had hunted for centuries. Like pagan incense rising from a sacrificial altar, the sweet smell of burning leaves hung permanently in the air, shrouding the countryside in a delicate veil of wafting smoke.

10

The sun, already a low fiery orb on the hill top, cast deep shadows around the small village that lay at the bottom of the winding descent. Another large tract of ancient oaks formed a protective arm around the houses, thinning out as the trees approached a tributary of the local river. Fine mist clung to the waters edge, its wraith-like form held fast by the poplars, adding to the illusion of unreality despite the fact that he was only a stone's throw from the motorway and some twenty minutes drive from the new city development in the next county.

Martin inhaled the last of his cigarette as he drew up the collar of his expensive cashmere overcoat. He was a city-bred animal, and although his eye could appreciate the subtle hue of a rustic autumn and his nostrils relish the crisp, fresh air, his ears could not come to terms with the awful silence. He was simply not attuned to the delicate symphony that hummed unceasingly amongst the tall, dried grasses of field and hedge-row. The cry of a bird broke his reverie and with a sigh of resignation he climbed back into the car to continue his journey.

At thirty-nine years of age he had earned himself a formi-dable reputation as a first rate columnist. His *piquant* style of celebrity interviewing was avidly read by Sunday supplement readers and his agent was inundated with requests from the 'glossies' for regular features. He had written two best selling biographies on currently popular personages and there was already talk of him taking over the editorship of one of the most prestigious monthly magazines (if the current editor, an ageing *prima donna* with a penchant for the bottle, fell down on the job once too often). Even though his features could not be classed as handsome, his looks and Jermyn Street elegance guaranteed him an impressive succession of attractive female company and a regular space in the gossip columns.

He already regretted his agreement to interview Charlotte Manning. There was no pleasure in the prospect of spending a weekend with an eccentric Madame Arcati, who had repeat-edly ignored all requests from the media. The interview had

11

originally been secured by Kate Ward for *Harpers*, but she had been rushed into hospital for an emergency hysterectomy and Alexander Martin was the only person to whom she would entrust the assignment.

"She's too damned elusive for me to miss it, Alex," Kate had gasped painfully from her hospital bed. "Everyone's into the supernatural these days and she's the best there is." So he had capitulated for an old friend and found himself buried in the heart of rural Northamptonshire, instead of attending a private dinner at Whites.

His interest had been re-kindled by the chance hearing of a radio debate, raising the question of the Papal Inquisition's historical crimes against humanity. He caught the name of Charlotte Manning and instead of switching off listened as she fenced words with the eminent theologian, Sir Mathew Roman. Roman, thrusting with scripture whilst she parried with historical fact, until total exasperation forced Theology to stalk out of the studio in a fury, leaving History victorious. The producer had cut the programme - but not before a low chuckle of triumph was replaced by courtly songs of the later fifteenth century.

The houses in Ashmarsh were built of mellow Northamptonshire stone, glowing golden in the late afternoon sunlight. Little altered from their original seventeenth century style, they blended perfectly with earlier cottages which still retained their thatched roofs. The village comprised of one long street, widening out onto a traditional green, complete with solitary oak and a duck pond. The High Street skirted one side of the Green, and on the far side of the grassy expanse was a Saxon Church; this was the obvious heart of the community where the Post Office was located.

A narrow lane ran alongside the public house down towards fields beyond and here were situated two rows of small red brick cottages that had been built for farm labourers in the days when local estates were the main employers in the County.

12

Stuck in a turn-of-the-century time warp, Ashmarsh appeared to have resisted the ribbon-building of modern houses and bungalows prevalent in the surrounding villages.

Reassured by the outward respectability, Alex decided to risk leaving his precious car outside the Saracen's Head public house and began to walk towards the church. He had not gone a couple of yards, when a large silver tabby cat appeared from under a bush and literally barred his way. The arched back and bristling of the animal's fur indicated its temperament was far from friendly and whilst not afraid of cats, he decided to give this one a wide berth.

As he stepped from the pavement into the road, the cat flew at him in a snarling, spitting fury, stopping only inches from his leg. Trying not to show surprise or fear, Alex remained motionless while the cat decided its next move. Finally, having made up its mind that the human was neither fleeing nor retaliating, the aggressive animal disappeared back under the bush - b ut not before bestowing the most malevolent glare that Alex had ever seen on the face of any living creature.

He continued his walk across the green towards the pond. A pile of damp oak leaves, lay drying at the waters edge. Although several cars were parked on the road, there seemed to be no visible signs of life in the village, except for isolated lamps being lit behind small cottage windows where deep stone walls prevented the afternoon sunlight from brightening the dark interiors. Nevertheless, he felt eyes watching him from behind the sightless windows. *"A hive of glass, where nothing unobserved can pass"* he quoted aloud to himself.

Turning back towards his car, Alex was greeted by a podgy sheepdog puppy, who whined piteously as he stroked its black and white head. The dog nervously wagged its tail and began following him towards the parked cars. He was about to order the dog to 'stay', when he realised the reason for the animal's agitation.

Five cats had materialised from under the parked cars, bellies close to the ground, ears flat against their skulls, as they eyed the dog. Alex tried to push away the fanciful idea that the cats were actually stalking the dog but he knew by the way the animal was shivering against him, that his suspicion was not far from wrong. He continued to walk towards his car, not knowing what to do with the dog when he reached it. He could hardly drive off and leave the sheepdog to face the five antagonists alone. As he drew level with the first of the cats, a delicate tortoiseshell, the animal growled threateningly.

The answer to his dilemma came almost immediately. "Patch, where are you?" a childish voice called. The puppy answered with a sharp bark.

A girl of four or five jumped down from the steps of a nearby cottage and began running towards him. "Your dog's been with me," Alex said to her, "He's been showing me around the village."

"Haven't you been here before?" The girl eyed him with the suspicion that country folk have for strangers.

"No, I'm looking for Mrs Manning's house. Can you tell me which one it is?"

The girl looked blank for a moment then her face brightened as she pointed with a chubby finger. "You mean the Cat Lady! It's the last house along there."

Alex thanked her and suppressed an involuntary shiver. After his experiences during the past fifteen minutes, the sound of the 'Cat Lady' felt unpleasantly sinister. He climbed into his car and looked around but the cats had vanished as silently as they had appeared.

Hunter's Moon was the last house in the village. A beautifully preserved Elizabethan farmhouse which, like its neighbours, had remained completely unspoiled by tasteless modernisation. The mellow stonework gleamed in the fading sunlight as a light autumn breeze pulled the last scarlet leaves from an ancient virginia creeper. As the house was situated on a sharp bend, Alex swung the Healey under the stone archway into an immaculate cobbled stable yard, rather than risk leaving it outside to the mercy of any passing local vandals.

In the shadows under the archway he noticed a door and instead of walking around to the front of the house, announced his presence loudly with the iron knocker. A light showed through the fanlight and above the glass he could see a carved wooden mask, coloured red and white - a Japanese charm to prevent evil spirits from entering.

The door was opened by a short, plump woman with bright robin eyes and greying hair that still showed evidence of an unsuccessful home perm. Almost totally enveloped by a large floral, wrap-over pinafore, she was engaged in removing flour from her hands with a tea towel. Half relieved and half disappointed at this seemingly normal apparition, Alexander Martin gave his name.

"Bless you dear, whatever are you doing coming to the kitchen door! Leave your bags and things, I'll see to those later. Come on in. I'll have the tea on in a jiffy."

The busy little woman removed his coat and Alex found himself propelled along the passage into a large main hallway with a simple flagstone floor, expensive rugs and an Edwardian table ablaze with an arrangement of copper and gold chrysanthemums. A bolt of grey fur hurtled past them and up the polished wooden staircase, stopping briefly on the landing to voice an angry hiss in their direction before disappearing into a bedroom.

"I hope you like cats, dear," the woman remarked in a resigned voice, "only there's rather a lot of 'em about. Now you make yourself comfy while I tell Miss Anna you're here. I'm Mrs Carradine and I do for Mrs Manning, cooking and such."

Alex studied his surroundings. He was a firm believer that personality and character could be determined by the furnishings and design of one's own home, and he was becoming more than interested in finding the key to Charlotte Manning's enigmatic *persona*. So far, nothing had been as he had expected.

The blend of warm colour and textures for the westerly facing room harmonised perfectly, complemented by rays from the setting sun that flooded in through open casement

15

windows. The furniture was good but inexpensive antique; the chairs and sofas were an assortment of styles, collected at different times and re-covered in matching chintz. One chair was occupied by a huge grey cat, who barely acknow-ledged his arrival.

Logs burned in the immense stone fireplace; the shelves on either side contained an impressive collection of rare books. A couple of signed Japanese silk prints adorned the walls but the only real extravagance in the room was a huge gilt mirror, flanked by large costly porcelain lamps. The overall effect was one of comfort before ostentation.

The door opened and a young woman entered the room. "Hello, I'm Anna Fenton, we spoke on the 'phone." She shook hands formally and indicated that he should make himself comfortable.

Turning on the tested Martin charm, he tried to counter her cool politeness. "I'm glad I agreed to make it a weekend, I had my doubts up until now."

The girl sitting on the arm of the sofa looked amused but did not respond to his flattery. She was an attractive red-head, perhaps in her late twenties with blue eyes and a perfect complexion that betrayed her Irish ancestry.

"Charly's been delayed in the clinic but she shouldn't be too long."

"Clinic! I didn't know ..."

"I think you'll soon realise that you know very little Mr Martin. But I'm sure your pre-conceived ideas will rapidly disappear after talking with Charlotte for an evening." Anna interrupted sharply.

Her sixth sense reacted to the urbane smoothness of their weekend house-guest and she was trying hard not to let it show. She objected to the confident manner and the patronising attitude. It was obvious that he considered this rural assign-ment a bore and would have mentally, if not openly, treat them like yokels. She knew her employer and friend well enough, however, to know that Charlotte actually found chauvinistic,

16

arrogant, 'bony-arsed' men attractive - and was more than capable of dealing with them.

"She runs an animal clinic," she added by way of an olive branch. "Not for ordinary veterinary problems but for the maimed, the mutilated and the mentally deranged! There are sights out there that make your blood run cold and most of the damaged was inflicted by so-called humans. Mind you, she has her fair share of human casualties too. Local mothers have a tendency to off-load their damaged infants on her instead of the doctor."

Alex pricked up his ears, curiosity prompted by another unexpected facet of Charlotte Manning's activities. "I didn't realise Mrs Manning was a vet."

"She isn't! And neither has she a medical degree but that doesn't stop her from using her healing powers if someone needs them. When I first came here, it was supposed to be part of my job to help in the clinic, but I haven't got the stomach for it. So now we have a girl from the village who comes in every-day."

Anxious to keep her talking, Alex nodded towards the grey cat, who was now staring into the fire, its amber eyes glowing red from the reflected flames. "He seems quiet enough."

"That's Aleister and, like his namesake, a bit of a monster," replied Anna, turning her head towards the window.

The journalist followed her gaze to the figure entering by way of the casement from the garden. "I'm sorry to have kept you, Mr Martin." It was an educated voice with just a slight hint of local accent. "I've been rescuing an injured bird from the barn roof and I climb better with bare feet."

Slightly taken aback, he reached out and took her beauti-fully manicured hand with its long, scarlet painted nails. "Thank you for your invitation."

Although he was only of medium height, barefoot she only came up to his shoulder and was forced to look up at him. Her dark hair was tied at the nape of the neck with velvet ribbon and across her face was a smear of dirt, giving her a waifish

17

appearance despite her thirty eight years. Her eyes were her most startling feature, deep pools of green flecked with brown and fringed with luxuriant lashes. Eyes that seemed to be studying him dispassionately, as if she were appraising blood stock.

Their mutual assessment was interrupted by a clattering from the direction of the hall door. Whatever Gwen Carradine lacked in appearance, she amply made up for with her culinary skills. An oak trolley appeared, covered with white linen and displaying a feast of buttered crumpets, home-baked fruit cake, scones with home-made jam and a selection of sandwiches made with fresh bread.

"Our Gwen's showing off," whispered Charlotte in an unexpected conspiratorial manner. "When she knew you were from London, she made up her mind to show you a thing or two about country cooking. If you take my advice, you'll not try to eat everything she puts in front of you, or you'll explode."

By now dusk had fallen and the heavy curtains had been drawn against the chill of the evening. More logs had been heaped on the fire and another cat had appeared. Accepting his third cup of Earl Grey, Alex related his rather strange encounter with the local band of fur-coated thugs. It seemed far away now and he was able to laugh at his own imaginative fears. His hostess was obviously experienced in handling anti-social animals and could probably offer an explanation for their behaviour.

"Any sensible person would never attempt to handle a strange, aggressive cat without proper equipment," she replied sympathetically when he had finished his tale. "Cats are fully capable of opening up an arm from shoulder to elbow with a smile on their face and without hesitation. As it happens, they were more than likely just tormenting the poor dog."

"So the cats in Ashmarsh have returned to their ancient status and are a law unto themselves?"

Charlotte studied him for a few seconds before replying, trying to decide whether she should ignore the possible mockery in his question. "Current archaeological evidence suggests that during the later dynasties, Egyptian priests kept colonies of sacred cats, purely for the purpose of selling the mummified bodies to suppliants of Bast. Judging from the number of remains discovered, this was carried out on a vast commercial scale and highly profitable for the priests concerned. Hardly reverence for the cat itself."

"I didn't know that," remarked Anna reaching for another scone, "it just goes to prove your theory that priests of any religion worship the fast buck."

"Were attitudes favourable in Europe at any time?" Alex asked by way of an apology but not missing an opportunity to introduce the subject he had come to discuss. "Surely cats were normally associated with Witchcraft?"

"It's widely accepted that Greek traders bought or stole cats from Egypt and due to their natural prolificacy they were soon sold throughout the Mediterranean. Pagan Rome was highly enthusiastic but Christian Rome was a whole new ballgame. Cats *were* later seen as Witches' familiars and thousands of the creatures were killed as a result."

"Back to the priests again."

"Precisely, Christian superstition and persecution, fuelled by the fanatical idiocy of the Dominicans decimated the cat population to such a degree that by the 1400s the species was almost extinct. When the bubonic plague-carrying rats arrived, there weren't sufficient cats left to deal with them. The cats had their revenge - two thirds of the European population died of the plague."

"Divine retribution or the judicial laws of Nature?" asked Alex, openly teasing her.

Charlotte grinned and shrugged her shoulders. "Each to his own theory but there will be some pretty horror struck faces on judgement day, if the Great Architect turns out to be a gigantic ginger tom, with a long memory."

"On the subject of the Dominicans, I caught part of your radio debate the other evening. How on earth did you manage to get involved in that?"

"Would you believe a dinner party dare," Anna answered with an impish grin. "A crusty old bishop offered the challenge, not for one moment expecting her to take it up and when it was, they wheeled in their tame expert ... the rest you obviously know."

"But why did you accept it?"

"Because she'll never miss an opportunity to sock it to the fundamentalists," interrupted Anna, "and it was a long time since she'd had any sport with 'em."

Alex looked in disbelief from Anna to Charlotte. "You did all that research just for *fun*?"

There was a small silence as Anna looked at her watch. "I propose that we let Alex settle himself in before hearing any more of your stories. I want a bath and you need one!"

"Thank you child," retorted Charlotte getting to her feet.

As he followed her along the landing to his room, Alex suddenly harboured the suspicion that Anna's interruption had been pre-arranged. All the cosy domestic talk about cats had cleverly thrown a smoke screen over those activities that really interested him. Authors in the horror genre weren't usually capable of entering into impromptu debates with theologians; they stuck to the research material required for their latest project, and that was that. He had been aware that she lectured on the paranormal, but it needed more than a passing interest in occultism before embarking on a live radio programme, not knowing what your opponent was going to use as ammunition.

Although his reception had been friendly and hospitable, from now on he would be on his guard. Especially if she had given a practical demonstration of her powers of control by manipulating him into a conversation on feline behaviour. In the recesses of his mind, there was the fanciful and rather ridiculous idea that she had possibly stage-managed the whole incident in the village to pre-empt it.

Chapter Two

Setting his breakfast tray aside, Alex threw back the duvet and climbed out of bed. Mrs Carradine had opened the window when she brought in his tray and the sharp perfume of a crisp autumn morning crept into the room. The bedroom overlooked the rear garden and from his vantage point there seemed to be no definite purpose or design in the rambling walled enclosure which surrounded a large natural pool with its own bubbling spring. The paved patio outside the sitting room spilled down through lawns and shrubs in a jumble of broken flagstones and strange moss covered rock formations.

As he leant on the window-sill savouring the pleasing nip in the air, his hostess ran across the flagstones towards the pool. Her outstretched hands over the water produced a series of swirling movements, as the enormous heads of Japanese koi carp, not yet ready for hibernation, broke the surface to take the food that was being offered. Returning to the house, Charlotte caught sight of him watching her from the upstairs window and waved. "Breakfast at nine," she called as she stopped beneath the window, pushing thick dark hair away from her eyes and squinting slightly against the sun. Kittenish behaviour in older women nauseated him but somehow her mannerisms were completely unconscious of effect.

"I've already had a tray."

"That was just to keep you going until the real thing." She replied and disappeared into the house.

As he showered and dressed, Alex compared the physical attractions of Charlotte Manning against those of Anna Fenton. Anna was certainly a beauty and the right age to appeal to him but it was the strange paradoxical quality of her employer that fascinated him more. Human nature being what it is, he mused on the direction his attentions would take if opportunity presented itself.

The previous evening had certainly been pleasurable, the dinner excellent and the conversation much more diverse than he had anticipated. It had been almost two o' clock before they had retired to bed and he had still not managed to broach the subject of her occult involvement.

Over breakfast, Charlotte offered to show him around the grounds and, anxious to be alone with her, he accepted. The house itself was considerably larger than it had first appeared in the gathering dusk of the previous evening. Only the dining room and kitchen overlooked the village High Street; all the other rooms were at the rear of the building, shielded from prying eyes by the huge stone wall.

Apart from the large sitting room, there was also a small morning room, through which they had to pass to reach Charlotte's study. If there were no guests in the house, the fire in the sitting room was not lit until late afternoon but the morning room contained a wood-burning stove that burned all night, offering a welcome warmth to insomniacs. This little room was unimposing and cosy, and from the obvious signs of wear, was used more than any other by the occupants of the house.

The study on the other hand was embellished with rich oak panelling displaying exquisitely mounted illuminated parchments of indeterminable age. Most were in Latin, while others appeared to be written *a la ancien Francaise*. Below these were an abundance of bookshelves, crammed with reference works and volumes of classical literature. An enormous antique desk was the focal point of the room and another log fire, already burning cheerfully, added to the comfort of rich wine-coloured draperies and the sombre hues of an old Persian rug. By way of contrast, the only concession to modernity was an extremely expensive computer system, cunningly concealed in an alcove.

Outside, a series of uninteresting buildings surrounded the stableyard but these were only pointed out to him from an upstairs window. Charlotte casually mentioned that her clinic was there but she was obviously not going to enlarge on its uses and Alex was not sufficiently interested to pursue the subject of rural animal husbandry. Pulling on a pair of stout rubber boots, she led the way through the garden to where a weathered oak door in the stone wall opened onto a whitewashed cow-yard. Here they found a teenage girl busily hosing down wire pens.

"Good morning, Gill," greeted Charlotte, "This is Alexander Martin, a journalist who intends exposing our fascinating life-style to the great unwashed."

The girl smiled shyly, obviously used to her employer's dramatic turns of phrase, and nodded her head in response. "I think that Springer puppy is ready for homing now, Mrs Manning. Shall I take him down to Mr Smyth when I go home for lunch?"

"Good idea. I'll look in on him first."

Charlotte opened a barn door, stepping into a clean, airy pen that contained a very young spaniel puppy. Barely able to fend for itself, the dog watched the intruders with large fearful eyes, its still bloody wounds naked and exposed despite the partial regrowth of fur. Very gently, Charlotte stroked the velvet ears, speaking softly in a low, caressing tone and using a strange incantation that Alex could not identify. Gradually the heavy breathing subsided and the dog snuggled down into the fresh straw.

"What happened to him?" asked Alex as they closed the door of the barn and walked towards the wire gate of the compound.

His companion thrust her hands deep into her trouser pockets and kicked a cobble stone. "He was shot with a crossbow bolt. Luckily our vet, Paul Kerrick, performed a brilliant piece of surgery that saved his life. One of the lumbar vertebrae had been fractured, but luckily there was no damage done to the spinal nerves and he survived. No one came forward to claim him, so we've been nursing him back to health until a good home could be found."

They walked in silence for a few moments. "And you don't know who was responsible?" prompted Alex.

"Oh yes. There was a witness to testify and EYES, the local animal welfare group, are bringing a court action." Then changing the subject. "This is the start of my land which has over thirty acres of forest, ponds, river boundary and some meadowland. We don't do much with it since I can't afford the luxury of a working farm. Most of this meadowland I hire out to a neighbouring small-holder and the woods are left to the wildlife."

"If it's such a responsibility why not get rid of it?" asked Alex quite seriously.

"Because this is the largest part of what remains of old Whittlewood Forest and right in the middle of it is a stone circle reputed to be older than Stonehenge. For want of a better explanation, I feel as though I'm the custodian of a slice of ancient history."

"Isn't that where those two young girls were murdered a couple of months ago?"

"That's right and the press had a field day suggesting all manner of ritual sacrifice and devil worship had taken place there. I'm afraid I don't appreciate that all publicity is good publicity and Ihave no empathy with tabloid journalism. Especially when they start one of their smear campaigns."

"Did they get the people involved?"

"Two of our local lads were arrested and are being held for a psychiatric report. It was a pretty bloody affair and quite horrendous for the families involved, so the least said about it all the better."

"You can't have a double murder take place on your door-

24

step and say nothing about it!"

"Why not? Everything that is written or repeated is just idle speculation. Only the people actually involved know what really happened and two of them are dead. I merely suggest that we wait until all the evidence is readily available before we start passing judgement. Perhaps then there will come a time for evoking a Higher Law."

Alex roughly took her arm. "What do you mean?"

"About what?" There was genuine surprise in her green eyes as she slipped from autocrat to innocent with consummate ease.

He released her abruptly, wondering how on earth he was going to attempt a serious interview with someone whose personality was as elusive as a butterfly. He should remember that she was a writer of occult fiction and that it was perhaps only natural that her vocabulary should take on a dramatic note. Perhaps she was studying his reaction for the plot of a new novel and the spiel about the double murder and taking drastic measures was rehearsed to set the mood. And in her book, of course, "evoking a Higher Law" could simply refer to *karma*. Nevertheless he found himself suppressing a shudder as a tendril of apprehension caressed his spine.

Skirting around one of the smaller pools, they came to the start of the wood, where the ground was already a thick carpet of bronze leaves. Thin sunlight filtered through the branches but once out of the warming rays, the morning air was chilly. Alex was conscious of that awful stillness as the Whittlewood closed in around them, and again he felt a slight tremor of apprehension. For sometime they walked through the trees in silence, the only sound the crackling of dry leaves under foot, until he could bear it no longer.

"Do you want me to write about your animal clinic?"

"No," she replied firmly, "I don't feel that you have the understanding or sympathy to tackle that particular story."

"There's been no complaints so far" retorted her companion, offended by her refusal.

25

They had continued walking through the wood and came to a clearing that contained an impressive stone mausoleum. What could be seen of the stone through the thick growth of ivy showed a dramatic frieze of nymphs and satyrs. The tomb was some twelve feet square with an iron grill embedded in the stonework to shield the only window from curious eyes. A solid wooden door with its compliment of iron grills and hinges was clear of the encroaching ivy but the most remarkable thing about the place was a life-size marble statue of the god Pan.

The statue was so perfectly executed that it was breathtakingly beautiful. Curved horns grew from a mane of curling hair which framed high cheekbones and a sensuous, but humorous mouth. The eyes, although sightless after the fashion of statuary, gave the impression of superior intelligence and hidden knowledge, too lofty for mere human minds to comprehend. The sitter had been a handsome youth, confident of his good looks and well developed body. The hands holding the pipes were slim and elegant, contrasting sharply with the coarse, curling hair of the goat legs and cloven hoofs. The overall effect of the statue was one of erotica rather than ominous idolatry.

"Don't you think he's beautiful?" asked Charlotte after he had stared at the figure for some time.

"Why do you leave it out here?" Alex responded, forgetting his annoyance at her rebuff.

"Where else should Pan be found but in woodland?"

Suddenly he became aware that her smile was an exact duplicate of that carved in cold marble. She stood with one hand on the arm of the figure and the other resting lightly on its shoulder, the scarlet of her nails like blood against the smooth sculptured surface. The combined expression of her mouth and eyes gave the same mocking intimation of secret knowledge. It was almost as though she had been practising the smile in a mirror and, remembering a similar passage from John Fowles' *The Magus*, he was certain now that she was using him in an experiment to gather material for her next book.

26

"Where did you find it?" The question came abruptly in order to stop her game.

Charlotte moved away from the statue with a characteristic shrug of her shoulders. "My Father found it outside a junk shop in Cumbria when he was researching some local legends. He thought my Mother and the Pan were so alike that he must have been a relative!"

For the third time that morning, Alex felt as though someone had walked over his grave. "People have told me that you are a witch!" It was a statement, not a question. She turned to confront him with an expression of distaste.

"Tell me Alex, why do you waste your time with all this *exposé* rubbish? You're a brilliant writer, that's why I agreed to see you, but why do you concern yourself with trivia just to feed the insatiable plebeian appetite for scandal?"

A flash of anger diffused his face. "Some of the top magazine editors in Europe happen to disagree with you."

"But what happens when you're no longer *fashionable*?" She made it sound like a dirty word and without waiting for the explosion, she pressed home her attack. "If only you would use it, you have the talent and the insight to delve deep into the entrails and search out the very soul of your subjects. Forget the grubby popular heroes who will be forgotten tomorrow and seek out those who know what it's really like to have life flowing in their veins! Everyone has a buried secret Alex, even you, and you wouldn't want your faithful public chewing on your bones. What gives you the right to do it to others?"

His grey eyes narrowed with fury. "You bitch!" was all he could reply in his confusion and anger at her unprovoked attack. "You know nothing about me."

Dumb with anger at this stranger's unexpected and unwarranted slur on his talent and achievements, his brain whirled in retaliation against Charlotte Manning and her softly spoken rebukes. If there was some dark secret that could destroy the unshakeable calm of this infernal woman, he would seek it out. Media-hype, directing public hysteria towards certain eminent

27

occultists, *had* culminated in victimisation, the burning of property and physical assault. This was the power he possessed.

Almost as though she were reading his mind, Charlotte reluctantly played her master card, demonstrating the unearthly power that *she* possessed. " How many people know that Sir Trevor Barnstaple's daughter was pregnant by you when she committed suicide?" she asked softly.

Alex felt his anger evaporate under the impact of words which activated a whirlpool of conflicting confusion, betrayal and pain of remembrance. Surprise weakened him and as he leaned against the wall of the tomb, his fingers entwined in the ivy for support, he could only ask weakly, "How did you know?"

"From the anguish you carry inside you. But that isn't important just now. I use it only to illustrate the pain and hurt *you* would suffer if it were made public knowledge. You would be judged by those who had no insight into the true situation and would be unable to defend yourself - or her." There was no threat in her voice, only a soothing balm of understanding and compassion.

Tears pricked at the back of his eyes as he fought to regain his composure. "We wanted to marry but the old man wouldn't give his consent. She told him she was pregnant and so he had her shipped off forcibly to a private clinic. She escaped before they could persuade her to go through with the abortion and tried to reach me. Her father got there first with a couple of his heavies and I spent the next month in hospital. When I got out, I found she'd thrown herself under a train. He'd told her that he'd paid me off and that I'd run with the money - because she couldn't find me, she believed him"

Gently her hand reached out and brushed the rumpled brown hair back from his face. "And it concerns no one but yourself," she said softly and for some deep instinctive reason he actually believed her.

Already the emotionally charged confrontation was receding as Alex realised he was experiencing a feeling of lightness on a subject that had been taboo for more than ten years. Not even his closest friends were aware of the painful episode which he had just related to a total stranger. It was almost as though she had drawn out all the inner pain of stifled emotion that had remained twisted and rotting in the dark recesses of his memory for a decade.

There was also a clearness of vision over the direction his career had taken. He had always wanted to be recognised as a great writer and he HAD sunk into a quagmire of popular journalism that afforded him no real satisfaction or sense of achievement, except for the fame and financial rewards. Charlotte was right, it *was* time to put the mundane and trivial behind him and achieve something worthwhile. Somehow, and for whatever reason, she had scraped down to bare bone and made him aware of his wasted talents.

The morning was clouding over as they walked back towards the garden gate and although Alex felt that a spark of warmth had been kindled between them, he could not ignore the suspicion he still harboured in his mind. He felt as though she had pushed him over a cliff in order to prove that he could fly; but why he had been pushed in the first place remained a mystery. Whilst he pressed her to discuss what had happened between them, she remained mute.

Later that day, Alexander Martin stopped the Healey 3000 in almost the exact spot he had chosen some twenty four hours before. Persistent autumn rain had set in just before lunch and through the fine drizzle, the village below was almost totally obscured by a damp haze. The journalist experienced a feeling of *deja vu*, as though time had shifted and he was coming out of a strange dream.

To pass the time until lunch, Charlotte had invited him into her study and in the warmth of the log fire, he had outlined his basic ideas for an interview, absent-mindedly stroking one of the strange grey cats as he talked. Anna had joined them for an excellent lunch and advised Alex to make a move while it was still light, due to the unexpected mists that occurred at that time of the year. He was not sure whether Charlotte had put her up to it, especially when his hostess made no attempt to delay his departure. Coffee was served in the sitting room but the intimate atmosphere of the study had evaporated with Anna's arrival. The conversation continued on the subject of Charlotte's work, how and where she found her ideas and what beliefs she actually held.

"I'm very much against putting labels on definitions of belief. If I were to seriously consider an established philosophy it would probably be similar to Buddhism, but like all organised religions that also has excessive ritual and dogma. Although less than most." She leant forward to refill his cup. "You?"

"Sceptic."

"What few journalists I have talked to, seem to prefer ideas set out in paragraphs, in words they can spell. For the benefit of your readership I'll quote you a passage by William James which is far more eloquent than I could ever be. Bearing in mind he made his observations in 1890, very few original ideas have actually been added since." She indicated with her hand that she wished him to use his small tape recorder and removing a book from the shelf, began to read:

"'The phenomena are there, lying broadcast over the surface of history. No matter where you open its pages, you find things recorded under the name of divinations, inspirations, demoniacal possessions, apparitions, traces, ecstasies, miraculous healings, productions of disease and occult powers, possessed by peculiar individuals over persons and things in their neighbourhood.

'We suppose that mediumship originated in Rochester and animal magnetism with Mesmer but one look behind the pages of official history, in personal memoirs, legal documents, popular narratives and books of anecdote, and you will find that there never was a time when these things were not reported just as abundantly as now ... a public no less large keeps and transmits from generation to generation the traditions and practices of the occult ...'"

There was a brief silence as she replaced the book.

"Do you want me to quote James?"

"As you wish, but I doubt if either you or I could explain any better where my ideas come from. I don't go in for gore, my style is to create a fictional story around historical phenomena that hopefully encourages people to consider the paranormal as something perfectly natural."

"Natural!"

"Just because there is no *immediate* explanation on tap, it doesn't mean that it's unnatural or that a solution doesn't exist. Accept that Jeanne d'Arc was merely an accomplished clairvoyant and a legend falls to pieces. Gilles de Rais is reported to have had some rather unsavoury habits but it doesn't make him a warlock. And the poor old Maquis de Sade. If his personal peccadilloes were so abhorrent, why weren't most of the French clergy and nobility incarcerated with him? He was simply imprisoned because his mother-in-law applied to the King for a *lettre de cachet*, which was a *quasi*-legal method of disposing of embarrassing relatives. Lastly, in our own time, Aleister Crowley. Was he an evil pervert or a genius? It merely depends on where you go for your source material."

Charlotte Manning remained an enigma. He was still unsure whether the different nuances of character and mood were a sort of game, reserved for strangers to see how they would react in her domain. Perhaps she cultivated spookiness in keeping with her professional image. Just as he felt he had begun to see the real woman, she slipped away from him like a wraith. Of one thing he was sure, on her chosen subject she was one of the most brilliant and fascinating conversationalists he had ever encountered. And if her brief, but effective, demonstration of telepathy had been genuine, then she was even more remarkable than he had imagined.

Still, he had his material and had promised to contact her when the article was ready for submission. He had indicated that he would be more than willing to deliver it for her approval but, like Fowles' magus, she had ignored his invitation to invite, denying him the opportunity to return to Hunter's Moon. As he drove out from under the archway, she was standing in the shelter of the stone doorway to wave goodbye and as the grey drizzle closed in around the car, he felt a brief pang of regret that their acquaintance had not been of a longer and more intimate nature.

Chapter Three

It had been a week since Martin's visit to Hunter's Moon and as no telephone call from Charlotte Manning had been forthcoming, he was left with no alternative but to post a copy of the finished interview for her approval, enclosing a brief note of thanks for her hospitality. Charlotte read through the typescript and then re-read the accompanying letter. Anna reached across the breakfast table for the neatly typed sheets of paper and after scanning the pages breathed an enthusiastic sigh.

"This is really very good. You should call and thank him. After all, he did have a pretty lousy time with you playing the wood-sprite and giving him the creeps. He must have driven off into the rain thinking the entire household was populated by lunatics and still writes a marvellously understanding and sympathetic view of your work. You don't deserve it."

Charlotte had not told Anna all that had happened between herself and the journalist in the wood but her companion was shrewd enough not to ignore the potent chemistry between them.

"Not only does he refer to you as the *High Priestess of Modern Gothic Horror* but likens you to Machen and Le Fanu. What does the letter say?" Charlotte handed it over but the letter only contained the normal civilities and a wish to meet her again in the near future. "You really ought to invite him back, if only to apologise. Besides, he's the first chap to come along since I've known you, to make any sort of impression. So I deduce that you must find him attractive."

"Admittedly he does have a certain animal magnetism."

"More so than Paul Kerrick?"

Charlotte frowned for a moment. "Paul and I are just friends."

"And I've never been able to understand why? However, the issue in hand at the moment is Alex and whether a break from all those cerebral types would be beneficial for you in your present condition."

"What condition?" demanded the writer.

"You're decidedly crabby at times and even more so since the Alex appeared on the door mat. I therefore diagnose an acute attack of frustration. I won't be back 'til late. Bye."

"Balls!" muttered Charlotte as Anna disappeared through the door.

For most of her twenty seven years Anna Fenton had confined herself to city living and if it had not been for the overwhelming backlash of an unhappy affair, she would never have applied for the position advertised in *The Listener*. The interview had proved successful and she had been invited to spend a probationary month at Hunter's Moon. The "responsible and demanding position" had offered her wider opportunities than her previous executive secretarial jobs and within six months, Charlotte had been so impressed by her efficiency and enthusiasm that she had been entrusted with valuable research assignments.

Although many editors had never realised it, Anna had ghosted many of the articles ostensibly written by Charlotte Manning for the various monthly magazines, because her employer considered them a waste of time and only agreed to produce a certain number because her agent demanded it in order to publicise her books. The only real setback had been Anna's reluctance to work with the animals that arrived at the house for treatment. This minor difficulty was overcome by employing Gill Cross, a sixteen year old village girl, who had no fear of the more unattractive aspects of nursing sick or injured animals.

That had been five years ago. During that period they had become firm friends and there was very little about Charlotte that Anna didn't know. Although she had been used to high-profile bosses, working for her new employer had opened up new horizons and challenges. Sometimes on Charlotte's behalf, she found herself travelling all over the country visiting public and private libraries, studying archives or exploring historical sites. She had also met some of the most colourful members of the literary profession.

As a result of the immense amount of research, she had also made one of the most important decisions in her own personal life. Having been brought up a strict Catholic, she now found herself questioning the articles of faith drummed into her head by the nuns at the convent-school. Charlotte's own books had exposed a raw nerve concerning the persecutions of witches and heretics by Papal decree, and the more Anna studied, the more revulsion she felt for the Church that had formulated her early thinking. Three years after her arrival at Hunter's Moon she had been initiated into the Traditional Craft.

Following Anna's departure, Charlotte mused over a message received earlier that morning and the concern over its contents was finely etched around her eyes. As so often happened when history was suddenly catapulted into the 20th century, it evoked strong impressions of strange places. The warmth and soft cushions of the morning room were replaced by the gloom and spartan facilities of a medieval garret. The thick stone walls ran with damp and high above in the darkness, seasoned timbers blackened from countless fires supported the broken tiles, through which, a shaft of weak sunlight filtered.

Idly she watched the thousands of tiny dust particles that danced in the solitary beam. The high narrow slits in the walls admitted very little daylight but the growing roar from the crowd outside travelled up through the narrow apertures and caused her to shiver with apprehension. Hostility hovered in the air but this was not the time for panic. Her face was veiled in shadow and her movements slow and deliberate as she mixed herbs with pestle and mortar.

The room was ill-furnished with one small straw palliasse that had seen better days, and apart from a crudely carved bench and table, the only item of any interest was the huge iron bound chest that stood against the wall. It was from this chest that she carefully selected phials and powders and administered them to folk who came begging for help in curing family sickness or the animals on which they depended for their existence.

The people had stopped coming since the priest in his black robes had caused such a fervour after being forcibly removed from the garret. In response to his thrusting, grimy hand between her legs, she had twisted free and competently kneed her molester in the genitals. From this episode had sprung malice. The acrid smell of smoke hung in the air and becoming aware of the subtle changes in the cacophony of sound outside, she detected the crackle of flames as they embraced the old timbers on the lower floors.

The howls from the mob grew louder as the fire reached upwards towards the lair of their prey. The garret was now full of smoke and through the ill-fitting boards, the scarlet tongues of flame could be seen igniting the timbers. It would only be a matter of minutes before she was cast down into the inferno below. Taking a phial of poison from the chest, she quickly drained the contents and slumped to the floor. There was a deafening crash as the fire ate its way through the timbers, bringing down the ancient stone walls as the supporting beams collapsed with the intense heat. As the showers of sparks flew into the air, her spirit drifted away into the light, leaving her persecutors to flounder alone in darkness.

Back in the present, Charlotte reflected that it still didn't take much to turn the mob against an individual or minority group - even in the latter part of the 20th century. The event she recalled so clearly had taken place five hundred years before, but a carefully orchestrated campaign by the media and religious fundamentalists had little difficulty in periodically inflaming public opinion against any form of occultism and its practitioners. Already the tabloid press had suggested that the murders of Alison Webber and Gail Masters were linked to Witchcraft, solely because their bodies had been found inside the Ashmarsh stone circle. For this reason, she was apprehensive about the message pushed under her door earlier that morning.

Anna had been encouraged to spend time with friends and, finding herself in the rare position of being alone, Charlotte told Gwen to take the day off. After a moment's consideration, she put away her files and reference books and slipped out into the cool of the late morning. The air was sharp and lifting her head she sniffed the wind, detecting the presence of rain. A tiny wren shrilled out a warning as she approached the ivy strewn wall.

She walked through into the clinic with its hundreds of bottles and phials of strange coloured liquids. This was her secret domain and not even Anna entered this *sanctum sanctorum*. Converted from the old dairy by her father so he could pursue his fascination with herbal medicine, the whitewashed walls had witnessed the perfection of the lore of natural magic. Here were secreted the medieval collection of grimoires and artifacts acquired over the years by Peter Neville and kept hidden away from curious eyes. Possession of such objects in former times would have consigned their owners to the flames.

When barely able to read the scrawling Latin and Old French herself, Charlotte had been taught the basic principles of preparing the potions for healing throughout her childhood. The knowledge she had learned had been used

37

to save the lives of many of the creatures that had come under her protection. Although she was never tempted to used the potions to benefit those outside her immediate circle, her father had been well known locally for his healing abilities and charmed medicines. As Anna had informed Alex during their initial conversation, Ashmarsh mothers still preferred to consult Charlotte rather than the local GP about childhood ailments and injuries.

The dreaded wolf's bane actually contained properties for curing gout and rheumatism; the leaves of the yellow-flowered agrimony and bark of ash cured jaundice and diseases of the liver or blood. The delicate wind flower soothed inflammation of the eyelid, whilst the juice of the beet was good for headaches and toothache. All these ancient cures and remedies that were once used as evidence of the ancient Craft were now carefully catalogued and recorded on computer.

After a moments hesitation, she passed through to the garden and into the woods, walking slowly and stealthily as her ancestors had done, using forgotten senses to catch the sound of a rabbit scurrying away in the undergrowth or the scent of a deer. Magpies screeched and chattered amongst the bare branches of trees at the edge of the wood, preferring open fields and hedgerows to the cover of the old forest. Long considered to be birds of ill-omen in Christian superstition, the pagan Iceni honoured them with tributes, for their harsh cries warned that wolves were in the vicinity and that men should protect their livestock. Although the Iceni weren't local people, many of their ghosts still haunted the Whittlewood.

November was fast approaching. The long bleak days steeped in persistent mists lasting until the weak noonday sun dispersed the last coils of dragon's breath from the land. This was the Celtic *Samhain*, the ending of the old year when all natural laws were suspended, giving spirits free reign of the deserted lanes and woodlands, and enabling the living to communicate with their departed ancestors. These were

38

the days when Herne the Hunter led the Wild Hunt across storm-cloud skies. Halloween and Bonfire Night were only a week away; two pagan festivals enthusiastically celebrated by modern man, unaware of the ancient gods to whom he still unconsciously paid homage.

Whittlewood Forest had occupied vast stretches of present Northamptonshire since pre-Celtic times. The dense oaks, the most sacred of trees, gave rise to legends of strange and fearful nature spirits who inhabited the sacred groves. Impassively the stately trees watched the passage of time and kings, and as the wooded acres diminished through the ages, the old fireside stories gradually lost their terror. Old gnarled trees that had stood for centuries, crashed to the ground and in their place, fresh green shoots pushed their way through the undergrowth towards the sunlight, maintaining the eternal circle of life. The mystic pulse of Nature was beating as strongly as ever.

Charlotte made her way to the Neolithic circle and allowed her mind to examine the impressions made on the earth and stones. She wanted to make a tentative exploration herself prior to the meeting scheduled for the late afternoon and was anxious that her judgement was not clouded by the recent deaths of the two girls. The circle had remained hidden amongst the trees for centuries and had been a boyhood discovery of her father's. Overgrown by bracken and brambles, and undermined by saplings, many of the stones had been uprooted by Nature encroaching on the sanctuary.

Peter Neville believed that the circle had been erected in a forest clearing already sacred to an earlier people, and that their Neolithic successors had merely utilised a former holy place, as was the case with the Rollright stone circle in neighbouring Oxfordshire. The Ashmarsh circle did not, however, attract visitors since the stones were buried to such a depth that the tallest stood only a foot above the ground, with others only inches above the grass.

Crouching down in the centre of the circle, Charlotte

39

placed her hands flat on the earth, immediately sensing a tingling along her arms which caused the hair on her neck to rise. There *was* a presence and a strong one, but she doubted whether the spirits of two teenage girls could produce such intense psychic activity. Both had been killed before the assassin had inflicted the multiple stab wounds, but even such a violent and terrifying demise would not cause a psychic disturbance of such proportions that it was still detectable to such a degree after a lapse of four months.

It was late afternoon before she returned to the house with senses sharpened and skin tingling from the invigorating exercise. The fire had burned low and as the flames licked around the fresh logs, Charlotte waited for her visitor. She heard a car pull into the stableyard and moments later Paul Kerrick came through the door of the morning room.

"Merry Meet," he greeted and she repeated the words.

As dusk deepened into darkness, they sat in the firelight drinking coffee and Paul finally revealed the reason for his mysterious message. "We need your help. The entire village has doubts about who actually killed the two girls and as you know, both Jennie Hughes and Barbara Masters are members of the coven. They both believe Michael incapable of hurting Gail whatever the circumstances. Anyway, Lydia decided to pay a private visit to the circle and attempt spiritual contact with anything that might throw light on the matter."

"I don't think I'm going to like what I'm about to hear."

Paul gave an apologetic grin. "You won't. Lydia made contact all right and received a blow in response that nearly took her head off. I've seen the black eye and it was a vicious one. She thinks she heard a voice talking in some strange tongue but she couldn't be sure whether it was inside her head as a result of the blow, or genuine communication. Fright and pain forced her to retire."

"Lydia is extremely accomplished I know, but you don't think she could have made a mistake with the evocation?"

"She says not. What she is also certain about are the

impressions she received. The presence didn't radiate evil. She felt a sense of outrage rather than malevolence. She also said that she had the notion that it was rather contemptuous of her efforts. That's why she's asked you to help."

"Lydia wants me to pull rank on our psychic visitor?" She leant back amongst the cushions on the sofa and gave a sigh. "You know I don't like interfering in coven activities but I don't suppose there's much choice. After receiving your message, I went up to the circle myself and there is definitely something alien there. It's too strong to be caused by the shades of two sixteen year olds, murdered or not."

"The main concern is that Michael and his friend are being questioned continuously by psychiatrists and social-workers and we all know what that will eventually produce. Both boys owned up to being there but neither claim to remember anything else that happened. The post-mortem showed that both girls had take quite a large amount of some hallucinatory drug, which also showed up in blood samples taken from the boys."

Although concern for the two boys in custody was of paramount importance, it was a relief that neither the police nor the media had discovered that the mothers of two of the youngsters involved belonged to a coven. There had been mention of 'ritual killing' in the original reporting but after the first rush of sensationalism this had petered out for lack of kindling for the tabloid fire. Both Charlotte and Paul were only too aware of the conflagration such revelations would produce. Nevertheless it was reassuring to know that Michael Hughes, as young as he was, understood the implications in confessing that his mother was a witch. It was up to the coven to prove that his faith was not ill-founded.

"Under the circumstances, I'd prefer not to have a full meet. Just you, Lydia and the two mothers involved. Don't look like that! We might not be burned at the stake but life can be made pretty unpleasant - and it wouldn't be the first time a coven had been betrayed by one of its own."

41

In the quietness of the night the voices of the old house gave tongue in an ancient language of creaks and groans as the timbers moved and stretched. Through the open window, nocturnal noises crept into the bedroom, a weird symphony of sound and silence but the night had no fears for Charlotte Manning, she had been alone for too long to ever be afraid of the dark. Having taken a bath of purification, she concealed her ceremonial robes under a hooded cloak and stepped out into the darkness.

There was a flickering candle lighting the window of the Neville family mausoleum. Patches of moonlight created by the overhead branches, cast elongated shadows across the clearing where the carved statue of the Great God presided silently over the discreet arrivals.

A ghostly white shape flew menacingly through the mono-chrome woodland as the powerful wings of the screech owl, tipped with fine down, moved silently as the bird listened for prey in the undergrowth. Casting a fleeting shadow over Char-lotte's face, the owl emitted a loud, piercing shriek and was gone.

The door to the mausoleum swung silently open to re-veal a stepped entrance in the marble floor. As she closed and bolted the door behind her, Paul Kerrick appeared from the subterranean depths, wearing the dark blue robe of the coven's Magister. Indicating that everyone had arrived, he blew out the candle in the window. By tradition while the candle was burning, members could freely enter but once the candle had been extinguished, the heavy door was bolted and no-one was permitted access. Charlotte dropped the heavy cloak on the floor and removed the rubber boots she had put on over her slippered feet.

"I hope these are consecrated gumboots?" whispered Paul facetiously, receiving a grin and an elbow in the ribs for his pains.

Charlotte led the way down the stone steps into the chamber below, as Paul sealed the entrance above their heads.

The room had been originally excavated by her great-grand-father, but it was the presiding genius of Peter Neville who transformed it into the Sanctuary when he founded his own coven prior to the war. A white marble floor was inlaid with a large pentagram, nine feet across, of black marble edged with bronze that gleamed in the lamplight. Exquisite Renaissance sanctuary lamps, acquired by archaeological barter, were suspended by chains from the ceiling and represented the four cardinal points of the compass and the four elements of Fire, Air, Water and Earth.

Neville had chosen his altar in the same white stone that lined the walls of the chamber - a huge rectangular block inscribed with the words *Ignotum Per Ignotius* - 'to reach the unknown through the still more unknown'. In front of the altar stood the forked stang of the coven, cut from the sacred ash tree and garlanded with arrows and greenery to symbolise the duality of the Horned God. Heavy incense permeated the air, banishing all negative influences and protecting the circle from any psychic attack.

The Lady, stepped forward and greeted Charlotte. Lydia Galbraith, also High-Priestess of the coven, was better known in Ashmarsh as the owner of a small handicraft workshop. She was visibly agitated and still sported an impressive mauve and yellow bruise on her left cheekbone. The other two women mirrored her anxiety but made no move to engage their famous neighbour in conversation. Without any unnecessary exchange of words, the four onlookers retreated while Charlotte drew her own protective circle; the only sound in the room was the rustle of her dark green robe as she finally settled in the centre of the pentagram.

Without further visual preparation, her mind despatched a telepathic message out into the woods in an attempt to make contact with the High Priestesses's assailant. Almost immediately, she came up against a powerful psychic barrier and although there appeared to be a willingness to respond, she was unable to decipher the unintelligible language of

43

the transmitter. It was obvious that communication could not be established on a purely spiritual level and so withdrawing, she prepared to make contact on the astral where all languages are one. In accordance with Lydia's own impression, she had also sensed the superiority of the presence and therefore it was necessary to establish a position of supremacy from the start. Drawing from the inner depths, Charlotte demanded that the presence appeared before her.

The atmosphere was charged with electricity as the confrontation built up in the subterranean chamber. Locked in a silent mental battle the protagonists poured their ungoverned will-power to focus in a swirling ball of fiery rage. A feeling of pent-up fury and resistance manifested itself in the form of amber eyes, glowing like coals against the shadows cast by the lamps. It was an emotion so intense that the observers, whilst not adepts of High Magic, were still able to sense the almost tangible existence of the irate astral presence outside the magic circle.

A faint luminous cloud began to form into an indistinct shape; a sliver of mist vacillating on the warm currents of air, faded and then grew brighter. Slowly it expanded and became denser, suspended in the air and exuding a slightly luminous blue light. The blue vapour increased in density, now appearing as a transparent membrane with moving bulges and empty spaces. Quicker now, the membrane began to develop substance and take on a life force of its own as it struggled to free itself from the invisible bonds.

The form was almost complete and easily identifiable to the onlookers. Wisps of vapour began to drift away from the mass and the membrane stretched, becoming more and more transparent until the shadowy figure of a man was revealed. His hair was worn long and unkempt, and his beard was matted but despite the primitive savagery there was intelligence and noble bearing. His clothes consisted mainly of skins and a simple woollen garment, and around his neck he wore the Celtic symbol of nobility - a heavy gold torc.

"Why have you come amongst us?" asked his summoner.

"The dead under my protection have been defiled. I require vengeance, Lady." The manner of his reply indicated that he had finally recognised and accepted her superior power.

"Who committed this desecration?"

"The Black One and only by his death shall their honour be satisfied."

Turning his face to the ceiling, he raised his arms, fingers outstretched and released a powerful boost of psychic energy which extinguished the sanctuary lamps as a demonstration of his own undefeated strength. Maintaining the stance until some outer demand lessened, his arms dropped wearily to his sides, before he disappeared through the walls of the chamber.

"Bugger it!" responded Charlotte Manning.

Chapter Four

The atmosphere in the Knightsbridge studio flat was far from harmonious. "Alex, you really are the limit! You must come to Anthea's party, after all, we did accept the invitation on your behalf."

Anyway, it won't be the same without you." Remonstrated a strikingly tall blonde girl, irritably twirling an elaborate silver and black mask by the velvet ribbons.

"Eleanor's right, if you're not doing anything else, why won't you come?" joined in her companion, a garish frog mask pulled back over his own stylish blond hair. They had arrived at Alex's studio flat half an hour earlier and had since failed to persuade him to accompany them.

Martin replenished the glasses of his three guests with champagne and generously filled his own. "I don't feel like a masked ball Serge."

"You can't break a ten year habit just on a whim. What will people think, if we turn up without you?"

"Tell them I'm working."

"You really are impossible" repeated Eleanor, flinging herself down on the couch, a pout on her normally perfect mouth, "We don't see *anything* of you these days."

"It's that witch woman," cut in the second girl, who had not previously spoken. "Ever since then, he's been off with all of us." Her blue eyes sparkled with malice.

"What witch woman?"

"Shut up Sam," interrupted Eleanor. " We don't want one of your bitching sessions just now"

Samantha Talbot sprang out of her chair. "Well it's true! He hasn't let me near him since he came back from that place. She must be a bloody good screw, considering she's old enough to be your mother!" With a toss of her head, she flounced over to examine her pretty face in a large, ornamental mirror.

"Perhaps we'd better let Alex get on with whatever he was doing." Serge Butler had seen the tightening of the muscles in the corner of his friend's mouth and knew the danger signals too well to ignore them.

"If that's your opinion Samantha, I question your cloying interest in *our* relationship," countered Alex, ignoring his friend. "Considering that Charlotte Manning is only a year younger than me, I find your obvious father fixation exceptionally unflattering. But then your childish tantrums are extremely boring."

The girl looked as though she were about to smash something or cry as Eleanor stepped in to disperse the discord. "I think I could do with another drink and then we really must leave." She linked her arm through Alex's, leading him towards the kitchen to look for another bottle of champagne. "That was very cruel."

"She deserved it," he replied stubbornly. "Just because I admire the talents of an extremely intelligent woman over the fleeting lure of a twenty two year old model."

"You always did like 'em sharp, witty and intelligent, to say nothing of mature. Well I remember the saga of Marsha Horton," she grinned.

"I thought we'd agreed not to talk about that embarrassing episode again," he laughed in response to her teasing, taking the chilled bottle from her. "*EVER!*"

Laughter between them came easy and dispelled the last lingering traces of anger. Samantha had left in a temper, slamming the door and muttering curses against them all.

The three of them had been close friends for years and the girl was not the first to feel resentful of their camaraderie. It was a bond that had begun at university when two 'socially disadvantaged' youths had teamed up against the snide comments and slightly inferior station allocated to them by their fellow students. It had continued through university, even surviving the advent of Eleanor Hamilton a first year student, who captured Serge's heart during his final year. From then on it had been recognised that an invitation would not be accepted if it did not include all three of them.

Disowned by her family for her association with someone of such inferior status, Eleanor gained her degree and moved in with Serge, changing her name to his in further defiance of her parents. In those few years she had been transformed from a lanky, fresh-faced country girl into a beauty who turned heads wherever she went. The combined physical and mental attributes of the Butlers and Alexander Martin ensured they were popular guests at any social event.

As tight as the bond was between them, Alex still felt unable to discuss the incredible hold that a virtual stranger had developed over him. Both had shown their unswerving loyalty when he had arrived on their doorstep a long time ago, bloody and beaten; through the long weeks of hospitalisation they had been with him constantly, never once requiring an explanation for his injuries. Now he felt guilty over forgetting a date that had been a permanent fixture on their calendar for years. The party had slipped his mind, but he had not forgotten that tonight was Halloween.

"I hope she's worth it," mused Serge shrewdly, finishing his Veuve Clicquot with appreciation.

After they had left, Alex examined the mask Eleanor had chosen for him. The sightless eyes stared back at him with an impassive blankness but even the faintly mocking curve of the mouth could not conceal the classic beauty of the features. He was looking into the haunting face of *Pan*. In a gesture of irritation he threw the mask across the room.

It was now three weeks since he had visited Charlotte Manning and although there had been lengthy conversations with her on the telephone, she had still not invited him back to Ashmarsh. As compensation he had turned to her books and lain awake long into the night, reading whatever his local library and bookshop could supply of her works. Suddenly he felt a stab of deep hunger that clawed at his intestines with merciless talons. He had thought himself well past the adolescent stage of secretly lusting after a woman but on several occasions he had woken from a deep sleep to find he had ejaculated and he was ashamed.

The lights in the studio were dimmed and as soft music poured out of the stereo system, Alex began to wish that he had accompanied his friends to the party. Charlotte's startling perception had forced him to evaluate himself and he had not liked what he had seen. With all the dexterity of a surgeon wielding a scalpel, she had sliced away the mundane and trivial trappings of his lifestyle and left him with a sense of freshness and rejuvenation. That twenty four hours had already changed his perspective of ambition and success. The atmosphere of his designer-furnished studio was chillingly sterile, offering him no comfort or warmth and, as had so often happened during the past three weeks, his thoughts turned to the welcoming hearth at Hunter's Moon.

He felt isolated and knew perfectly well that there was only one antidote for his acute emptiness. "Damn you!" he said aloud and within the hour the headlights of the powerful Austin Healey were burning a path through the dark Northamptonshire night.

Away from the motorway, a deep enveloping blackness swallowed the road and against the inky backdrop, wind-blasted branches stretched their bony arms towards the car as it raced past. Shortly after ten, the dim street lamps of the village gleamed like a beacon through the leafless hedgerow. Light drizzle glistened on the stonework as Alex swung the car under the archway and with a final roar the

49

engine died in the cobbled courtyard. A dim gleam showed at the fanlight of the side door and before he had reached the step, a golden warmth flooded the gloom.

"You're just in time for supper," she calmly stated as he entered the narrow passageway.

All the resentment and anger faded at the sound of her voice. "You speak as though I were expected."

"You were."

She walked ahead of him into the lighted hallway, her lithe body concealed beneath a blue embroidered caftan. As she turned to take his coat, he was again surprised by her stature, barely reaching his shoulder in her bare feet. Gently, in spite of the urgency he felt, Alex took hold of her by the shoulders and pulled her towards him. As his mouth met hers for the first time, he held her close in a strangely familiar way, as though there had always been intimacy between them. The wanting that had consumed him was evident by the uncontrollable reaction of his body to the subtle caress of silk and fine perfume.

"So you sent for me and I came," he murmured into the darkness of her hair.

"Perhaps you are merely predictable," she replied coolly.

Her tart response broke the spell and he felt a certain inward relief as she calmly suggested they have supper. As always, Charlotte seemed to have him at a disadvantage. Did she *really* know that he was coming or was she merely quick witted enough to turn an unexpected situation to her advantage? However, supper for two *had* been set in the panelled alcove off the kitchen. The warmth from the huge blackened range seeped into his bones, as his unfathomable hostess ladled enormous helpings of home -made game soup into pottery bowls. The formality of his previous visit now comparing slightly less favourably with the present cosy atmosphere permeating the old kitchen.

Apart from heavily upholstered alcove and the black range which occupied almost half of one wall, the rest of the kitchen had been left in its original state. The flagstone floor and huge scrubbed oak table were also obviously original features. The rough walls were painted white and Charlotte had resisted the current trend to transform the place with fitted units. Like the rest of the house, the kitchen had not been brutalised by modernisation.

"We only really use the dining room when we have company," she remarked, reading his thoughts. "When they cease to be guests, they come in here. I think it's far more civilised," she added.

Throughout supper they talked of abstract things but there was an ease between them of old friends meeting after years of separation, slipping comfortably back into their old familiar relationship. Having demolished the large steak that was set before him, plus two slices of Gwen's well-remembered plum pie, Alex lit two cigarettes and passed one to Charlotte.

"*'If I were now to die, 'Twere now to be most happy; for, I fear My soul hath her content so absolute, That not another comfort like to this Succeeds in unknown fate'*."

"*'The heavens forbid but that our loves and comforts should increase, even ...*' Why are you laughing?"

"I remember quoting Shakespeare to a girlfriend once. She looked at me with a pained expression saying that it wasn't surprising I never sold anything if I wrote stuff like that."

Charlotte laughed in response, drawing up her feet and resting her chin on her knees. "I know exactly what you mean, I dragged my first husband away from painting our rather dismal rented flat in Islington to see this fat peach coloured harvest moon. I can see him now. Paint brush dripping white gloss onto the concrete path of an overgrown garden, furiously muttering 'You dragged me out here just to see *THAT!*' It was the beginning of enlightenment, I assure you."

"How many times have you been married?" asked Alex pouring more wine into her glass.

"Twice and neither time successfully," she answered,

encouraging no further discussion on the subject.

The conversation drifted to other topics and during a lull in the rain that had been lashing furiously against the window all evening, they heard the church clock strike one. Alex rose to his feet and stretched out a hand in invitation. Without taking her eyes from his, Charlotte took his hand and allowed him to lead the way to her bedroom.

The large room was richly decorated in cream and gold, unexpectedly luxurious in comparison to the simple decor of the rest of the house. The heavy brocade drapes were pulled back to reveal tear-stained window panes. Magnolia coloured walls boasted an impressive collection of gilt mirrors, all reflecting the iridescent gleam of crystal from the lamps and small chandelier, while erotic French miniatures occupied the wall space over the bed. Alex studied the room thoughtfully for a moment. Here was a clue to the secret Charlotte - perhaps she had a touch of the French whore in her after all.

In the softly lit room they made love tenderly, without blind passion or recklessness, and without the uncertainty of first time encounters. Hands and mouths enjoying the exploration of soft, perfumed flesh; legs intertwined, two parts becoming a whole, even though some hours before they had been virtual strangers. Soft pliable breasts surrendered to hard muscle as appreciative hands traced the pattern of natural symmetry across belly and thighs. The voyage of discovery amid tangled linen sheets was long and pleasurable, culminating in copulation, an act of worship as old as creation.

In the darkness of the early hours, Alex drifted in and out of sleep. He had woken suddenly from a vivid dream in which some large animal was about to spring at his throat, leaving his heart racing and his body covered in sweat. To his relief he discovered that the heavy weight on his chest was the bulk of the large grey cat, its amber eyes reflecting eerily in the darkness.

Charlotte lay on her side in a deep satisfied sleep, her

mouth slightly open. There was sharp burst of rain against the window, followed by an unearthly scream that made Alex's skin crawl. Echoing through the night, it was a wild, drawn out cry of pure terror and he would have put it down to the remnants of his nightmare except for the fact that the cat was now staring out through the rain for the cause, its tail bristling and twitching in agitation. He tried to wake Charlotte but got no response to his shaking. For some time he lay there, straining his ears for further sounds, but the pouring rain drowned any noises from outside and finally he dropped into a fitful rest until morning.

Feeling mentally and emotionally bruised after an unscheduled and eventful night, Alex looked at the small gilt clock, the hands of which showed that it was almost nine thirty. From his previous stay he knew that the household were early risers and what was even more strange, was the fact that there were no noises or breakfast smells coming from the kitchen. Creeping down the stairs he found that Gwen had not yet arrived and the fire was almost out.

Recalling the working of his grandmother's antiquated range, he piled on the logs and after fiddling with the damper to draw the flames, he managed to start a cheerful blaze while the electric kettle boiled. Carrying the tea tray carefully back upstairs, he walked into the bedroom as Charlotte came out of the bathroom, pulling a sweat-shirt over her head.

"Have you seen the time?" she demanded. "Where the hell's Gwen and Anna?"

"Tea is served madam."

Her irritation vanished with an apologetic grin. "Sorry, but I've never known Gwen to be late. Perhaps I should ring and find out if there's anything wrong."

"You'll know soon enough," he replied. "Finish getting dressed and I'll be cook."

As it was late they breakfasted on hot bread rolls, with home-made preserves, swilled down with plenty of strong tea. Charlotte kept glancing at the clock and frowning; not

53

until she heard the side door opening and footsteps in the passage did her face show signs of relief. Flushed and breathless, Gwen Carradine entered the kitchen as fearlessly as a minesweeper.

"Sorry I'm late dear. Hello Mr Martin. How are you? Terrible, just terrible. When did you arrive - and had to get your own breakfast too!" Gwen Carradine unwound a colourful headscarf from her damp, frizzy hair.

As calmly as she could, Charlotte interrupted. "What's made you so late, I was worried something was wrong?"

"Bless you, you needn't worry about me. My Brian would have popped in if I was poorly and not coming. Is there any tea left in the pot or shall I make a fresh one?"

It was obvious that Gwen would not divulge the reason for her lateness until she was properly ensconced with a fresh pot of tea. Charlotte sat drumming her nails on the table top while Alex lit another cigarette and studied the hair-line cracks in the ceiling plaster, in an attempt to conceal his amusement at Gwen's prevarication and Charlotte's growing impatience. The daily help was not one to be hurried.

"Now then, when Brian was off to see to the chickens, early it was and still raining, he saw a police diversion sign and they said he couldn't go through to his bit of land. Well, my Brian's not one to let the hens suffer, so he left his bike in the ditch and took a short cut through the wood, and do you know what he saw?"

"No, but I expect we'll get there eventually!"

Gwen passed over her employer's acidity and continued, spooning a vast heap of sugar into her tea. "A body!" she announced triumphantly.

Remembering the scream in the night, Alex sat up interested. "What sort of body?"

"A dead body," answered Gwen incredulously, not quite sure that she was hearing him correctly.

The sound of Anna's car drawing into the courtyard, brought a further sigh of relief from Charlotte. Hurried footsteps crossed the passage and Anna burst into the kitchen. She had dark circles under her eyes and was obviously tired from a late night, but this could not suppress her excitement.

"Hello Alex. Come down to investigate our murder?"

"We've only just heard about it."

The girl looked speculatively from one to the other before carrying on. "They've blocked of the road from the end of the lane right up to the junction on the hill. I had to go all the way to Towcester to miss the police diversion."

"You should have left the car in a ditch and taken a short cut through the wood," replied Charlotte with a edge of sarcasm.

Anna grinned and ignored her. "I did better than that, 'cos I got stopped by this divine detective who wanted to know where I lived and where I was going ..."

"And what *are* you doing tomorrow evening?"

"Apparently the victim was old Barney, the poacher. He didn't say too much but I gathered the killing was pretty horrific."

"But old Barney was harmless enough. He only used to take what he needed to keep himself alive."

"The police wouldn't tell my Brian anything," said Gwen, slightly indignant about police lack of confidence in her husband.

"Perhaps he hasn't got red hair," offered Alex

Later that afternoon Paul Kerrick arrived at Hunter's Moon only moments after the police. Detective Inspector Morris was a burly man used to handling himself around the old dock areas of Liverpool but he had decided to move south with his family to give his two sons a better chance. A competent detective with many years of experience, he was nonetheless totally unprepared for the case he had in hand. He was used to street violence and was never surprised at the grievous injuries one man could inflict on another - but this was different.

Paul called on the pretext of collecting some herbal medicines and, excusing herself for a few moments, Charlotte led him through to her workshop. Handing a couple of bottles of natural laxative to support his story, Charlotte stood by the window to see if anyone had attempted to follow them. The police would be convinced by his visit, but she wanted to keep him away from Alex.

"Do you think this has anything to do with our truculent Celt?" he asked, his lean face furrowed in thought.

"I don't know," she responded, "but it might take the pressure off the boys if the police are investigating another murder. Do you know anything about it yet?"

"No. I came here as soon as I heard and judging by the rumours the whole business is pretty gruesome. It could be the same killer, or it could be the old Celt starting his campaign of vengeance but the police won't welcome news of either."

"Has anyone had any thoughts on this Black One we're seeking?"

"Well, the Traditional Craft have the Man in Black, who's the clan mediator but I don't think he would be of interest to our chap. All we can think of is an ethnic black or someone dressed in black. It's given Jennie and Barbara fresh hope about Michael, at least."

"Good. Look, as soon as I can, I'll get down to some serious research and see what I can uncover. He hasn't just turned up out of the blue. Trouble is my pre-Roman history isn't too hot, it was one of my Father's preserves, but if I find anything in his books, I'll ring you. Now let me go and sort out the law."

Paul's car was parked under the archway behind Anna's and, having seen him off the premises, Charlotte re-entered the house by the side door as Mrs C. was busily dispensing tea to the waiting detectives. Like a dog sniffing the wind, Charlotte detected an underlying presence of suspicion and malice, especially from the younger man. It was a reaction

56

she was used to in outsiders and decided once again to ignore it. It was easy to become paranoid over ignorance.

"Perhaps you know the deceased, his name was Barney Smiles?" the CID officer was asking.

"We know him," interrupted Charlotte, "He's poached in these woods for as long as I can remember. He was slightly dotty but harmless."

"How did he die?" Alex also sensed the Inspector's agitation and assumed that the nature of the killing had something to do with his thinly disguised revulsion.

"Until the coroner's had a look at him we won't know for sure, Sir, but whoever did for him certainly had a taste for killing." On this ominous pronouncement, the detective took his leave, apologising for the interruption, but warning them that he would be asking for their co-operation in future enquiries. "It's already been suggested to me that I look towards the local witches for the culprit," he added looking directly at Charlotte "but I don't hold with wild accusations. I might need your advice on another matter though, since I understand you've had plenty of experience with this cult nonsense"

The three of them sat in silence after the police had left. Already the heavy drapes had been pulled shut against the persistent, rain sodden evening. Fingers of flame caressed fresh logs in a passionate, consuming dance, as each of them pursued their own train of thought concerning the murder that had been committed virtually on their doorstep. Alex remembering the scream in the night; Anna thinking of the mutilated bodies of the two teenagers; Charlotte desperately trying to recall any scrap of information that would help identify the Celtic shaman and the reason for his sudden manifestation.

"Did the Inspector mention that old Barney was done to death near your stone circle?" asked Anna finally breaking the silence.

"No. He didn't mention that," answered Charlotte softly.

Chapter Five

For the next few days speculation ran rife in Ashmarsh, each person proffering their own theory as to what the police were actually trying to conceal, for local people knew better than to believe the renewed newspaper sensationalism suggesting Witchcraft. Most had grown old with a member of the family still following the Old Ways and understood that there was nothing to fear from it. The Post Office became the hub of curiosity and for hours on end, groups of villagers could be found crammed into the dimly lit shop to hear the latest news.

"Done to death with a meat axe, he was."

"My sister's nephew's wife, who cleans for a Inspector over at Towcester says it was an animal."

"Don't talk daft Ruby, we haven't got any wild animals big enough. And there's nowhere for one to escape from."

"Heard he owed somebody money over Nether Heyford way."

"Them damned newspapers always like to think they know everything, and when they don't, they like to cause trouble."

Gwen Carradine was the star orator, having listened to the conversations that had taken place in the kitchen of Hunter's Moon earlier in the week. Her pantry at the house was always well provisioned but on several occasions Gwen decided it was necessary to make a few purchases from the

Post Office. She was not repeating anything that had been spoken in confidence. She would never gossip about any *private* matters that she was privy to, like the fact that the journalist fellow was sleeping with Charlotte Manning. That was family.

She had been in the kitchen preparing lunch during the whole of the Inspector's second visit and had not been instructed to remain silent. Her kitchen was becoming congested these days due to the fact that Anna, Charlotte and Alex had suddenly taken to have their mid-morning coffee in the breakfast alcove. That morning she been more than irritated when young Gill Cross came in with two cat cages, plus occupants, and had to be told severely not to put them on the kitchen table!

"Just collected them from the vet's and officially they're both dead. This one is Benjamin," her fingers caressed an enormous black cat through the bars. "His owner had him for eight years and then moved to that posh housing estate where Ben didn't fit in. She told Mr Kerrick that she wanted him to go to heaven!"

Charlotte snorted with exasperation as Gill continued. "And this is Oscar, an extremely bad tempered rabbit who, according to Mr Kerrick is ancient, possibly a museum piece. Some woman turned him over to the vet to be put down because he'd bitten one of her grandchildren."

"Some folk aren't fit to live," muttered her employer. "Okay, Gill take them out to the barn. Let them settled in for a few days and then we'll have another look at them."

Gill nibbled at an already well chewed thumb-nail, a nervous blush colouring her fresh, Anglo-Saxon complexion. "Mrs Manning, I'd rather like Ben myself. As you know, my Dad doesn't like animals, so I'm renting Brook Cottage and Ben could live there with me. Is that all right?"

"Of course. I suppose you'll want a salary increase to help with your additional expenses?" The teenager's face lit up with delight. "Go on, I'll come down to see you later"

59

"You spoil that girl," commented Gwen as the side door closed. "Her Dad, won't thank you for it."

"Mr Cross can go screw himself," replied Charlotte.

There had been no love lost between her and the local dentist, Jeffrey Cross ever since Gill had started working at Hunter's Moon. The girl's father considered that a manual job, working in an animal clinic, was beneath his family's station and had unwisely told Charlotte so in no uncertain terms. Furious beyond belief, she had retaliated with such ferocity that Jeffrey Cross has swiftly abandoned his normal Wednesday evening session in the Saracen's Head, much to the amusement of his drinking cronies.

There followed several sharp exchanges between father and daughter, culminating in a swift box round the ears that had sent Gill scurrying to Charlotte for protection.

"Charly, the Vicar called to see if we're going to the bonfire party. Oh, this one's all right," said Anna, laughing at Alex's pained expression. "She normally steers clear of the clergy, but the Rev. has an enquiring mind, so he joins the ranks of privilege."

"Actually the Rev's a pretty decent human being and it's good fun if you wrap up warm," Charlotte told him.

"Sounds good to me," he lied.

"Right. I'll phone Margaret and order the tickets." Anna got to her feet as the bell pealed at the front door and a few moments later, she steered Inspector Morris through to the kitchen.

The detective was greeted with fresh coffee and another plate of sugared doughnuts was produced, as if by magic. "We've heard the gossip Inspector," purred Alex, his journalistic habit dying hard. "What's the truth?"

Morris wiped grains of sugar from his mouth with a monogrammed handkerchief and sighed. "I wish I could say, Sir, but even the coroner's confused. All the evidence points to an attack by a powerfully built man but there were no tracks or prints in the mud anywhere near the body."

"Could he have been killed elsewhere and the body dumped?" prompted Alex.

"Not according to the forensic lads. The pathologist's report states that he died of a heart attack, probably brought on by fear or shock. He'd been strung up in a tree, and his balls cut off and stuffed in his mouth. Not content with that our murderer had the old boy impaled!"

"Oh my God," cried Gwen Carradine, dropping a cast iron preserving pan which made them all jump.

A muscle twitched slightly near Alex's mouth as he pressed the Inspector for more details. "Does it suggest any connection with the two who were murdered here in the summer? I mean, mutilation seems to be the common denominator." He wasn't aware that Charlotte had communicated the thought to him telepathically.

Morris frowned slightly before answering. "The weapons weren't the same if that's what you mean, Mr Martin. But I don't believe in co-incidences of a nature that give me three bodies, all done to death near a stone circle and then mutilated."

Anna studied the smear of jam on her napkin and felt a little sick. "I don't believe it either."

"And neither do you Mrs Manning, and that's why I've called to see if you can help me. According to the current theories in the Incident Room, I'm either looking for a group of homicidal Witches indulging in ritual killing, or an individual who wants us to *think* that it could be the work of local Witches. On the other hand, it could be that the victims were there out of sheer bad luck and there's no sinister hidden agenda."

Charlotte remained silent for a moment, studying her scarlet fingernails against the polished wood of the table top and thinking carefully before she spoke. "I would rule out the first suggestion as totally ridiculous. Whatever you may have heard, Witches do not go in for ritual rape, or blood sacrifices of any kind, it goes against their creed of 'And it

61

harm none, do what thou will'. Your second question of whether certain parties are attempting to make you think it's the work of a coven, is a possibility. Some fundamentalists would stop at nothing to discredit occultism in general, regardless of the consequences to innocent parties. The end would justify the means."

The detective shifted uncomfortably, "Any suggestions?"

"Well, since it's already been suggested you investigate the local Witches, I can only retaliate by pointing you in the direction of the evangelicals. Some are more fanatical than most but there's not been any first hand experience of it around here. And that leaves us with the possibility of your third suggestion taking into account that the victims were teenage girls and an elderly man."

"There have been reports of fundamentalist attacks on occult premises, businesses and psychic fayres, Charlotte," suggested Alex.

"But they've never killed anybody. And I'm not going to start bandying about false accusations to implicate them out of spite. Which is what it would amount to. The police have wasted enough time chasing their tails over fundamentalist propaganda in the past, and that's why Inspector Morris is here. He's not going to risk his investigation or his career by chasing around after Witches without any positive proof."

"I think its best to keep quiet over the more gruesome details, but the powers that be have already released the information to the press. The public have a morbid curiosity that I find frankly sickening at times."

On which note, the Inspector took his leave.

The Reverend Archie Branston was a popular man in the community, who kept his dog-collar and sermons for the Sunday service and who was usually seen about the countryside inconspicuously dressed in tweeds, helping and comforting those who needed him. The older characters in The Saracen's

Head liked him for not mentioning God outside his church, and because he could sink a pint of ale with the best of them. He had served briefly as a chaplain during the Aden crisis and, following his front line action had adopted a personal creed that comfort should be given to any sufferer, regardless of denomination or belief, and this was his own chosen way to serve his Maker. His wife Margaret flatly stated that she would not have married him in the first place, if he'd been a normal parson.

The Bishop considered that the Rev. Branston conducted himself more like a social worker than a minister of God and had permanently consigned him to the depths of rural Northamptonshire. He had lived in Ashmarsh for over thirty years and was well liked by old and young, even by Charlotte Manning. He respected her for her untiring devotion in the service of dumb animals - a feeling that was reciprocated by Charlotte herself, for precisely the same reasons. She considered his flock in the same light.

Dusk had fallen and high winds were keeping the land dry underfoot. For days anxious young helpers had been collecting rubbish for the bonfire, which was always held in a small paddock behind The Saracen's Head. Trestle tables held an assortment of food for the party but the main attraction was the Vicar's portable barbecue, acquired from a nearby USAF base many years before. Mouths watered in anticipation of plump sausages, chops and burgers, grilled over burning charcoal. Any profits from the evening went towards the needy of the Parish.

At exactly seven o' clock, the church bells pealed out across the countryside and the villagers left their homes to walk to the party. The Ashmarsh bell ringers performed their repertoire as the Vicar officially lit the bonfire; reminiscent of the days when beacon fires flared on hilltops and bells had rung out in warning as Dane and Saxon met in bloody combat in forest clearings - or of the earlier fire-festivals of the Old Ways. The fire roared up around the 'guy' slumped in an old chair, awaiting his grisly end. As the wind caught at the sparks, throwing them high into the air, the first volley of rockets hurtled up into the blackness to announce the start of the display. Cascades of coloured stars showered down on the onlookers and the small crowd responded with their customary 'ooohs' and 'aahs'!

As Charlotte pointed out while they sipped mulled wine - the whole affair was managed with military precision that would be the envy of NATO. The timing, safety precautions, the order of the display and the catering were so discreet that hardly anyone was conscious of being organised. The elderly brigade of the public bar sat in a row along the rear wall of the public house, appearing unimpressed by the spectacle but their comment after every bonfire party summed up the feeling of the whole community.

"Vicar put on a bloody good show."

By ten o' clock most of the children had been taken home and the fire was being tended by the small group of teenagers who were playing rock music and clearing away the remainder of the food. Charlotte exchanged a few words with Gill a nd her new boyfriend, while she tactfully avoided the sight of Anna dancing cheek to cheek with the young detective who had come to the house during the murder enquiry. For some reason he irritated her immensely but she put the feeling down to her inbred distrust of authority and dismissed it.

"Shall we go?" asked Alex.

"Not that way," replied his companion, pulling him away from the firelight and into the shadows. "We can cut through the woods and it's a lovely night."

Climbing down a steep bank to where the stream was narrow enough to jump, they made their way across the fields to the house. The moon gleamed bloated and mis-shapen over the trees, its eerie reflection staring back from the inky depths of the first pool. Bare branches raised their gaunt arms to the glowing orb in worship and underfoot, crushed damp leaves perfumed the night with the sweet, perfumed smell of decay.

Without speaking, Alex stopped and pulled out a packet of cigarettes. "I have a strange feeling of ... timelessness," he said finally. "We're standing here now, looking at the same moon that someone was looking at, standing exactly on this spot, thousands of years ago. It's a beautiful and frightening thought."

Charlotte took the cigarette he offered her and narrowed her eyes as she watched him through the smoke. "Perhaps you're experiencing the first glimmer of your cosmic Self. A view of life as it really is and not merely how it appears. The Roebuck in the Thicket."

"That smacks soundly of paganism." In his mind's eye he held the image of her standing by the statue of Pan during his first visit.

"What is the alternative to organised religion? The eternal search after truth, to stand with your feet in the earth and be at one with the universe and nature, to feel the power of the elements. I can think of no better focus for worship."

The mournful cry of night birds trilled out in the darkness as they continued to walk in silence, hands stuffed deep into coat pockets, breathing in the sharp beauty of the moonlit night. Charlotte was leading the way through the woods along a narrow track towards Hunter's Moon when they both became strongly aware of the sudden drop in temperature.

"It must be the chill off the water," whispered Alex, looking out over the moon-flecked surface of the pool.

Charlotte hunched her shoulders and shivered. "Why are you whispering?" .

"I don't know. Listen!"

The only audible sound was the night wind in the reeds, a rustling of dead leaves and in the distance, the haunting cry of a barn owl. In the silence, more night noises assailed their ears, the call of other night creatures, wet bark groaning as branch rubbed against branch, the footfall of a solitary predator. Some way off, about fifty yards in front of them, the path between the two pools was obscured by a fine mist that appeared to be moving towards them.

Suddenly Alex gripped her hand, causing her rings to cut deeply into her fingers. "Do you hear that?" Nervousness transformed his whisper into a hoarse croak.

Charlotte stood still, staring into the rapidly approaching mist. "No, but I can see it!"

She could feel her heart pounding as the form drew stealthily nearer and nearer. There was nowhere to hide and even if there was, she instinctively knew this was no living, breathing, flesh and blood creature. Rooted where they stood, the mist parted to reveal the ghostly apparition of the ancient Briton. Briefly their eyes met in silent communication but as Charlotte shifted her gaze away from the patch of mist to see if Alex could see it, the figure disappeared, the temperature lifting noticeably.

"What the hell was it?"

"What ever it was, it's gone now," she replied, extracting her fingers from his grip.

"Did we really see something?" demanded Alex.

Charlotte thought for a moment before giving her answer. "Yes, we did and I think I would like to get back to the house before it comes back. Quick, this way."

She set off rapidly across the compound and Alex found it difficult to keep up with her. The swiftness of her pace prevented any conversation and before he realised it, they were closing the garden gate firmly behind them. There were no lights on in the house, showing that Anna had not yet returned from her date with the amorous detective; with relief they entered through the door in Charlotte's study.

Alex went to make the coffee and carried the steaming mugs back to the study where he found Charlotte staring into the fire. There was a question that he wanted answered and tonight he was going to insist that she told him the truth,

66

no more games and evasions - he also wanted to know what she - what *they* - had seen out there in the woods.

They sipped coffee as the fire crackled in comforting fury; the unease of the last half hour already receding. "Are you really psychic, Charlotte?" he blurted out, immediately annoyed with himself for his lack of subtlety.

Slowly she turned her head to face him, as though she was considering whether to be truthful. "I have ... gifts. Not just the power of clairvoyance but the ability to see into the very depths of a human soul and it's a very disturbing phenomena I can assure you. I can see and divine many things that science dismisses as superstition; I can walk in other worlds and heal by touch. I am well versed in herbal lore and magic. I suppose by your definition, you could say I was a Witch." It was not the whole truth, but it was good enough for now.

"Have you always been like it?" asked Alex curiously.

"Always."

"Since you were a child?"

"Oh, certainly since then. I used to embarrass my parent's guests by announcing aloud what they were thinking and in later years would continue conversations long before my companions had actually opened their mouths. Some found it disconcerting." Suddenly she rose to her feet, her eyes flashed with anger as she continued. "Let me give you a practical demonstration! You are thinking that it would make a damn good story but you don't believe a word. You can only accept what you can touch and see, or have explained in scientific detail. But you'll humour me and see if you can find out more."

"Why the hell are you so angry with me?" he demanded, resenting what he considered to be another unprovoked attack but also nervous, because she had read his thoughts correctly.

"Because you are afraid to step outside your narrow, smug little world of glossy trivia, populated with inflated egos and plastic smiles. Can you open your mind Alex and receive the knowledge that's there for the taking? Tonight, just for a moment, *you* glimpsed the Infinite. And if you weren't receptive you wouldn't have been able to see the shape in the woods."

"I don't understand this at all," he answered sulkily. "It's all superstition and fairytales, as far as I'm concerned."

"And your mind now explores the possibility that perhaps I am mad and that it was a mistake to become emotionally involved with me!"

Alex leapt to his feet and took her roughly in his arms. "Okay you've proved your point, now stop it!"

She laughed hollowly, resting her hands against his chest as the anger flowed out of her. "Alex, you are very sweet but you really don't understand, do you? Can you imagine what is like to have unlimited psychic or occult power?"

"Then try to tell me," he answered gently, stroking her hair in an attempt to restore the harmony between them.

"Let's have a brandy first. I'll try but I don't expect you to understand or even believe. However, as you wish to know ..." She broke off to pour two generous measures of cognac.

"If a black human mates with white, the offspring will usually have a fairer complexion than the parents. If those offspring continue to mate with white partners only, through the generations then the end product will be descendants who are white without any noticeable black characteristics. Admittedly there are genetic throwbacks from time to time but this is merely a simple hypothesis.

"Psychic genetics are the opposite. In the course of ... rebirth, transmigration of souls, reincarnation ... call it what you will, the powers are intensified with each earth-life. It is even possible, under the right set of circumstances, to produce a 'magical child'. Think of the brain power of a prehistoric shaman, whose spirit has been rattling around for thousands of years, the amount of psychic knowledge and power that would be at his command."

"I thought the theory was that you progressed spiritually until you reached Nirvana?"

Charlotte brightened a little at his comprehension. "Only if the soul has reached perfection, suppressed all desire and attained a oneness with Self and Godhead. Some reach that state but choose to remain earthbound in order to show others the Path. These are known as The Lightbearers or Watchers. However, occultism, like all branches of natural and scientific law, can produce the fluke, the mutant or the renegade."

"You mean that the spirit isn't quite good enough for eternal peace. Perhaps the ego is too strong to surrender totally and cannot be considered perfect enough to be absorbed into Godhead."

"Exactly! A mind of that calibre could probably split the atom through sheer brain power! There are safety measures against this type of thing occurring, of course, but they're far too complex for us to discuss now."

Alex thought for a moment and with a scarcely concealed smile asked. "Are you trying to tell me that your mind is like that?"

To his relief she laughed and accepted a cigarette. "The spirit's previous existences are usually blocked out to prevent over-load and confusion in the present life. They occasionally have glimpses of what's been before but these are fleeting and few are actually sure whether they've dreamt it or not. There are safe-guards."

"And you have existed before?"

Charlotte nodded and sipped her cognac. "Many times and always with inner knowledge."

"You must have been burned as a witch as few times," laughed Alex and then wished he hadn't, as she might take offence.

She turned her gaze away from him and smiled a secret smile as she murmured softly. "They tried ..."

Chapter Six

In the glow of the dying embers, Charlotte sat rigid and alert, her sharp brain trying to tune in to the telepathic message coming to her from the outside world. She and Alex had been about to reach a mutual climax; the tension in his body indicative of the passion that amounted apace with her own, when a single word reverberated in her brain - *Iceni!* Stripping away any thought of physical gratification, she waited until Alex drifted into a deep sleep and slipped soundlessly from the bed.

Now, an open volume of *Britannica* lay in her lap as she turned over in her mind the possibility that the apparition was indeed one of the ancient followers of the heroic Briton. There was no response to the mind probe that she sent out into the darkness, so she returned to the entry that charted Boudica's short but courageous history. The story was familiar enough to any schoolchild - the retaliation against heavy-handed Roman rule, the march on London and the destruction of Colchester, the massacre of over 70,000 people and the annihilation of the 9th Roman legion.

What even local people did not realise, was that the final battle between the East Anglian Britons and the army of Suetonius Paulinus was thought to have been near Towcester, on the Watling Street, only a few miles from Ashmarsh. The entry in the encyclopedia stated that thousands of Iceni perished in the confrontation "or were hunted down in a ensuing guerrilla warfare." The term 'guerrilla warfare' implied that remnants of the Iceni went into hiding - and what better place for concealment than the ancient Whittlewood which in those days spread for some 35 square acres along the Watling Street.

In the deep shadows of the water course, Death in its most terrifying aspect lurked in the darkness. The clearness of the night reflected the icy brilliance of the stars while the moon hung golden and serene behind the trees. Nature's nocturnal world was alive with rustling and scurrying, the stealthiness of poetic movement, occasionally broken by the shrill scream of dying. Eyes watched and gleamed, claws and teeth ripped and savaged as warm blood splashed onto dead leaves. Suddenly there was an eerie silence.

A shadowy figure left its hiding place to search out and kill as it had promised. The fine mist that hovered over the surface of the rippling brook consolidated into a savage throwback to Celtic times, bent only on the destruction of those who would defile a sacred site. A light breeze still carried the faint traces of wood smoke and gunpowder which did not impair the ancient sense of purpose. The hide-bound feet left no imprint on the damp grass as nearer and nearer the shadow crept towards the haunts of humans. In the stillness, the intake breath was audible to its fellow night prowlers who carefully avoided its path. Amid the dense tangle of overgrown brambles, a solitary dog with teeth bared in a snarl and bristling fur challenged its presence but it stalked on, ignoring the confused canine.

A door opened, partially illuminating the untidy yard with a dull glow as the bulky figure of a woman stepped out into the night. She had no thought for the beauties of the universe, the only motive for her quietly surveying her sur-roundings was to ensure that none of her neighbours observed her actions. Seeing a figure half concealed by the darkness, she turned, picking up the pail of icy water she kept to hand

71

for such a moment. She had guessed that the bonfire party would bring out the courting couples, and the narrow lane behind the cottages was a favourite spot for adolescent petting.

"Come," she cooed in a soft Irish brogue. "I'll soon cool you down, you randy little beggers. The good Lord'll not be offended on my spot of ground."

As she drew back her arm to drench the unlucky pair, death leapt, drowning out the human scream of terror in a gurgle of blood. A sharp blade stabbed and tore through cloth, sinews and muscle, leaving gaping bloody holes where once there had been white flesh. Within minutes, a mutilated corpse was discovered hanging from an apple tree by a neighbour who had heard the screams, but the assailant had faded back into mist and moonlight as silently as it had appeared.

A watery sun limped apologetically through the open window as Charlotte slipped out of bed, leaving Alex asleep. As she dressed, she hungrily ran her eyes over the slim, firm lines of his naked body, recalling with pleasure the intensity of the previous nights love-making - before the interuption. Noises on the landing had disturbed her and as she opened her door, she heard Anna talking softly to someone in the hallway below.

"I hope you didn't keep that poor boy out all night," she called down as Anna closed the door after her visitor.

"It seemed such a pity to let him go home all alone in the dark," her assistant retorted, walking through into the kitchen.

Charlotte followed her. "Was it discretion or panic that made him leave so hurriedly?"

"Neither. His bleeper went off ..."

"How untimely."

"His bleeper went off," Anna repeated, "because there's been a murder in the village. From what I gathered from a one-sided conversation, it's identical to the last one."

"Who was it?" asked Charlotte cautiously

"I'm not blessed with a morbid curiosity, I didn't ask."

"Pity."

"Why don't you 'phone and ask?" replied an exasperated Anna.

"That won't be necessary, I'm sure Inspector Morris will appear as soon as he's visited the scene of the crime."

"Why on earth should he?"

Shrewd green eyes looked fully into the youthful blue ones. "Because he's got nowhere else to turn, unless he's forced by the press to go on a witch-hunt. And that I intend to avoid at all costs."

"Do you know who it is?"

"No, but I think I've got something for us to work on. Don't worry dear, you very thoughtfully provided us all with an alibi by sleeping with your detective."

"You really can be a cow sometimes."

"I'm practical. Twenty per cent of the adult population in the village are Witches - you should know you meet them regularly enough. Everyone for miles around knows of my talents for healing. All roads lead to Hunter's Moon."

"No one in Ashmarsh would snitch."

"No, but there are those in other villages who would. People don't change just because we happen to be in a different period of history than the witch-trials. Human nature never changes."

In the comforting warmth of the kitchen the two women sipped tea talking softly about neighbours and friends in the locality who might fall under suspicion if the press started snooping about in earnest. Anna was thankful that there was someone to speak on her behalf, while Charlotte privately recalled the conversation she and Alex were having the previous night when Anna and her guest interrupted them.

"Look, without going into a lot of detail, I want you to do some immediate research on Boudica. Concentrate on the final battle the Iceni had with the Romans which supposedly took place near here. I want every scrap of information you can find, no matter how trivial and don't leave out the legends, crackpot theories or unsubstantiated references."

"Is this to do with a new book, or the murders?"

"The murders. Drop everything else, this is more important if we're to stop it before anyone else dies."

If there was a power at large which could manifest itself so effectively after 900 years, then she was annoyed with herself for not having detected it before but more than that, she was afraid of the repercussions if she'd got it wrong. It was so long since it had been necessary to call on her *own* powers that her brain had atrophied, become sluggish and dull through want of stimulus. Living in the twentieth century didn't give you a lot of scope for magic! Nevertheless there was little point in carrying out a banishing ritual if she had no idea from whence the power came, or exactly what she was banishing - and to where.

It was well after lunch before Alex was able to catch her eye to indicate that he wished to speak with her alone. Her prediction had been confirmed on Gwen Carradine's arrival, followed only minutes later by Morris. There was a great deal of cordial conversation but Anna betrayed her agitation to Alex by her furtive glances in Charlotte's direction. The Inspector was more than a little put out on discovering that one of his men had slept with the delectable Anna, but he let the matter pass. He did however, inform them that the injuries to the body appeared to be similar to those inflicted on the old poacher, but this time the victim had died on her own doorstep.

In silence Charlotte and Alex watched two of the grey cats chasing leaves across the lawn in a moment of kittenish folly. Attacking immediately by stating that he had observed Anna's behaviour, Alex accused her of knowing the identity of the murder victim before Morris's arrival. The killing had been almost identical in nature to the previous one but this victim had not been afforded the luxury of dying of heart failure.

Death appeared to have been caused by the savage attack itself, which the medical examiner found to be extensive wounds to the throat, chest and stomach. The woman's breasts had been removed and rammed into her mouth, while a sharpened pole had been pushed through the body lengthways.

"Since Anna's given the game away, I suppose I'd better tell you. She's scared that the continuing publicity in the newspapers will bring the wrath of the media on the village. There have now been four particularly nasty murders in less than six months, and that makes for good copy. It's only a matter of time before they turn up en mass."

"But why on earth should that bother Anna? She's got nothing to hide."

"Because Anna is a Witch and so are most of the families in Ashmarsh. They have been for generations and it's fairly common knowledge around here, so any keen journalist will have no trouble in getting outsiders to talk. A suggestion of Witchcraft, four murders with three of them in the locality of the stone circle, and the pencil wielding brigade won't have far to look to invent a whiff of sulphur."

They sat down on the broken stone wall. "In the cold light of day and after a good lunch, I find myself remembering that you never did say what we saw out there last night," Alex remarked casually.

"Are you sure you want to know?"

"Do you have to answer every damned question with another one?" he snapped. "Just give me a clear, concise, one line answer."

"Your journalistic patience is slipping," countered Charlotte sweetly. "Okay, short and sharp but you won't believe it. I've no proof yet, but I believe it was the manifested image of a 900 year old Celtic shaman!"

"Shit!" cried Alex, slapping his hand against the damp stones.

She ignored his outburst as thought recalled the figure

that had appeared out of the mist. "It was constructed of some kind of mist or gas but there was a luminous tinge to it. It was a huge man, covered by a goatskin cloak, and as it came towards us, I could even see the fine lines etched around the eyes."

"I do not believe we saw the ghost of a long-dead Celt!"

"Neither do I and don't blame the Vicar's punch either,"

"But ..."

"Alex - the thing isn't real, it doesn't exist!"

"Hallucinations now! But I even heard it breath!"

Charlotte firmly led her lover back into the house. Anna was in the study absorbed with Charlotte's latest research project, so they sank into the deep chairs in the morning room, basking in the warmth from the fire, enjoying freshly brewed coffee. With her eyes half closed in concentration, Charlotte leaned back against the cushions and began to explain her theory.

"Have you heard of Dion Fortune?"

"Didn't she belong to the same bunch of lunatics as Aleister Crowley?"

"The Hermetic Order of the Golden Dawn, but don't dismiss them entirely as lunatics. Crowley may have been a randy, ego-maniac but his achievements aren't to be treated with scorn. Most of the stuff you read about occultists are written by people who have never seen the inside of a magician's circle and can't be taken as reliable sources.

"However, I digress. Dion Fortune was a bit of a rebel herself and managed to upset a few of the old stalwarts in the Order. As a result her household was afflicted with a plague of black tom-cats, who fouled the place to such an extent that the stench became unbearable. She states quite categorically that it was not an hallucination, as the neighbours shared their affliction and the caretaker was forced to remove the animals from the window-sills and doorsteps with a broom."

"Hardly to be classed as irrefutable evidence of occult phenomena? More a case for the Cat Protection League."

76

"Agreed, but as part of the same scenario she also experienced meeting a gigantic tabby cat, twice the size of a tiger, which moved towards her and then vanished. She realised it was a *simulacrum* or thought-form being projected by someone with occult powers."

"Charlotte, wait! Just suppose for one moment that I concede that a thought-form could be seen, heard and even smelt - but damn it all, the victims in our case have been butchered! Don't ask me to believe that a figment of the imagination can be responsible for carving up two people. It's sheer madness."

Her dark hair had fallen across her face concealing her annoyance but she made a concentrated effort at patience and took a deep breath before continuing.

"The story is not confined to mere thought-forms. Dion Fortune was well versed in the art of astral travel, which apparently she practised with some regularity. Her antagonist engaged her in astral combat and she later discovered that she was scored with vicious claw marks from neck to waist. When she related her story to friends of similar persuasion she was told that it was her antagonist's favourite method of dealing with offenders and that she was by no means the only one to experience it."

"I'm sorry but you've gone off into the realms of fantasy and you won't convince me that what has been going on around here can be credited to occult phenomena. It's one thing to study the paranormal, even to teach it to university students, but to claim to believe it!"

"Would you prefer it left in the hands of occult historians who are incapable of viewing the subject outside its historical context and who know nothing of initiated magic?"

"I'n view of the circumstances, perhaps that's the best place for it," retorted Alex sulkily.

"Then what's your explanation?"

"I'm certain that some pathological killer is on the loose and that blood-lust drives him to attack anyone who frightens or surprises him."

"Then how do you account for the fact that even though the ground is sodden after all this rain, there have been no tracks found to identify who or what did the killing?"

"I haven't got an answer but I can't accept your theory."

"You realise of course that our dear Inspector suspects me of concealing information about the killer?" asked Charlotte changing the subject.

"That's plain idiocy."

"He's convinced that I know more than I'm letting on, which of course is true. But since a celebrated journalist dismisses my idea as lunacy, why should a narrow-minded policeman be any different?" She got to her feet and walking over to the bookshelves, selected a slim red volume from her collection and handed to him. "I'm going for a long soak. This is a more detailed account of Dion Fortune's story, and Alex ... I know the whiff of ectoplasm when I smell it!"

Alex stared into the fire as the scarlet flames rose around a fresh log. If Charlotte were correct and he had no doubt as to her ability to read minds, then Morris would not rest until he had unearthed something to satisfy his enquiring mind. Her explanations concerning psychic phenomena could not convince him and he doubted whether they would impress the detective either. His own research into her background for the interview had revealed the fact that she was held in high enough esteem to be invited to lecture students of parapsychology and anthropology. It appeared that she had unlimited knowledge of Witchcraft and Demonology, and considered most aspects of the paranormal to be within the realms of possibility.

From what he had learned of her family, her father had been eminently respected for his knowledge of the ancient history of the British Isles and Charlotte had cut her eye teeth on *The Old Straight Track*. He was acknowledged to be an expert on stone circles and his colleagues harboured the suspicion that his covert occult knowledge was even more

78

impressive.   His wife did not share her husband's Celtic obsession although she was herself Welsh, but their home life was secure and happy until their untimely death in a 'plane crash when Charlotte was seventeen.

Anxious to avoid having a guardian appointed to curb her freedom, the teenager had managed to coax an old friend of her father's into letting her join an archaeological trip to Crete and from there she had pursued her studies of comparative cults and religions. She had always maintained her family home but it was not until she was nearly thirty, with two unsuccessful marriages behind her, that she'd returned to Ashmarsh to live and begin her new and lucrative career as an occult authority and novelist.

She was proud, stubborn and extremely independent, which meant that any assistance he could give, would have to be without her knowledge or consent.   The power of the press could be a formidable opponent if used to her advantage, with this in mind he went through into the study to borrow Anna's typewriter. The copy of *Ritual Magic in England* lay discarded on the sofa. He did not know it then, but he had just taken the first steps in creating another legend in the annals of crime.

The Hon. Paul Kerrick, the local veterinary surgeon, had his home and practice in Marsh Halse some three miles distant. He was an exceptionally handsome man, greying at the temples with the fine features of centuries of good breeding. He was acknowledged to be the best horse vet in the county but his own personal passion was for natural medicines. It was this common passion that had first brought him and Charlotte Manning together; the mutual occult interest was a later discovery.

There had been talk across the county that they were romantically involved but the gossip and speculation came to nothing, soon dying away.   In fact, they had been very much involved but their identical personalities proved a stumbling block and they both agreed that it was not an ideal base on which to build a permanent relationship. This had in no way impaired their friendship, nor the magical relationship, which had grown in strength over the years.

Now, Charlotte sat opposite him on the edge of a cupboard, waiting for him to finish writing his clinic reports. Finally he put down his pen and walked across the room. Strong arms slid over slim denim clad legs and cupped her firm buttocks, as his mouth came down fiercely on hers. For a moment she surrendered to his demand before resisting by gently pushing him away.

"Paul, don't do this to either of us."

He released her with a grin. "You obviously received my message?"

"Your message! The timing was perfect."

"I thought it might be. We tend to forget that the Iceni met their end around here, and there doesn't seem to be anything else of major importance during that period. Love and hate wouldn't last for 900 years but duty would. Only loyalty could induce a shaman of this capability to protect his dead for so long ... and who would inspire that kind of fealty?"

"Let's not get too ambitious for starters. I've got Anna ferreting out all she can find on Boudica. Once we have a better idea of what we're looking for, we'll be in a stronger position to deal with our friend. By the way, I saw him again after the bonfire party - on his way to the next victim."

"Damn. Why couldn't he be more explicit!"

"The dead aren't known for their verbosity when it comes down to communication with the living, they've always been particularly perverse in matters relating to instructions. That's why I've never seen any point in necromancy. Anyway, all we know is that he requires a particular human life in retribution for the desecration of his dead and the Black One is responsible."

"And it looks as though he's going to pick off anyone in the vicinity, just so's we don't forget. Have you seen this?"

A folded newspaper was handed over with the article outlined in red ink. The tabloid headline screamed 'Ashmarsh Beast Stalks Villagers' , suggesting that in view of the number of anonymous tip-offs directing the police in the direction of localised Witchcraft, this might be a smoke-screen designed to conceal the fact that the murders were being carried out by a religious fanatic. The author went on to expostulate that the suggestion was not preposterous, since the nation-wide satanic ritualised-abuse scandal had been promulgated by Christian fundamentalists, and for four years had Establishment departments convinced that the phenomena actually existed before finally being proven to be a hoax.

The author of the article, a certain M. Ander, went on to cite the case of the priest who was sent to America as a form of 'rehabilitation' after sexually molesting altar boys in the UK, where he had promptly 'sinned' again, and had to be returned to Europe. A leading newspaper had claimed that the Church, knowing that an international man-hunt was taking place, had ferried the priest around Europe to hide him from the authorities. Was it possible that following the collapse of the anti-occult campaign, that an over zealous fundamentalist had decided to take the law into his own hands and that family and friends, or members of the clergy, could be shielding a serial killer?

"Not his usual style," offered Kerrick as Charlotte got angrily to her feet. "But it gets better, or worse, depending on your viewpoint."

The second newspaper, one of the even more tackier tabloids, had picked up on the story with 'God-Squad Blamed for Circle Deaths'. "These will have Morris camped on my doorstep," muttered Charlotte darkly. "What the hell does he think he's playing at?"

"He's just trying to protect you, my love," reasoned Paul gently.

Inspector Alan Morris did not actually feel that Charlotte

Manning was deliberately withholding information. He did, however, realise that her help could be invaluable in understanding and tracking down the killer if there were *genuine* occult connections. Despite the dozens of anonymous letters informing him that Ashmarsh was a nest of Witches and devil worshippers, Morris was not going to make the same mistakes as some of his Northern colleagues who had been caught up in a maelstrom of anti-occult hysteria. Charlotte Manning emphatically denied that any of the deaths could be laid at the door of any witch-cult and he believed her - but he instinctively felt that she had her own ideas about the murders; he wondered how long he would have to wait for her answer.

Morris drove to a lonely fire access in the Whittlewood and mulled over the facts surrounding the four deaths that had occurred on his patch. The chill November afternoon drew the folds of its cloak around him and, as he stared thoughtfully through the windscreen of the car, tongues of fog spread tendrils of misty vapour amongst the gnarled boles of the oak trees. The gloom of a woodland dusk strongly resembled the opening scenes of the Gothic horror movies of which he was so fond. Superstitious by nature, a trait inherited from his Scottish mother, he was half inclined towards a theory of a non-human agency but his logic forced him to think otherwise.

The household of Hunter's Moon drew his attention time and time again. Locals stated without fear or rancour that the lady of the house was, if not exactly a Witch, then someone who certainly possessed extraordinary but indefinable powers. Even the Vicar who, if not denying his neighbour's abilities, was a staunch defender of her character. Charlotte Manning's sponsorship of village welfare work was a well publicised activity; nothing sinister there but he had to take into account the other unlikely suspects he had encountered during his career.

He did not think for one moment that she had anything

to do with the actual killings, but could she be protecting someone? One of the dead girls and the boy suspected of killing her were from Ashmarsh and the village was known for its close-knit community. The boys had been remanded by Magistrate, Horace Ambrose Lawton, despite a lack of forensic evidence to support the case against them. Mind you, thought Morris idly, he himself had often had cause to doubt the reasoning of that particular gentleman on several occasions.

And what was the reason behind that writer chappie producing that ridiculous article. *The Ashmarsh Beast* indeed! What was he trying to achieve? And the Hon. Paul Kerrick, second son of Lord Whatshisname? Morris had the distinct feeling that the whole lot of them had been laughing at him, or was that his imagination? Damn, if D.C. John Sinclair had kept his hand on his dick instead of dabbling with the secretary and providing them all with an alibi! He could do without his men getting their leg over in the middle of a murder case.

Never in his entire career had he seen wounds like those inflicted by the killer of Smiles and Trasker. The old man had been mutilated after death, but the woman's killer needed immense strength to strike a blow sufficient to smash through the rib cage, straight into the heart and then withdraw the weapon to strike again and again. He had seen two cases where the knife had become wedged between the ribs, and the killer had insufficient leverage to remove it, neither of them had been weaklings. Although there had been plenty of blood on the ground from the slashed jugular, there was nothing leading away from the scene to even show in which direction the killer had made his escape.

The dusk had now turned to an inky blackness in the shadow of the tall trees and Alan Morris started the car engine, anxious to get home before the cursed November fog blanketed the countryside. Despite the powerful heater the detective shivered again as superstition replaced logic.

83

No matter from which angle he looked at it, there was no answer to the nagging question of how the attacker was able to leave no tracks in the damp ground.

Chapter Seven

Alex sat on a bar stool, staring at his mirrored reflection through the barrage of brightly polished glasses. "You're a serious journalist Alex," his agent had told him, "leave this sort of thing to the news-hounds."

It had taken a lot of persuasion to convince Sam White-man that no national newspaper had the Ashmarsh story and the fact that he been on the spot when the second and third murders occurred was the only reason the agent accepted it, but not without reservations. Alexander Martin was at the top of the journalistic pile and Whiteman was reluctant to damage that hard earned reputation. By way of compromise, they agreed to submit the article to a leading daily under a pseudonym - Alex did not tell Whiteman that he suspected there was more to come. That would have been too much, and the wily agent would have wanted to know why he was so sure. Even so, the story had been run on the second page of *The Express* and if it helped Charlotte, so much the better.

She did not need his protection.

In fact, she needed nothing from him at all, as far as he could see. She was a rugged, isolated island that he had been allowed to visit but never really felt he had explored; this did not prevent him from feeling guilty at leaving without saying goodbye. The atmosphere at Hunter's Moon had become so oppressive with the constant referrals to the paranormal that he felt the need to escape to the saner more tangible world he knew. He had packed his belongings and fled, leaving a brief note to the fact that he would call her in a couple of days. That was why he was sitting alone in a tiny bar off Covent Garden waiting for his friends to arrive.

If the term 'beautiful people' was still in vogue, it would have been applied to Serge and Eleanor Butler. Both were tall, elegant with smooth blonde good looks and refined features. They were Alex's closest friends, caring deeply about him in return. He had spoken to them on several occasions from Ashmarsh but the conversation had been guarded and he now needed the freshness of their bright humour as an antidote to the sinister darkness that he felt was closing in around him.

Eleanor threw her long arms around his neck and kissed him enthusiastically, to the envy of a handful of businessmen in the bar. Serge bought another round of drinks and they retired to a booth for privacy and comfort. "It's nice to have you back," purred Eleanor still holding his hand.

"You sounded awfully mysterious on the 'phone," added Serge pouring tonic over cracked ice in his glass.

"And then we saw the piece in the paper."

"Can we talk about it when we get back to your place?" Alex pleaded. "I don't want anyone to overhear what I don't believe myself."

Eleanor immediately turned the conversation to gossip about mutual friends and after another round of drinks, suggested they go back to the flat before supper was spoiled. Their flat was located near Shepherd Market and as Alex followed the tail lights of Serge's BMW towards Piccadilly, he almost felt as though he were claiming sanctuary. His brief interlude of rural living had shaken his normally cool composure and it was essential that he unburden his story on two people who, even if they could not understand, would at least listen. He was immersed in something beyond his own powers of comprehension.

Sensitive as always to any tension amongst themselves, both Serge and Eleanor kept the talk light and easy while they ate. When his appetite was satisfied, Alex toyed with the remains of his salad, while Eleanor poured the coffee. He declined Serge's offer to open another bottle of wine, he did not want to be befuddled with alcohol while he related the story. It was ridiculous enough as it was.

"And she really is psychic?" asked Serge to break the silence that followed.

"That much I do believe."

"The rest is incredible. I don't know what to say."

"Alex, come away from there," pleaded Eleanor.

"I am away."

"I mean, don't go back. What if this ... this thing, whatever it is, attacks you?"

Ignoring his partner, Serge phrased his question carefully. "What if the first two victims were the catalytic force needed to activate this ... this thing. Does it seem credible to you that it wasn't human agency?"

"But she's saying she saw it!" Eleanor raised her voice.

"Correction, she stated quite definitely to Alex that she couldn't have seen it, because it wasn't real."

"What does that prove?" asked Eleanor crossly.

"If you're going to be negative ..."

"Hey," broke in Alex. "I didn't come here to have you two falling out over it."

Both of them broke into a laugh and Serge reached out to take her hand. "She just over-reacts sometimes," he joked. Eleanor hit him good naturedly with a cushion. "So what you're saying is that the police should be looking for a knife wielding assassin, who leaves no prints in muddy ground and who, in fact, does not exist."

"Shouldn't be too difficult." Eleanor tried to lighten the conversation.

"Or someone *else* with extremely powerful occult knowledge," said Serge softly.

87

"Which is the most plausible?" sighed Alex.

"The second, in view of the lack of footprints or ground disturbance. And the rights to the film's screenplay," Serge suggested.

"This may seem like a stupid question to you avid disciples of magic, but surely if Charlotte Manning *really* is psychic, she should be able to sense if there is someone sending out psychic energy signals?" asked Eleanor.

"Not necessarily, if there is someone with power of that magnitude, then they would have no difficulty in blocking off a mind probe from a lesser or unsuspecting power." said Serge.

"Wow," exclaimed Alex laughing for the first time since his arrival. "I'm impressed."

Relaxed laughter turned the conversation to other matters, including the suggestion that Alex stay with them for a few days, instead of going back to his own flat. Although he had desperately wanted to get away from Ashmarsh, by the time he reached the motorway, he had already decided that he did not want to be alone and their invitation was eagerly accepted.

While they were waiting their turn in the bathroom, Eleanor tucked her arm under his. "What are you *really* afraid of? Charlotte?"

"Myself," he answered and slipped into the bathroom ahead of her, as Serge opened the door.

Later, unable to sleep, Alex turned over the events in his brain. He was glad that their conversation had ended when it had, he did not want to say that on her own admission Charlotte had stated that her own psychic powers were a result of centuries of accumulated knowledge, or was *he* over-reacting? Had she really said that? No, she hadn't, she had only given an example of the possible mind-power of someone who HAD been reincarnated several times over. But she did say she had lived before, said an inner voice.

Several days later, a mentally and emotionally recharged

Alex agreed to accompany Eleanor on a shopping expedition to Fortnum's. After collecting some personal belongings from his flat, he also took the opportunity to pay a visit to The London Library in St James's Square. He knew he wouldn't find the answer to the dozens of questions that perplexed him but at least he could acquaint himself with some Celtic history. An hour later he had made pages of notes relating to Celtic Britain.

Charlotte had referred to a 'shaman' and this he learned was a magician or healer who was in contact with the deities and spirits sacred to his people. The more he read, the more he realised how far her world was removed from his own, for Charlotte accepted things which he considered fanciful, as a reality. One point that did attract his interest, but he did not know why, was the shaman's ability to commune with ancestral spirits and escort the souls of the dead to the otherworld. It appeared that shamanism was a particularly powerful brand of magic - if you believed in such nonsense.

A chill wind greeted him as he walked into Piccadilly, pausing to look in shop windows, where assistants were changing the displays in readiness for Christmas. By prior arrangement, he and Eleanor were to meet in Richoux's for lunch and he was pleased to see that she already occupied a booth at the rear of the small restaurant. Several regular lunchers who knew them both came over to indulge in a brief gossip, for the word was on the street that Alexander Martin had a new interest in his life.

"Don't you miss all this?" she asked, expertly picking at her stir-fry vegetables.

Alex shrugged and refrained from answering. When he was in Ashmarsh he had sometimes longed for the buzz of fashionable London but now he had found himself missing the log fires and the excellent food that was to be had at Hunter's Moon. For despite the reasons behind his sudden departure, in the few days since his return to the City, he had actually found nothing to compare with the peace of that strange country house.

"I miss you and Serge rather than London," he replied. "Anyway, there's nothing for me to go back to. She's not the sort of woman you walk out on."

"Alex" a voice called over the gentle rumble of conversation.

"Hello Charles."

"Saw your piece old boy. Thought you were more suited to writing about fallen heiresses, not covering a recalcitrant psychopath terrorising the darkest Midlands."

The famous muscle twitched at the corner of Alex's mouth and he was only seconds from hitting the man.

"Charles," interrupted Eleanor sweetly. "Why don't you crawl into a corner and fester!"

"Charming," came the reply, but the hint was taken and the offended diner ambled off.

"Don't worry," Eleanor stroked the back of his hand.

"That article was supposed to be by an unknown freelancer and everyone appears to know I wrote it!"

"Sam wasn't too clever with the choice of pseudonym and gossip has already linked your name with Charlotte."

In the small restaurant, listening to other people's conversations was unavoidable and Alex felt uncomfortable; but he was glad they hadn't gone to The Groucho Club where the media-junkies would have been out in full force. He sensed rather than heard Charlotte Manning's name mentioned and it suddenly came home to him what a small, petty, sham world it was. Cruel jealousy and cutting jibes were considered witty conversation between people whose intellectual abilities were only a thin veneer. Charlotte was correct in what she had said that first weekend - what right *had* these people to sit in judgement and whisper.

The old cliches about jungles came to mind; the kicking and clawing and biting to survive and be top of the heap by these superficial but deadly butterflies. He had only had a brief glimpse of that other jungle through a flimsy veil.

Another jungle of another time, where primitive man stalked the darkness waiting for the kill, where the heady perfume of decaying leaves and wood smoke was far more pleasing than the belch of exhaust fumes. The glossy bright people of this world could not survive in that other far, remote place; they would quickly wither and die in such an environment. Had he forfeited his right to return?

"Are you going to leave me sitting here?"

"Sorry pet, I was far away for a minute."

Alex settled the bill and they walked back to Fortnum's. Eleanor's classic beauty turned heads and Alex enjoyed the prestige of having such an elegant woman on his arm. Her short cropped hair, coloured a delicate ash provided a flattering frame for her expressive grey eyes. The perfect bone structure and flawless make-up coupled with the tailored mink-coloured coat with matching accessories were the envy of many a younger woman in the store. It might not be the height of high-street fashion - but Eleanor had her own distinctive style.

She could have had any of the men in London at her feet but she still only had eyes for Serge. The daughter of an old county family she had abandoned the life-style so loved by her parents for Serge, who was strongly disapproved of by her father and dismissed as a 'sponger' by her brother. When she had announced her intention to live with him, her father's wrath knew no bounds and much to her brother's delight, she had been ordered out of the house. Now it was only possible for her to visit the family home when there were no weekend guests and her father was absent. Serge was forbidden to even enter the drive.

"I've been thinking about Charlotte," she said as they piled into a taxi. "I do believe she's been to dinner at The Grange on several occasions. Wasn't she going out with Paul Kerrick, the local vet, at one time?"

"What on earth are your parent's thinking about, entertaining the local vet and a novelist?" Alex remarked, half in jest and half in resentment.

"Oh, Paul's father is a baron, although his elder brother inherits the estate and the title, so he's definitely good county stock," replied his companion, knowing full well what he meant. "Charlotte's family were landed gentry, I think. How much do you know about her?"

"Not a lot," he confessed. "On her own admission she's had a couple of husbands and has travelled around the world before coming back to Ashmarsh. I didn't know the vet was an old flame, though," he added.

"What a lovely old fashioned expression."

Over dinner that evening they regaled Serge with the gossip and details of the days activities, finishing off with Eleanor's remembrance of Charlotte's name as a guest at her family home.

"Obviously the lady has better connections than me," said Serge without a trace of malice. "I have not been idle. I spoke to a couple of people on the 'phone but they couldn't, or wouldn't, be very helpful. They did admit to knowing of your lady-friend, and although no-one was very forthcoming, I got the impression that we were talking serious stuff."

"They wouldn't give much away to a casual enquirer."

"I brought these home for you," said Serge, offering two thick paperback volumes. "Read these and nothing will surprise you ever again."

Alex frowned at the prospect of ploughing through the contents. "But will they help?" said the voice of scepticism.

"I have a whole library if it will help. I keep them at the office."

"And they can stay there!" came a voice from the kitchen. "I thought you'd stopped reading that rubbish."

"My dear girl, I may be a humble Somerset lad but I assure you that my blood is pure Celt. The paranormal is not rubbish."

"I didn't know you read this," said Alex.

"He's what is commonly referred to as 'into it'," replied

Eleanor serving juicy chicken pieces, "and he would give his eye teethto get into that damned woman's company!"

Alex had been away from Hunter's Moon for over a week and whilst he had made several telephone calls, he had never managed to speak to Charlotte. He had a desperate need to hear her voice and to apologise for running out on her. He missed her body in bed but more important, he missed her throaty laughter, her frown of concentration and all the little, foolish things that make a relationship important. He accepted the fact that he missed being with her and that he was actually forcing himself to stay away. For the third time that week, he flung the receiver down in exasperation as he listened to the precise tones of Anna's voice on the ansaphone.

Eleanor and Serge had been invited to a weekend party and reluctantly, Alex agreed to join them. He was half tempted to drive to Ashmarsh and demand to know why she was constantly unavailable, but common sense and the fact that he had only known her for a few weeks prevailed. He had no claims on her time or person but his ego would have liked to have known if she was sulking or angry because he had left her.

The party was well under way when they arrived at the Cheyne Walk apartment. Rich curtains were pulled back and through a vast panoramic window, the dark waters of the Thames flowed icy and glittering with reflected light. Their host was a client of Serge's, who had selected the guests with as much care as the food and wine. There was something for every taste. Morsels to be taken up and sampled. The buzz of conversation and laughter filled the room like a gigantic hive.

Those males who had not brought along their own partners, cast envious glances at Eleanor, coolly turned out in white, but the protective presence of her lover was enough to persuade them to look elsewhere for their fun. Those who knew the couple, lost no time in asking Eleanor to dance and Serge was left to fend off the remaining predatory females. The Butlers were so sure of each other that jealousy was not included in their make-up. Perfectly matched, neither had any fear that their partner would be attracted to someone else.

Alex, on the other hand, had a reputation for appreciating good champagne and fine looking women and both were in plentiful supply. In contrast to his friend's strong virile appearance, Alex could have made a successful second career as a model. With a physique that was any designer's dream, he stalked catlike amongst the guests until he was accosted by an elfin West Indian girl. The grey cashmere suit showed style, as did the rest of his appearance and she appraised him hungrily. Aware of the dark liquid pools that followed him across the room, Alex wasted no time in pulling the girl onto the dance floor.

The rhythmic writhing of her supple body against his as they danced, made him suddenly think of another woman, with dark hair and green eyes who had the same pantherian grace. Another woman who would be contemptuous of this colourful, fast living, pleasure loving crowd. Annoyed with the unsummoned apparition, he was determined not to let her stand between him and his prey, and he dismissed the vision from his mind. Almost rudely, he suggested that they leave the party for somewhere quieter and the girl eagerly agreed.

Their coupling was frenzied and urgent. A tangle of dark and light limbs, holding, intertwining with animal lust and uncontrolled passion. Here there was no room for gentleness, no spiritual release that belonged to that other world; the one he had chosen to ignore for a few fleeting, unimportant hours. His need to dominate and possess overruled his natural inclinations as he asserted his virility on the willing body of his dusky companion. Thoroughly sated with alcohol and sex, he slept fitfully and beset by demons.

The cold, uncompromising light of a November morning flooded the room as Alex pushed back the crumpled sheets on a strange bed and stumbled towards the tiny bathroom. His head felt as though it were already in two halves as he turned on the shower's biting spray and flushed the used condoms down the lavatory. The hot water revived him and as his head cleared, he was aware of a sharp sensation of pain across his shoulders. He heard a cry of astonishment from the open door and as he half turned, he caught the expression of revulsion in the girl's wide eyes.

"Your back!" was all she could say by way of explanation over the noise of the water.

Grabbing a bathtowel Alex pushed past her into the bedroom. An overpowering smell of stale sex and incense hung in the air and where he had slept, the crumpled sheet was covered in blood. Nausea and panic swept over him as a large mirror reflected the deep scratches that disfigured his skin; from the shoulders down over his buttocks there were deep claw marks. For an instant he was about to blame the girl but he knew these were of no *human* origin. Quickly he pulled on his clothes and to the girl's obvious relief, he left for the sanctuary of the Shepherd Market flat.

"You look like hell," greeted a rumpled Serge, who was just pouring himself a strong coffee. "Have fun?"

Without speaking, Alex removed his jacket and turning, peeled off the shirt which was now sticking to the bloody wounds. Wincing with pain as silk tore away from drying blood, he threw the ruined garment on the floor.

"Christ man," breathed Serge in mock admiration, "I didn't realise you were that good!"

"Shut up!" screamed Eleanor who had heard Alex come in. "Look at him!" She burst into tears, flinging herself into Alex's arms, sobbing almost to the point of hysteria.

Between them they managed to get him to the bathroom to vomit before he passed out. From the depths of the darkness he was pursued by gigantic black cats, their green eyes flashing with anger, jaws gaping wide to show the terrible curve of strong white teeth. ` Hissing and spitting, their screams of challenge echoed through his brain and amid the noise and terror he heard a familiar deep throaty laugh.

All the fury of hell vent itself on his numbed brain allowing him no rest. As he drifted in and out of troubled sleep he was at least sure of one thing - she cared! She cared enough to hate him, reeking vengeance in such a terrible manner, that there could be no doubt who was instrumental in inflicting those appalling injuries. She was guilty of one of the deadliest of human sins. Jealousy. A candle flickered briefly at the end of a long, dark tunnel. If she cared that much, then he would be a fool to turn his back on such passion. Was this a summons to return?

Alex passed Sunday in a haze, he was aware of Serge's gentle touch as he removed the rest of his friend's clothes and bathed the wounds. He half recalled Eleanor's tear-stained face as she sat by his side, holding his hand. The following day, she insisted that he remain in bed and by evening, he was ready to join them for dinner. During the meal none of them referred to the night of the party. There was an embarrassed silence as each felt the need to talk about it but not wanting to be the one to start the conversation.

"Let's talk it out," said Alex finally.

Serge helped himself to a liberal slice of pie. "Have you told him?" he asked Eleanor, almost too casually.

She twisted her napkin around her finger. "I spoke to my Mother about Charlotte Manning and apparently she spent the weekend from Saturday afternoon with them and Paul Kerrick."

As they sat facing their friend, both Eleanor and Serge felt a desperate need to express their feeling for him in some way. "Well, at least she didn't get laid Alex. No one is allowed to in that house. The doors are bolted from the outside upon retiring, when you are issued with a chamber pot and copy of *Country Life*," remarked Serge in an attempt at humour.

96

"What are you going to do?" asked Eleanor gently squeezing his arm.

The expression on his face reflected his inner hurt as the grey eyes narrowed. "I'm going back to Ashmarsh, it appears that I might be wanted after all. And if I don't go now, I'll never find out for sure."

.

Chapter Eight

It was late afternoon before Alex managed to leave London. Eleanor had done everything in her power to prevent his returning to Ashmarsh but finally he was on his way northwards on the motorway. There had been thick fog that had failed to disperse all morning and as he left the security of the continuous stream of slow traffic, he found himself driving along the narrow country lanes towards the village. The sun hung in the sky but the blanket of fog prevented the fiery light from pervading the gloom.

In the eerie yellow glow, the roads and hedgerows were unfamiliar and menacing as tendrils of fog wrapped themselves around the Austin Healey. The silence was broken by the shrill cry of a bird, whose voice trilled out in the cold afternoon air. A large cock pheasant ran out from the hedge, causing him to brake sharply. Fortunately for the bird, he was driving slowly and with a squawk of indignation it vanished into the hedge.

Like a cross-roads spectre, the white signpost for Ashmarsh pointed in the direction of the heavens, due no doubt, to some recent earth subsidence. However, this sign was only three miles from the village and he would soon be out of the damnable fog. His eyes burned from staring into nothingness and the pain from his wounds, aggravated by his hunched position over the steering wheel, was beginning to affect his concentration.

With relief he swung the sports-car into the courtyard and at the sound of his key in the side door, Gwen Carradine came out to greet him. Her round ample figure and the familiar smell from her kitchen greeted him with a feeling of maternal welcome and returning home. Already the warmth of Hunter's Moon wrapped itself around him, drawing him into its heart and banishing all the haunting doubts. He felt a little foolish at his flight.

"Managed to get back for the party in spite of the fog, Mr Martin," she beamed, "You get rid of that coat and come into the kitchen for a cup of tea."

"Is Mrs Manning in?"

"No love, the pair of 'em went into town to collect some things for tonight but they shouldn't be long. It's the fog you see," she added quite unnecessarily.

Alex suppressed a grin. "Of course."

While she made the tea, Gwen prattled on about the effect of the murders on the community. Although Smiles had been a good-for-nothing poacher and bible-punching Emily Trasker had been thoroughly disliked by her neighbours, the villagers were canny enough to see the connections between the two killings and no-one walked out alone after dark. Fathers demanded that daughters be brought home to the doorstep, encouraging all manner of nocturnal couplings on cottage hearthrugs by insisting that boyfriends not cycle home alone through the dark woods. Being discredited *was* better than being dead.

After accepting tea and a couple of slices of Mrs C's excellent cherry cake, he excused himself and went through into the sitting room. As usual, the grey cats had selected the best places near the fire and took no notice of his arrival. Unceremoniously dumping the big grey on a sofa, Alex ignored the malevolent stare and pulled the chair closer to the fire. He was enjoying the peace when Anna's voice brought him back to earth.

"Hello you," she said, lightly kissing his cheek. "Where have you been?"

99

"I've been up to London avoiding the Queen" he replied in a slightly sour tone.

Anna shrugged. "We've been away, too. Charly needed some research on the Iceni for her next book but it was too damn cold to do anything. Why it can't be set in summer, God only knows."

"When did you get back?" he asked casually.

"Saturday morning. She had some plans for the weekend." There was a hint of malice in her tone.

"With Paul Kerrick!"

Her eyebrows rose slightly but she gave no other hint of being taken aback. "That's right, you'll be able to meet him tonight."

The bitching session would have continued if Charlotte hadn't chosen that moment to enter, followed by Gwen and the tea trolley. For a moment they studied each other warily from across the room. It was Charlotte who broke the tension.

"Hello darling," she cried with artificial gaiety, "why didn't you let us know you were coming?"

"I've been talking to your ansaphone all week."

"You didn't leave a forwarding number so it wasn't possible to let you know of my arrangements," she replied, still smiling but the eyes were as cold as the basilisk's gaze.

The conversation continued with clipped, unspoken recriminations, offered first by one and then the other until Alex began to wish he had not bothered to return. After all, *she* had been away for the weekend with another man and if he were here tonight, it would be extremely embarrassing. It was with an inward sigh of relief that he found an excuse to follow Charlotte upstairs and escape Anna's amusement at his expense.

As soon as the bedroom door closed behind them, Alex pulled off his sweater to expose the cruel scratches, now a mass of crusted blood. "Look at this!"

She appraised him impassively. "Most impressive, did you remember to leave *her* your 'phone number?"

100

"Damn it Charlotte, these aren't human finger nails and you know it."

"I can only speak of your tastes as being rather conservative. Whatever your persuasions are away from here, they're none of my concern."

Alex smashed his fist against the window-sill in exasperation and stood silently staring out into the dusk. Darkness had fallen and fog blanketed the house. Emotional, in addition to physical, hurt swept over him with the acceptance that she was not offering him the peace he had been so desperate to find. He had convinced himself that by returning to Hunter's Moon everything would be seen in a different light.

"I shouldn't have come back." Weariness disguised his hurt.

"No-one ever wanted you to leave," she answered, the inflection in her voice softer but still remote. "That was entirely your own decision."

For the first time since his return, she stared him full in the face and he felt the tenderness flooding out of her like an electric current. Her own eyes mirrored the intense hurt she must have felt at his sudden departure and he felt guilty for causing her so much pain. He sank gratefully into the padded chair and leaned his head back against the cushion.

"I had to go. I thought I was going out of my head with all that talk of bloody psychic phenomena. I needed to find my own level of normality. The panic, the running away, the girl - it was an exorcism."

Her hand reached out and lightly brushed his hair. "And did it work? Did your friends help you rediscover yourself?" There was a slight edge to the question but it was good natured mockery.

He shook his head and laughed with a note of bitterness. "No. Serge was more interested in your capabilities and to echo the thoughts of Mrs Lamb, Eleanor thinks you're mad, bad and dangerous to know." He managed a weak smile and taking her hand, gently kissed the palm.

Charlotte knelt by the chair, running her hands gently over his naked chest as her mouth sought his. The familiar urge of desire twisted like a knot in his groin and he communicated his need by growing hard at her touch, despite the intense pain from his wounds. Between kisses she suggested they share a hot bath, and as the warmth of the water soothed away the last jagged edges of anger that had held them apart, fingers and toes explored slippery curves under a froth of perfumed bubbles.

"I did miss you," she whispered huskily as she lay against his chest in the deep water.

"I'm sorry for going without telling you. It was a cruel thing to do."

The conciliatory kiss conveyed more than words or promises and, for the first time since knowing her, Alex actually believed that she did care for him. She was an exceptional woman and it would take time for their relationship to grow, but at last he knew he had met someone with whom he could consider sharing his life - if nothing else happened to spoil it!

"Let me see those cuts," she murmured as she dried the inflamed wounds with a soft towel. "I think I've got something for that."

She returned from the bathroom with a very old, glass stoppered apothecary bottle, containing a dark green liquid. The sharp, astringent smell of wet leaves and spring hedgerows caught his nostrils as she smeared the soothing medication on his skin. Within seconds the raw, burning sensation disappeared and the muscles along his back relaxed under the soft strokes of the cotton wool.

"Does Gwen brew that in the bath?"

"No. This is my own recipe made from belladonna."

"That's poison!"

"Don't panic, this is made from the leaves not the berries."

Under her gentle touch, the pain from the lacerations dispersed, leaving only the strong need for *caring* sex. "If I

102

remember correctly, The Beast maintained a positive belief in sex magic. How about taking an added precaution, just in case your potion fails?"

"Oh, the belt and braces approach," she answered with a laugh, untying her bathrobe and throwing it aside.

The scent from her skin carried the warm, spicy fragrance of clove and carnation. Firmly he confined her arms above her head, one hand securing her wrists, while the other kneaded the firm flesh. Not until he was sure her desire matched his own, was he content to release his grip and take her in his arms, holding her close while they made love.

"What's the party in aid of?" he asked sleepily as Charlotte dressed again in the lamplight.

"It was Paul's idea. Our dear Alan Morris is still making a bit of a nuisance of himself over our local Witches and I can hardly take him along to an esbat. So, as I usually have a drinks party around Yuletime, Paul thought it was a good idea for the Inspector to be invited. That way, neither he nor I have given anyone's name and the murders will be a fairly normal topic of conversation. The Inspector can observe and question all he likes - and the Craft will have the opportunity for an off-the-record chat about the anonymous letters."

"Good idea and then, like Hercule Poirot, at the end of the night he can denounce the guilty party," murmured Alex as he drifted off into a deep sleep.

He awoke over an hour later in the darkened room. Someone had turned off the lamps while he slept but he was conscious of the deep rumbling purring of a cat. As his eyes became accustomed to the dark, he could make out the shape of the large grey whose place he had usurped earlier, curled at his side. A chink of light from the hall crept into the room, turning the amber eyes to an evil glowing red. The purrs seemed to fill the room, indicating that its mood was friendly but he could not ignore the sharp pressure of the needle sharp claws against his skin. This was the first time the cat had ever shown any liking for his company and as he nervously stroked the satin head, Charlotte arrived with a strong black coffee.

"How are you feeling?"

He felt surprisingly well and free from the discomforting scratches "Here's to Witchcraft," he toasted her with the coffee cup.

"'So mote it be' is the correct response. You have half and hour before Paul arrives for supper. The rest of them don't arrive until eight."

She was dressed in a dark green velvet gown; her dark hair tied back with a black velvet ribbon and the only piece of jewellery was a heavy rose-gold chain at her throat. Certainly not fashionable, but extremely elegant.

For the first time in his life, Alexander Martin dressed to compete with another *man*. Anna had talked about Kerrick on numerous occasions and barely concealed her attraction to the debonair vet. He already had a mental picture of the smooth, sleek, immaculately tailored Paul Kerrick, whose impeccable taste would be impossible to match. For sheer contrast, he selected the grey cashmere suit that he had purchased whilst out shopping with Eleanor.

It was a loose cut, hardly suitable for the country but it was good quality, highly fashionable and with the correct accessories would make him stand out in any crowd. When he was ready, he took a final look in the mirror to study the effect. His choice of a yellow and blue shirt, worn with a loosely knotted tie and soft grey leather casual shoes was an ideal choice for the West End but he was not sure about Ashmarsh. His stylish brown hair was teased into a casual style to flatter his angular face and generous mouth.

Paul Kerrick rose from the sofa immediately he entered the room and advanced with his hand outstretched. "Alex Martin? Paul Kerrick. What can I get you to drink?"

For a few seconds while the drinks were poured Alex took the opportunity of appraising his rival. He had been cor-

104

rect in his assumption that the vet would be elegant and though he knew of his background, he was nevertheless impressed by the fine, aristocratic good looks of the man. Every move, every gesture reflected refinement and good breeding. It was his frank brown eyes that made Alex dismiss his previous misgivings and decide to like him.

"I expect you find us strange animals down here," Paul reflected as they sat by the roaring fire. "Some aspects of our life-style are still positively archaic."

Alex laughed easily. "It's taken some getting used to, especially knowing what to wear. That was a problem and still is," he gestured to the grey suit by way of an apology for any lack of taste.

"On the contrary, we dress to suit our neighbours, our environment and to conform to an uniform code of behaviour that others in our group recognise as their own. If I were to mix in your circles," he indicated his own clothes, "I would be dismissed as *passe.*"

"Not entirely but I take your point. However, county people do seem to have a certain distinctive style and that is important."

Paul laughed. "Don't be fooled by appearances. Most of us would pull on the first thing that comes to hand. It reflects generations of being totally dependent on a valet. I inform Evans of my weekly engagements and the appropriate clothes are laid out for me. He will occasionally observe that certain items need replacing and makes the necessary arrangements with my tailor or outfitters. A very simple system but most of us would be in a devil of a mess without it."

Their conversation was interrupted by Anna announcing that dinner was served and that Charlotte was waiting for them in the dining room. Heavy drapes were closed against the damp December night and the sombre tones of richly carved oak panelling reflected the splendour of a bygone age. The only light came from the fire and two enormous candelabra set at either end of the huge table. Each

105

holding a dozen tapering candles, the candelabra shed a flickering brilliance on the fine crystal and silver. It was not only moonlight that suited her, reflected Alex, as he took his place on the opposite side of the table, candle-light could also be used to her advantage.

As usual the food and wine were excellent and the conversation animated, with no awkward moments. Alex made up his mind to persuade Paul to agree to an interview. He was interested in this youngest son of a baron, who had built himself a successful veterinary practice with a formidable reputation among the county-set, which amply supported the life-style to which he was born. He felt the vet would have far more to say than the latest craze in the world of popular music or football; here was a man with life flowing in his veins and as Charlotte had predicted, he felt he was fully capable of bringing that life to the printed page.

"My father refused to speak to me when he learned that I'd entered Veterinary College, he thought I was in the Guards." They all laughed in response, although Charlotte and Anna had obviously heard the story before. "However, my dear Alex, anyone who has managed to capture this elusive lady in print has my grudging respect and I will most certainly agree to become your victim."

Before they had finished coffee, the first guests arrived, which meant Anna and Charlotte left the men to finish their port and cigars. There was a hum of voices from the hall, trailing off into the distance as the new arrivals were shepherded into the sitting room.

"The first of my adoring public," said Kerrick in the resigned tone of a man who was a firm favourite amongst elderly ladies.

"I understood you were a horse doctor."

"I am but my first love is the cat. Cruel, vicious and only a paw print away from the wild, but there isn't a creature on this earth more beautiful. Although I was virtually born on a horse," he continued, "and a reasonably competent point-to-point competitor in my younger days."

"And hunting?"

"It's a subject that's taboo around this dining table," he answered, glancing sideways, "but yes, I hunted."

Seizing on the past tense, Alex pressed home his question. "And what made you stop?" It was not idle curiosity, he sensed it had something to do with Charlotte, and he hoped he wouldn't offend Kerrick by pressing the point.

Paul studied the end of his cigar for a moment as though he were carefully considering his answer. "It wasn't conscience I assure you. I had hunted since I was a boy and it was second nature. I was also at Eton with the Master of Fox Hounds and had been invited to the traditional Boxing Day meet. Our remarkable hostess remained at home but begged me not to ride that day because my life was in danger. I ignored her warning and as you probably know by now, Charlotte's is not a voice to be ignored. My mount shied at a stone wall and I was thrown onto a chain harrow, severely injuring my back. I have never ridden since."

"You don't believe she had anything to do with it!" asked Alex incredulously before he could stop himself.

Paul made a strange sound. "Obviously you're aware of her powers, but be realistic - as I had to be. The animal was a favourite of mine, she may have sensed the danger on the other side of the wall, they certainly outrank us when it comes to a sixth sense. And as is the case with any rider of experience, it was not the first time I'd been thrown. I don't doubt Charlotte's power of clairvoyance, she's demonstrated it too accurately in the past but to cause the accident ... No!"

There was a silence as the vet refilled Alex's glass. "Were you lovers?" he asked before he could stop himself.

His companion, didn't even flinch at the forthright question. "We had been for many years. She disagreed with the doctors who said I would be paralysed and fortunately I believed in *her*. Perhaps I needed to believe in something after doubting her warning and it was not misplaced. She

107

helped me through those first difficult months but from then on our affair was ended - but not our friendship," he added firmly.

Alex raised the crystal glass. "To a fellow victim"

Paul raised his glass with a hollow laugh. "I hope you are never afflicted the way I was." A masculine voice joined the group in the sitting room and before the journalist could reply, Paul got to his feet. "Let's join the good Inspector and observe the suspects."

Several hours later, five people sat around the fire drinking coffee. The fog had driven Charlotte's guests home early and those remaining were discussing the events of the evening.

"So, on which Witch of this parish does your suspicion fall?" Paul asked of Alan Morris with amused candour.

Morris was more amiable than he had been for weeks. "Alright, you've all made your point. I will admit that it is highly unlikely that any of those here tonight would be capable of this type of murder. But I appreciated their frankness. And to give them their due, no-one tried to convince me it was the fundamentalists!"

"Can you imagine the Misses Green and Osbourne tearing a man limb from limb?" laughed Charlotte as Anna and Paul joined in her merriment, relating the story for the benefit of the others.

The septuagenarian pair lived in a small cottage in Woodford Halse, which was also home to an assortment of cats. Their genteel upbringing had not equipped them for holding conversations with a man on the subject of feline sexuality and it usually took Paul Kerrick a vast consumption of tea and home-made cake before he managed to discover the reason for his visit. Neither of them would remain in the room whilst he conducted an examination as, on the first occasion the elder, Miss Osbourne, had fainted dead away when Paul had taken a rectal temperature recording from one of their pets.

108

"But not all Witches can be good guys?" quizzed Morris with a twinkle in his eye.

"Of course not," replied Anna. "In fact there are a lot who like to refer to themselves as Witches, but who have never really made any real study of the Craft. Unfortunately, it always seems to be that variety who get themselves in the papers or on television, and do nothing to convince the public that the Craft isn't an outlet for promiscuous behaviour."

"There's no possibility that a group of these ... amateur witches ... could be the ones we're looking for?"

"I wouldn't think so," interrupted Charlotte. "There's been no attempt to tart up the deaths to *look* like a ritual sacrifice and if that *were* the case, I'd have expected a couple of pentagrams to be painted up somewhere, at least. And that argument holds for any form of fundamentalist frame-up too."

"I take your point." Morris sighed and accepted another drink. "So we can discount the theory you so clearly expressed in your newspaper article Mr Martin."

Alex had the good grace to blush.

Chapter Nine

After a couple of days, the damp creeping fog lifted and the warmth of the sun helped to dispense some of the trepidation surrounding Ashmarsh as the village people went about their daily routine. Children played on the Green whilst vigilant mothers kept an eye out for any strangers who might approach.

Although no-one was tempted to venture out alone after dark, none of the inhabitants really suspected his neighbour of the murders, laying the blame squarely on the shoulders of some unknown assailant; an opinion now shared by those daily newspapers whose banner headlines had originally implied devil worship and Witchcraft. The Ashmarsh Beast, now stoutly identified as a religious fanatic, was a reality in the tabloids and drawing a considerable amount of flack from the established Churches, who resented the allegations.

At Hunter's Moon the morning sun spread a welcome glow on the crisp linen of the dining table as the household finished their breakfast. A large pile of mail lay unopened by Charlotte's plate, the garish colours of Christmas stamps prompting her to ask Alex about his own plans for the holiday.

"Oh God," groaned Anna, "We're about to be organised." Hastily swallowing the last of her coffee, she grabbed the mail and fled from the room.

Charlotte looked mildly offended and Alex poured another coffee to cover his amusement. "I hadn't really thought about it," he lied.

"Don't you normally spend it with your friends?" she asked, a little too casually.

"Normally yes, but I thought perhaps you could ask them here instead. I'm sure you'd enjoy their company and Serge's dying to meet you." Charlotte looked doubtful. "You know Eleanor's family - Colonel and Mrs Hamilton at The Grange."

For once Charlotte was surprised. "The Hamilton girl?"

"Hardly, she's well over thirty."

"And learned little in those thirty odd years."

"How can you say that when you don't even know her?" retorted Alex loyally.

Her green eyes studied him patiently and calmly. "Because she leaves the entire running of the estate in the hands of that moronic brother, who will destroy the place within six months of his father's death."

"Excuse me, but her father booted her out because she loved Serge," Alex almost shouted in reply.

"Correction! Your friend left home in a school-girl huff because her father objected to her living with a penniless art student. He can be forgiven for wanting better than that for a daughter who could have been the belle of the county."

"Eleanor would have gone back if Serge had been allowed in the house. They wouldn't give him a chance." Alex was seething at the unwarranted criticism of his closest friends.

Charlotte sighed. "Paul and I have tried to educate you in the ways of county matters. The Colonel is old school, professional army man and all that. To have his daughter living with a man she's not married to is only one step up from prostitution in his eyes. An archaic attitude in these enlightened days, I agree, but that's how the old boy thinks. Believe me there's not a day goes by that he doesn't wish his daughter back."

"How do you know?" asked her lover without thinking.

Her expression did not change, neither did she answer. "What about him?" Meaning Serge.

"You and Serge would get on extremely well. He's basically an extremely talented artist who clawed his way up from a farm labourer's family to reach the top of the pile in a very cut-throat profession. Marketing might be a dirty word but those who are on top are damned good at it. He does have one of the largest agencies in London. And he's not occult-illiterate," he added as bait.

Gwen came in to clear away the breakfast plates, filling the room with her cheerful bustling presence. "Have your friends decided whether to visit us for Christmas, Mr Martin?" she asked.

"I wasn't aware ..." began her employer.

"Mr Martin told me a couple of days ago that you might have company. I'm sure a Christmas away from London will do them the world of good ..." She prattled on, reminiscing about her childhood memories and her own children growing up until Charlotte suggested a walk.

"You've obviously joined forces with Gwen in taking over the running of the household and she's just ended the dilemma of what to do for Christmas."

Alex helped her into her sheepskin coat. "'Oh, what a tangled web we weave'." Good naturedly she kicked his shin in reply.

The harmony spilled over into the garden as they walked hand in hand across the paddock, cocooned in a silence that only happens between new lovers, comfortable with their own happiness. The woods were quiet with pale sunlight filtering down through the bare branches of beech and oak, gnarled and knotted through centuries of existence. Twisted and deformed, some blasted by lightning, but each spring pushing forth the pale green shoots of life. The sound of voices sent a pair of wood pigeons hurrying to the safety of the upper branches with a whirr of strong wings.

A lone oak tree, whose massive root system had created a

112

ridge in the forest floor, presided over a gigantic rabbit warren. The Ashmarsh rabbits had somehow escaped the deadly plague of myxomatosis in the '50s, maintaining their isolated existence and immune from the fatal virus transmitted by the rabbit flea. This part of the old Whittlewood Forest was a haven for rabbits and their paths criss-crossed the ancient forest floor creating a series of tracks that could be followed for miles.

Suddenly the screams of child in pain shattered the peaceful morning. Fearful of what they would find, Alex and Charlotte ran as fast as they could through tangled undergrowth and whip-like saplings, in the direction of the ridge, where the path through the forest had been widened by horses. There amongst the bracken, a small girl lay screaming in terror, her foot held fast by the vicious jaws of a gin-trap, while a boy, only a few years older struggled in vain to release her.

"Put the pressure on the metal plates but don't get your hands anywhere near the teeth," instructed Charlotte as she pushed the boy aside.

The girl's cries echoed through the woodland as the trap sprung open and released the lacerated leg. While he held the metal jaws apart, Charlotte pulled the girl away and as Alex released the pressure, the trap snapped shut with a sickening crunch. He had read of illegal gin-traps but this was the first time he'd ever seen at first hand the damage such contraptions could cause. The girl had been wearing high rubber boots but the leg of an animal would have no such protection, and the image of a defenceless creature caught by those terrible teeth made him shudder.

"Let's get back to the house," ordered Charlotte and with the tearful bundle wrapped inside his coat, Alex carried the girl while Charlotte sent the boy on ahead to warn Mrs Carradine about the accident. Slowly they trudged home, and although their conversation turned back to plans for Christmas there was little enthusiasm on either side.

By the time they reached the house, Gwen had set up the first aid box and provided towels, bandages and plenty of hot water. Sitting the girl on the kitchen table, Charlotte set about removing the ripped boot with strong scissors, so that she could get at the wound. It was difficult cutting through the stout rubber but eventually the boot was cut open enough to pull it away from the mangled flesh. With a dirt streaked face, and dried leaves in her hair, little Katie Watson gazed at them with her large hazel eyes.

"Katie, this is going to hurt but until I get the boot off, I can't do anything to make it better. Can you be a big girl and not cry while I'm doing it? Hold Mr Martin's hand tightly and if you feel like yelling, squeeze hard, got it?"

The tear stained face wobbled slightly as Charlotte began to ease the remains of the boot over the foot. The inside was soaked with blood and as it was removed, the girl gripped Alex's hand as two large tears forced their way through tightly closed eyelids but there was no sound or complaint. Her brother hovered by her side, a worried frown on his face.

"Good girl. Danny is your Dad in?"

"Dunno Mrs Mannin' he was to go to the hospital today for a check-up and me Mum's up at the Grange."

"Katie, we'll get your Mum here as quickly as we can but I just want to make sure that the leg's not broken. It will hurt for a while but I'll be as quick as I can."

As Charlotte gently manipulated the ankle and felt around the wounded area, Katie flung her arms around Alex and sobbed silently against his neck. Unfamiliar with handling small children, he returned what he hoped was a reassuring hug to the brave little soul. Nevertheless, he still found himself experiencing a revulsion for the skinny arms and poor quality clothing. Grubby, frightened children, with tear stained faces and runny noses were ghosts from his own past - and he didn't like it.

"Shouldn't she go to hospital?" he asked, trying to conceal his feelings from Charlotte.

She merely looked exasperated. "Look, if I thought the bone was broken she *would* go! But the boot actually prevented any serious damage, and all that's necessary is for me to clean it up, add some magic liquid and Katie will be as right as rain."

Into a bowl of steaming water she poured a generous measure of the green liquid she had used to heal Alex's scratches and began to bathe the leg by letting the hot water run over the wound. Almost with a surgeon's precision she used her long fingernails to dislodge bits of rubber and fabric from the torn skin. Her patient watched in fascinated silence as the wound was cleaned, smeared with ointment and professionally dressed.

Alex thought about a similar incident two mornings earlier when a frantic mother had brought another child to be tended for a cut finger. Afterwards, asking why a cut had been allowed to turn so black and messy, Charlotte had replied with a grin that the mother had used the old remedy of putting a cobweb over the wound to stop the bleeding. In answer to his disbelief at modern mothers using such medieval quackery, she had explained that farmers used the method to stop bleeding when livestock were injured and emergency treatment was needed.

"There we are! Now Alex, could you run Danny up to the Grange to fetch his Mum because Katie can't walk."

"You mean I can go in your sports car!"

"Well, I didn't mean for you to run behind," she replied. "Anyway you'll need to show Mr Martin the way since he hasn't been to the Hamilton place before, have you darling? It will give you the chance to case the joint."

Sitting in the morning room after a quick lunch, Alex started to quiz Charlotte about the Watson family. "I'm surprised kids that young are allowed to roam about in the woods on their own. In London the social services would be on to them."

"Why? We've all grown up in those woods and the kids in the village know them like the backs of their hands. Be-

115

sides, they were only looking for holly. We're not talking about latch-key kids, Alex. This family's had a rough time. Tim Watson was a first class farrier but there were too few horses about to provide him with a decent living when he wanted to get married. He said if he was only going to turn out fancy ironwork, he might as well work in a factory and not have to worry about looking for business. He did, and as a result of an accident, he's now a cripple and unable to provide for his family at all."

"Surely there was compensation?"

"No. Modern society being what it is, no-one saw anything and Tim was blamed for the accident. That's why Tricia Watson works at the Grange when there are extra hands needed, and you've got to be desperate to work under Mrs Lacey, their housekeeper."

Alex thought about the interior of the small cottage which he'd visited when taking the family home. Like many others in Ashmarsh, it was cramped and although the furnishings weren't luxurious, it was a warm, friendly home to walk into. Then he remembered ...

"They have enough to buy a colour television and video."

He had little sympathy with tales of poverty; for those who claimed such low standards of living, were usually far better off than the meagre living eked out by his mother during his own childhood. There had been nothing left over for luxuries and he resented the Watson's their status of having Charlotte's sympathy.

"No they don't," replied Charlotte softly. "Compassion isn't your strongest asset Alex ..."

"So where do they ..." he interrupted and then he knew.

A few hours later found Charlotte concealed in the stone arbour away from the cool afternoon breeze. Sitting with half closed eyes, her knees drawn up to her chin, she turned her mind back to snow clad peaks soaring up to meet a matchless blue sky. Sunlight reflected the glare of the deep white snow and from a distance the chant of prayers assailed her ears. The dull boom of the prayer bell reverberated along the monastery walls and echoed across the valley. Those were the days of the first peace, of the first remembered enlightenment, in a world where brutality and cruelty were only the trade marks of nature. A delicate hand of a young man with old eyes, spun the prayer wheel, musing on the thought that the transmigration of the soul had no regard for gender or position in any future rebirth.

The throaty call of a rook returned her thoughts to the present. The Black One, in striking at those unfortunate youngsters had re-kindled a spark of primitive magic far more effective than anything modern occultists could create. As a result, the demand for vengeance had been reinforced by two more deaths and if the Black One were not apprehended, it was obvious that more would follow. If Paul's intuition was correct and the shaman was indeed Iceni, then it would be necessary to find his grave and neutralise his power. He was a powerful enemy, but nevertheless Charlotte had a healthy respect for a spirit-force that could hurl itself into the 20th century because the dead, over which he had stood guardian for 900 years, had been violated.

Thousands of years had passed since man had emerged from the primeval wilderness and still he had not learned his place in the system of things. Greed, brutality and a lust for killing and destruction had placed him apart from all those who had been created equal. In those far off days, when he had huddled in terrified silence, confined to a hole in the ground throughout the hours of darkness, his worst fear had been of the spirits that haunted the night world. Now man's worst nightmare had returned to the earth to meter out justice for an unspeakable act of desecration.

With both Anna and Alex busy with their own work, Charlotte decided to share a pot of coffee in the clinic office with Gill Cross and to see if she had any suggestions as to who could have set gin-traps on her land. She had already

117

had a couple of shouting-matches over the telephone and was furious that anyone should dare trespass on her property.

Gill idly played with the spoon in her mug. "Anything could have been caught in those snares, Mrs Manning, do you think there are any more in the woods?"

"There's sure to be but my main concern was to get Katie Watson back here."

"Can't we go up there and look? I'd hate to sit here waiting for something else to get caught in them and do nothing."

Taking Gill's battered old van, they drove along the lane, flanked by the tall trees. The old rabbit warren was within easy reach of the road when you knew where to look. Much of the under- growth at the foot of the ridge had been flattened when they had released the Watson girl from the trap but in widening the area, there was still a large amount of tangled foliage to be investigated. The immediate area around the burrows was bare, as the rabbits had stripped all the vegetation within reach, including any young tree shoots. She only permitted certain local people on her land to cull the rabbit numbers before they became unmanageable - and none of them used traps.

Following the path, Charlotte suddenly had the wild idea that someone may have been laying the traps in the area of the stone circle in an attempt to snare the murderer. The ridge was fairly near the circle and trying to keep the same distance from the Neolithic site, she tried pacing an outer ring.

After ten minutes of careful searching she found another trap on a wide rabbit track, its vicious jaws open and menacing, which she snapped shut with a stick. Similar to the one that injured the child, this one was also extremely rusty and obviously not used for some considerable time. Instructing Gill to walk in the opposite direction, but following the same line, she started off again and a few moments later found another empty trap - but this one had been sprung.

Gill was some distance from the ridge when she uttered a choked cry. Charlotte reached her side just as the girl vomited into the bracken and the sight that met her eyes forced the bile into her own throat. Mangled remains of what was once a man, lay strewn across a narrow gully. A frenzied attack had left the corpse almost unrecognisable as a human being, the body having been torn apart with amazing ferocity.

The head was almost severed from the body and crows had already removed the eyes from the bloody sockets. The stench rising from ruptured intestines was vile enough to turn any stomach and as the body had lain there for some time, it was obvious that passing woodland creatures had looked upon it as an unexpected meal.

"Gill!" Charlotte shook her roughly. "Go back to the house and 'phone Inspector Morris. I'll wait here. Go on, hurry!"

Gratefully the girl ran through the trees, fighting back the tears as she left her employer alone with the body. A battered canvas bag spilled the remaining rusty gin-traps amongst the undergrowth, and Charlotte had no doubt that this was the man responsible for the accident to Katie Watson. Carefully poking through the contents of the bag with a stick, she could discover no evidence to suggest that the dead man was intent on poaching. The only plausible explanation for anyone setting traps in the vicinity of the stone circle was an attempt to bag a killer.

The woods, silent in the presence of Death, suddenly increased her awarness of an inner sharpening of her senses. Modern living made little demand on her esoteric knowledge, restricting her practice to instructing students of parapsychology and herbal healing. Nevertheless, she could feel a surge of strength in the inner recesses of her mind, similar to those an athlete would experience when exercising muscles long out of use.

The telepathy she had used to bring Alex to her had used very little of her psychic energy. It was strange but not

119

disquieting. There had been talk of little else since the murders began and daily she had been called upon to explain some mystery. Alex questioned continuously for explanations; Anna was researching the Iceni connection; so it was not surprising that her mind was opening up to the vast inner store that had lain dormant for so long.

She was standing alone in a forest clearing over the body of a sacrificial victim, as her ancestors had stood thousands of years before. This remnant of the vast acreage of the Whittlewood had once extended to some thirty four square miles of royal hunting forest. Her ancestral roots were planted firmly in the soil before Norman or Plantagenet wore the English crown; before Roman Legions tramped the old Watling Street her people had met in sacred oak groves or within the shadows of holy circles, burying their dead in earthen barrows.

Legend claimed that amongst the sacred oaks of Whittlewood the formidable Queen of the Iceni, Boudica finally took her own life by poison, after the massacre of her people by the Romans. Over 80,000 Britons fell that day; the legionaries spared no-one. Even the women and children, who were normally sent in triumph to Rome to be sold as slaves, were speared. Their bodies thrown onto the pile of butchered baggage animals; blood mingling with that of husbands, brothers and sons, staining the earth to a depth of several feet. Whose grave was the shaman guarding? Boudica, or perhaps her daughters who seemed to have vanished from history after their violation sparked off the Iceni vengeance. Or nobles of the tribe?

On the periphery of her vision, Charlotte became conscious of a group of people in strange attire, watching her from the shadows. The image was indistinct, as if viewed through a filmy veil and if she attempted to look directly at them, the figures merged into the rough bark of the trees. As soon as she looked away, the images returned. Priests in long robes entered the clearing, carrying sickles and mistletoe boughs, the leaders of the throng chanting a weird yet familiar paean. These ghosts from the past were accepting the blood sacrifice made in honour of their Goddess.

The slamming of car doors tore her attention away from the haunted wood and back to the present. As she turned away from the corpse, the figures vanished completely as Alex, together with uniformed police, ran towards her through the trees.

Chapter Ten

As a result of the fifth death, a war of hysterical resentment divided the village communities. Those devotees of the ambitious life-style, the spiralists, whose expense account salaries had purchased derelict properties and brutalised them out of all recognition, lobbied councils, the police, set up protest groups and committees. The media flocked to the South Northamptonshire villages eager for news of the latest serial killings that threatened the peaceful existence of the country folk. The spiralists spoke to the newspaper reporters, the television and anyone else who would listen.

The countrymen talked to no-one - not even the spiralists. They had always been uneasy bed-fellows with their campaigns and conservation programmes but now the 'natives' were openly hostile. The coroner's report confirmed that the man had been killed with the same remorseless method as Smiles and Trasker but added that he could not account for the ferocity needed to tear a body limb from limb.

Unfortunately, the body had been eaten in part by wild animals and it was difficult for forensics to state exactly how the 'person, or persons unknown' had dismembered the body without further examination. While the spiralists talked, the countrymen took down their guns and organised a shoot across the meadow lands and dark woodlands.

The victim had been identified by a blood-soaked wallet found amongst the mangled flesh. It transpired he was a married man from Northampton who was a cousin of Peter Jeffrey, still being held in connection with the initial murders of the two girls. The reason for his being in the Whittlewood remained a mystery until Charlotte Manning told Morris of her suspicions.

Further enquiries showed that Dennis Quinnell had told his drinking cronies that as the stone circle was the focal point of the murders, the only way to catch the killer was for traps to be placed at intervals around the circle. His friends had scoffed at the idea but he'd been proved right, even if it had cost him his life, and there was bitter regret that he's been held up to ridicule.

Alex had no choice but to immediately telephone a report to his agent on the latest murder, which meant that *The Express* had again carried the headline before the rest had even heard of the connection with the Ashmarsh Beast, as it was now officially labelled. When it was known that Martin was staying at Hunter's Moon, the house was under siege from reporters, all demanding that he talk to them. It was impossible to leave without reporters clamouring for information and several of them even found their way through the woods to the stone circle which everyone claimed was at the heart of the mystery.

Charlotte, Lydia and Paul were furious over this second desecration of what to them was a sacred place and in exasperation, Charlotte ordered a local fencing contractor to erect a high wire fence around the circle. Ostensibly this was to protect the ancient stones from damage, but in reality they hoped to heal the magical aura of the place once the morbid interest had died down and, in the meantime, prayed that it had not been damaged beyond repair. The fence did not deter the press but they had to be content to take photographs through the mesh.

Out of loyalty to Charlotte and a feeling of guilt in bringing the media's attention to the murders, Alex volunteered to join the night patrol searching for the killer. Alan Morris had tried to persuade the men not to carry guns but to no avail. Gun laws were becoming an emotive political subject but since they were hunting on private property and not breaking any law, Morris had to be content with allowing one of his men to accompany each group. He didn't want anyone taking it upon themselves to shoot the killer if the opportunity arose. Alex expressed his regrets over the sensationalism to one of the hunting party as they shared a flask of brandy, but the man bore him no ill will.

"Don't worry, boy," answered the gruff farmer. "They'd have heard sooner or later and anyway, at least you credit us with something we can shoot at - not a bloody ghost. And who knows, it might get rid of all the bloody commuters!"

In the season when greeting cards and church sermons preached goodwill, the gulf between the natives and the newcomers widened into unconcealed loathing. The local people resented the encouragement the spiralists gave to the media in their attempts to gain satisfaction from the government, the police force and in some cases, the Church. Resentment outweighed fear in the battle of neighbours.

The week before Christmas the weather, although still dispensing brilliant sunshine, turned bitterly cold and with no further deaths to sustain the excitement, the reporters were driven from the villages by the freezing conditions. Still smarting from the onslaught of outsiders, the locals hid themselves away and ignored any strange cars that drove into the village. The latest visitors to Hunter's Moon felt the distinct coldness, which was nothing to do with the weather.

"Thank goodness old Mr Pocock recognised me or we would have driven miles out of the way," laughed Eleanor hugging Alex against her cold cheek. Due to the unwanted publicity, the Ashmarsh locals had either removed or altered the signposts surrounding the village.

"You're looking well," remarked Serge as Gwen came out of the kitchen, ostensibly to take their coats but her real purpose was to be the first to examine Eleanor and Serge at close quarters.

"It's all thanks to Gwen's cooking. Once you've tasted that you'll never want to leave." The daily help blushed scarlet, elbowing him in the ribs, before scuttling back into the safety of the kitchen.

Alex led them through into the sitting room where Charlotte was waiting beside a blazing log fire. He had to admit that her stage management was perfect and she certainly knew how to create an impression. Her dark glossy hair was smooth to perfection, the make-up flawless and the cream silk leisure suit merely hinted at the curves of her body.

There was just enough plain gold jewellery to flatter and again she had used the subdued lighting of the room to her own advantage. She had none of Eleanor's classic beauty but she had none of Eleanor's nervousness either. The introductions were made and right on cue, Gwen Carradine wheeled in the sumptuous tea trolley. She accepted their appreciation as her due but never took her eyes from Eleanor.

As the door closed behind her, Alex said in a low voice. "What's the betting she'll run out of sugar in the next ten minutes."

"Five," responded Charlotte, beginning to pour the tea.

Not four minutes passed before Gwen returned with her coat over her customary flowered pinafore. "We're a bit short of sugar, Madam, so I'll just pop down to the shop."

Alex could barely contain his mirth until she was safely out of the way as Charlotte explained. "Our Gwen is the Ashmarsh Oracle. She will report in detail to her cronies in the Post Office every detail of what you are wearing, how you look and what you've eaten. It was obviously so important, it couldn't wait, she won't normally pay the prices locally, she's been spoilt by bulk buying."

Serge had to be restrained from eating. "I've never eaten home-made cake like that," he wailed as Alex removed it from his reach.

"I don't know what's being prepared for dinner tonight but the whole exercise is hinged on the fact that only good reports will go back to Mrs Lacey at The Grange," Charlotte informed them. Mrs Lacey was cook to Eleanor's parents and each woman considered her own position to be the superior. Gwen's idiosyncrasies served to break the ice as Alex told a few more stories about the much loved daily housekeeper.

"I suppose I'll have to go over. They're bound to be told I'm staying here."

"They already know. You don't think Gwen could keep that quiet do you? Besides we've all had an invitation for Boxing Day." Charlotte helped herself to another scone as casually as though her remark had concerned the weather.

Eleanor was astounded. "*All* of us?"

"To quote your father, "If that writer chappie is going to be here, you might as well bring the arty one as well!""

Eleanor sat back in her chair. "What on earth have you done to my Father?"

Her hostess grinned impishly and shrugged her slim shoulders in a typical Gallic fashion. "The invitation's for dinner but I've told them that the decision is entirely yours. Talk about it tonight and then I can call them."

A tear pricked at the corner of Eleanor's eye as Serge squeezed her hand. "I don't know what to say, I want to go of course ... but I'll have to think about it. What's the plan for the holiday?"

Alex lit a cigarette as though he were giving the matter a great deal of thought. "Tonight we have dinner at home. No doubt when Gwen returns she will continue to prepare a gargantuan feast, the after effects of which are guaranteed to keep you comatose until late morning. You will be awakened with tea, followed by a traditional country house breakfast, after which we will escape from her devilish clutches into town, to avoid being fed further until dinner."

"If everything tastes like that cake, I'm going to ask Mrs C to marry me," enthused Serge.

The cold winter sunlight glowed richly on the stonework of All Saints Church, on whose altar the Norman barons swore fealty more than 700 years before. The strains of a Salvation Army band could be heard playing carols under the great portico, where old John Bailes was buried, having been born in the 16th century, lived through the 17th and died in the 18th. The weathered statue of Charles II high above the open parapet and clad in Roman toga, stared out over the heads of the Christmas shoppers passing the spot where the poet John Clare, who used to wander down from the asylum, used to sit in the shadow of the huge round columns.

The Market Square was alive with colour and sound as the vendors plied their trade, whilst heavy laden shoppers picked their way carefully over the cobbles. Hurricane lamps hissed and stuttered, the smell of methylated spirit mingling with other smells of a busy market. Holly decorated the stalls and eager children watched as weary mothers filled baskets with juicy tangerines, crisp apples and the traditional assortment of nuts for cracking or roasting.

Sitting in the corner of the dimly lit wine lodge, the walls above the dark wooden panelling stained with age and cigarette smoke, Charlotte and Eleanor waited for their men to return. The coloured glass windows and flagstone floor gave the room the appearance of being much older than it actually was. On market days it was full of life and of deals being done; during the rest of the week, it was the current fashionable place to be seen in.

"I must say that Alex looks exceptionally well. His work has improved immensely and he's happy too. That's the important thing," Eleanor smiled her gratitude.

She had been terrified of his return to Ashmarsh but now she had seen him again and met Charlotte for herself, the last remaining doubts vanished. Eleanor was a practical person and she banished all their previous discussions on occultism as fanciful imagination. During dinner the previous evening and afterwards, she had been able to observe the natural chemistry that flowed between them and enjoyed the verbal fencing they seemed to delight in.

"He's learned there's more to life than being fashionable," replied her companion, swirling the ice around a large gin 'n tonic.

"It's not just that. How much do you know about him, his background, I mean?"

"He comes from a less than salubrious part of London and was the illegitimate son of a Billingsgate porter. Mother struggled to bring him up and to give him a reasonable education. I understand she died the week before he graduated."

Eleanor nodded, a sadness in her eyes as she remembered those far off days. "None of us had anything then but we managed to get by. I think what brought us all so close together was the fact that none us had any family, so to speak. Serge and I were lucky, we had each other but Alex had no-one. He's always seemed to be looking for something more from life but everything always fell short of his expectations."

Several people whom Charlotte knew came into the bar and after the introductions, a great deal of complimentary small talk and a refill, Eleanor lit a cigarette. "Serge thinks we should go on Boxing Day."

"For dinner?"

"The whole hog!" replied Eleanor with a nervous smile.

Charlotte leaned back against the wooden panel and studied her house-guest. "I know it's your home but I think I should fill you in on some recent family history. I don't believe you are aware of the Colonel's heart condition," she carried on quickly before Eleanor could make a reply. "He forbade your Mother to mention it and although it's not serious, the thought of dying has obviously crossed his mind. You should remember that the Colonel is all bluster and bellicose but underneath he is a very sad, lonely man and I'm very fond of him."

"There's something else though, isn't there?" For the first

time in years, Eleanor allowed herself to give full attention to her family's affairs. She wrinkled her nose in thought for a moment.

"Roger!"

"Exactly, the Ethiopian in the fuel supply. When did you see him last?"

"Ten years. When he was sent down from Cambridge, he stayed with us for a while but he and Serge didn't like one another. Only fleetingly since then."

"No one could like that moronic little twerp," snapped Charlotte, surprising her companion with her candour. "Baby Roger has grown into a real bastard. His main aim in life is to get you disinherited and he will do anything, and I mean *anything*, to succeed. The Colonel loathes him to put no finer point on it and realises that within six months of his death, Roger will sell off the estate to the highest bidder and pocket the takings."

"But he's got to get rid of me first, is that it? Funny," she added, "I thought I *had* been disinherited."

"Roger's too stupid to see how your Father really feels. You always loved The Grange and he would have liked nothing better than for you and your children to live there when he's dead and gone. It was your Father who called me to make the invitation incidentally."

Eleanor turned everything over in her mind. "Has he told you all this?"

The green fathomless eyes sparkled with barely concealed mirth. "How much has Alex told you about me?"

"Enough!" Eleanor answered with mock resignation. "Are you going to tell me I've been wrong all these years?"

"Stubbornness and pride on both sides, I should say. He's easy enough to manage, I argue and flirt with him, which keeps him happy and your mother amused."

"Flirt! What on earth *have* you done to my Father?" she asked incredulously for the second time since their meeting.

As Anna had predicted, they were organised with military precision. The remaining days before Christmas Eve were alive with childish excitement as gifts were wrapped, the tree decorated in the sitting room and enormous burnished copper pans were filled with holly. Everything at Hunter's Moon was an indulgence of what every dream of Yuletide should be.

The side door was permanently open to delivery vans and each driver was offered a drink and one of Gwen's excellent mince pies. Tantalising smells issued from the kitchen and if Serge was missing, he could be found with a finger in a mixing bowl, sampling the contents. Not a day passed without Gwen telling Eleanor what a lovely boy he was.

Serge stood with his arm around Charlotte, admiring their handiwork over the luxuriously decorated tree, glimmering in scarlet and gold. "And do you realise, I don't even know you're organising me," he remarked happily,

Serge, most of all, had been uncertain of how to react to a traditional country Christmas. During his childhood there had been neither money nor inclination to celebrate the holiday, even in a modest way. He guessed, rather than knew, that Christmas was treated as something special in other households but he doubted that it would ever hold any pleasure for him personally. Normally, he and Eleanor went abroad with Alex for the holiday, and he had only accepted the invitation out of curiosity and a need to meet his friend's new mistress.

"What's next, chief?" he teased, spinning his hostess around by the shoulders and kissing her on the nose.

"A light tea, then the Vicar's carol service, followed by supper at the Vicarage."

"You're not serious! I thought you were a Witch? Christ, you are!"

In the crisp, inky blackness, broken only by a few solitary street lamps, the four of them walked through the village to the beautifully preserved Saxon church. No curtains sealed off the cottage windows tonight, as warm shafts of yellow light streamed out into the road. Each home had a Christmas tree glowing with tinsel and coloured lights, from a two foot miniature on a window ledge to a monster that took up a whole corner of the room.

Some of the older inhabitants still festooned their rooms with coloured paper chains, whilst others experimented with decorations purchased from the local department store. Of the forty-three homes in the village, from the humblest to the most wealthy, not one was left out of the festivities.

"This is incredible," remarked Serge, his arm linked through Charlotte's as they followed Eleanor and Alex across the Green. "I lived in a village like this when I was a kid but no-one would have cared if you ate dried bread for your Christmas dinner."

"Most of these people were born in the village and a lot of them will die here. They've worked on the land and they've grown old on it. Even the younger ones who go away to work in the town feel a certain security in coming home to friendly faces. What's a few groceries and decorations compared with that?"

"How do you keep the outsiders, out?" he asked, referring the problem in some of the surrounding villages over the newcomers.

"Easy," she replied, tucking her coat collar under her chin. "Between us, the Colonel and I own all of the properties."

They burst into laughter as a peal of organ music floated out into the cold night air Serge finally realising the full implications behind the invitation to The Grange. He wasn't bothered about the money, his business earned enough to keep himself and Eleanor in a comfortable life-style, however, he understood what would happen to Ashmarsh and its community if the surrounding land was sold off to developers.

They were still laughing as they reached the church door to be welcomed by Archie Branson. The beautiful little church was only half full as they were shown to their seats in

131

the front pew by a choirboy, dressed in a red cassock, trimmed with lace surplice. Eleanor leant back against the hard wooden seat and looked around her.

Nothing had changed since she had come here with her parents as a small child for Sunday service. She felt the tears prick her eyes as she experienced what Charlotte had referred to as the "timeless perpetuality" of Ashmarsh, allowing its remembered warmth to course through her veins and into her heart. She squeezed Serge's hand, glad that she had come home and he felt a sudden protective urge toward the people she'd grown up amongst.

Its foundations laid in the seventh century over an even older holy well, the church had sprung up amongst an isolated forest community. Rounded arches were all turned with rich red Roman tiles, probably taken from an ancient garrison site on the old Watling Street. The windows were a mixture of Saxon and Norman architecture and over the years, local gentry had enriched the simple church by donating some fine stained glass. The dark oak pews, worn by centuries of use, were carved with strange figures of demons and curling tendrils of vines. Alone in the Lady Chapel, lay a stone effigy of a medieval knight clad in surcoat and chain mail, his noble features casting an eerie shadow as the candle-light fell across his tomb.

The church was ablaze with candles and the ladies of the village had spent most of the morning arranging beautiful displays of evergreen and holly. On the altar the highly polished cross and candlesticks gleamed, reflecting the glory of colour and movement in the nave. Angelic choirboys in newly laundered surplices took their places as the church filled to capacity. If Archie Branson accepted that he preached to a quarter filled church on most Sundays of the year, it was worth it to see his flock willingly coming to the fold every Christmas Eve.

The local people, from Ashmarsh, Farthingham and Greens Abbot came as a gesture to a man they valued as a friend, rather than a priest. The whole population of Ashmarh was represented, Christian and Pagan, bringing with them the sons and daughters who had moved away, returning with a new generation of grandchildren. The carols were all the old favourites, refraining from the new of current fashion, so that everyone who came could give full voice to old familiar tunes and words.

"I like your Vicar," admitted Serge as they walked towards the Vicarage after the service, "not one mention of God and no sermon."

Flushed from her efforts in the kitchen, Margaret Branson quickly ushered them out of the draughty hall into the large untidy sitting room, where a huge log fire was blazing. Charlotte made the introductions as the number of guests swelled to some forty persons around the buffet table. Although Rev and Mrs Branson were hosting the party, it was to Charlotte Manning that people paid their respects, each greeting made discreetly and to a casual observer, almost unnoticeable.

Alex had been watching this for some time, particularly surprised at the manner of a grand old lady, who was now sitting beside the fire in a shabby, over-stuffed armchair. Judging by her face, she must be at least ninety years of age and her black dress was beautifully embroidered with tiny jet beads that came from an age long before mass production.

Her jewellery denoted a comfortable background and fascinated by her, Alex asked if he might replenish her glass. She graciously accepted his offer and on his return with a dry sherry, invited him to sit beside her. Discovering that she lived some way out of the village in an isolated Queen Anne house he inquired as to whether she had any fear about the murders.

Her eyes sparkled with merriment. "I'm too old to worry about dying but in any case nothing will happen to people from this village." Alex fancied she glanced in Charlotte's direction but he could not be sure.

"The woman who died lived in one of the cottages."

"Unmourned by anyone Mr Martin. I can assure you there are a good few folk who have wished that damned bible puncher in Jericho at times. She was from the village, not of the village. Ben Trasker left here for a time when his first wife died and returned with that woman."

"You speak as though it was some form of retribution."

"Do I? Take no notice of me, Mr Martin, I'm getting old and I don't go out very much these days. My husband was the local doctor and he died thirty six years ago on Christmas Eve. He lies buried in the churchyard and I come every year to listen to the carols and think of him."

Alex helped her from the chair as she tried to rise. "Thank you young man for your company. My car will be here soon and I must say goodbye to Charlotte."

Proud and upright she crossed the room, barely leaning on her ebony stick, her fingers resting lightly on Alex's arm. He had the impression she was laughing at him. They came to where Serge and Charlotte sat together in conspiratorial fashion on a window seat.

Alicia Howard, clasping Charlotte's shoulder as she leant forward, kissed her on the cheek. "Bless you my dear, for all that you do. I hope you and your friends have an enjoyable Christmas." Charlotte smiled her reply as the old lady turned to Serge. "Are you the young man who stole our fair Eleanor away?"

"Yes, ma'am," he replied, a little uncomfortable.

"Then I hope you do right by her and her family. And you too, young man," she added, patting Alex's hand. "Standards may have altered since my day, but in the country these things still matter. Charlotte, be good enough to see me to my car."

As the two women walked away, Alex asked his friend if he had noticed the strange atmosphere with everyone paying attention to Charlotte, instead of the Bransons.

"What's surprising about that? The Vicar keeps a little black book on all the Ashmarsh families and every year they

134

get a hamper depending on their personal needs from the Parish fund. The Vicar collects the information and your old lady foots the bill if there isn't enough in the kitty."

"Of course," replied Alex a little foolishly.

Serge slapped him on the shoulder "Come on pal, you're beginning to look for a mystery in everything. You'll be writing horror fiction next."

Chapter Eleven

For the first time since her guests arrived and the holiday started, Charlotte found herself alone for a few hours. The morning was clear and bright with a filmy sun casting pale shadows around the house. She had drawn up a chair in front of the fire, surrounded herself with her cats, and lapsed into a semi-conscious doze.

The rest of the household had accompanied Paul Kerrick to the traditional Boxing Day meet and on the grounds of personal abhorrence, Charlotte had elected to stay at home. In fact, it was the first time for months that the house had been empty and she was enjoying the peaceful solitude.

The hypnotic effect of the flames plunged Charlotte's mind into a deeper trance, producing a strange, half familiar, half forgotten, floating sensation. A log slipped, sending a shower of sparks into the inky blackness of the chimney and the sweet smell of charred timber lingered in the room. Since leaving the cloistered life of the East, she mused, fire had dogged her footsteps throughout Europe. In previous lives she had seen life through the eyes of man and boy, woman and girl; from humble peasant existence to high spiritual and academic attainment but from the very beginning, fire had always been a harbinger of death.

The sudden mental picture was so vivid that the sharpness of wind on the mountainside almost brought tears to her eyes. The boy, leading four middle aged men on the hazardous nocturnal climb down the precipitous cliff face of Montsegur, carried his own precious burden no less valuable than the secret books of the Cathars. The siege would soon be over and it was important that the men be well out of reach by the time the soldiers of the Albigensian crusade looted and burnt the citadel.

The small party had volunteered to make the dangerous journey, carrying the holy books to safety, knowing that their loved ones would be slaughtered unmercifully when the soldiers entered the city - those accursed followers of Dominic de Suaman would see to that. On the following night they rested in a cave and on the calm of a soft spring breeze, the screams of those left behind, echoed across the valley. From sunset until sunrise the five Cathars watched the glow of the flames silhouetting the rocky citadel on which their fortress had stood. For nearly forty years their people had been systematically butchered on orders from Rome and each knew that no-one left in the citadel had a chance of escape or mercy.

The picture blurred and refocused on a warm spring day; the beauty of which was marred by the stench of burning flesh. Medieval Paris was in the throes of an orgy of death, for today was execution by slow roasting to death of the Grand Master of the Order of the Knights Templar, Jacques de Molay. The pyre for de Molay and his companion had been erected opposite the royal gardens, so that the King might have an uninterrupted view of his arch rival.

A tall, bearded man watched the fire burn up around his comrades in arms, and tears ran down his cheeks unchecked. No one paid any heed since the acrid smoke caused many eyes to weep as they watched with morbid fascination. With one last supreme effort the voice of the Grand Master rose above the roaring of the fire and silenced the crowd: "Pope Clement, Chevalier Guillaume de Nogaret, King Phillipe, I summon you to the Tribunal of Heaven before the year is out, to receive your just punishment ..." The man in the crowd bowed his head in prayer - and smiled.

Unbidden, half forgotten mental images passed through Charlotte's mind. Her inner strength was expanding day by day, releasing the dormant powers of her brain, drawing deep from the fountain of hidden senses. Encouraged by Rome, the rabid Dominicans in their detested black robes had spread the insanity of the Inquisition across Europe, even more efficiently than any plague rats. Their hapless, and mostly innocent, victims were brutally tortured and maimed to extract their confessions, before meeting death by fire in some market place, watched by jeering crowds.

The true Wise Ones, quietly stole away from a world gone mad, leaving the populace to suffer the agonising mental and physical torments of the Black Death, abandoned by their church. The pleasure loving priests refused to give comfort to the dying, afraid that they themselves might contract the dreaded disease and left the victims to die unshriven. And out of the ashes of the funeral pyres, the Faith of the People was reborn and grew stronger.

Charlotte turned her thoughts to the present and reflected on the change in public attitudes. During the past century the average person had become more and more inquiring over matters relating to the occult. Unable to accept scientific dismissal of the paranormal as mere superstition, the public had clamoured for more information on the arcane, and horror fiction had become a popular genre. Charlotte herself had furthered this enlightenment by producing some ten fictional best-sellers, culminating in her most impressive work to date, a serious discourse on the subject, *By Mist and Candlelight*, the book that had brought Alexander Martin to her.

After weeks of psychic stimulation, the inner eye was opening and light coursed from the secret recesses of the brain, producing a sharp tingling sensation in her veins. Incorporeal energy coursed through her like a mountain torrent swollen by melting snows. She was one of those who,

138

even in ancient times, had attained the true goal on the Path of Ultimate Enlightenment; unhampered by gender, the power had continued down through the ages in various forms and incarnations.

Getting up from the chair and crossing to the open casement, she looked out over the flagstone patio. The morning was cold and clear, withered leaves still clung to some of the shrubs and in the bushes sparrows argued furiously. High above, in the denuded rowan the crystal sharp song of a robin trilled on the breeze. Everything looked and smelt different at this time of mystical replenishment.

Encouraged by mild weather and the silence of the house, a large brown rat ambled carelessly across the grass, his thick winter coat glossy and well cared for. The creature's natural instincts had fattened him up for the cold months ahead and his rotund middle bulged from good living. Accepting that all creatures have their place in the Cycle of Life, Charlotte had no pathological hatred of the destructive rodent and remained perfectly still as the animal walked towards her. Suddenly aware of the presence, the brown rat sat up on his back legs, displaying an immaculate grey under-belly as he stared disdainfully in her direction. After a few moments of surveillance, the animal went on its way and disappeared into the tangle of dwarf conifers by the edge of the pool.

"It's the two legged variety that threaten us," muttered Charlotte as she drew back and closed te window.

Arriving home cold and hungry, her guests fell on the ample lunch that awaited them. Steaming bowls of thick soup quickly disappeared as everyone had a second serving, suspending conversation until the circulation had returned to chilled fingers and toes. A rich game pie with a crust gleaming golden brown, accompanied by baked potatoes, saw a return to normal meal time conversation as they gossiped about who had been at the meet.

John Sinclair, Anna's detective lover had become slightly more used to their company and now, over his initial shyness, proceeded to imitate a grossly overweight local solicitor's wife who had been riding side-saddle. There had been a few ribald remarks made and Sinclair was hoping that the solicitor would not recognise him at some future court date. He glanced oddly at Charlotte a few times, but she ignored it, only giving a fleeting thought to the idea that perhaps he was looking for signs from his hostess that he had overstepped the mark. There were times when he made her feel distinctly uneasy but she put this down to her age-old distrust of law enforcement officers.

Paul Kerrick took his leave as soon as the meal was finished, as he was flying to Norway the following morning for the cross country skiing and was driving down to London that afternoon. He joked with the company about preferring to take his vices away from the prying eyes of local busybodies. John was taking Anna to meet his family over at Daventry, so the remaining four took their coffee through to the sitting room, to spend a lazy afternoon, recovering from the after effects of a hectic Christmas Day and the vigours of a chill Boxing Day morning.

From early the previous morning, over the opening of presents with champagne and smoked salmon, to the midnight chimes of the church clock, the old farm-house had resounded with laughter. The grey cats, normally haughty and aloof, had joined in the fun by demolishing the pile of torn wrapping paper each time it was piled up for removal. One even applying a well sharpened claw to the bottom of the plastic rubbish bag as Alex lifted it, resulting in another cascade of litter being deposited on the sitting room floor. Bows and ribbons were later discovered all over the house, where the cats had carried them off.

People had called for pre-lunch drinks; after-lunch drinks; afternoon drinks; all served with mincepies and everyone could understand why Charlotte preferred to serve dinner at six in the evening. There had been a dozen guests, mostly local people who had joined them for a feast of traditional cooking. The dining table, its heavy linen cloth shimmering with polished silver and crystal, brought cries of delight from the ladies and Alex, seated at the head of the long table with Archie and Margaret Branson on either side, secretly relished his role as host. Not long after the diners had sat back with coffee and liqueurs, the first guests for the evening began to arrive.

Both Alex and Serge were surprised to discover that they were actually enjoying participating in the traditional party games. Inspector Morris, his diminutive wife Meg and their two boys, all shy at first, were soon roaring their answers to Charlotte's talented miming in charades. The house was full of people enjoying an excellent buffet supper, with hot punch and the luxury of blazing fires. The heat from the burning logs drying the holly, so that the leaves fell into the flames, wafting a delicious scent into the room.

The ladies were resplendent in a dazzling array of evening gowns that normally only saw daylight for the annual hunt ball. Although many of the styles were out of fashion, the dresses were elegant and beautifully made, complemented by an enviable collection of diamonds, sapphires and pearls. Most of the men wore dinner jackets originally purchased from dignified bespoke tailors and slightly discoloured with age. All in all, it was a distinguished gathering of the local gentry.

Good manners in the country has always been knowing when to leave and as the church clock chimed midnight, Charlotte's guests said their goodbyes. Most were people she had known for years who found themselves alone over Christmas now that their families had left home. They were privately grateful for the invitation, returning her compliment by dressing for the occasion and treating her party as one of the most important social events of the Yule season.

Even on Boxing Day, some were still suffering from the after-effects. "I will never be able to move again," groaned Serge, throwing himself into a comfortable chair, balancing his

141

coffee cup carefully on the arm and undoing his trousers.

"We did warn you," remarked Alex smugly

"True," his friend replied wistfully, "but I can't leave the food alone."

Eleanor leaned over the back of the chair and patted his stomach. "You'd better go for a good run and loose some of it before tonight. Charly has told me that Gwen and Mrs Lacey are deadly rivals so tonight will be another feast, guaranteed to impress the prodigals."

"I think I'm going to be sick," wailed Serge taking her hand. "Worried about tonight, princess?"

"A little," she admitted with a weak smile. "Daddy can be so damned difficult at times."

"You'd better give me a list of all taboo subjects."

Eleanor laughed, "It's endless: The modern generation, socialism, the cost of cattle feed, pheasant shooting, the local council and the modern housing estate. You are per-mitted to mention his regiment, his prize winning bull and if you want a favourable reaction, compliment him on the rose garden."

"In December!" retorted Serge despondently, still search-ing for a way to impress Eleanor's father.

"Of course, there is one way of making sure that the evening is a total success," enjoined Charlotte.

"And what's that?" Alex asked suspiciously, not liking the gleam in her eyes.

She turned to him, wide-eyed with the innocence of her remark but the twinkle still gleamed. "By Serge announcing that he's going to make his daughter an honest woman."

"Steady on!" cried Serge. "You are joking, aren't you?"

"Absolutely not. Ask the Colonel for his daughter's hand in marriage and I guarantee all will turn out fine."

Serge slipped further down in the chair staring at the fire. "Are you trying to add me to the Colonel's hunting trophies?"

His hostess stood in front of him, her hand extended. "A magnum of Dom Perignon to a full Stilton, I'm right."

Serge recalled the conversation he'd had with Charlotte at the Branson's party on Christmas Eve. She'd made him understand why it was so important to curry favour with the Colonel but he wasn't sure about her method. "Done."

"Just a minute you two!"exclaimed Eleanor. "This is my future too, you know."

"Sorry babe, but a bet's a bet."

She looked helplessly from Serge, to Charlotte to Alex. The joke, if joke it was, had gone too far. "You're worse than horse traders!"

Dinner was always served at seven prompt at The Grange and with Alex driving Serge's car, the party drove silently towards Eleanor's childhood home. The night was again sharp and clear, each star standing out brightly against the dark of the night sky with the hump-backed moon still to rise above the trees. Powerful headlamps scythed through the darkness as the car followed the narrow country lane. Gaunt, leafless hedges flanked the lane like a phalanx of infantry, shields interlocking so that none should pass. The naked arms of the trees stretched overhead creating a vaulted cathedral of interwoven twigs, branches and silence.

Charlotte was the only one who was aware of the mysteries being performed out of the beam of the headlamps The darkness was alive with night creatures who sought out their food under the cover of the darkness. A complicated ballet of life and death enacted for Nature by the hordes of insects, birds and mammals, all completing their nightly rituals.

Her inner senses also enabled her to tune into the undercurrent of trepidation that hovered inside the car. Both Serge and Eleanor were in a state of nervous excitement, both fearing for different reasons, that the evening would go disastrously wrong. Like two small, terrified children, they sat in the rear seat, each holding tightly to the other's hand, not daring to speak in case a tremor in the voice betrayed their apprehension.

143

As the car swung into the gravelled drive of The Grange and tyres crunched on the stone chippings, a curtain twitched slightly behind a leaded pane. The heavy door swung open, spilling a warm welcoming glow and two amiable dogs onto the driveway. Eleanor felt a lump in her throat as she stared at the creeper covered house of which there were so many happy childhood memories and reassuringly, Serge squeezed her hand.

Charlotte was the first out of the car, treading carefully on the gravel to avoid injury to her sandaled feet. The Colonel and Mrs Hamilton were waiting by the door; his face was impassive but his wife showed her nervousness by twisting her lace handkerchief in her fingers. The immense bulk of the proud military man was enough to put the fear of God into anyone, mused Alex. A thick mane of silvering hair and a neat moustache framed the coldest blue eyes, he had ever looked into and he doubted very much that Serge would find the courage to win his bet.

Charlotte kissed them both on the cheek before introducing Alex Martin - "And Serge Butler."

There was a glint in the old man's eye as he shook Serge's hand but it was difficult to detect either hostility or any other emotion. "Glad you could come," he muttered gruffly, unable to take his eyes off his beautiful daughter.

In the long years that Eleanor had been away, she had been transformed from a pretty, lanky student into an extremely elegant and beautiful young woman. During her brief visits home, her father had not been aware of this metamorphosis, not even wanting to see her when she called on her brief and infrequent visits. Tonight a special effort had been made for a very important occasion and Eleanor was glad Charlotte had insisted on evening dress. One look at her father's face showed all the hurt and longing of the years of separation but most important to her, it showed love.

"Daddy!" she cried, flinging herself into the old man's arms.

Tears she had been determined not to shed couldn't be held back and the others turned away as a solitary tear appeared on the Colonel's cheek. Ever the perfect hostess, Jayne Hamilton led them into the drawing room to allow her husband to recover his equilibrium. All day she had been both dreading and longing for this moment and never before, in all their years of marriage, had she seen her husband lose his self control.

"Thank you," she whispered to Charlotte. "Mr Butler, may I offer you a drink?"

Sitting with her guests and talking politely about the Christmas holiday and country life in general, Jayne Hamilton kept a nervous eye on the door. Eventually the Colonel joined them, his hand holding his daughter's so tightly that it conveyed more than words ever could. The happiness on both their faces was a joy to behold. Somehow the old man did not look quite so large and forbidding.

Quickly, Serge made his decision. If finally bringing Eleanor home was this easy after all the years of hurt and animosity, he would tolerate the Colonel's antipathy in the future if it meant that Eleanor was happy. Nervously he moved from his place by the fire to stand between the Colonel and his Lady. Squaring his shoulders and like a man about to face a firing squad, Serge embarked on a venture which he hoped they would not regret.

"Sir, I would like to thank you for inviting us here tonight, firstly, because it gives me the opportunity to apologise for my behaviour. I've always thought you were unreasonable in the way you treated Eleanor, but I now realise just how much we must have hurt you and your wife." Eleanor's mother gave a surprised smile of encouragement but the Colonel remained impassive.

Serge took a sip of the scotch Alex handed him, desperately avoiding the amused laughter in his friend's eyes. "And secondly, I would like to ask your permission to marry your daughter. It's a belated gesture but it's sincerely meant."

145

Alex looked from one to the other, not missing one glance or expression, Serge looked even more like the man who had dared deliver the bad news to Rome and was expecting a death blow at any moment. Both Eleanor and her father looked amazed but for different reasons, while her practical mother was already arranging the wedding. He was appalled that Charlotte could register such a display of innocence.

"If I refused, would it make any difference?"

"No Sir!"

Determined not to lose the unexpected opportunity of her only daughter's wedding, Jayne Hamilton leapt from her seat and hurried from the room. Reared from generations of good county stock, she had been brought up never to dare openly to overrule her husband's judgement but tonight was worth a little courage and she returned holding out a small red leather case to Serge.

"I know this has happened rather suddenly and I hope you won't take offence ... Serge," She used his name uncertainly for the first time, "but would you mind if Eleanor wore her grandmother's engagement ring?"

Eleanor was more astounded by her mother's daring than her lover's proposal. With his most disarming smile Serge took the case to open it, revealing a beautifully cut stone. Eleanor remembered the large flawless sapphire in her tiny hands when her mother had occasionally allowed her to look at it, before putting it away again for safe keeping. The stone must be worth a fortune and it was her mother's way of showing her approval.

Taking her hand, her newly acquired fiance removed the ring from the case and slipped the sapphire over her finger with a slow, reassuring smile. "Mummy, it's beautiful." Now there were more tears running freely down her cheeks and everyone beamed with satisfaction.

"I'll give you ten out of ten for stage management," whispered Alex to Charlotte. In reply she kicked his ankle.

The Colonel still not giving any true indication of his

feelings on the matter, or on his wife's defection, rang for Mrs Lacey who, like her arch rival at Hunter's Moon, was usually within earshot of the family's private affairs. As the last peal died away she presented herself in the sitting room.

"Was there something you wanted, Colonel?" Her sharp, bird-like eyes missed nothing.

"Yes, Mrs Lacey. Can you delay dinner for half an hour and bring me *two* bottles of champagne." The house-keeper's face showed even further amazement when he added, "Not that muck young Roger drinks, I want a good one, out of the cellar!"

Chapter Twelve

Alex lay sprawled against a pile of cushions, idly watching the flickering firelight through the amber liquid in his glass. "I imagine you're quite pleased with yourself the way things have worked out. Funny, I hadn't got you marked down for a matchmaker."

"What on earth are you talking about?" replied Charlotte, a bemused look on her face.

"Come on! You've got yourself a nice little country wedding, with everyone living happily ever-after. Don't tell me that wasn't what you planned. I'm even starting to believe in this magic business," he teased.

"Do you think I arranged all this for my own amusement? Yes you do! Look! Most aspects accredited to magic are merely illusion and quite a large proportion of that is down to the onlooker who believes he's seen more than he actually has. Which is exactly what you're doing. It's also taking an unexpected situation and using the effects to your own advantage, which is exactly what Serge did. The Butlers are your friends; she also happens to be the estranged daughter of a neighbour of mine. And it was your suggestion that they came here for the holidays."

"You suggested Serge marry Eleanor," he responded with a pained expression.

"But I didn't force him. He took the initiative. Anyway, that's not what we're discussing. What I do know is that

Eleanor's brother has already started negotiations for the development of The Grange and its land for a leisure complex. This means that as soon as the Colonel's dead, the land adjoining the village will be sold for building and we'll have dozens of ghastly little boxes on our doorstep."

"There's such a thing a planning permission."

"True but I've learned through experience that you never trust the word, or integrity of the establishment. Anyhow with Eleanor re-united with her parents, AND soon to be respectably married, The Grange will pass to her - not Roger!"

Alex stared at her in silence. "You scheming, manipulating little bitch. I thought there was a touch of sentimentality in you."

"There is but there's an overriding sense of self-preservation that's even stronger. Ashmarsh and its inhabitants have pursued a secure and traditional way of life for many generations. You've been here long enough to see the schisms caused in other villages around here by outsiders' disrupting influence. Before long there would be complaints to social services and the education department about children being raised outside the Christian faith. Farmers wouldn't be able to leave their tractors on the Green while they had a quick lunchtime pint because the conservationists would complain to the council."

"So it wasn't out of kindness?"

"What on earth do you think I am? Eleanor is part of that tradition, whether she consciously accepts it or not, and so are the Hamiltons. Serge understood."

Alex wasn't sure. He was now, more than ever, convinced that the Hamiltons and the Butlers had somehow been manoeuvred into a situation over which none of them had any control. If there was a puppet-master, then it was Charlotte who was pulling the strings and her assurances that nothing of the kind had occurred did not persuade him otherwise. Nevertheless, he had always been attracted to strong-willed women and this sinister ability to manipulate people, acted as a powerful aphrodisiac.

"Aren't you glad we gave up our tickets?" asked Alex when Serge and Eleanor returned to Hunter's Moon. He and Charlotte were curled up together on a sofa in front of the fire and judging from their rumpled appearance, there had been a great deal of scurrying to get dressed before their guests arrived home.

"I truly appreciate the sacrifice," groaned Eleanor, saluting them with a welcoming cognac.

"What have I let myself in for?" sighed Serge. "I was surrounded by all these old biddies demanding information about a wedding that was only agreed on the day before! They were positively frightening. I've negotiated inter-national contracts with less fear than I experienced wedged up against the piano in the back room of a provincial town hall!"

"Serves you right," retorted Eleanor. "If you hadn't made that bet with the Witch of Endor here, you would have passed by unmolested."

Overnight thick snow fell, blanketing the countryside in a mantle of quiet. Confined for so long by professional and social conventions, both Serge and Alex felt the irrepressible urge to indulge schoolboy inclinations and get out into the woods. They set off across the paddock towards the ponds where dead rushes held captive by the frozen water rustled in the wind.

The snow had fallen so heavily that even in the wood, the drifts had piled high between the trees, cunningly concealing dips and hollows. Icicles hung from dripping branches and high above the wooded tangle, the heavy slate blue sky promised further snowfalls. The pure, untouched snow was breathtakingly beautiful and, as if in tribute, the sweet, melodious song of the robin trilled out on the frosty air.

Unobserved, boyish enthusiasm was unleashed in a violent snowball fight as they hurled the compressed snow at each other. Ducking behind trees to avoid his friend's missiles, Alex fell into a snow covered ditch from which Serge had to extract him. Lying side by side on the trampled snow they fought to regain their breath and get the circulation back in their fingers.

"God, it's years since I had a snowball fight."

Alex grinned sheepishly. "And we always thought ourselves so sophisticated."

"Don't knock it," breathed his friend, "You know I think I'm going to be able to do it - the country bit, I mean. When I left home, I wouldn't have cared less if I never saw another cow in my life but Ashmarsh is different."

"Yes because we're on the other side of the fence now, mate," replied Alex. "Would you want to go back to how it was?"

"No. But then I'd got no standards to judge anything by. Now I can recognise for myself the differences between people like Charlotte, Paul and the Hamiltons and the rich cats we've associated with over the years. I'm beginning to understand what tradition means to people like these and why they're so desperate to hang on to them. Thank God Eleanor made me realise it is important - can you imagine what the folks here would lose if The Grange was sold for development?"

Leaning back on his elbows, the bottom of his face hidden inside his collar against the cold, Alex confessed his own misgiving. "I didn't think I'd care one way or the other if I was accepted by these people, but living here it's different. All your impressions and opinions change. And I know you're not doing it for the money, either," he added, answering his friend's unspoken question. "Still, we haven't done too badly for two kids from the other side of the tracks, have we?"

Serge showed his even, white teeth as he pulled Alex to his feet and put his arm around his friend's shoulders. "Perhaps we're just lucky at picking the right women and no amount of money can equal that."

The reply was flippant enough but both were fully conscious of the other's true feelings. Getting the education had been hard enough, but the hard knocks and put-downs

151

they had suffered in their respective careers had honed their ambition to the razor sharpness of a *samurai* blade. Neither of them had to thank anyone for their successes or apportion blame for the failures, but when success had crowned them with laurels, they both felt that they could be forgiven for a little show of arrogance now and then. Having someone to share it all with was the added bonus.

"I just wish my Mother could have lived to see it," added Alex wistfully, half to himself, in a rare moment of nostalgia.

"Yeah. I don't even know if my parents are still alive but I've no desire to find out. Somehow, I've got the feeling that all this is going to work out for all of us. Perhaps this is where we get to start over again, with a proper family life, a home, things that matter. I just hope the Hamiltons really like me - for *my* sake."

Fortified with cognac from Serge's hipflask, they trudged through the snow in the direction of the old mausoleum. Here the snow was almost three feet deep but standing tall and proud with a diadem of ice was the statue of Pan. The dark lushness of the ivy covered walls contrasted sharply with the bleak vista of the countryside and against the rich backdrop, the god of woods and pastoral places accepted their silent homage. The sightless eyes returned their scrutiny.

"Impressive sort of a chap. Is he any relation?" Serge inclined his head in the direction of the house.

"It was the first thing I noticed, too."

"Alex, changing the subject. If you had something important to confess, would you do it now or wait till the wedding?"

"Depends on the nature of the confession, some things are best left unsaid but what on earth have you got to confess that Eleanor doesn't know about?"

Serge lit a cigarette and sucked the acrid smoke deep into his lungs. "I'm afraid she'll die laughing at the altar."

"Then it can't be that bad."

"It is to me," retorted Serge, a frown on his handsome face.

152

They were walking back towards the larger of the ponds, the centre of which was still a gaping black hole where the ice had not covered the water completely. Rooks whirled overhead, their raucous chanting harsh against the snow bound silence. The depths of the ancient forest gaped behind them like a gigantic primeval cavern, awful in its silence and occasionally the screech of a pheasant reached their ears.

Serge made his confession. "My real name is Sidney Butcher."

"Sidney Butcher!" Alex tried to look and sound sympathetic but the injured expression on his friend's face was too much for him. Laughter burst from him and the rooks flew off in fright.

"It's not funny."

"But it's beautiful. Where on earth did the 'Serge' come from?"

"From a French classic we were reading at school."

"But even at University you were Serge. How on earth did you manage it?"

"It was easy enough, no-one ever took any interest in my schooling and I just altered a few papers here and there. Same initials and Butcher is easily transformed to Butler if the writing's bad enough. Even at the age of sixteen, I knew I wasn't going anywhere with Sid for a handle. As soon as I was old enough I changed it legally by Deed Poll."

Barely suppressing his laughter, Alex placed his hands on Serge's shoulders, and, being slightly shorter than his friend, had to stretch to place a kiss on his brow. "But I still love you in spite of everything."

A muscle twitched at the corner of Serge's eye and without warning, Alex found himself flat on his back in the snow, as Serge kicked his feet from underneath him. There followed a brief wrestling match, which ended with them both gasping for breath.

"What on earth are you two laughing at," remarked Eleanor as they staggered into the kitchen, faces flushed from the cold and their exertions.

"The thought of freshly baked bread, roast coffee beans and you my love," replied Serge, caressing her buttocks as he slid into the dining alcove.

Eleanor was instantly suspicious. "I've known you both for too long. You're up to something, I can tell."

Placated by a quickly fabricated story, Eleanor seemed to be satisfied with the explanation but it was difficult for either of them to stop laughing as they sat down for a light lunch. Alex was pouring the coffee when Anna walked into the kitchen. Her arrival was unexpected and the visible signs of a prolonged bout of crying disfigured her pretty face.

"Hi. You're back early, anything wrong?"

Her normally sparkling blue eyes were red and swollen. "Everything, where's Charly?"

"Here." Charlotte's brow furrowed with concern as she concentrated her efforts on the source of Anna's distress.

Her secretary struggled with her handbag as she extracted a crumpled blue folder, which she handed over. "Read it."

The novelist removed the sheets of handwritten notes and photographs from the folder and quickly perused the contents. An angry growl escaped as she continued to read. "The little shit!"

Alex began reading over her shoulder although he knew from previous occasions that it was a source of annoyance to her. Silently, she handed him some of the top sheets. His lean face showed a succession of emotions from amusement through annoyance and anger. D.C. Sinclair's meticulous notes recorded every conversation that had been carried on in his presence by the occupants of Hunter's Moon. It was an in-depth report to support the claim that Charlotte Manning and her guests were a group of powerful devil-worshippers, who were probably responsible for the murders in and around Ashmarsh.

"According to the dossier, this is a nest of devotees of the black arts. He has faithfully recorded the lengthy conversations that Serge had with Charlotte on voodoo and the ability to kill by auto-suggestion. He has observed that both parties appear to possess an abnormal depth of knowledge on the subject and recommends that further enquiries be made into their respective backgrounds. He goes on to further to suggest that the deaths in the neighbourhood be seriously considered as ritual killings. And there is even a devil's altar here."

"I don't believe it."

"You mean he accepted your hospitality ..."

"But all this is in his imagination."

"And I didn't even smell him."

Charlotte was annoyed with herself for overlooking the deception. She could never understand what Anna had seen in him from the start but she had never really bothered to probe him and as a result, his insignificant personality had successfully shielded his unscrupulous ambition. There had been several occasions when he had made her feel uneasy but she had dismissed this as being due to her natural suspicion of policemen.

Alex had taken the remaining sheets from her and continued reading. "It gets better. Not only is Charly accused of being a practising witch but she has also been written off as someone who purchases power and popularity with important people in the area by acts of pseudo-kindness and generosity. And in the red corner, our friendly neighbourhood warlock, Serge Butler, is named as a confidence trickster for having lured away the Colonel's daughter by unknown means and he now seeks to advance his financial position by ingratiating himself in the family's favour."

"I'll ingratiate the little bastard if I get my hands on him."

"Don't bother, Charlotte will lend you some plasticine and pins for the job."

"It would appear that you have some hold over Eleanor and live off her money as the flat in London was purchased in her name and he also recommends that your business affairs be looked into ..."

"That was a tax dodge!"

Alex continued. "Eleanor is classed as very beautiful but very little else. Anna fairs little better and is dismissed as existing in someone else's shadow and basking in their fame. As for myself, my presence here is suspect as a long standing friend of Serge and Eleanor and even more so, since on the 2nd December I paid a considerable sum of money for an original set of Crowley's *Equinox*."

"What on earth for?" asked an astonished Charlotte.

"They were supposed to be a present for you but didn't arrive in time for Christmas."

"Where on earth have we got a devil's altar?"

Anna enlightened her. "That's my fault. Over Christmas we went for a walk in the woods and he saw the statue and decided that Pan was definitely satanic. I'm sorry all of you for bringing this on you."

Alex put an arm around her shoulders and planted a kiss on her temple. "It's not your fault, Blossom, don't let it get to you."

"But it's cleverly put together," remarked Serge, reading through the offending pages. "Everything he's quoted actually happened. Don't you remember I made some idiotic remark about playing my cards right and having the family fortunes in my grasp? *All* these conversations took place but not as he's represented them - lucky for us witchcraft is no longer a burning offence! He's even got photographs of each of us."

"That boy will go far," observed Eleanor. "What's to be done with the report?"

"This," said Anna savagely, snatching up the papers and thrusting them into the red hot coals of the range.

"Now you've destroyed the evidence," cried Serge with mock severity.

"It can't if it's not true and it's not an official police file. Anyway, I've only called in to show you that and collect a few things. I'm going to London to stay with my sister until after the New Year, so if he phones, you can tell him what you like."

"My pleasure," replied Serge.

"Good idea. Alex and I are going back with Serge anyhow. There's a party on New Years Eve and both of us have appointments with the respective people who pay us money from time to time for our creative genius. So we'll also be missing for a few days. Ring when you're coming back. And don't worry."

For the first time since she had walked in the door, Anna forced a smile and left the kitchen. From the moment she had found the file hidden under the seat of John's car she had not had respite from the mental anguish his betrayal had caused. Not only a betrayal of herself but of those she loved best. If only she hadn't tried to adjust the car seat she would have remained in ignorance of his treachery and on finding the dossier, her only thought had been her loyalty to Charlotte Manning. The thought of him touching her while all the time he was plotting against them, forced the bile into her throat.

"Poor kid."

"Something should be done about friend John."

"It's not worth the bother."

Even though there was nothing for him to discover and the reports in the dossier were a complete fabrication, Charlotte was uneasy about police infiltration into her home. There was nothing to link anyone at Hunter's Moon to any illegal practices but her first-hand knowledge of persecution left her in no doubt that John Sinclair was not the only policeman capable of manufacturing evidence to secure an arrest. The others might take the affair lightly but she was fully aware of the serious implications.

The Christmas holidays had taken people's minds off the murders for a few days but police investigations continued without respite. Five grisly deaths had aroused community distrust and although the villagers of Ashmarsh held to their original belief that no one from there could be responsible, the inhabitants of other villages were not so reticent.

Gossip and rumour pointed out that the Ashmarshers had "always bin a bit queer" and the Neville family's penchant for herbal remedies did not escape comment. Despite the regularity with which the fingers pointed back to Ashmarsh, the villagers themselves could, or would, offer no solution. "We all know one another," they answered, "and it's not one of us."

Accusations flew fast and furious until Alan Morris was reduced to screaming pitch. He was intelligent enough to see for himself that much of the ill-feeling amongst the forest communities stemmed from the fact that the ordinary people of Ashmarsh were slightly more affluent than their neighbours. This affluence manifested itself in help with private education for promising pupils, financial assistance in times of difficulty or private health care, and of course the thing that was foremost in everyone's mind - the personal Christmas hamper for each family. It was understandable that the petty jealousies of the less fortunate were targeted at Charlotte Manning for her generosity.

Amidst the turmoil Morris received another stomach-churning piece of news. An eleven year old girl from Ashmarsh had not come back from walking the family dog. The parents, who had not worried until the terrier returned home alone, immediately called the police. The winter solstice had passed but there were too few hours of daylight left to give Morris time to organise a police search, especially with so many men off duty for the holidays. For a moment panic began to build, until he noticed the telephone number for Hunter's Moon scribbled in his diary.

In the time it took Morris to round up any available on-duty policemen and get to Ashmarsh, Charlotte and the Colonel had mobilised the entire village and estate to search for Tracy Walker. Again, in view of the political repercussions, Morris was nervous about the number of guns carried by the villagers, particularly as his own men were unarmed but he wasn't going to waste time arguing. The sun was already beginning to sink and before long, the countryside would be plunged into that eerie half light that distorted hedges and tree stumps into demons. He would just have to pray that no strangers appeared to tempt an itchy trigger-finger; and that the tabloid press would keep their distance - there was going to be enough flack as it was.

Serge, Alex and the Colonel joined the long line of guns that would sweep across acres of wood and farmland north of the Watling Street. The impressive sight of over a hundred men and dogs, dark shapes against the fierce whiteness of the landscape, attracted the press in droves. Their vehicles bogged down in drifts, they were forced to follow on foot across the snowbound terrain. Almost immediately Tony Walker found what he believed were his daughter's tracks, following her favourite haunt along the banks of the stream. The searchers had not gone a hundred yards when the footprints vanished, leaving the solitary paw prints of the dog clearly visible.

The news was being passed along the line of guns when Alex and Serge suddenly found themselves alone in the eerie silence of the ancient Whittlewood. Only moments before there had been men to the left and right of them and now there was nothing, not even the bark of an excited dog. For as far as they could see, there was no movement between the trees and although logic told them that there were over a hundred armed trackers within hailing distance, both felt a distinct tremor of panic. High in the branches, a bird suddenly gave voice to a high pitched, piping melody resembling the reeded instrument of a pastoral deity.

Serge stopped and shivered, recalling a story he'd read as a child but he couldn't remember the title. *"The piper at the gates of dawn ..."*

"Eh?"

"The kid's book, you remember ... " He stopped and grabbed Alex's arm.

159

From the twisted shell of a blasted oak, a child's body protruded; the bright orange anorak and blue jeans jarringly unreal against smooth, unruffled snow. The figure lay perfectly still and since Alex had seen Quinnell's body after the killer had finished with it, he needed to take a deep breath before finding out whether the same fate had overtaken Tracy Walker. Serge, however, had run on and dropped to his knees beside the recumbent figure, giving a loud cry.

"She's okay!"

The girl was unconscious but there were no signs that her clothing had been tampered with, nor any cuts or bruises visible on her face or head. Neither were there any sounds from the rest of the party and despite Alex yelling for help, no-one came. There was no alternative than to carry the senseless child back to the village. Unsure of how they had become separated from the rest of the search party, doggedly they plodded on, taking it in turns to carry the limp figure of the girl until they came out into the uneven tract of a ploughed field covered by the snow.

Again they were in the company of men to the left and right of them but for an instant, in that small remnant of old Whittlewood Forest they had the strange experience of being utterly alone. A shout went up and suddenly, faces that only moments before had been grim and tense, were now wild with joy and relief. Tony Walker took his daughter in his arms and dropped to his knees, tears coursing down his face.

By the time the searchers returned, the television cameras were waiting in Ashmarsh where the landlord of the Saracen's Head had opened the bar to serve hot soup and coffee to the weary search party. Most were too frustrated or exhausted to bother with reporters but there were those who did not come from the village who were willing to be interviewed, even though they had not taken part in the search. Loud voices argued and quarrelled as gratefully Alex and Serge found an anonymous corner, away from the noise

160

and shouting.

The fire in the bar attracted the assortment of dogs, who had accompanied the party, from experienced gun-dogs to hounds and terriers. Apart from a few initial growls while they vied for position, the floor in front of the hearth was carpeted with dozing canines. Occasionally there would be a whistle and one of the animals would sit up, listen and then join his master who was about to leave.

The Colonel who, despite having been warned by his doctor not to take part, was looking remarkably healthy. His ruddy complexion glowed from the exhilaration of the chase and the warmth from the fire. He was on his second brandy when their party was joined by the large, jovial farmer who owned the land adjoining Hunter's Moon.

"Well, George, I must confess it's not an ending that I expected. I thought we'd find the lass dead."

"How the devil did she get from the stream to that part of the wood without leaving any tracks?"

"Don't ask me, man. Some of these dogs are the best in the county and they couldn't flush her out. We'll have to wait 'til she comes round to see what happened." He whistled up two Springer spaniels who climbed over the prostrate bodies of their companions. "Good day to you all, I'd best be off or the Missus will think I've left home. We appreciate you turning out 'cos there's not many here that would," he added meaningfully to Serge and Alex.

"Praise indeed," replied the Colonel, pleased that the chap who was to be his son-in-law had found favour in the eyes of a local man.

"Only when it's deserved, George. Anyway I'll be getting along before those bloody reporters get around to my turn. Least said the soonest mended is what I say."

Alex nodded in response but an idea was beginning to form in his mind. It was true that not one of them had expected to find Tracy alive but the girl *had* been left un-harmed in the woods. Nevertheless, the fact that there had been no tracks in the snow confirmed the suspicion that her abductor was none other than the Ashmarsh Beast.

Suddenly he found himself remembering Alicia Howard's strange comment that the second victim was "from the village, not of the village".

Chapter Thirteen

The moon cast her ethereal light over snow covered farm-land, creating a mysterious monochrome world of light and shadow. A silent, frozen tranquillity invaded the countryside, transforming the woods into glacial cathedrals. The cry of an owl; the sudden flurry of a rabbit as blood splattered on the snow in homage to the pagan moon, so low and heavy in the sky that she seemed to be resting on the brow of the hill. A dog fox trotted out of the wood, his muzzle to the ground as he sought his prey. Suddenly he stopped, ears pricked. With one paw raised he listened as the thick fur ruff rose along his spine. In a flash he turned and ran towards the cover of the trees.

Two men trudged through the snow, the drifts almost covering the tops of their boots as they cast long shadows in the moonlight. Muffled against the raw cold, they brought with them a dog whose reluctance for the night's excursion was noticeable by the way its tail drooped as he plodded slowly through the snow.

The Staffordshire Bull Terrier is known for its courage and tenacity, and this particular animal was a seasoned fighter from the illegal dog fighting circuit that operated in the neighbouring counties. This uncharacteristic nervousness puzzled his owner but the man was too intent on reaching the old barn silhouetted against the skyline, at the edge of the copse.

The stone barn had been used for storing winter cattle

feed but the farmer to whom it belonged now transported fodder to his livestock by tractor and the barn had not been used for some time. Taking care that no light should show, the two men entered the barn where a younger man was waiting. The walls of the building were heavily lined with sacking to prevent draughts and to stop any light from escaping to attract the curious. The floor of the barn was littered with straw, and the arena, made out of corrugated iron sheets, was held in place by wooden stakes and straw bales. A powerful overhead lamp cast shadows, large and grotesque, against the walls as they moved about in a shadow-play of preparation.

As Geoff Hickson stepped outside to urinate into the snow, Maurice Whitehead removed their next victim from its box. Sensing the blast of cold air, the cat made a last bid bid for freedom. Twisting and writhing in the man's grasp, razor sharp claws met with bone as the terrified animal lunged at its captor's face. With a scream of agony, Whitehead dropped the cat, which immediately bolted for the half opened door and disappeared into the night. Normally the dog would have sprung to attack a loose cat but tonight it sat shivering as his master screamed with a mixture of pain and rage.

Sloshing whisky onto a not too clean handkerchief, Scotty Wilson handed it to his companion. "What the hell's going on? The bloody dog didn't even move!"

Clamping the alcohol soaked rag to his face, his partner waved a hand to indicate his ignorance. The Staff moved towards its master and with a low whine, wagged a tail in apology. Ignoring the dog's overtures, Whitehead aimed a kick at the animal and with a yelp of pain, it retreated to a corner. In all its four years, the brindled terrier had never been treated in this manner. He was a perfect specimen; muscles tuned to perfection with a smooth coat that hardly showed any traces of injury from the numerous fights from which it had emerged the victor. The thick barrel chest contained a heart that would burst with loyalty, if it were ever put to the test.

Geoff Hickson knelt down beside Boss in the straw and patted him. "I don't think he's well. I noticed when you came in that he was nervous and all of a tremble. Perhaps he's picked up a chill."

"Well, he'd best get rid of it and quick," replied the whisky swilling Scot. "He's fighting the night after tomorrow."

"He can't fight like this," protested the youth.

"Are you telling me my business boy?" roared Scotty, unbuckling his belt. "I'll liven the bugger up!"

The two men glared at one another, Scotty clenching and unclenching his fists in a threatening manner. He was known for a bully in the less salubrious public houses in the nearby town and Hickson knew he would be no match for those enormous hams if Scotty hit him. Instead he got to his feet and dragged the dog towards the door. Boss hung back and as Geoff reached down to get a better grip on his collar, the double doors of the barn crashed open.

A loose plank of wood knocked the boy to the ground with a savage gash on his temple and as he drifted off into emptiness he was aware that in the lamplight a huge man cast an even larger shadow on the walls. Dressed in a shaggy goatskin cloak, the giant was menacing enough without the dramatic entrance that had demolished half the door. Wilson's immediate reaction was one of glee, for in mistaking the bearded man for an animal-rights protestor, he only had one thought in mind and that was to teach the long-haired know-all a lesson he wouldn't forget in a hurry. The man was big, but he'd fought bigger - and won.

Instinctively Scotty pushed his accomplice away, to widen the gap between them and hoping that Whitehead would have the presence of mind to lay the intruder out with a plank of wood if the opportunity presented itself. He had also spotted a pitchfork against the wall and he knew that he would only be given one chance to kill the giant, for from underneath the cloak, there had appeared an evil looking knife, its edges gleaming in the grimy light of the lamp. The roles

165

had been swiftly reversed, and instead of an easy victim, the men weren't slow to realise the precariousness of their position. Scotty was a bully but he had an animal need to survive and even in the situation of being menaced by, what he now recognised as the possible killer of five people, his naked courage did not fail him.

Perspiration and blood ran down Whitehead's face as the Iceni edged nearer and nearer, with all the precision and cruel grace of a cat stalking a mouse. The man was so close that he could almost feel his breath but fear had paralysed his legs and he could no longer move. Without realising it, he had cornered himself by the straw bales and cut off his own means of escape. A terrible stench caused him to retch and he realised with a flush of shame that his sphincter had failed him and that he had emptied his bowels.

There was now a gap of some ten feet between himself and Scotty, whose hand was slowly reaching for the pitch-fork. His fingers brushed against the smooth wood of the handle and he scarcely dare breathe in case the implement slipped from his grasp. Firmly, his hand gripped the shaft, his knuckles white with tension as he lifted the fork to strike.

Lunging at the intruder with a tremendous thrust, to his satisfaction Scotty saw the iron prongs sink into the man's chest. With a snarl of unbridled fury the Iceni raised the hand brandishing the knife and in the split second before the lethal blade cleaved his skull, Wilson realised that the pitchfork had passed straight through the human form, its prongs embedded in the floor of the barn. The body slumped to the ground, spilling blood and grey matter from the fragmented bone.

Maurice Whitehead was already unconscious through sheer terror when the shaman began hacking at his prone body; ripping at the clothing and slicing through his genitals. Briefly he regained consciousness but mercifully the full horror of being castrated whilst still alive caused his heart to give out.

Geoff Hickson's eyes opened to see the Iceni competently butchering the remains of his companions. Maurice Whitehead's mutilated body already dangling from the rafters. Not three feet from him lay Scotty, his brains slipping out onto the floor of the barn. He was briefly mesmerised by the idiotic expression of surprise on the dead man's face. Forcing himself not to vomit, the remaining victim inched himself slowly across the floor, towards the doorway.

Quickly pulling himself to his feet, he leapt out into the clear, cold darkness. The deep snow impeded his flight and turning, he saw the man following him through the drifts. Silently the Iceni tracked him, feet barely touching the smooth blanket of whiteness. Finally Hickson could go no further and sank to his knees against the bole of a tree, realising that the dog had followed close by him and as the boy's strength failed, Boss whirled to face the attacker. Ears flattened and lips drawn back over his teeth in a snarl, the dog bravely blocked the killer's path. Even in the middle of his own terror, Hickson had to admire the dog's courage in its futile attempt to protect him.

Only feet apart, man and dog faced one another. Growling and snarling rent the chill night air as the antagonists challenged one another in the snowbound amphitheatre of woodland. It was so bright that Boss cast a deep shadow as he circled the man, but his opponent cast no shadow and left no tracks. The dog positioned himself for the attack and with a cry that was part bark, part howl he hurled himself at the man's throat. The Staff blinked in surprise as nothing checked his flight. Where the man's chest should have been there was thin air and his teeth snapped together, holding nothing. The force of the savage leap had pitched Boss headfirst into a snow drift.

Geoff Hickson began whimpering with fear as the man moved towards him. The Iceni was so close that the terrified boy could see moonlight glinting in those contemptuous, merciless eyes. Slowly the killer reached over to him and a scream forced its way up from his lungs, filling the night with abject terror. The powerful arm raised high in the air, came down with such a force, that the blade of the blood-stained knife hacked several inches of bark from the tree to which Hickson was clinging. Unconcerned by the boy's screams the killer stood motionless for a moment silhouetted against the clear night sky and then was gone.

The dog shook snow from its coat and ran to where Hickson was still screaming hysterically. The dog whined, licking his friend's face in comfort but it was of little use. The youth's mind had been unhinged by the horrors of the barn and with the sight of the murderous Iceni still imprinted on his brain, he was unable to register that the killer had vanished. His screams echoed over the still countryside until finally a curious farmer came out to investigate. One look at the carnage told him all he needed to know but even his presence could not stop the fearful screaming. With eyes bulging and spittle running down his chin, the last of the dog fighting team would need to be carted away in a straight jacket, a gibbering, mindless idiot.

It was some hours before the doctor and ambulance team delivered Geoff Hickson to the county asylum. The screaming had finally stopped but the boy still opened and closed his mouth in the manner of a stranded fish gasping for air, making pathetic mewing sounds. Alan Morris had been called immediately but there was nothing to do except wait until the boy calmed down. Morris had already been to the scene of the attack and he had the horrible feeling that he wasn't going to like what Hickson told him.

The doctor led the policeman back towards the reception. "Don't know when he'll be able to tell you anything. His brain has received such a tremendous shock."

"Has he said anything ... anything at all?" asked Morris buttoning his sheepskin coat.

"Not really, Inspector, just rambles on about travellers

He's being kept under sedation in case he attacks one of the nurses. It may be weeks before he's fit to be interviewed."

Morris stabbed the young doctor firmly in the chest with his index finger. "Look mate, he *saw* whoever killed his companions and I want him off those drugs and lucid. I've got to get into his head and find out exactly who we're lookin for. I've now got *seven* people dead and at least he'll be able to give us a description we can circulate. I don't give a damn how you do it, but just get him back in this world for a few minutes, okay?"

"Then you'll be responsible for the consequences?" The doctor's tone was openly hostile at the policeman's intrusion into hospital routine.

Morris was not going to be intimidated by a white coated smart-arse. "As responsible as you'll be if we land up with more bodies because you won't co-operate," he replied with a jaunty wave.

Much to his frustration, he discovered that Charlotte Manning was still away and not expected to return for a few days. He sat in his car with his mind and the engine racing. He now had *seven* unsolved murders: two boys held on the flimsiest of evidence, a madman and an aborted abduction of a child on his hands. A serial killer - how he hated to use the popular expression - but there was no other description that fitted the pattern. Ominous rumblings were coming from the direction of the Superintendent's office and he knew that it would not be too long before the Chief Constable insisted that outside help be called in.

"Balls to the Grimme Reaper," he muttered to himself.

He had his own specialist to consult. Why he felt that an occult novelist could succeed where forensics and professional investigators had failed, he could not answer. *Seven bodies and and one idiot* and no clues as to the identity of the killer. A killer who left no tracks in virgin snow *had* to be a bloody magician and somewhere in Charlotte Manning's vast reference library there must be some logical explanation. He'd also been looking into some of her other activities, and there were a couple of proposals he wanted to put to her.

The snow still lay thick and deep under the steely grey sky, faithfully recording the movements of the individuals involved in the latest of the bizarre murders. Until the Scene Of Crime Officers had finished their investigations, suspicion had naturally fallen on Geoff Hickson as his foot-prints were the only ones leading away from the barn. It was originally suggested that he had killed his companions in a moment of frenzy and then fled into the night. Enquiries found that he had an alibi for the other nights in question and as forensic evidence showed that the killer's *modus operandi* was the same in each instance, SOCO were forced reluctantly to look elsewhere. However, in the meantime, they still had their original suspects safely under lock and key in the Remand Centre and Hickson in the loony bin.

The pressure was now on to release the two boys because in addition to the lack of evidence, during hours of intense questioning both were adamant that they had not killed their girl friends; and though neither had had the opportunity to corroborate, the stories were remarkably similar.

The post-mortem showed the girls had been killed and mutilated with a long thin single-bladed knife - while the others had met their end by the services of that distinctively wide, double-edged blade. Morris was becoming increasingly concerned that in the hunt for the Ashmarsh Beast, the real killer of Alison Webber and Gail Masters would be overlooked. There had always been a nagging doubt in his mind whether the boys had carried out the murders, even though the pathologist's report showed that the semen found in each girl, came from their corresponding boyfriend. But if they weren't responsible, that meant two killers on the loose!

Now he had the histrionics of John Sinclair to contend with. The detective had been furious when he discovered the theft of his painstaking report but his chagrin had turned to elation over Anna's obvious complicity, as he reported the details of his findings to his superior. To his surprise, Morris had not seemed duly impressed by his diligent infiltration of the household at Hunter's Moon.

"She would know a lot about black magic because she earns her living writing about it. From what *my* investigations tell *me,*" he emphasised the point, "she even lectures at the Universities on the subject. Are you suggesting that anyone who conjured up a pretty authentic black mass for the book buying public should be implicated in the murders? Should we arrest them too?"

"Sir, I believe there's evil in that house."

"Well, you've spent enough time in it," retorted Morris "and so have I. I'm not surprised Miss Fenton took off with your report, she probably thought it was an act of base treachery by a supposedly upstanding member of the community. You've only known her five minutes, do you think that is enough to replace her loyalty to her employer?"

"Manning and that London fellow, spent nearly the whole of one evening arguing over the non-existence of the Devil," replied Sinclair mulishly.

Morris frowned slightly and then his mind cleared. "Which church do you belong to, son?"

"Evangelical, Sir."

The theological argument that to maintain there was no Devil was to call Christ a liar was a well publicised anathema to those of fundamentalist persuasion. In his time Morris had heard all sorts of pleas offered by the defence; that the court should take the defendant's religious background into consideration, or that the accused truly believed that the Devil had directed his actions and was therefore not really guilty of crime. Morris did not hold with the opinion that people should not be given more personal responsibility than they can rightly claim as their own. If anyone committed a criminal act then they should pay the penalty; there might sometimes be mitigating circumstances but as sure as there was snow outside, Morris would not accept pleas of devilish interference -

171

no matter how good the lawyer!

"You'll find as you go through life that there are many that oppose your way of thinking, be it religious, political or moral, but it doesn't mean that they're wrong or bad. I knew a man once who was an sworn atheist, hated church and God alike but when it came down to acts of charity to his fellow man, he was more Christian-like than most. He would have been insulted to the core if you'd called him one though. You can't judge all men by your own beliefs."

"Should I apologise, Sir?" The offer was insincere.

"No, leave well alone, I'll speak to Mrs Manning but I should keep out of the way if I were you. No running around after Anna or you might get yourself turned into a toad."

He sat there cracking the bones of his fingers, a habit that annoyed his wife intensely. In view of Sinclair's attitude to Charlotte Manning, Morris decided to request that he be taken off the case and for once the Superintendent had seen the sense behind the request without asking for a triple page report. Sinclair would have difficulty in accepting the decision but he had no intention of having religious bias whispered in his ear at every turn. In Sinclair's place he'd been assigned D.C. Carole Marchant, a quietly efficient brunette, whose background revealed no definite religious viewpoint. His new assistant had been sent to the hospital to wait for the opportunity to speak to Tracy Walker.

Two hour's later she arrived back at the station, flushed with cold and success. Not only had she brought him a mug of hot soup but a artist's sketch of Tracy's abductor and a taped recording of her interview with the girl. By way of showing his appreciation, Morris put his arm around her and gave her an affectionate squeeze - and hoped he wouldn't be reported for sexual harassment of a female detective. The sketch showed a face of strong character, despite the thick shoulder length hair and shaggy moustache. The artist had paid particular detail to the eyes, which the girl had insisted were the most remarkable feature about him.

172

D.C. Marchant had found Tracy none the worse for her ordeal only rather confused by all the fevered activity and questioning. She remember meeting the long-haired stranger by the stream but had no recollection of anything after that. The voice on the recording was bright and confident, insisting that at no time did she feel frightened or threatened by her abductor. She described him as a very big man, although the only other firm description was of the clothes he was wearing. Tracy had insisted he was wearing a coat like the one her dad had worn in a photograph at home. Later investigations showed this to have been a large coloured picture of Tony and Diane Walker, taken at one of the first open air rock concerts in the company of The Rolling Stones. Tony, also long haired and bearded, was wearing what Diane referred to as an 'Afghan' coat.

"Tracy always loved that photo," explained her mother. "I think it was because Tony and I had once met a few famous people. Everyone seems to think the '60s were a real swinging time and no matter how many times we tell her that we only went to one concert, it's got some glamourous image for her."

Carole Marchant continued with her report. "There's no signs of any sort of sexual interference; not even a slight scratch or bruise. Although she couldn't describe the man, she obviously has a very strong impression of him. To begin with, Jeff drew a young thin-faced type but she was adamant that he was older, with what she called "a proper face". As soon as Jeff started to add the character lines, she was quite sure that it was a fairly accurate impression. She even asked for a copy!"

"Not the sort of reaction you'd expect to a bloke who's put paid to seven people?"

"I don't think this has anything to do with the others."

"Then how do you explain," replied Morris, hoping he didn't sound too patronising, "the lack of footprints in the snow? Get the picture circulated to the papers and maybe we'll get some response."

"Too late Sir" D.C. Marchant unfolded the late edition of the local evening papers which both ran a full front page artist's impression of Tracy's abductor and banner headline: Jesus-Freak Sought By Police and Gun-Law Reigns.

Alex and Charlotte knew nothing about the latest developments until the morning newspaper arrived at the Butler's flat. Alex stared long and hard at the sketch before handing it to Charlotte, who was still in bed. "That was the face in the woods on Bonfire Night!"

She took the paper and a low whistle escaped through her teeth. "And a good likeness. Pity they won't be able to identify anyone from it. Or are you still insisting on human agency?"

It was the first time the subject of the shaman had been brought up since Alex's hurried departure and although he was aware of the amount of time she was spending trying to discover the reason behind the sudden manifestation, he had tactically withdrawn from any discussions. Now he could ignore it no longer and as the newspaper article had pushed the subject into the foreground, he was forced to ask how far her research had progressed.

"We believe that our nocturnal prowler is an Iceni who was killed by the Romans after their last battle. There's little enough evidence to go on but the Iceni were recorded as stringing up their victims in sacred groves as a sacrifice to their goddess Andrasta. The women had their breasts cut off and stuffed into their mouths, while long skewers were thrust through their bodies lengthways. There's no mention of what happened to male captives but I think we can supply the answer to that question."

"So what set him off?" Alex wasn't convinced but he felt he ought to make the right noises.

"The first deaths seem to be the key. If he is the guardian of Iceni dead, then the killing of Alison and Gail, or the

174

location of the murders, must have taken the form of a desecration of the burial site. The problem lies in locating his burial place and releasing him."

"Releasing him! Christ, Charlotte, if what you say is true then this ... Iceni ... has been running around the countryside hacking folk to bits! Surely you should be talking about destroying him?"

Charlotte sat up and stared thoughtfully. "You can't impose 20th century morals and laws on a man who died around 60AD. Anyone from that period desecrating a burial place would probably have been executed and he's only reacting according to his lights. I know those who died weren't responsible for the desecration but I can't see my way to condemning him for his actions."

In total exasperation Alex turned his attention back to the newspaper so that he wouldn't have to face her. There were times when he considered her to be totally amoral and rather than face another fight, he continued to read the cover story. The current victims had been identified as coming from the nearby town; the lone survivor was reported as being an Ashmarsh boy ... *from the village but not of the village* ... echoed again in his mind.

Chapter Fourteen

It was several days later when Charlotte Manning returned to Hunter's Moon - alone. Alex could delay his own assignments no longer and had flown out for a round trip to Lisbon, Florence and Tunis in pursuit of the subjects for his personality profiles. His agent was howling for material and although Charlotte was suffering from a severe chill, he was forced to attend to his livelihood or be without an agent. He reflected during the journey to the airport, that until he had met her, nothing had stood between him and the racy, biting interviews for which, only the bravest or most foolhardy publicity seeking celebrities would volunteer.

His piece on Charlotte, scheduled for February publication, had been one of the most difficult he had ever encountered. It was not because she was a awkward subject but because he had found her almost as impossible to capture in words as an artist attempting to recreate the iridescent beauty of a butterfly on canvass. They had lived together under the same roof for two months but his interview, written after only a few fleeting hours of her company, did nothing to capture the magnetic life force surrounding her, affecting anyone who came into her sphere of influence.

The aura surrounding her generated its own electricity and not for the reason that she was gregarious; in company her expression was that of a mask, the remote smile identical to the one worn by the statue in the wood. Her cool politeness neither encouraged nor discouraged; his own friends were unable to understand his attraction to such a diminutive icicle. They had spent the New Year with Serge and Eleanor, who were now such firm disciples that they would walk fire for her if asked and at the theatre, in restaurants and at parties, Alex had become increasingly aware of the interest shown in his mistress. Wherever they arrived, all attention in the room would focus on her as though she projected some strange animal magnetism to which all were forced to respond. She was no great beauty and her stature was far too short to make her impressive but she carried with her a certain mystique which none seemed to ignore.

Alex often found himself wondering just how long he would be able to carry on in the role as a live-in lover, without demanding something more from her. He had found it amusing to watch from the side-lines as Serge had been manoeuvred into marriage but now he was finding himself envious of his friend's new found happiness. Both of them had once agreed that marriage was unimportant in a relationship and he was hurt by Serge's defection to respectability. He was *almost* certain that he did not want to marry Charlotte but at the same time he felt the need of some declaration of permanency in their relationship.

The only woman with whom he had ever considered marriage had been the dead Katherine but in retrospect, how much of that desire had been prompted by the fact that she was expecting his child. Would it really have worked if she hadn't died so tragically? At least he could remember her without guilt since Charlotte's relentless attack on his ego during that first visit. But Charlotte had been *le belle dame sans merci.*

Charlotte had travelled back to Ashmarsh by limousine, much to the delight of Gwen Carradine, who was waiting for her on the doorstep. Amid clucking and scolding, she was forced to retire to bed while the chauffeur was attended to and with

177

no energy to protest, the mistress of the house collapsed gratefully into her familiar bed. Even the most potent of ancient magic had no remedy for the common cold.

On the third day, after a lengthy call from Alex from his Florentine hotel, Gwen announced that Alan Morris was downstairs, wishing to speak with her. After fussing around and straightening the heavy brocade bed cover, where the cats and a pile of books formed a cocoon around the invalid, the housekeeper ushered the detective into the room. Taking her time to withdraw in case some titbit of information was forthcoming.

"Sorry to hear you've not been well," he commiserated as they exchanged pleasantries. "No doubt Mrs Carradine has filled you in with the details of our latest murders?"

"She tried but I cut her short," she gave a weak smile, "Butcher's shop narratives were the last thing I wanted this week."

"If you're feeling better I'd like to go over it with you, because I'd like your advice on one or two ideas of my own."

When Alan Morris had completed his summing up, they sipped the tea which Gwen had thoughtfully provided, fussing around until she was dismissed with the suggestion that she was already late in getting home to arrange her husband's meal. Grinning like conspirators, they listened to her heavy bulk descending the stairs and after a few moments the side door closed with its customary thud.

"I've got one lad locked up in Berry Wood and two more in the Remand Centre and if we carry on like this, half the youth in the county will be behind bars."

"But *you* don't think any of them are guilty?"

"No. I've been onto Surrey University to the chap who's proved to be pretty good at psychological profiling and he's come up with his ideas of who we should be looking for. According to the Professor, a criminal leaves evidence of his personality through his actions in relation to a crime. And nothing here fits either of the boys, or Hickson. There's an artist's impression too."

He handed her a thick manilla envelope containing enlarged pictures of the barn murders. "As you can see, three men and a dog went into the bar and only one came out - plus the dog. The snow shows where Hickson ran and then turned, the foot prints indicate that he was facing back towards the barn. He fell, regained his feet and then finally collapsed where the snow was churned up by him thrashing around in a panic. There are the dog's paw prints but nothing else. We've got the girl's description and it's imperative that I get a description out of Hickson."

Charlotte studied the other enlargements that showed the scene inside the barn. The bodies and the pitchfork, its prongs still embedded in the ground, had not been disturbed. There were other forensic photographs that showed the injuries sustained by the victims and she was half prepared for the artist's impression which was a perfect likeness of the Iceni who had appeared to her on two separate occasions. The profile was even more alarming, since it identified a man in his mid-thirties, a loner, highly intelligent, probably with a strong religious or moral background, who reacted strongly to any actual or unintentional infringement of his own strongly held convictions.

The Iceni shaman's spirit was around 900 years old, but he could have been around 30 years of age when he died; his appearance seemed much older but 30 was a good age in an ancient Briton. His position within the tribe would also require a high level of intelligence and aloofness. "And the girl actually saw him?" She asked, covering her surprise by pretending to read a transcript of Tracy Walker's description. "I'm not sure why you're telling me all this."

Morris moved the chair nearer to the bed in a conspiratorial manner. "I want to get into young Hickson's head and find out what he really did see. It's time we knew what the hell we're looking for! If it was the same chap as went off with Tracy Walker, then why the devil didn't he kill her too?"

"I take it you did not discuss any of your ideas with the Professor?"

"Or with my SIO either."

"You intrigue me."

Morris fumbled for his pipe but remembering he in was in a lady's bedroom, changed his mind. "Down at the station they think we're finally onto our man, but I can't completely subscribe to that theory. I don't think that the two girls were killed by the same person who murdered the rest. It's not unknown for a murderer to change weapons if he finds something more effective, but I don't think so in this case. I believe there are two killers who are so remotely distant from one another that I'm not sure that I even believe it myself."

"Go on!"

"Young Hickson hadn't a spot of blood on him, except for a cut on the head and there is no way that a man could be done to death like this ..." He tapped a photograph with the unlit pipe, "and his assailant not be covered in gore. We've taken the blasted barn to bits and there's nothing concealed inside, the snow doesn't show any evidence of clothing or weapons being taken outside and on top of it all, there are still no tracks belonging to the killer. *Discounting* the two girls, we have five people butchered and not one shred of forensic evidence to help us. For all intents and purposes, they might just as well have murdered themselves!"

"So you obviously ruled out the Hickson boy as a homicidal maniac?"

"Scotty Wilson's skull was opened up by a blow from the front. If the boy had gone for him, he wouldn't have stood a chance if Wilson could see it coming. He was a nasty piece of work, as some of my lads well know."

Charlotte leaned back against the creamy pillows, her mind as suspicious as a Borgia. "So what's your theory?"

Morris had the good grace to look uncomfortable. "In your line of writing you've obviously come across every type of theory about magic. Just suppose that there was a single or multiple personality so powerful that it could create a presence capable of drawing its energy from the mind of its creator. Like a generator, feeding on the impulses to such a degree, until it could manifest itself on a physical plane at the time of the kill."

"Good God, Alan, what on earth have you been reading?"

"*A Grave Undertaking.*" He answered sheepishly, naming one of Charlotte's first novels. He would also avoid mentioning that the local library had been instructed to supply him with every one of her books.

She found it difficult to conceal her surprise at Morris's candour, especially as her mind probe found that the man was perfectly sincere in his request for help. She had suspected some cunning idea formulating in his subconscious but the man's mind was free from guile. Neither was there any trace of a desperate man clutching at straws. Her hand casually stroked one of the sleeping cats while she measured just how much help she should offer.

"Individuals of The Golden Dawn were capable of manifesting both mental and physical effects but I doubt if there's been anyone in the last 200 years with the sort of power you're seeking."

"You stated in your book that hatred was a dynamo which could power such a phenomena."

"True Alan, but it was also fiction. My books are based on documented cases of occult happenings, but I can't answer for the reliability or credentials of the fictional characters."

Morris looked deflated and seemed somehow smaller than his normal six feet. "Do you think I'm barmy?"

"On the contrary, I think you are showing a remarkably enlightened viewpoint on the whole affair but it's not one that I would recommend you to voice to your superiors. The paranormal is either terrifying or ridiculous to those who have no interest in discovering what is probably the oldest and most satisfying science in the history of man. How else can I help?"

181

"I want to prove to myself that Hickson saw something or somebody. If he's says it was a Martian with a meat cleaver then we're buggered. But if he describes the man in this picture, then I know he's telling the truth because he's been in the nuthouse under sedation since the attack and I've given instructions that he's not to see a newspaper."

"But how does it involve me?"

"Do you know a reliable hypnotist who would be sympathetic to a bit of skulduggery in the interests of science?"

"Professor Robson-Fforbes and I have presented a double act at Aberdeen University but he's out of the country at the moment. He's the only one I know personally in that line, who is seriously interested in parapsychology."

"What about you? Couldn't you talk to Hickson?"

"I'm a writer not a medic."

"Charlotte, I'm desperate. Couldn't you at least talk with him, try to explain that we do believe him, anything to get collaboration. You have a way of talking to people, they seem to open up to you."

"Why didn't he die along with the rest of them?" she asked aloud but the question was directed at her subconscious.

"Only Hickson himself can tell you that," replied Morris, hoping to whet her appetite.

Against her better judgement, the following afternoon found Charlotte Manning in a barred waiting room deep in the confines of the local asylum. The walls were painted the colour of cabbage water and everywhere smelled strongly of disinfectant. Alan Morris had come up against some strong opposition to the proposed visit to Geoff Hickson but he had appealed to his Senior Investivating Officer and Masonic wheels had ground into action. He had concocted some cock-and-bull story about Mrs Manning knowing Hickson's family, and the SIO, with no other leads on which to act, had reluctantly agreed to give them access to the suspect.

Although Charlotte knew she was now far from suspect

herself, she felt it expedient to be one step behind the detective during his investigation, in case it should be necessary to place herself one leap ahead. Morris had issued the invitation and she was unable to refuse it. The bleak greyness of the world outside was magnified a hundredfold in this seething cauldron of mental anguish.

To allow the mind to probe only briefly brought a barrage of tormented souls clamouring to be heard, the atmosphere electrified with the shrieks and moans of silent torment. Charlotte gave an involuntary shudder and exchanged a wry smile with her companion as they waited for admission to the inner sanctum of madness.

In the week since his nightmare started, Geoff Hickson had been transformed from a quiet, fresh faced country lad to a furtive caricature of his former self. Of light build by nature, his confinement following the killings had caused him to rapidly lose weight, leaving his clothes hanging on his meagre frame, his eyes and cheeks sunken. Warily he watched the two visitors as he sat rigidly on the hard chair, his hands gripping the seat until the knuckles gleamed white. Against the doctor's better judgement, the patient had been taken off the drugs originally prescribed and Geoff Hickson was left to face their questioning and his memories with no means of retreat.

Charlotte perched informally on the edge of the table and offered him a cigarette. It was forbidden for patients to be given cigarettes but in the brief unguarded moment of surprise Hickson snatched it gratefully and as he inhaled the smoke, she began to delve into his mind. The strength and stability of her psychic influence washed through him, offering a brief glimmer of hope and respite from the nightmare ridden days since the killings.

"I'd like you to tell me what you saw up on the ridge on the night your friends were killed." Her tone was low and soothing, as though she was talking to a frightened animal.

"You a copper?" his eyes darted from side to side, the wariness briefly returned.

183

"You know who I am."

"Why should I tell you anything, don't you know that I'm supposed to be mad?" A gleam of bitter sanity flared under the narrow lids as he inhaled the cigarette. "They think I killed my mates."

"I don't think you're mad and neither does Inspector Morris, that's why he asked me to come and see you. He doesn't think you killed your friends either. I can help you convince other people that you're innocent," she added.

The youth dropped his guard and showed blank astonishment. Everyone, even his mother, had said he was mad and it was easier to go along with their way of thinking than try to explain. The drugs they administered stopped him from dwelling on the reality of what had nearly turned his brain but now he was denied the luxury of tranquillised escape. Confused and frightened his eyes turned once more to Charlotte and a single tear spilled onto his cheek.

"Tell me!" The voice was commanding but soothing.

Slowly the stricken youth began his story, hesitantly at first, then gathering momentum. Charlotte sat with her back to Morris, who, in listening intently to Hickson and recording the conversation, was unaware that her hypnotic green eyes were drawing out the boy's inner hurt whilst she probed his memory. She held him in a deep hypnotic trance but to Morris, the sightless stare would be accounted for by the boy's near madness.

"We were up in the barn with Boss, that's the dog, and I went out for a piss." His forehead furrowed as his memory conjured up the fearful images. "There was something wrong with Boss that night. He's a brave dog but he was whining and shivering and getting himself in a right old state. I remember saying that he was ill and as I was looking him over, the door crashed in on top of me and hit my head. I don't know how long I was unconscious, but when I came round I could see this bloke ... cutting up ..." His voice faltered and wavered as the scene vividly came to life in front of his staring eyes. "Scotty

184

was dead with his brains splattered over the floor."

"Go on," she urged gently. The voice modulated, holding firmly on to the boy's self control.

Digging his fingers into the wasted muscles of his thighs, Hickson continued. "I don't know how I ran. He chased me across the snow and it was deep, pulling me down into the drifts. I remember Boss being there as I fell. He stood over me and old Boss stood up to him, snapping and snarling, trying to protect me. Then he flew at the bloke's throat. He kept right on going, he jumped right through him as though he wasn't there. Just nothing. He turned on me then and I really saw him for the first time because he was outlined against the moon."

"Could you describe him?"

"I'll never forget him. He was big. Much bigger than Scotty with long hair and a beard. He had these staring eyes that made him look as though he was angry at me and he wore a thick coat of some animal skin. Every night he stands over me and I start screaming all over again ..."

The horror of the story telling over, she relaxed her hold and gently slid mentally away from him. His ghosts had been laid by the retelling of his story; there would be nightmares in the months to come but they would recede. Hickson's face had lost its grey, haunted look as he continued speaking, and he gave a flickering apologetic smile. "He looked like one of those flower-power people from the '60s."

"Why didn't he kill you?"

"Dunno."

Silently Morris handed her the drawing. "Is this him?" she asked holding the plastic folder in front of Hickson.

The boy gaped at her in amazement. "How did you know?"

"Because someone else has described him exactly as you have done and this is an artist's impression of what she saw. Geoff, this may seem like a stupid question but do you believe that the man was *real*. I mean a flesh and blood human that you could have actually touched?"

For the first time since their meeting, he looked her squarely

185

in the face. They had led him to understand that they believed his story and if the man had been seen by someone else then it meant that he really wasn't mad. If he told the truth they could keep him locked up for years. His throat constricted and felt dry, it would be so easy to lie.

"He weren't real," he replied firmly. "Boss jumped right through 'im."

Charlotte slipped off the table and gently placed her hand on the boy's shoulder. "You'll have to stay here for a couple of days, Geoff, but I'm sure the Inspector will have you out as quickly as he can. But if I hear of you involved with dog-fighting again, I'll see you back in here. Do you understand?"

The boy nodded dully in reply. He was crying freely now, but the tears came from relief. "Thank you," was all he could manage.

There seemed to be a sudden lightness in the sky and the intense cold that had held the countryside in its icy grip was loosening. The slight breeze that moved the frozen branches of the rowan lacked the honed cutting edge of the previous week. In the bare chestnut trees, two magpies, as elegant as Japanese fans gossiped and shrieked like fishwives, their insane laughter mocking the inmates confined behind the high walls.

"It will thaw soon," commented Charlotte as they walked towards the car, her keen senses detecting the faint drift of spring in the air.

"And with it goes any chance we have of tracking the thing down" said Alan Morris ruefully, as he opened the door for her and walked round to his own side.

"You can't track down the paranormal by it's footprints Alan and that's most certainly what you're up against."

"No, but it'll give the rest of 'em something to look for and keep the investigation open. While the rest chase their tails, I'll carry on looking for the murderer of the two girls. I'll leave the other one to you," he added grimly, looking her straight in the eye.

Chapter Fifteen

With the latest spectacular spate of murders, the press descended in droves on South Northamptonshire for a fresh onslaught. Isolated victims done to death in rural surroundings were normally consigned to an inner page but the previous exclusive front page story of the macabre Ashmarsh killings featured by *The Express* spurred them on. Especially when the man who had been the prime suspect was released and a police statement issued to the fact that they were satisfied he was not the murderer of his companions but an innocent victim.

Geoff Hickson returned to his home in Ashmarsh but the ceaseless barrage of cameras and microphones soon began to affect his mental stability, already seriously undermined by his traumatic experiences. In desperation Mrs Hickson finally packed him off to her sister who lived in the remote Highlands of Scotland, with an address that no-one could locate on a road map. Faced by this formidable woman wielding a broom, the reporters backed off and like a pack of terriers began to worry at the heels of the neighbours for stories of Hickson's background.

With the fresh police enquiries underway and the relentless pursuit by the press the whole atmosphere in the village changed. In the early stages of the investigation they had politely listened to the questions before disclaiming any knowledge of the victims, now they were openly sullen and hostile. The few people who had been willing to talk retreated behind a blanket of silence and suspicion; both police and press were faced with a unified wall of non-co-operation.

Amid the fervour, Alexander Martin returned to Hunter's Moon and, stopping at the Post Office to mail a letter, he was surprised to have one of the local men spit on his car. Furious at the insult, he leapt from the hired car to confront the culprit, who coloured up under the walnut weathered skin and stammered an apology.

"Sorry Mr Martin, we thought you were another of those bloody reporters." Carefully Cyril Johnson wiped the spittle from the car with a grubby handkerchief.

"I am," he answered with a wry grin.

"Not like those buggers," retorted another labourer.

Alex listened to the aggrieved villagers and piece by piece the story fell into place. A band of reporters had taken over the saloon bar at the Saracen's Head and had badgered any local who might be persuaded to talk to them for the price of a pint. At first the men saw this as a bit of sport and solemnly regaled the press with bogus village gossip and speculation. They drank cheaply for a few days but then became bored by the persistent hounding for gossip concerning their neighbours.

This rash of reporters had even reduced the mild mannered Rev. Branson to swearing aloud and declaring that the Vicarage was out of bounds to the gentlemen of the press. The icy weather did not prevent the autocratic Mrs Howard from instructing her chauffeur to stop the car whilst she gave them a dressing down in her most regal manner. They shuffled with embarrassment at her infringement of privacy lecture but continued to accost anyone who hesitated for a moment.

Every house and cottage in the village had been called upon and even children were stopped as they got off the school bus for any titbits of gossip that their elders may have repeated. One reporter had already been pushed into the duck pond by one irate mother, for approaching her child.

By way of an apology for the behaviour of his less

reputable brethren, Alex invited the three men to join him for a beer. He had got to know most of them reasonably well during the months he had lived in Ashmarsh and was grateful that they did not treat him with the manner usually reserved for newcomers.

The fire in the bar gave a welcoming blaze, as did the pleasant, round faced landlord, Bob Burton. "What can I get you gentlemen?" he asked. His manner contained its usual ring of joviality, but his eyes held a warning glint as he gave an almost imperceptible nod in the direction of the alcove as he pulled four beers.

"Didn't know you were thought of as a local, Martin." A middle-aged man in a loud sports jacket strolled over to where Alex stood with Cyril and his friends.

"I live here, yes."

"Beat us all with the first scoop didn't you but we're not leaving until we get a story. There must be someone who has something to say."

"Perhaps they don't know," replied Alex patiently.

"They're only being friendly with you to keep you sweet," retorted another reporter, slightly the worse for drink. "These village communities are all the same, they'll cover up all the shit going if they think it's one of their own who's suspected."

"I don't think anyone in Ashmarsh has anything to worry about," answered Alex icily.

"Funny, they all say that. As though they feel that the place is protected. It's a different story in the other villages though, all those fancy properties going on the market so that the owners can move back to safety of the towns."

"Each to his own," replied Alex turning back to the Ashmarsh men, listening impassively to the exchange.

"You seem to prefer to rub shoulders with peasants nowadays. Remind you of your Billingsgate origins?" The man who came towards him was drunk, but not drunk enough to have made the comment without giving a great deal of thought to the reaction. "Perhaps you'd rather tell us something about the fancy piece of tail you keep here."

The knuckles on Alex's hand whitened as he gripped his glass but it was his only visible reaction. Carefully he replaced the glass on the polished counter and glancing quickly in the mirror behind the bar to see exactly where the man was standing, he whirled and followed through with a savage punch that sent his antagonist sprawling. Bar stools fell as customers tried to move out of the way.

"Get out, all of you! If you can't behave like civilised human beings then keep away from those who can."

"Look here, Martin ..."

"Get out!"

Alex hoped that none of the others would start anything. Even though they had felt uncomfortable at their companion's goading, he could not rely on them not to retaliate. He hadn't physically hit anyone since his school days and felt a trifle foolish at losing his temper. Mumbling threats, the felled drunk was dragged from the pub as the landlord produced a large brandy and Alex downed it swiftly.

"Thanks Bob, I'd better be getting home before this gets back."

"Too late, mate," grinned one of his companions. "Gwen Carradine was in the 'jug and bottle' when you hit him and she took off like a stag. Guess you'll be in a bit of trouble for brawling when you get home."

"Never mind lad," added the second who was only senior to Alex by a few years. "We'll tell her it was for a good cause."

Accepting their good-natured banter, Alex went out into the crisp afternoon air, but there was no sign of the pressmen. The sky was a beautiful blue with large fluffy white clouds that occasionally blotted out the sun, creating large dark patches on the rolling green landscape. Much of the snow had melted from the roads and south facing slopes, but in pockets and hollows sheltered by the trees the deep drifts still lay. The gentle slopes of the meadows stretched away from the village towards the river. In several cottage gardens, tiny snowdrops nodded in the sunlight, breathing in the brief warmth of the day.

Charlotte was waiting for him in the sitting room and with her customary passion for fresh air, the windows were thrown open. She was watching the cats as they examined the fresh sights and scents in a garden that had recently cast off its mantle of snow. Large clumps of snowdrops and aconites bloomed under shrubs and bushes, providing vivid splashes of colour to the sombre garden.

Her greeting was as casual as though they had only parted that morning, instead of being apart for a week over thousands of miles. Not for the first time was Alex resentful of her casualness towards their relationship. If only she would throw herself into his arms in welcome. Roughly he pulled her towards him, crushing his mouth against hers as he held her tightly in a powerful grip. For a brief moment she struggled, then relaxed her mouth, returning his kiss as he transmitted his desire for her in the old familar way.

The slightness of her body allowed him to throw her easily across his shoulder and carry her off in the direction of their bedroom. The afternoon sun warmed the room with a delicate glow and in the all-enveloping peace of that gold and ivory room they made slow relaxed love. Lying in a close embrace they patiently rediscovered one another; gently stroking and caressing the softness of a breast; the warmth of a thigh and delicate curve of hips. He was pleasantly surprised at the urgency of her touch and after the first flush of gentle surrender, he took her savagely. Until now they had not exchanged one word and it was Charlotte who spoke first.

"Is this a continuance of your new macho image?" She murmured drowsily as she lay in the curve of his arm.

"Gwen got here first?"

Charlotte stretched her arms above her head and lay amongst the lace pillows with her eyes closed, the long lashes like butterflies against her cheek. "It hasn't been easy here for any of them."

191

"I understand you interviewed the survivor with Alan Morris." This much he'd gleaned from bar-room gossip.

"Hardly an interview." She sat up and reached for a peach satin robe. "Considering that he was in a mild hypnotic trance at the time."

"I'm surprised Morris allowed it."

She swung her legs off the bed and tied the belt around her waist. "He didn't know. He expects hypnosis to be induced by waving a finger around in front of the subject's eyes, I sat with my back towards him and used my mind. Not enough to freak the boy out, but just enough to open up his memory without him feeling too much pain."

"And...." He was slightly perturbed by this casual confession.

She sat on the edge of the bed with the rapt expression of enthusiasm, that seems to be the prerogative of academics having just rediscovered an extinct species or an ancient manuscript. Her eyes glowed with eagerness as she relived her experiment.

"It really was fascinating, Alex," she concluded. "I could actually see the mind pictures forming in his brain as he related what he had seen. He transferred even the slightest detail to me, so that I saw exactly the same as he did through his own eyes. The Iceni has grown considerably larger than when we first saw him."

"Surely Morris doesn't believe the thing is supernatural?"

"Wavering. But he doesn't know how to deal with it."

"And you do?"

She turned her large green eyes on him with a slightly tragic look that could have been comic if the killings weren't so horrifically real. She knew for the first time in her present lifetime, that she had found a man whom she could truly love but even that love was not strong enough to strip away the inborn self-preservation that had kept her, and her kind, alive throughout their long existence. Suspicion of their fellows had often denied them love and companionship; the

192

trust on which normal people built their lives, had all too often been betrayed by those closest to them.

"I have the theory I've explained to you, that's all," she lied and again the lie hurt.

She would have given anything to be able to tell him the truth.   He only half believed what she had told him about herself. She thought of the morning spent with Paul Kerrick, trying to find a way of laying to rest the tragic Iceni, whose guardianship of the dead had been transported into the 20th century by the immense psychic energy generated by a man dead for nearly one thousand years! At least Paul understood her reluctance to destroy and didn't consider her amoral.

These thoughts flashed through her mind in the second that it took to reach out a hand towards her lover. "Alan doesn't think that the girls were killed by the same person."

"And what about what we saw in the woods?

Charlotte slipped her arms around his naked waist. "Alan has left that in my capable hands. Science and Commerce always cock a snook at Nature but she usually comes up with some unforeseen retribution that rocks 'em back on their heels. Perhaps this is one of her little jokes but it's more suited to my powers of detection than his."

Alex kissed her nose. "I suggest a long and leisurely bath while I tell you all the gossip from my trip, then, when you're suitably jealous I'll allow you to make wild unrestrained love to me - but first a present."

She sat with childlike expectancy while he unfastened his suitcase. The gift was wrapped in elegant black and gold paper with matching ribbons. "What is it?" she cried impatiently.

The open box revealed exquisite silk and lace lingerie, coloured a deep forest green.   As the sun's rays caught the fabric, the silk shimmered like the plumage of a mallard. "It's beautiful," she breathed, throwing her arms around his neck.

In the days that followed they had the house to themselves for Anna had still not returned from her self-imposed exile.

193

Alex sat by the window in Charlotte's study, transcribing the material that had taken him across Europe. He had always possessed a flair for words but now his rich application of the English language flowed like poetry. People whose names were unknown to the general public, came bursting into life as his fingers flew over the keyboard. There was the American cattle heiress who had escaped to a bougainvillaea strewn villa in Sidi Bou Said, some 20 kilometres from Tunis, and who had propositioned him within ten minutes of his arrival. The Florentine opera star dazzled him with her flamboyant life-style before inviting him to her bed. While the elderly Polish count in exile in Lisbon, received him graciously and lamented the fate of his homeland as he stroked Alex's thigh with an elegant hand.

With the discernment that had made Alexander Martin something special in his field, he heard about a talented young French actress who embodied the talents of the glorious Colette in a film destined for the Cannes Film Festival. Such were the praises, that he was determined to secure an interview before she became famous in her interpretation of *The Vagabond*. His unscheduled stop-over in Paris had produced amazing results and a startling interview - and another proposition.

He had come a long way since he had been living with Charlotte. Now there would be no mention made of the advances, each of the subjects had a fascinating story to tell and it was this aspect of their personalities that would make such brilliant reading in future monthly 'glossies'. Their personal vices remained their own affair. As the fire crackled and licked around the logs, he structured his articles so that the vibrant personalities of his subjects leaped from the page. So intimate were his observations that it was almost possible to smell the heavy scent of jasmine, as the talented soprano poured out the story of her struggles to become one of Milan's most popular stars. The reader would become enchanted and the *diva's* success assured when she next visited Covent Garden.

Outside, the sharp January sunlight coaxed the slim buds of the crocuses to open, and across the walled garden, splashes of purple and gold appeared. There was a great deal of peace to be found in the old farmhouse, and from the cocooned warmth of the study, he watched the slim woman who had become so much a part of his life. If Serge and Eleanor were to live nearby, it was doubtful if he would ever wish to return to London to live, although he was mindful of the fact that Charlotte had still not mentioned a definite future for them. He was not foolish enough to take her for granted.

Being there with her had sharpened his creative powers and it was apparent in the work he was producing. His mind had expanded, his vocabulary had increased a hundredfold and his vision far reaching. He was at a loss for the reasons, feeling that the cause hardly mattered in view of the results. If he were honest with himself, he was becoming dissatisfied with the repetitious scandal-mongering, even before Charlotte had tactlessly forced him to face up to it during their first meeting. A few extremely tempting offers had already come his way but he had the feeling that there was something else about to happen, and he wanted to wait.

Gwen came in each morning to tidy the house and prepare breakfast but had been instructed that until Anna returned, Charlotte would prepare their evening meal. She was, surprisingly enough, a good cook and it made a pleasant change to eat casually at the kitchen table or from a tray in front of the fire. Their very real need to be close to each other while the house was empty manifested itself in their frequent afternoon love-making sessions, a situation that was almost impossible when there were so many other people about. If one was working, then the other would sit quietly in the same room, with a book or turning over ideas for future publications. Turning his thoughts back to the work in hand, he vigorously attacked the manuscript and some hours later, with a satisfied sigh he leaned back in the chair, stretching his arms behind his head. Country life was certainly satisfying and productive, he reflected.

Out in the hallway the telephone rang for some time before Charlotte answered it. There was a buzz of conversation and shortly afterwards she appeared with a tray laden with tea and hot buttered scones. "Anna will be back the day after tomorrow."

"Has she recovered from her disappointment?"

"Don't be cruel. I don't think it was him letting her down that bothered her too much, it was the implications made against the rest of us. As far as she was concerned, it was her responsibility."

"It goes to show that you can never really know anyone deep down," reflected Alex, helping himself to a large spoonful of jam.

"That my love, is true."

It was just passed midnight when Charlotte slipped out of the house and made her way through the woods. The night was dark with rain clouds blotting out the stars, and since fear of a terrifying death kept neighbours at home, there was little chance that she would be spotted. Amid the blanket of fear and suspicion, it would not do for either Paul Kerrick or herself to be seen near the stone circle after dusk. She had even ordered that the coven should not meet at the mausoleum until the murderer had been apprehended, in case the esbat aroused unwelcome interest. Tonight, however, she and Paul needed the concentration of Temple power generated by the circle in the Sanctuary.

The tiny window was in darkness but her instinct told her that he was waiting for her inside the tomb. As she entered the oak door swung shut and iron bolts slid into place. A hand reached out in the blackness as the door to the underground chamber opened noiselessly at her feet. Relying solely on touch and familiarity, Charlotte slowly walked down the stone steps as the door closed above her head. Suddenly the room was filled by the beam of a powerful lamp, as Paul helped her off with her cloak.

196

"How are we going to stop this maniac?" he asked in a low voice, lighting the lamps and throwing incense into the burner.

"Appeal to his finer instincts," she replied as she began a ritual of purification of the circle.

Oblivious to the suppurating chill of the underground chamber, she sat cross-legged in the centre of the circle and began to slowly control her breathing. So adept had she become at this practice that within moments, her voice called out on the astral and commanded the Iceni to appear before her. Almost immediately, a fine misty vapour gathered in the corner of the room, producing the now familiar form of the ancient Briton. His stature had grown considerably larger since their first encounter but his demeanor was almost humble as he greeted her.

"You summoned me, Lady?"

"I forbid any more killing of my people."

"Those sacrificed were not of your people, Lady."

His economy of language explained why the lives of Geoff Hickson and Tracy Walker had been spared. Charlotte tried a different approach. "By what name are you known amongst your own people?"

"I am called Antedios."

"Well, Antedios, I will help you keep your oath of vengeance, and providing that no more people die, I will seek out the Black One and destroy him. But first you must tell me all that you have seen of him."

"I did not awaken until blood was spilt in the sacred place. The youths had brought the maidens there in love but the Black One only had hate in his heart. At first I thought the youths had been killed but I found this was not so. While they lay as if dead, the Black One turned his knife on the maidens and began to cut their flesh."

"Did you see his face?"

"He had no face. Only blackness within his heart and without."

197

"We will speak again." Charlotte dismissed him formally.

The form wavered and hesitated. "You have the power Lady, why do you not destroy me?"

"I have no desire to destroy you, Antedios," responded Charlotte. "If a man keeps his faith with an oath taken nine centuries ago, he shows himself to be honourable and true to his word. I will help you, not destroy you."

"Then there will be no more killing, Lady," the Iceni inclined his head in a salute and the form vanished.

Returning to her body over which Paul had been keeping guard, she was relieved to find that her projection had only lasted five minutes. There was a danger that Alex would wake before she returned, since the drug she had administered was only a mild sleeping draught.

Quickly she repeated what the Iceni shaman had told her. "It's a possibility that we're looking for someone wearing a black balaclava, it's the only explanation for him not having a face."

"That could be anyone!"

"True, but it supports our belief that the boys are innocent of murder. Someone must have been watching them."

Paul allowed a chuckle to escape. "Yes, but I can't see the jury being convinced by a witness who's been dead for nine hundred years!"

Chapter Sixteen

"How on earth can a woman be so incredibly boring?" muttered Alex in exasperation. He was trying to complete a biography for a twenty-three year old rock singer, whose raunchy stage act had brought her international stardom. "I spent hours talking to her and there wasn't one thing of substance in her character. She was more interested in screwing than interviewing."

Anna stood behind him and began to read the draft over his shoulder. "That's what comes of putting finances before personal integrity. Mind you, I think you'll get The Purlizer if you manage to inject any life into that creature. Can't you get by with lots of pictures and captions?"

Alex slumped down in the chair. "I've taken the money so I've got to come up with something. Do you realise that if this offer had been made after I'd met Charlotte, I'd never have accepted. She made me face the fact that there's more to success than a healthy bank account but how the hell do I get out of this mess? I can't drum up any sympathy for the subject, and that's fatal."

"Come out of the way and let me have a look at it," replied Anna. "You don't realise how many times I've had to ghost things for editors because Charlotte thinks it's a waste of time. I think we're talking about the same level of readership, so I might be able to suggest a different angle."

"I'm in your hands," grinned Alex as he threw himself

down on the comfortable sofa.

"Actually we're both in Charlotte's hands. It takes a while before you realise just how much influence she has over the way we think or act. She changed my whole concept of living by encouraging me to find my own way. Just by being there, she taught me to think and question, to explore parts of myself I didn't know existed."

"And she brought you into her coven?"

Anna frowned slightly as she turned over the notes. She didn't want to speak out of turn but there was something that Alex had misunderstood and she felt she should try to explain. "Charly, isn't a witch," she began hesitantly. "Her Path is that of High Magic, a Magus. She belongs to an ancient esoteric Order but I'd rather she told you about that. I'm only saying this because I know your scepticism dismisses the possibility of magical power. But I've *seen* that power at work within the coven. I know it's real. One day you'll understand but please, don't treat it as some kind of joke or crackpot theory."

Her blue eyes were bright with unshed tears and Alex put his arm around her, realising that her outburst was a reaction to the recent experience with Sinclair. There were times when Charlotte exasperated him with her matter-of-fact attitude to all matters physical but Anna was far more intense. This was the first time they had even discussed her coven involvement but she obviously felt it was important to convey her own sincerity in her belief, if only to convince him that Charlotte's work was something to be taken seriously.

"Sinclair really got to you, didn't he?"

Anna ran a thumb nail around the edge of a folder. "Apart from still feeling emotionally bruised, I'm really suffering from acute embarrassment. I knew it wasn't the big *IT* but I thought it was at least a meaningful relationship."

"It's happened to us all, sometime or another."

"I appreciate that, but this involved you, Charly and even Serge and Eleanor. They must think I'm a first class idiot."

"Not really, after all if you can't trust a policeman, who

can you trust?"

"I've heard Charlotte make a similar caustic observation about the priesthood, so don't pretend to sympathise. He even came to my parent's place looking for me," Anna continued. "Sitting in his car outside the house until the early hours of the morning."

"He's never called here."

His companion laughed bitterly. "He wouldn't. He was really convinced Charly was the Devil - or worse - and half expected the odd glimpse of a cloven hoof! Anyway, what I'm really trying to say is that I don't think we've heard the last of him and I'm apologising in advance."

On the surface, life at Hunter's Moon was a constant round of literary activity. Alex's agent was delighted by the subtle changes in his client's style and although his old familiar astringent quality was still there, the razor coldness was tempered with a new richness of language. His subjects found themselves drawn out, expressing opinions they would normally not discuss with a stranger and the resulting interview showed a different dimension to their personality. "I didn't realise I was so fascinating," remarked one of his subjects following publication in *The Tatler*.

Anna spent hours sifting through Alex's notes and taped recordings in an attempt to add some new dimension to the stilted biography. Instinctively she was able to piece together a profile that would enhance the rock star's image and although the volume would be a slim one, it was not an unflattering portrait. Until the business of the Iceni was out of the way, there would be no further work carried out on the next novel and she was glad to have something different to occupy her mind.

Meanwhile Charlotte worked on the complex jigsaw of instinct and meagre fact to support the gut feeling surrounding the appearance of the Iceni shaman. Considering that Boudica had left behind such a powerful

201

legend, there was remarkably little recorded about her in the history books from which to draw any definite conclusions. The two classic sources that provided the basis for the majority of academic works were those of Tacticus and Cassius Dio, a Roman and Greek respectively, whose works were completed some years after the Iceni uprising and showed little sympathy for an autocratic Queen avenging a wrong done to her people. One modern historian even going so far as to describe her as a red-headed, arrogant, loud-mouthed bitch. In resisting the seizure of her late husband's property, Boudica was stripped and flogged like a common criminal, while her daughters "as spoils of war, were raped by all and sundry".

As a result, the Iceni rose up against their oppressors and settled the account by destroying what is now Colchester, London and St Albans, slaughtering the inhabitants unmercifully - Romans and Britons sympathetic to Roman rule. The Britons took no prisoners - theirs was not a fight for gain. Rarely did any historian raise the point that the Iceni were defending their freedom against a 'barbaric' foreign domination and exploitation. Their enemies perished by 'sword, gibbet, fire and cross' but whatever bloody rites were carried out in the sacred groves in homage to their deity, they were no worse than the mass execution of innocent people in the name of entertainment in the Roman arenas.

The outcome of a Roman battle was dependent on the seriousness of Roman casualties and even those who threw down their arms and pleaded for mercy were rarely spared. And the Iceni had the destruction of the Ninth Legion to their credit! Neither classic nor modern sources were able to identify the site of the final battle between the Iceni and Romans, although the majority of historians appeared to agree on some point on the Watling Street, with several volumes citing Towcester as being as good a choice as any. Ironically, there were no legends as to the true fate of Boudica herself. Tacitus claimed she took poison, while Dio suggests she fell ill and died; another scholar suggesting that she made it back to East Anglia. But whatever the outcome, Boudica was not taken to Rome in chains - the fate that awaited her kinsman Caratacus.

Neither was there anything to suggest that the remains of the Iceni Queen had been left in the Whittlewood, no matter how long and hard Charlotte re-arranged the information in the computer. She tried every configuration of available data but nothing seemed to offer a solution as to why the shaman had chosen to remain at this spot since that last spring-time of Iceni freedom.

This deep concentration was interrupted when two rather unkempt persons of indeterminable sex were shown into her study and introduced by Gwen Carradine as Cindy Webster and Marc Numan, the latter wearing a beard. His companion was completely swamped beneath a rather old battered combat jacket, several sizes too large. The close cropped hair, desperately in need of a shampoo made it difficult to identify her as female. The man was little better.

They eyed their surroundings with the attitude prevalent amongst the young, whose education had promised better things but their background decreed otherwise. Frustration bore fruit in the shape of resentment, levelled at authority in any guise and the wealthy, who seemed to have it too easy. Their transparency inwardly amused their hostess but she could also detect an undercurrent of desperation that had prompted their visit. Her annoyance was soon replaced by curiosity: why should people such as these appeal for help from the very class they despised?

"We think we've got some information that might interest you about the murder of those two girls," began the youth. His tone was belligerent, a demand, thinly disguised as a request answered her unspoken question. "But we can't go to the police."

"Why come to me?"

There was a gleam of malice in the man's eyes as he replied. "We know that two of the kids' mothers are witches

203

and that you're the head of their coven."

A tight smile of contempt showed on her face. "Really! And who gave you this precious piece of information?"

"We heard the kids talking in the woods."

"Rather a sordid and perverted pastime isn't it? Spying on adolescent couples necking in the woods."

"They were doing more than necking," sneered the girl.

"Fine. So they were indulging in a bit of under-age sex which, incidentally was shown up by the postmortem. So where's this little charade getting us?"

"Do you think we would waste our time if we didn't know something?" retorted Marc Numan rudely.

"Then go to the police - or the newspapers. I assume that's your next suggestion. Well, Mr Numan, we've been besieged by reporters for weeks, so a few more won't matter. I've been publicly branded as worse than a witch before now and if you think the threat of adverse publicity worries me, you're both sadly mistaken."

The girl was unable to meet Charlotte's glacial stare, so she turned her cold green eyes back to the man. "Now since your abortive attempt at obtaining money has failed miserably, I suggest you leave before *I* call the police."

"Come on, Mark, we can't get involved with the police and we're not going to get anything here," the girl's voice trembled slightly.

"What did you expect?" snapped Charlotte, strongly sensing there was something else that both were anxious to reveal. "If you've heard anything about me at all, you should know that I do not tolerate bungling amateurs in anything - not even blackmail."

"We're desperate!"

Charlotte's voice was raised to such a pitch that Alex could hear the conversation in the next room. "Really, then why the hell don't you do something about your condition? If you're going for the sympathy angle, forget it. Do you realise the full extent of your stupidity?"

"I don't think ..."

Charlotte's voice had changed from ice to fire as she interrupted the girl. "Exactly, you don't think! You want to prove to the world that you can rock the establishment, flout the rules, run headlong into the law and wave your banner of freedom. Well, it doesn't work. You have no true concept of oppression or suppression, they're just words. Your freedom to choose has reduced you to a snivelling drug dependency that will eventually kill you. If you wish to tell me what you know about the deaths of Alison and Gail I can get you into a clinic where you can attempt to regain your self-respect, but that's the only help you'll get from me."

"We'll manage without your help," Marc Numan was still defiant although clearly he had not expected to be dismissed with such contempt.

The youth was ready to storm from the room but Cindy prevented him by clinging to his sleeve. "Mark! They were only kids, they didn't deserve what happened to them. It's not *HER* fault."

Marc Numan scowled at his friend but made no further attempt to leave; Cindy pressed home her appeal. "Mrs Manning, if we weren't drug addicts we wouldn't have been around to see what happened. We were travelling through to Birmingham and stopped off in the woods to spend the night. We got near to that old stone circle and heard voices, so we hid in the undergrowth. It was only four teenagers and judging from the noise they were making, we guessed they'd been drinking. They were larking about, taking their clothes off and disappeared into the undergrowth for a while. I guess they were having it off."

There were tears forming in the girl's eyes as her companion mellowed and placed a firm arm around her shoulders in support. "The kids were otherwise occupied, so we crept out and went through their belongings. There was only a few quid in their pockets but there was plenty of coke - and good stuff too," he finished the tale.

"Cocaine? Are you sure?"

"Positive. As I said, it was good stuff, not the usual shit that gets palmed off on schoolkids."

"Where did they get it?"

Numan shrugged his bony shoulders under the shabby coat. "The stuff's sold in the playground these days."

"So you stole their money and removed the drugs?" Both looked at the floor in embarrassment and nodded. "Why have you kept quiet all this time?"

"We went up to Scotland and it wasn't until we were on our way back that we decided it was worth a try ... to come to you."

Cindy bit her lip. "You see ... we think we may have seen the man who killed them."

Charlotte's head shot up. "Describe him!"

"That's the problem. We can't. He was dressed all in black - trousers, poloneck sweater and one of those knitted masks that terrorists wear to cover the entire face. All we can say for certain is that it was a man; he was crouching down but I guess he was quite tall and well built. He was watching the circle and didn't see us."

Much to Gwen Carradine's disgust, she was requested to feed the pair and give them a well stocked hamper to take them on their way. Charlotte was fully aware that they would clam up the moment the police arrived and she believed there was nothing further they could add to the identification of the Black One. Except now she understood why Antedios had referred to him as such; the black figure-hugging clothes and mask would seem peculiar to someone who had awoken after 900 years straight into a bad dream.

"Are you sure you're doing the right thing?" asked Alex having overheard her request for Alan Morris to arrange a meeting with Michael Hughes. "Two drug addicts pitch up on the doorstep and admit to having seen the killer. Doesn't it seem a little far fetched to you?"

"On the face of it, yes. But there's nothing else to go on.

Perhaps I can jog Michael's subconscious into action."

"You and Morris still believe there are two unrelated murderers on the loose?"

"I know there are. And I have it on good authority." Her expression dared him to repudiate the claim of outside psychical stimulus.

"And you trust Morris?" He still refused to allow himself to be convinced by Charlotte's claims of supernatural powers at work, even if Alan Morris was beginning to echo this opinion.

"As much as I trust anyone who sets themselves up as a guide or protector of the populace at large. I have an inherent suspicion of such motives. Personally I think it indicates some concealed personal inadequacies but Morris is refreshingly intelligent."

"I suppose you're going to tell us you had some run-in with the law in Rouen in 1447, which has subsequently made you mistrustful of all enforcement agencies!" Anna was familiar enough with Charlotte's history to poke fun at her boss and dared pass comments that from Alex would offend.

"I have perpetually been at odds with both the law and the clergy, and after rattling around the vaults of eternity for a few hundred years, I feel as though I can speak with some authority. I loathe priests and I mistrust a copper, even nice ones like Alan Morris," countered Charlotte good naturedly.

"But you've got something up your sleeve," added Alex with a degree of trepidation.

The novelist dismissed this with a wave of her elegant hand and a grin. "Perhaps a practical display of psychic power."

"Don't you bloody dare!" yelled her secretary. "The last time you demonstrated the powers of mediumship, the Vicar got drenched with a vase of water. Anyway you don't believe in seances, you just like showing off."

"A brief scientific demonstration of telekinesis cannot be classed as showing off. It doesn't need any assistance from the spirit world, they're all too busy with their own astral activities to be bothered about popping down here for a quick cabaret turn."

"Piss off," replied Anna to her employer's teasing. "The dead have too much sense than to communicate with you!"

By pulling a few more Masonic strings, Alan Morris managed to procure entry to the Young Offenders Institution where Michael Hughes was being held. He was more than a little annoyed with Charlotte for not reporting the arrival of two key witnesses, but he knew as well as she that they would have denied all knowledge of seeing the murderer if the police had been brought in to question them. As it was, Charlotte had given them time to get away and Morris had subsequently affected a half-hearted search for the pair but there was no trace of Mark Numan and his companion.

"Why do you want to see Hughes?" Morris asked. "He's the one that's been the least co-operative of the two. I think you'd be better off talking to the Jeffrey's boy."

Charlotte decided quickly. "Because Michael's mother is a witch and so is Gail's mother. This lad is keeping to the tenets of his mother's faith in keeping silent. Because he's been brought up in such an environment, it's possible that his psychic abilities aren't as suppressed as those of Peter Jeffrey. I want to trigger off something in his subconscious to confirm the existence of ..." she was about to say 'The Black One' but refrained. "... of the killer."

"Why the hell couldn't you have told me this before?" muttered Morris angrily.

"Because if the psychologists got hold of that, they'd turn the boy inside out and you know it. Michael hasn't got anything to fear from the truth but he has been taught about his need to survive."

Michael's imprisonment had transformed the boy into a sullen, uncommunicative adult. Days of endless questioning by police, social workers and psychiatrists had taken their toll but his inner strength had not deserted him. " Merry

Meet," intoned Charlotte as she sat down.

He gave a surprised glance at Morris before answering softly "Merry Meet."

"I've explained to the Inspector why you won't talk but we need to know if you can provide us with a particular piece of information."

"Forget the under age sex and drugs, boy," added Morris gruffly by way of assurance. "I happen to agree with Mrs Manning that you didn't kill your girlfriend but the only help I can give you is to find out who did."

A wary light showed in the boy's eyes. "What do you want to know?"

"Was there anyone else near the circle on the day of the murders?" asked Charlotte. "I want you to concentrate, go back over the events leading up to the time you passed out and see if there's something there that you've forgotten."

"I can't!"

"Yes, you can. I'll help you. You don't need to be afraid. Now, look deep into my eyes and remember, fix your mind on when you all met up on that day, think of nothing else ..." The soft hypnotic intonation soothed away the weeks of tension and Morris watched fascinated as the boy began to relax. He accepted a cigarette from Charlotte and after inhaling deeply, he began to talk.

"Gail and I went over to the pub on our bikes and left them round the back in the bushes. Pete had joked about going up to the old stone circle for a party; he knew Gail and I were interested in the Craft but we'd never let on that our mother's actually belonged. He's the only one old enough to drive a car and after a few drinks we all piled in and drove up to the wood.

"He'd plenty of drink in the boot and I think we'd got through quite a bit of it when he produced some cigarettes he'd brought off a bloke in the pub. We passed a joint around and started larking about - just kids stuff but it seemed to affect the girls more than us. Pete told me to wait a bit

209

because he'd got some really heavy stuff from the same bloke and he wanted to try it out."

"What was this heavy stuff?"

"I'm not sure. We had a lot more to drink and Alison and Pete went off into the bushes. Gail started to get nervous and kept claiming that someone was watching us. Eventually I persuaded her to go into the bushes with me and she did. A bit later Alison came back without any clothes on and began dancing around the circle, pretending to be a witch. She'd read a few books on the Craft so she thought she knew all about it. I was a bit embarrassed since she was making a complete idiot of herself, but Gail was furious. They had quite a heated row. I left them to it and went to take a leak and that's when I blacked out."

"And then ..."

There was dumb misery in the boy's face as he relived his nightmare. "I was lying on the edge of the circle, just outside the stones and my head felt like it was in two pieces. As I got up, I saw Alison and Gail lying in the middle of the circle. Gail's dress and things had been torn off and she was cut all over. There was blood all over her face where someone's hand had been over her mouth. He'd cut her open ... I fainted and when I came to, Pete was kneeling next to me shaking and crying."

"You said 'He'd cut her'. Why do you say that?"

"I don't know."

"Think! This isn't a trick question. Gail told you she thought you were being watched. Was there anyone else?"

"I can't ... I ..." he faltered as a glimmer of memory stirred.

"There *is* something. Stop blocking it and let it come through."

"Look, this sounds as though I'm making it up."

"Come on lad, think" added Morris gently. "This is important."

Charlotte gave the detective a warning glance. "Concentrate, turn your thoughts inward and seek."

210

"I saw a shadow.   Only it wasn't a shadow because I felt the tremor of a footfall on the ground as it passed over me. I felt the vibration of footsteps on the earth. I couldn't open my eyes properly because the sun was shining in my face and I couldn't see ..."

"Describe the shadow."

"I can't because it was all black."

"All black!"

"Like a *ninja* in those Japanese films!"

"Holy shit!" breathed Morris. "You're a genius Charlotte Manning!"

Chapter Seventeen

Bird song filled the lanes as the first lambs tottered about the meadows, their soulful cries carrying for miles on the gentle breeze announcing the pagan festival of *Imbolc*, the beginning of the Celtic lambing season. The fresh beauty of early spring mornings were a sharp contrast to the nightmare that stalked the countryside under the cover of darkness during the long winter nights. For now humans listened attentively to the night sounds, lest some fearsome creature should spring on them from the shadows.

Some miles away, a battered van was parked outside the Cooper Brother's yard but any signs of activity were concealed by thick sacking nailed across the grimy windows. The open sheds gave little cover to the skins that came for curing and around the whole place the pungent odour of ammonia had permeated the very mortar of the buildings. Rusted farm implements were stacked against the walls and beneath the piles of rubbish, rats lived undisturbed. Straw from broken bales was scattered all over the floor of the barns and spilled out into the untidy yard.

In one corner of the huge shed, in a small room that served as an office, three men sat talking in hushed voices. The spluttering yellow light from the lamp only partially illuminated the small room, casting no light on the dilapidated state of the old farm-yard. Heavy black cobwebs accumulated over the years, sprouted like strange plant life in the cavernous gloom of the rafters.

"Mind what you're doing with that bloody lamp!" Snarled Joe Cooper as the youngest of the brothers spilt methylated spirit onto his trousers. "The whole bloody place could go up."

"Do you think I'm stupid or something?" came the reply, as Martin Cooper threw him a piece of sacking.

"You were daft enough to light a fag in Ben Adam's haybarn."

"And they never did find out who done it," answered Martin with a certain pride.

"Shut up and pass us a beer. We've got to decide whether or not we carry on with moving those stones or not. I reckon it's time to lay low for a while and let the fuss die down." The eldest brother, Harry, most resembled his late father in both build and temperament. Although he was rough and uneducated, there was at least a modicum of common sense.

"You frightened of a few old witches, Harry?"

"No, I bleedin' well ain't but as the whole damned countryside is on the lookout for a murderer, I reckon it's best not to take any more risks being seen near them stones."

In the dimness of the barn, the shadows thrown by the flickering lamplight cast the coarse features of the men into primeval meanness. Used to making their living through the death of other creatures, they had no respect for life - there was money only to be found in death. If a local farmer had an animal die, then he sent for the Coopers to remove the carcass. They cured inferior sheepskins for the cheap glove and slipper trade and had, over the years, operated a clandestine trade in antique garden statuary, stolen from local parks and gardens.

Harry Cooper brooded on the events of the past weeks. If that damned Sunday paper hadn't got hold of the story, business could have gone on as normal. It had all started when the buyer and several heavies had come around demanding delivery of the promised witches' stone circle and Joe hitting one with an axe handle. The police had been called to restore

213

order but it was obvious that their sympathies did not lie with the Coopers. Barely literate and immensely strong, Joe was almost unmanageable when he was angry or drunk, as several of the police officers answering the call knew to their cost.

It had been lucky that the elder Cooper had prevented the attack from being more vicious than it was. The middle brother was said to have a volatile nature but it was merely a polite way of commenting on Joe's obvious mental instability. As a child he was prone to bouts of excessive violence and was even suspected of having caused the death of a younger sister through jealousy. Old Mrs Cooper had protected her young as savagely as any she-bear and the authorities had given up trying to convince her that Joe needed help. On their isolated farm, the Coopers had lived rough and run wild and now, in adulthood, there would be no changing them.

The youngest, Martin, still wore a dirty plaster to conceal the wound dealt him by a flying brick. The cut had healed but the youth liked the effect of displaying his injury. Of all the brothers, Martin was the family pet, good-looking and according to the regulars of the Royal Oak, was "all right on his own side", especially when it came down to attracting the attentions of the village girls. One local girl had been soundly thrashed by her father for announcing that she was going steady with the youngest Cooper.

"I'm not going to let no London toughs frighten me," he bragged. "Anyway no-one knows what the fight were about."

"That blow on your head didn't improve your brain any, boy," responded Harry. "No-one's talking about being frightened off. If we want to continue with that side of the business we've got to be a bit clever and not draw any more attention to ourselves. After all, we did take the man's money and 'e hasn't got his goods."

Joe grinned maliciously, showing his blackened teeth. "Or could it be that Ma threatened to take a stick to you if any more reporters turned up at the farm."

"All I'm saying is, that ... are you listening to me, boy?"

214

Martin raised the sack covering the window and peered out into the night. The old buildings were too far from the main road for the street lamps to shed much light and the gloomy buildings were swathed in shadow. Even the brilliance of the moonlight could not brighten the dismal scene. Generations of filth caked the cracked panes of glass, obscuring his vision even further. Squinting through a broken window, the yard looked quiet enough.

"I thought I heard something out there."

Joe leapt to his feet. "Those bastards again."

His progress was halted by his elder brother's massive forearm across his chest. "Martin, get the lamp, we'll all go out."

The three men stepped out into the yard but not before Joe had picked up the double-barrelled shot-gun that had been propped in the corner. Hastily loading it with cartridges, he followed his brothers out into the night. The cold silence was spooky after the intimate closeness of the small ill-kept office and Harry experienced a slight prickle of fear. Old Man Cooper hadn't been afraid of the Devil himself, and had made sure that his sons followed in his footsteps but for all the old man's teaching, Harry felt someone walk across his grave.

Together they examined the deep shadows of the partially derelict cow sheds, still ankle deep in straw, but found nothing. A search of the other barns also proved fruitless but none of them could escape the unreasoning presence of menace that reached out from the shadows. Joe was about to call to his brothers, when primitive cry echoed in the silence. He raised the shot-gun in the direction of the sound but nothing moved in the darkness as the brothers approached from opposite sides of the yard.

Martin moved forward just as a arge man dropped from the slated roof. The youth had barely time to cry out before the deadly knife ripped into his throat, slashing the jugular and releasing a fountain of rich, warm blood that sprayed the walls of the barn. Releasing his hold on the lamp, features con-

215

torted with horror, the younger Cooper's hands pushed feebly against the incredible bulk of his attacker. The Iceni slashed again and a final gurgle of life bubbled in the throat of its victim.

In the second that it took for Joe to raise the gun and fire both barrels at point-blank range, he saw Harry opposite him clutching at his stomach, a look of pure amazement on his face. The eldest Cooper slumped to his knees; blood oozing through his fingers as the colossus pitched forward and lay still.

The lamp that Martin had been carrying had fallen into the straw and the leaking spirit was spreading the flames across the floor of the barn. Joe was oblivious to the wall of fire behind him. The horrific death of young Martin; the fact that he had fired at the intruder and the shot had passed right through him and killed Harry was too much for him to comprehend. As the flames grew higher, the flickering light turned the ancient Briton's eyes a fiery red as he advanced on the lone survivor. Dropping the rifle, Joe backed away, nearer and nearer to the fire as suddenly the flames, feeding on the spirit soaked trousers, transformed him into a screaming, whirling pillar of flame. Staggering blindly, the human torch ignited the rest of the rubbish that lay scattered around the yard until the whole place was ablaze.

Against the flames of the Cooper's funeral pyre, the Iceni raised his arms above his head in triumph and roared his victory - the sweat along his arms glistening in the flickering light. For a moment the muscular body, silhouetted against the background of fire in an attitude of pagan homage seemed to hover in the heat haze and was gone. The fire attracted the attention of the small housing estate opposite and people began to appear in dressing gowns and various states of undress. These were the occupants of the newly finished executive homes and there was no love lost between them and the Coopers.

"Has anyone called the fire brigade?" asked a voice.

"Let it burn," replied another.

"Christ, don't let anyone put it out now it's going!" This enjoinder brought a burst of merriment.

As they watched, a small explosion, possibly caused by discarded paint tins or petrol, caused the roof to cave in sending showers of ash and sparks high into the air. The old timber rafters heaved and groaned before collapsing, pitching the tiles down into the flaming yard. The shrill sound of the local fire brigade resounded through the night but by the time the engine pulled to a halt there was nothing to be done other than to let the conflagration burn itself out.

The fire at the Cooper's yard was the talking point of the county, particularly when the police announced that three charred bodies had been removed from the smouldering ruins. The people from the housing development who had watched the fire, perhaps to ease their own individual consciences, tried to convince themselves into believing that someone else should have been calling the fire-brigade. The fire had seemed God-sent to a community whose only bone of contention was the evil smell emanating from the buildings and that despite complaints to the public health department, the business had still continued to function. The fire had purged the site for good and the Cooper's were considered no great loss to this community.

The one person who mourned their loss and questioned the reason for them being there, was their mother. Old Mrs Cooper refused to believe that all her boys were dead and if they were, then someone else had to be responsible. They had been lured into a trap and murdered; it was up to the police to apprehend the culprits, and hand them over to the old harridan for justice. Despite three hours of frustrating but patient questioning, the detectives handling the the case were none the wiser about their activities.

Doris Cooper insisted that her boys were only high spirited and that the other farmers' sons were jealous of them. Battle-weary, the detectives refrained from pointing out the

217

damage caused by the phalanx of marauding Coopers on a Saturday night rampage. There had been numerous assaults and claims for damage laid at their door but it was useless to talk about this to the tough farmer's widow. She grieved but she would not, or could not, shed a tear for them. The police left the ramshackled farm and put a call through to the local doctor, asking him to call.

Because there was no reason to connect the fire with the Ashmarsh murders, Alan Morris was not involved and Alex learned of the whole sorry affair from Gwen Carradine as she ploughed through her weekly baking marathon. While mixing the rich fruit cake of which he was so fond, she regaled him with all the local gossip about the Cooper's. Three charred and blackened bodies were found out in the yard and as the roof had caved inwards, it had been impossible to identify them. It was only when the police visited the Cooper farm about the fire that they discovered all three brothers were missing.

The police believed that the Coopers had been meeting someone at the yard, knowing from experience that the brothers conducted their illegal activities after dark and were often to be found there late at night. Perhaps some disgruntled client had returned and extracted their revenge for non-delivery of the promised goods. It was even possible that the place had been set alight without anyone realising the brothers were inside.

Evidence given in the coroner's court, however, had added an even more startling and sinister angle. The rifle used to kill Harry Cooper had been thrown or kicked away from the raging fire and clearly on the stock were Joe Cooper's finger prints. Another theory was offered that the second son had finally gone completely insane and killed his brothers. Doris Cooper leapt from her seat in protest, screaming obscenities at the coroner, the police, and anyone else who came near her, until she was physically removed from the courtroom.

The pitiful old woman, straggling grey hair escaping over

her face from beneath a knitted woollen hat, sat forlornly in the corner of the saloon bar of her local pub. There was no-one to offer any words of comfort and the story that Joe had been responsible for the death of his brothers came as no shock. There was hardly a farmer's son or labourer in that part of the county who had not fallen foul of the Cooper temper at some time or another and they could be forgiven for taking the attitude of "good riddance to bad rubbish."

"There y'are Missus." The landlord placed another bottle of stout in front of the bereaved mother. He was the only man in town to have beaten both Harry and Joe in a fair fight and he could afford to be compassionate. With fists like hams and bulging biceps, he stood no trouble from the raucous teenagers who frequented the Saturday night dances at the Town Hall.

"He never done it, Ben."

"Perhaps he did and perhaps he didn't," replied the inn keeper tactfully, "but you've got to face the fact that Joe was always a bad lot. That temper of his has always had him in trouble."

"Comes from his father's side." Doris Cooper dismissed the fact that she had broken the nose of a policewoman as she had been removed from the court.

Reading the newspaper over breakfast the following day Alex casually asked Charlotte what she thought about the evidence surrounding the Cooper deaths. Her wide green eyes were cool and unconcerned. "They were a bunch of thugs who probably did one crooked deal too many. I know nothing of them, so I can't pass judgement."

"According to Morris, the one clue that didn't find its way into the papers was that a genuine Celtic pin with a peculiar design had been found amongst the rubble and the police assume that it was part of an antiques haul. The motif was a cross between a boar and a horse ..."

He had expected a sign of interest; what he was not

prepared for was the mask of pure fury that suffused her features. Morris had left the vague message without any further explanation, hoping that Alex would pass it on without question. Like an avenging goddess Charlotte rose from the table, flinging down her napkin and stormed from the room, leaving him staring after her in amazement.

She flew out to her workshop and slammed the heavy oak door. Rage made it difficult for her to concentrate but within moments she had controlled her breathing and pulse rate, before projecting her form across the astral. Antedios was waiting for her in the glade near the circle, his face grey and drawn with inner torment. The abject appearance of the normally arrogant Iceni cooled her anger as she realised he had not willingly broken his promise but she needed to retain her supremacy over him and her voice was icy.

"You have broken your word Antedios."

"They were going to destroy the sanctuary, Lady. They were here once before trying to remove one of the stones but it was buried too deep. They talked of a tool that would dig right down into the earth and tear the stones from their roots. I'd given my oath to protect them ..."

Following the pointing finger, Charlotte saw that the fence surrounding the stones had been cut through with wire cutters and the earth around the largest of the stones freshly dug. Suddenly Charlotte understood.

"You guard the resting place of the daughters of Boudica? They were buried here in the circle after being killed by the Romans?"

A deeper anguish lined the face of Antedios who shook his head. "The Romans did not kill them, Lady. They took poison from my hand so that they would not suffer the humiliation of being taken as slaves and ravished again. I swore to the Queen that I would never desert them and that I would avenge any defilement by death. We were unable to escape the soldiers but I have kept my word."

Charlotte's anger evaporated with compassion for the

220

unfortunate Iceni who was tied to the earth by an oath made in honour so many years before. "And if I find a way to release you from your oath?"

"I am tired Lady but I cannot rest until I have the life of The Black One who desecrated their resting place. I gave you my word but my oath to the Queen is the greater obligation. Forgive me if I offend you."

"There is nothing to forgive Antedios but slay no more, or I will be forced to use my power to destroy you without mercy and that I do not wish to do. I can free your spirit but only if you trust me."

Without a word Antedios bowed his head deeply and faded from view, leaving Charlotte deeply moved at his unswerving loyalty to Prasutagus's family. His sacred oath had bound him to the earth and instead of being released by a Roman sword, the Iceni had been unable to follow the natural path of death and rebirth in the footsteps of his ancestors.

Alan Morris slumped in his favourite armchair, his mind still turning over the details of the Cooper case. Although there was no evidence to connect the Coopers with any of the other deaths under investigation, he felt deep down in his own mind that there was some juxtaposit linking them. The investigation had been dealt with swiftly and efficiently by a colleague and the findings heard in the coroner's court required no further examination. Still, Alan Morris was not a happy man since he was the only one to appreciate the significance of the Celtic pin found amongst the ashes.

For the first time in his career, Morris seriously considered retiring from the force. He and Meg had grown up together amongst the beautiful fells of the Lake District and when Alan had realised his ambition of becoming a policeman, they both saw that promotion would be waiting for 'dead men's shoes' if they stayed where they were. They were married a week before he took up his new posting in Liverpool, probably the toughest city in the Kingdom.

Alan Morris hated the grimy streets, presided over by those two ridiculous birds perched on top of the Liver Buildings, but the chance for such a young man to transfer to CID was too good to be missed. He rose quickly through the ranks, earning himself a formidable reputation amongst the local villains and several commendations but he and Meg were never really happy. Finally, on reaching his thirty fourth birthday, he decided that if they did not make a move there and then, he would find himself buried on Merseyside.

The whole family had settled down well to small-town living; the boys were doing well in school and Meg had made more friends in the village than she had ever known in the North. The work was easy and there was no longer the permanent undercurrent of violence and unrest that had dogged his footsteps for so many years. That was until his latest case of the damned phantom killer. *The Ashmarsh Beast* - he could quite cheerfully murder Alexander bloody Martin himself for labelling him that!

For the umpteenth time, he started to run through the deaths in his mind. Examining the facts, rearranging them, trying to form a different picture but each time he came up with the same answer - nothing! His men had investigated every fundamentalist group in the county and police forces throughout the UK had been requested to conduct a similar investigation within their own areas. Militant fundamentalists were a dangerous breed and capable of fire-bombing occult shops, picketing psychic fairs and campaigning for the removal of occult publications from newsagent's shelves, but rarely did they confine their activities to one small area. Each time, the finger pointed to someone within the immediate locality of Ashmarsh.

Arthur Smiles, convicted poacher and still up to his old tricks when he met his grisly end in Whittlewood Forest, lived in a ramshackle cottage in Greens Horton, only three miles from Ashmarsh. Lucky for the old boy that his ticker gave out first but the mutilations matched those on the body of the second victim, Emily Trasker. The Coroner was adamant over the immense strength of the attacker. Surely anything with that sort of strength would carry enough weight to make even the smallest impression on the damp earth.

He had been definite too, over the ferocity of the attack made on Quinnell and had graphically described the injuries as being similar to a terrier tearing a rat apart. Several of the women had looked quite green by the time he had finished his report, Morris recalled with grim humour. Still, he'd seen Quinnell's remains himself and had been glad that it wasn't part of his job to go around picking up the bits, especially after wild animals had already begun the mopping up operation.

No sympathy to spare either for Scotty Wilson and Maurice Whitehead. If ever two buggers deserved to die, those two had it coming, thought Morris with uncharacteristic viciousness. Fancy using a noble beast like that terrier to tear an opponent apart in the name of sport. The dog was still in the police pound and Alan Morris had already let it be known that if the dog had no -where else to go, then he would offer it a home. If the animal had tried to protect the Hickson boy against the killer, then the dog deserved to be given a chance.

The whole sordid crime had been recorded on the floor of the barn and outside in the deep snow but there were still no clues to give the SOCO team even the merest hint of where to start their investigations. Five bodies. and not even a bloody suspect! That was why his Scottish blood had stirred in his veins, telling him that if the answer could not be found in this world, then he should look outside it for the solution. And the best person to isolate supernatural phenomena was Charlotte Manning; he just hoped she'd come up with something before the SIO summoned him.

Which brought him to the fatal fire at Cooper & Sons. The three Coopers were veritable giants in size and strength, and the suggestion that an unknown assailant could be responsible for their deaths struck him as ludicrous. He had been in the area long enough to learn of the legendary might

223

of the brothers.   True, the shot found in the charred remains
of one body matched that coming from the shot-gun carrying
Joe's finger-prints. But what if Joe had fired at something else?
Something big, and strong enough to kill three men.   His
memory did not have to go back very far to remember the pitchfork that Scotty Wilson had used in an attempt to defend himself.

He firmly believed that none of the deaths attributed to
The Beast could be linked to the murders of Alison Webber
and Gail Masters, and furthermore he agreed with Charlotte
Manning that neither of the boys were responsible. Therefore
it meant that two killers *were* still on the loose - and one of them
was definitely human! However, there was a glimmer of hope.
Following their visit to Michael Hughes, Morris had interviewed
one of Peter Jeffrey's friends about the man who had supplied
the boy with drugs. He finally managed to drag a description
out of the terrified schoolboy, which added an even more
sickening solution to the crime.

Chapter Eighteen

Eleanor Butler relaxed in serene contentment amongst the hay bales in the stable-yard barn, her elegant hand plucked a long straw and placed it between her small, perfect teeth. As a child, she had always sought solitude in the barn when things in the adult world became too difficult to manage; and now she was avoiding the continuous stream of well meaning friends and relations who were calling with wedding gifts and congratulations. Her mother, with uncharacteristic energy and enthusiasm, intended that every detail surrounding the wedding should be perfect.

There had been endless animated discussions about the selection of bridesmaids, as the only small children in the family were cousins twice removed and any permutation was guaranteed to upset someone. The catering was left entirely in the hands of the capable Mrs Lacey, whom everyone knew would provide a banquet fit for royalty. Eleanor had finally balked at the suggestion that her mother helped to choose her gown, and partly out of stubbornness, silently vowed that no-one would see it until she walked down the aisle on her father's arm!

The service was to be held in Ashmarsh Church. With the exception of the carol service at Christmas, it would be the first time Eleanor had set foot in the church since her confirmation, when the aged Bishop of Zululand had droned on ceaselessly about the Battle of Jutland to the white clad assembly, gathered there to receive his blessing. The accommodating Rev. Branson questioned neither her beliefs nor motive for being married in his church. In his own view it was a celebration of a family reunited after years of anger, and that was praise enough indeed in the sight of his God, if not in the eyes of the Diocese. In the dark days of fear and murder, he welcomed the diversion of a lavish wedding in his parish.

The bitterness felt towards her family during her years with Serge had dimmed her memory of the happy days of childhood, when she spent hours in the stable-yard, helping with her father's horses. Although the old cavalry man still cut a fine figure in the saddle, his appearances grew fewer as the months slipped passed. Now there were only two mares and her father's chestnut gelding left in the stables and the yard had a empty, hollow ring.

There was a rattle of iron shoes against cobblestones as a truculent voice disturbed her peace. "Don't tell me how to manage a horse, boy!"

Rising on an elbow, Eleanor could make out through the dusty window, the red-faced anger for which her brother was well-known. She had seen nothing of him since her engagement had been announced and each time the Butlers visited The Grange, Roger had been absent. The mare he had been riding had foam dripping from its mouth and the beautifully groomed coat was flecked with lather, showing that the horse had been galloped recklessly for some considerable distance. The reins were being held by young Tommy Haycock, a thin, under-developed local boy who looked after the horses at The Grange. The grey's eyes rolled as the powerful forelegs reared off the ground at the rider's approach.

"Let me take her and calm her down, Sir, you're upsetting her." Nervously Tommy kept himself between his beloved charge and the drunken, infuriated bully.

"Upset her, be damned," shouted Roger, aiming a blow at the boy's head with his riding crop. Instinctively, Tommy lifted his arm as the crop raised a savage weal across his wrist.

At sixteen, Tommy stood a head and shoulders shorter than Roger Hamilton but in spite of the pain he bit his lip, forcing himself not to cry out. A tear crept from the corner of his eye but he refused to give any ground, still firmly holding the reins of the nervous grey. Angrily the rider approached the mare, who let out a terrified whinny as his crop was raised again.

"That's enough Roger!" His sister had bounded across the yard and tried to wrest the crop from his hand but he pushed her easily away.

"So you've come home to start giving orders and playing Lady of the Manor, eh? Perhaps I should find some sordid little labourer's daughter to bring home for a big county wedding to impress the guests." His eyes glinted dangerously and Eleanor remembered just how calculatingly cruel he could be when angry.

"You're drunk," replied his sister, contemptuous of the way he had allowed his once handsome features to become so bloated.

"So would you be if you'd been informed that all you were to inherit was a lousy trust-fund administered by the bank. Why the hell couldn't you stay away?"

Attempting to use the crop as a weapon for the third time, Roger deliberately aimed a blow at his sister's lovely face, intent on marring her flawless skin. Tommy lunged at the raised arm, deflecting the lash that fell viciously on Eleanor's shoulder. Incensed beyond all reason, Roger flung the stable boy away as carelessly as a dog shakes off a flea.

Forcing Eleanor against the wall with the crop pushed against her throat, he seized her breast, spitefully kneading the pliable flesh with his free hand. "So, you like a bit of rough trade, do you?" His rancid breath, foul from stale drink, caught her full in the face and she retched.

Suddenly, a strong hand gripped him by the shoulder, spinning him round enough for Serge's fist to connect with his chin. Although out weighed by Roger's bulk, Serge had learnt to defend himself in less salubrious surroundings, where there were no rules in a street fight. A smirk crossed the larger man's face, as he saw the opportunity to teach the upstart a lesson. With blood pouring from a split lip, Roger lunged at his future brother-in-law but in his fury he tripped over Tommy's outstretched foot and fell sprawling.

Seizing a handy pitchfork, Roger hauled himself to his feet and charged like a maddened bull, the prongs of the implement embedding themselves in the stable door as Serge moved aside. Serge was not going to waste time reasoning with a drink addled brain and aimed a cruel kick to the groin, which dropped Roger to his knees. The face contorted with pain as Serge followed through with a vicious smash to Roger's nose, which shattered in blood and broken bone. Finally, he toppled over and lay still in the mud and manure that was waiting for removal.

As he put an arm around his future wife to comfort her, a shadow fell over them and to his dismay, Serge looked straight into the cold blue eyes of the Colonel. "I'm sorry Sir," was all he could offer by way of an apology for brawling in the stableyard with his future brother-in-law.

Suddenly old again, Roger's father nodded a weary head. "Should have done the same m'self a long time ago. Take Eleanor up to the house and take the boy, too."

The Colonel walked over to where his defeated son lay groaning and picking up a pail, dashed the icy water in his face. No-one knew what passed between the Colonel and his son, but within the hour, Roger had left The Grange and no further word was spoken about the incident.

Tommy Haycock, however, wasted no time in telling the story to his mother, who in turn became the centre of attention in the Ashmarsh Post Office. This was a story for everyone to relish. Local farmers' daughters and village girls were safe from Roger's predatory attentions and fathers seeing the white BMW parked in the lonely lanes, need no longer fear that it was their own daughter being forced to succumb to Roger's amorous and ungentle persuasion. The Colonel had suffered many embarrassing moments when confronted by his tenants and fellow farmers on a personal matter involving a molested daughter, but who wanted to take the matter no further because of their esteem for the Colonel and his wife.

"Roger the Ram" had been vanquished and Serge's stock stood even higher with the villagers. It would have been embarrassing if one of their own had given him a good beating, but since justice had been kept in the family, they could congratulate Colonel Hamilton on his choice of a son-in-law who had shown himself to be a *man's man*. The local people had taken a liking to Serge during the Christmas holidays and were glad to find that the man who would eventually take over the management of the estate, was one who was willing to fight to protect what was his, despite the consequences. Mrs Haycock embellished the tale to her own satisfaction and Serge would have been surprised to learn that he had saved the stable boy from an attack that only just stopped short of murder.

It was actually Serge who bloomed radiant in the days leading up to the wedding. From his origins in a derelict cottage in a poor Somerset village, he was about to enter into marriage with one of the most important county families. Jayne Hamilton shyly clung to his arm, half afraid that this vision of happiness might vanish and was already half in love with her good-looking and talented son-in-law. If she were twenty years younger ... she announced to a shocked bridge party.

"... And it's all your damned fault!" Eleanor informed Charlotte as they shared a bottle of wine in the writer's study. "My Mother's half ready to marry Serge herself and Father's so puffed with pride that his future son-in-law has made it on his own and with no hand-outs from anyone. They're as pleased as though they'd chosen the bridegroom themselves."

229

"Well, to echo the sentiments of the redoubtable Gwen ... He's a lovely boy."

Eleanor sighed. "I know and I should be over the moon because everyone thinks he's wonderful. I'm just terrified that marriage will change everything between us and I couldn't bear that. I loved him the way we were, when we only had ourselves to bother about. Perhaps I'm just being selfish."

"Would you rather turn the clock back?"

"Too damned right I would," laughed Eleanor, "and to have had all this, then!"

Charlotte smiled, leant over and took a sheaf of papers from her desk draw handing them to her visitor. "Art not being my strong point, you'll have to reply on photocopies and rough sketches, but those are a few suggestions for the gown."

Her guest studied them for a few moments. "Charly, they're *all* beautiful, but which one do I choose?" Her new friend leaned over the back of the sofa to rearrange the sheets. "This one is almost identical to the gown worn by Margaret of Anjou on her marriage to Henry VI; and this, chosen by Elizabeth Woodville when she was first presented at Court. Either could be made out of natural silk and worn with a matching silk cap, covered with seed pearls. Both would be extremely breath-taking, if that's the effect you wish to create."

Eleanor turned and knelt on the sofa, flinging her arms around Charlotte's neck. "That's exactly what I want to do!"

"Then let's drink another toast to the wedding of the year," laughed Charlotte, extracting herself from the affectionate embrace. She still had trouble coping with the closeness of people and Eleanor's unconscious gesture had made her feel uncomfortable for a moment.

"I envy you the information you store away in your head. You obviously research so much historical detail for your books and you seem to retain it all so vividly. Who else would recall what every well dressed lady of the fifteenth century was wearing on any given occasion?"

"Finer details make the novel more interesting and that's what the public wants" was her non-committal reply.

Three weeks later, Eleanor Butler drew up in front of Ashmarsh church in a sleek black limousine, hired for the occasion from the local undertaker. She knew instantly by the gasps of admiration that the gown was a success. The design she had finally chosen was a copy of one worn in Florence at the turn of the fourteenth century, which flattered to perfection her tall, willowy figure. The ivory silk was embroidered with gold thread in a motif of lilies and vine leaves that left only her hands and throat bare. A tiny cap of gold mesh and seed pearls against her blonde hair could not detract from the perfection of her bone structure and fine grey eyes. A simple spray of white lilies completed the picture of simplicity, but as Charlotte had predictedthe effect was breathtaking.

As she passed beneath the lych-gate, the villagers who had not gone into the church for the ceremony, greeted her with smiles and good wishes. Her father, beaming with pride, held his daughter's hand firmly against his arm in a gesture of not wanting to give her to another man, only having just rediscovered her after the years of separation.

Especially tidied for the occasion, the churchyard offered a profusion of spring crocuses in yellows, purple and cream, and clumps of fading snowdrops against the crumbling stone wall nodded their bell heads in the gentle breeze. Even the yews seemed less sombre than usual in the morning sunshine. Children were seated irreverently on the lichen strewn tombstones, the names of the occupants completely obliterated by those eager for a glimpse of the beautiful bride as she passed into the church. Her family was part of their lives and all were thrilled that she had chosen to be married in her local church, rather than a fancy London wedding.

At the door Eleanor felt a lump rise in her throat as her eyes became accustomed to the gloom after the sharp winter sunlight. Although it was only mid morning, dozens of candles had been lit, sending enfeebled shadows dancing up into the ancient rafters. The whole church was filled with flowers, their astringent fragrance blending with the heady French perfumes of the guests. As the organ announced the arrival of the bride, her cousins, with Anna as chief bridesmaid, fell in behind her, blocking her flight.

Slowly she began the long walk on her father's arm and as heads turned to admire her fairy tale loveliness, she caught sight of the rapt expression on Serge's face and knew there was no further need for any doubts. He and Alex standing in front of the altar, elegantly attired in morning coats, watched her with open admiration. Unable to take her eyes from his, Eleanor walked towards Serge, oblivious to the flattering whispers, although she found time to send Charlotte a brief smile of thanks.

The Rev. Branson, freshly laundered and smiling, led the voices in the celebration of matrimony and finally, with the ceremony over and the register signed, Eleanor and Serge stepped out into the sunlit churchyard to a crowd wreathed with smiles. Neither had yet stopped to consider that their union symbolised the continuance of a local tradition, and those employed on the land could rest easy with regard to their future. After the photographs had been taken, the bridal party set off for the wedding breakfast which was being held at The Grange, followed by the cavalcade of guests.

It was many years since the village had seen such a celebration and Mrs Lacey had loftily refused her employer's offer to employ outside caterers, so that the housekeeper could attend the wedding as a guest. In her opinion they needed someone around to make sure that everything was perfect and she wasn't having strangers messing up her kitchen. It was the only personal gift she could give young Miss Eleanor and she intended to supervise every single aspect of the wedding breakfast herself.

The whole ground floor of the old house had been set out with small groups of tables and chairs, so that the guests could sit with whom they chose. As they arrived, Mrs Lacey, with her stern eye on the girls brought in from the village to help for the day, directed the flow of traffic through to the buffet table in the dining room. She and Gwen Carradine exchanged curt nods of politeness but there would be no relaxing of the rivalry that the two women felt for each other.

The vast drawing room was unrecognisable from its normal gloomy appearance. Every item of furniture was highly polished and around the lamps, huge bowls of fresh spring flowers reflected warmth and light. A roaring log fire added to the welcome and even the Colonel, who never normally noticed such things, wondered why they didn't use such a charming room more often. Both the sitting room and morning room had been festooned with flowers and in small groups, guests gossiped and exchanged news over the suddenness of the Butler wedding after years of cohabitation.

Drinks were served and toasts made as photographers spent film after film on the bridal pair. *The Tatler* and *Harpers* took care of the society coverage, while the reporter from the local *Independent* was unexpectedly, treated to a few moments of Serge's precious time. When most of the guests had filtered through to the dining room to sample Mrs Lacey's culinary skills, Serge sought out his friends, who had taken refuge in the Colonel's study. This was the only room in the house not to be disrupted and the Colonel had forbidden his wife to set foot in there. Damn it, a man needed some escape!

"Not bad for a village lout, eh?" He asked, kissing Charlotte's cheek.

"Here's to my favourite lout," she responded kissing him back.

"Now I'm a respectable married man, can proposition my best friend's bird, without let or hindrance?"

"Shouldn't think so for a moment," volunteered Alex, cutting an extremely elegant figure in his morning coat. "You'll need to conserve all your energies for producing the expected heir."

His friend halted his glass, half-way to his mouth. "Do you know something I don't?"

Alex took his glass and refilled it, before placing a protective arm around his friend's shoulders. "Look, you don't really think all those people out there were pleased just because there was a charming society wedding going on, do you? You represent the continuance of the Hamilton family and they expect you to accept that responsibility by presenting the Colonel and Mrs Hamilton with a couple of grandchildren as soon as possible."

Serge took a gulp of champagne. "You are joking, aren't you."

"'Fraid not," responded Charlotte equally straight faced. "Old county families are on a par with royalty and so an heir is a must."

"Christ! Eleanor and I have never even thought about kids." He finished his drink and a slight flush appeared on his cheeks. "I'd better go and find her."

"Serge ..." Alex's voice stopped him as he got to the door. "I think it can wait a *little* bit longer."

With a pained expression Serge passed through the door and it was all they could do to stifle their laughter as they both collapsed into the Colonel's armchair. "That was cruel."

"True, but I felt it my duty to warn my best friend of his responsibilities. Besides, that will teach him to poach on my preserve." With difficulty Charlotte wriggled out of the chair, as Alex's hand slid along her stocking clad thigh to the cool flesh above.

"I think it's time we visited the buffet."

By now most of the guests had settled down into small groups, and they so they joined Paul Kerrick and the Morris's. The detective and his wife had been astounded to receive an invitation to the wedding and felt a little out of place amongst such glittering company, although they were thoroughly enjoying themselves. Anna had gotten rid of her precocious charges and was engrossed in conversation with a distinguished looking man, who Paul identified as the family lawyer.

Apart from some of the most well known families in the county, the guest list had been supplemented on Serge's side by business friend's whom the couple had known for many years. If anyone felt it was a little strange that the bridegroom had no other family to offer, no-one made their observations aloud. The day had been a huge success and no mother could be more proud or happier than Jayne Hamilton as she stood beside her smiling husband to receive the compliments of the guests.

Charlotte was about to help Alex to another slice of beef wellington when Eleanor caught up with them. "What on earth have you been saying to Serge, he's positively white."

"You look lovely," answered Alex, kissing her cheek and avoiding her question, "and I'm sure Serge will have no problem in performing his duties admirably."

"You two are the most Machiavellian, scheming, double-dealing, conniving pair I've ever met. You could out-Borgia the Borgias! And I love you both. Thank you for everything."

"Go and enjoy your wedding, Princess," laughed Alex. "Besides, old Serge looks as though he needs rescuing from one of your Great Aunts."

While he waited for Eleanor to change into her travelling clothes, Serge walked with Alex through the bare rose garden. The afternoon sun was losing its warmth and would dissuade any of the guests from venturing too far from the house. Whilst the day had far exceeded his expectations, Serge was conscious that a door was closing on his past and he felt a stab of panic.

"Look, Alex, I don't want you to take this the wrong way but I want you to think about something while we're away. We've talked about selling the flat and coming here to live and ... well, I'd be happier doing that if I thought you were just down the road."

"What are you trying to tell me, Serge?   That you want me to propose to Madam, just to make *you* feel secure?"

"You know that's not what I mean. She's right for you, man, don't ruin it all because you're too bloody proud or stupid to ask her.   Christ, Alex, you're all the family I've got, I just want you to be happy too."

Serge flung his arms around his friend, holding him in a firm embrace and Alex felt the tears pricking his eyelids as he hugged him in return. That simple gesture voiced all the words they had ever needed to say to each other and never found the opportunity.

"I know, but let's not rush things, eh?   Now go off on your honeymoon and enjoy yourself. And rememeber, Ashmarsh expects ..."

A few days later, when the editor from the county magazine was selecting photographs for the next issue, she by-passed one taken of the crowds outside the church with a shudder. The photographer had caught the bride arriving and in the background, over Anna Fenton's shoulder, was a man's face so distorted with hatred, that it completely ruined the harmony of the picture.   Without another thought, the editor dropped the photograph in the rubbish basket.

.

Chapter Nineteen

"Eleanor was lucky she didn't wait until this week for the wedding," remarked Anna, her forehead pressed against the cold window pane, watching the leonine fury of the March winds.

"And they're ensconced in Bermuda until the 15th. How's your romance progressing, by the way?"

Anna shrugged and forced her hands deeper into the pockets of her bulky cardigan. The fire drew her closer and she squatted down on the floor next to where Charlotte was attempting to sort through some papers, hindered by the cats who were obviously resentful of the intrusion into the sitting room during the daytime.

"It's hardly a romance but it was exactly what I needed. For someone else to find me attractive, I mean."

Charlotte eyed her carefully for a moment. "You only have to look in the mirror."

Her secretary smiled at the compliment. "I mean attractive on the inside. Like you. You really are one of the most beautiful people I know and it's because you're beautiful on the *inside*. Mrs C knows it and so does Paul, Serge and Eleanor. Alex, poor soul, doesn't understand you but he loves you for the same reason. All the villagers hold a high opinion of you and not because you've got money and land but because you're a good person. And every one of your mangy old cats know a good thing when they see it."

"With my philosophy on life don't you find it strange? It should be exactly the opposite. Wicked Witch of the West and all that."

Anna frowned and chewed at her bottom lip. "You know, to be honest I've never really known whether all the things you say I believe or not. About previous lives and things. You know so much, too much really, and none of us know whether you're joking or serious when you rattle on. But I don't think I'd really want to know for sure."

The novelist continued to examine her papers without answering. Anna was merely thinking aloud and her conjecture called for no positive response. "That was the strange thing about John. I would repeat things you'd done or said, either to impress or amuse, I don't really know which. But he became paranoid about it. He would ask all sorts of idiotic questions and half the time I gave idiotic answers just to wind him up. He really thought we were a nest of devils."

"I hope you didn't conjure up a picture of Gwen leaping naked from her broomstick to attend a sabbat in Ashmarsh church-yard." The thought of Gwen Carradine's ample bulk in its natural state, participating in a satanic rite, reduced both of them to laughter and Anna's reflective mood vanished.

Senior Investigating Officer, Superintendent Hubert Grimme, known throughout the ranks as The Grimme Reaper, read through the report in silence. A nervous tic at the side of his mouth was the only indication of the anger that boiled inside him. Finally, he closed the file with a snap and eyed Detective Inspector Morris with some distaste.

"You came to us with excellent recommendations Morris but I find little to recommend in the way you've handled this business. We've more bodies than we know what to do with and you've let the only suspect retire to the Highlands of Scotland for the benefit of his health! Now you want to release those two boys for no other reason than you don't believe they were responsible."

Grimme heaved himself to his feet and began to pace the room. "I have only one suggestion to make Morris, get every man that can be spared out into those villages and interview every single person, eliminate no-one. From now on, everyone is suspect. Do you understand me?"

"I understand Sir, but would *you* like to inform me what we're supposed to be looking for?" There was an edge to the Detective's voice.

"Don't be bloody insolent, Morris. You're looking for a muderer! Now go out and do the job you're paid to do instead of hob-nobbing with the county elite." Grimme sank back into his leather chair. "That will be all."

Instead of accepting the dismissal, Alan Morris leaned over the desk and this time his voice was pure ice. "Forensics can't give us any information. SOCO have no clues, no tracks. There hasn't been one single lead on any of the killings. The psychological profile doesn't match up with anyone in the area *if* we're supposed to match it to the description given by Tracey Walker. Now if you're so bloody clever as to have risen to Superintendent, perhaps you would like to give me a more constructive order other than to tie up the entire force on a wild goose chase! Sir."

Apoplectic rage shook his superior but Morris pressed home his case. "I am perfectly willing to discuss the case in a constructive and logical manner, but I'll be damned if I'll take your offensive criticism because you need a scapegoat for the Home Office. Now, if I can draw on the benefit of your experience, I'll listen but I'll not listen to any more bellowing and bullshit."

Grimme rounded on him in fury. "You can begin by handing in your resignation, Detective Inspector Morris. In fact ..."

Morris forestalled him by placing a long white envelope on the blotter. "Already done, Sir. Written out after spending a whole weekend trying to work out where I've gone wrong. I reckoned if I hadn't got a lead after seven deaths, then it was about time I packed the job in. Which just about voices your sentiments, I think, Sir."

Hubert Grimme was a tough superior but he was not an unfair man and as he slowly read through the detective's resignation, he kept a careful watch on Alan Morris's face. He had no doubts that Morris was a good officer, they all were on his team. If he had any complaints about the way a case was being handled, then a good roar at the officer in charge usually brought about the desired result. This case was different, however, and Morris obviously felt strongly enough about it to bawl back.

"Sit down Morris," he said wearily.

"Sir?"

"I said sit down. Unless you're deaf as well as incompetent." The words were sharp but the inflection carried a tone of sympathy. "Do you really want me to accept this?"

Morris shook his head. "I've been a policeman all my life and I don't know anything else but this Ashmarsh Beast business is getting to me."

"Right. Tomorrow morning, nine thirty sharp, I want you to bring all the information you've got relating to these deaths. Including the details not included in your report," he added wryly. "We'll sit down together and go through everything. Warn Patterson in Forensics that I'll want to talk to him and while you're at it, ring the Coroner. If there's anything at all, then we'll find it. Now go and sort out your files and when you're done, take the rest of the day off."

Over the next few days Alan Morris saw a glimpse of the brilliant analytical mind that had earned Grimme his reputation. The man was obviously bored with the routine of administration and meetings, and the challenge of working on a case again had fired his enthusiasm. He pounced on obscure facts and worried at them with all the tenacity of a terrier, until he had extracted all there was to know. From Morris's notes, he took thumbnail sketches of the persons involved and built up a whole character analysis. After three days, Morris actually admired the man who, prior to their fiery interview, had only been a sinister dark figure, stalking the corridors of the building.

"Well Alan," sighed the SIO as he sipped his coffee. "I must confess that I owe you an apology, but answer this one. Do you think there is any possibility that any shred of evidence could have been overlooked by the Scientific Support Officer?"

"No, Sir." Morris's response was immediate. "I don't believe Janice Milbrook could miss a vital clue in seven different murders. Nobody could be that incompetent, especially in snow. There was nothing to find." He still hadn't voiced his suspicions over the deaths of the Cooper brothers.

Grimme allowed himself a smile. "But there's something you're holding back?"

Morris's own theory had been carefully avoided since the discussions with his superior had begun and now they had come full circle. "I'm not sure that you'll want to hear what is, at present, only a theory. And I doubt if you'll approve of the methods used to obtain the lead. The only concrete evidence is here is these files and I've gone over and over it. I've got nothing else to offer on the Beast but I do have something I want to follow up on the circle murders. I just do not accept that they are connected."

Grimme replenished his cup and offered the detective a refill. "I don't know, Alan. After forty years of policework, I have to confess, that I don't know every answer. But I do have a suggestion, I want to put another man on the case. Someone who doesn't know these people, a fresh pair of eyes, so to speak. Going through all this," he tapped a pile of paper with his spectacles, "it's obvious that you've already explored every angle open to you but someone else just may see something we've missed. This isn't a criticism of you, I want you to understand that, and I shall make it perfectly clear at the briefing tomorrow."

In fact Grimme was better than his word. As a colleague candidly put it in the canteen, Morris came out smelling of violets. Pressure from the Home Office demanded more positive action and so both uniform and plain-clothed police were detailed to make house to house enquiries in every village in a twenty mile radius of Ashmarsh.

"You lucky bugger," swore one of his colleagues as he was about to pile into a squad car. "We tramp the villages in the freezing cold, while you drink coffee with the Grimme Reaper."

"Well Adams, old Hubert and me are the brains behind the whole operation." Adams muttered something un-complimentary and drove off.

"Alan, what can you tell me about this Manning woman, who seems to continually crop up in your investigations?" Grimme held up his hand to prevent any interruption. "Firstly, four of the murders are committed on her land and one in Ashmarsh itself. Now we've had accusations and counter-accusations of witchcraft and fundamentalist conspiracy. But you've got your suspicions that the two girls' deaths aren't linked to The Beast. I've also got my suspicions that you suspect someone. Am I correct?"

"Yes, Sir. But I still don't want to stick my neck out just yet."

Grimme nodded. "I know you have become extremely friendly with the parties concerned but have you any reason to suspect that they might know more than you think? This may seem like an idiotic question, Alan, but in your opinion, could she have hypnotised Hickson and Hughes? Planted their stories telepathically?"

Alan Morris's mouth dropped open in astonishment. "She didn't do anything, just talked to them and I was there all the time. The boys certainly weren't in any trance. Can I ask why Sir?"

"Mrs Manning, by all accounts, is an extremely accomplished lady when it comes to matters of the occult. From my own enquiries I find that she has been a willing subject of investigation by the Psychical Research Society and that she regularly advises on parapsychology experiments at the

Universities. I don't believe in such rubbish m'self, but there are those that do, and those people are usually gullible enough to be influenced. Besides, whichever way we look at the evidence, all the clues lead back to Ashmarsh."

Morris shook his head vehemently. For one idiotic moment he thought Grimme was suggesting that something supernatural was responsible for the murders. The relief that the Ashmarsh Beast was no longer his concern had made him almost light headed with euphoria and he had no intention of making himself look foolish now. The notion that the unknown slayer of five humans was not a creature of this world he kept firmly to himself. He wanted a clear run at pinning down the man who killed and mutilated two schoolgirls and the net was closing in.

"They all have unshakeable alibis. Damn it, one of my own men was screwing the secretary in the house the night of one of the murders."

"Yes, I heard about that, and I strongly disapprove Alan. I don't want to hear of any more of your lads sleeping with suspects when there's an enquiry going on or there'll be disciplinary action taken."

"Yes Sir. The affair's over now anyway. Slight religious disagreement, I believe."

Grimme's eyes narrowed for a second. "Is this where your enquiries are taking you Alan? If so, make damn sure you're right."

If it was time for Alan Morris to discover that his boss *was* human, it was also time for Alexander Martin to discover that his lover wasn't. Dusk had not yet fallen when Alex drove out of the courtyard at Hunter's Moon. They were expected at The Grange for the evening and Eleanor wanted to show Charlotte her new hunter. They had only travelled a few yards along the High Street when they came upon a group of people standing around something in the road.

Before they could ascertain the reason for the hold-up, a

small girl dashed up to the car, babbling hysterically, with tears streaming down her cheeks. The child struggled at the door handle which resisted her efforts; it was Katie Watkins, whom they had rescued from the gin-trap some weeks before. Charlotte only had time to open the car door, before the little girl seized her hand, pulling her towards the group of villagers. Through the choked sobs, Charlotte learned that the girl's puppy had been knocked down by a passing car and had been seriously hurt.

A woman who was obviously the driver of the vehicle, stood amongst the villagers crying that she had not seen the dog run into the road in time to brake. Everyone was ignoring her, waiting in respectful silence to see what would happen next. As Charlotte approached, the girl's mother tried to pull the child away, whilst apologising for the nuisance but Katie would not budge. Her deep violet eyes, red and swollen, pleaded for the life of her pet.

As Charlotte knelt down in the road, gravel ripping her stockings to shreds and blood smearing the hem of her skirt, the child's eyes were riveted on her face. Alex stood behind her, but he could see that the dog was so badly injured that there was little hope of its recovery. The black and white puppy lay in a pool of its own blood, the thick white ruff around its neck scarlet from a vicious, gaping throat wound. The poor creature's life was ebbing away, and it could barely lift its head to whimper for help.

Charlotte knelt with her eyes closed for a few seconds with her right hand over the dog's heart. She took a deep breath and plunged her left hand into the matted bloody mess at the animal's throat. The blood continued to pump, although the flow had lessened, and her beautifully manicured hands were now drenched as it seeped through her fingers in a scarlet stream. The child's eyes had never left hers and Alex was touched by the blind faith that shone from the eyes of innocence. If faith could move mountains, he thought, then Katie Watkin's faith alone should be enough to save her pet.   What a pity that life's cruel disappoint-ments had to be experienced so early in life he reflected sadly.

The puppy gave a whimper and a tremor ran the length of its body as Charlotte looked directly at the little girl and, for the first smiled a slow, secret smile. Wonder radiated from the young face as Charlotte leaned forward to whisper instructions. Pulling the covers from her doll's pram, the girl handed them shyly to Charlotte, who used them to wrap around the still form.

"Come on Charlotte," Alex leant over and touched her arm. "There's nothing else you can do now."

"No," she agreed, her voice tired. "There's nothing else."

Gently picking up the puppy, she placed its bundled form into the girl's arms and with further whispered instructions, the child carried her precious charge home. A neighbour offered to help but Katie quite firmly shook her head in re-fusal. She had been given her instructions and she intended to carry them out to the letter.

Tricia Watkins squeezed Charlotte arm. "Thank you, Mrs Manning," she smiled in gratitude. "She loves that dog more than any of her dolls."

The crowd dispersed, the other villagers mumbling amongst themselves as they drifted away, leaving Charlotte and Alex with the woman who had hit the puppy. "It really wasn't my fault, you know," she said when the last person had left the scene. "The dog just ran out in front of me and I only stopped in time to miss the child."

"Don't worry, children and small animals are known for their foolishness as well as resilience."

"Do you think I should offer to get the little girl another puppy, or would it be wrong?"

Charlotte looked puzzled, before realising that the woman was a stranger. "He'll be up and running around inside two weeks"

"But I thought it was dead!"

"Far from it. He'll have to be kept under sedation for a few days to stop him from moving too much but apart from a sore throat and a headache, he'll be fine."

The woman looked doubtful and slightly suspicious. "Would the family mind if I called back, just to make sure?"

"I'm sure they would appreciate it," replied Charlotte, seeing that the woman did not believe her but not really caring. "Now if you'll excuse me, I really must go and change. We're expected at friends for supper and I can hardly turn up looking like this."

She ruefully studied the dark red stains that were already drying on her clothes and hands. There was also a smear on her face. "You look disgusting," remarked Alex "and you smell even worse. You're not getting in my car like that!"

Charlotte stuck her tongue out at him. "Bet I'm home before you can turn this heap around," and she took off like a hare, leaving the startled woman gazing after them, as though they were both mad.

She was already on the telephone to Paul Kerrick when Alex walked in the door. "While I shower, call Eleanor and tell her we'll be a bit late," she called, running up the stairs.

In the bathroom, she stripped off the bloodstained garments and flung them in the bidet to soak. The hot water of the shower helped to disperse some of the tiredness that threatened to overtake her. The impromptu working had left her depleted, since it had taken a tremendous effort to heal the puppy's wound, especially under the watchful gaze of her neighbours; but the trust that had flowed out from Tricia Watkins' little girl had been too strong to ignore. The story would spread round the villages like wildfire. Wrapping herself in a huge towel she walked back into the bedroom as Alex came through the door, a curious expression on his face.

"Okay Alex, say it."

"How did you do it? That dog was as good as dead when we got there. There couldn't have been a drop of blood left in its veins and yet you diagnose that it will be up and well in a fortnight!"

"Thaumaturgic healing is a fairly common practice."

"That wasn't faith healing, that was raising the bloody dead! Damn it Charlotte, its throat was cut from ear to ear. I know what I saw!"

Idly she selected a fresh shirt from the closet. "But I'm at a loss to understand why you're so upset about it all. I've told you repeatedly that I have powers others don't possess and the gift of healing is one of them."

Alex ran his fingers through his hair in exasperation. *WHAT* the hell *WAS* he getting so fired up over? Was it because he now had to face up to the fact that her abilities, which he had so effectively convinced himself were purely academic, were real after all?

Chapter Twenty

The long-circulating rumour concerning Alexander Martin being offered the editorship of a leading magazine became a reality on 1st April - April Fool's Day. In the same post was an invitation to discuss the possibility of hosting a new weekly current affairs programme for a well-known commercial television production company.

Impassively he re-read the letter, looking for some signs of a hoax, before handing it to Charlotte over the breakfast table. "Have you seen the fee they're offering?"

"For a contract giving you free rein and no restriction on your own journalistic commitments, you'd be mad not to accept."

"How do you know I'll be any good?" The Martin ego never suffered from self doubt, he merely wanted his companion's flattery.

Charlotte smiled inwardly, reading his thoughts. Resting her chin in her hand, she studied him carefully for a few seconds. "Ignoring your obvious talents which over the years have earned you a handsome living and a formidable reputation, I would say in a nutshell 'old fashioned sex - appeal.' Whichever way you look at it, you've worn well for your age and will pull a readership or viewing audience from nineteen to ninety. Without being good looking you have a certain charismatic lifestyle that will communicate itself to the impressionable teens, the avaricious twenties, the budding thirties sophisticates, up to the still suave grand-fathers. Whatever you do, you can set a trend and there's that..." She leant over and placing her hand on his crotch, squeezed meaningfully. "That would come over best on television ..."

"You're telling me they're paying all that money for my obvious libido?" There was a slight edge of irritation in his voice.

"Don't be naive," she replied. "The one obvious advantage you've got is the old animal magnetism - so exploit it! The magazine is already a bible for whatever happens to be de rigueur in clothes, food or entertainment. The publishers want an editor who reflects that image. Television wants someone who looks good and offers something to the serious minded. Only you can decide which is your true metier. And as long as we don't have Hello magazine on the doorstep, I can live with it."

Before he could make a reply Gwen came in to remove the breakfast dishes. "Mrs Carradine, what do you think to the idea of Mr Martin having his own television programme?"

"Funny you should ask that, Mrs Manning. I was only saying to my sister, the other day, that Mr Martin here should be on the telly. I mean, he's a nice looking boy and speaks better than most. You're not as handsome as Mr Butler but, well ... you've got something else. If I were twenty years younger, I'd go for you myself." She added, chuckling at her own daring as she went out of the room.

Amused by Gwen's response, Alex laughingly took Charlotte's hand. "As I'm obviously accepted by the inimitable and redoubtable Gwen, don't you think it would be a good idea for me to commemorate the new development in my career by making an honest woman out of you?"

He hadn't given a thought to Charlotte's reaction but he was totally unprepared for the unveiled horror that showed in her eyes. He had expected surprise but never once did he anticipate the colour draining from her face in such a manner that her rejection of his proposal needed no words of confirmation. He had made up his mind shortly after Serge's marriage, that if the contract came through, then he would ask Charlotte to be his wife. He had never dreamed she would refuse.

Charlotte sank down in a deep hollow, carefully choosing a spot surrounded by oaks. A reassuring smell of damp earth and the astringent odour of rotting leaves perfumed the air where her feet had churned them from the ground. Danger and uncertainty had always been an occupational hazard, emanating from jealousy, hatred, suspicion, envy and even love. At least she assumed he loved her, having made that ridiculous proposal in the manner he had, catching her off-guard. She accepted that her feelings for him were stronger than any emotion she had experienced for a long time, but how could she convince herself that he would not harm her in the end. Everyone else had.

Alex had come to terms with his earlier belief that her occult knowledge was purely academic. The affair over Katie Watkin's puppy had forced him to accept that her claim to healing power was a reality. He still felt uncomfortable discussing it but now sat back with barely concealed amusement throughout her occultic discourses. Nevertheless it terrified her to think how he would cope with the eventual discovery that he was married to an entity who was barely human!

The soft greenness of the foliage above whispered on the gentle spring breeze and in through the fine veil of unfolding buds, came the ripple of a stream. Amongst the lush foliage on the floor of the wood, delicate anemones and violets bloomed. The pagan goddess Eostre presided over the rebirth of Nature, her very essence felt in the stirring of bees and the jubilant call of the wren.

Charlotte stretched out on the ground, and summoning all of her inner strength, forced her mind to expand beyond the realms of her present existence, her breathing becoming shallower as she drifted away. As her inner self began to soar upwards, she was conscious of her earthbound form mingling with the damp earth below. Her very bones seemed to develop a life-force of their own; protruding through her flesh to graft onto the powerful root of the oak that reached beneath the ground. Her hair flowed over the moss, until her whole being merged into the living carpet of the forest floor.

High above in the comforting velvet blackness, her mind explored and expanded; seeking answers, questioning. The darkness slowly lightened, until it was ablaze with the fiery red of brilliant sunlight; a cool breeze gently enfolding her as she hung suspended in time and space. Light wings and unseen hands seemed to bear her ever upwards, whilst in her ears echoed an unearthly, hypnotic chant. A litany in some strange, ancient tongue that bore no resemblance to any earthly form of prayer. As the glowing sun died, the light was veiled by a soft, shimmering mist, accompanied by the gentle sound of water murmuring over smooth pebbles in a crystal stream. Finally, the mist cleared to reveal an iridescent rainbow of such sublime colours that it dazzled the senses, whilst leaving the mind clear, cool and at peace.

Slowly, Charlotte felt herself descending once again into the dark void where the scurrying of feet could be heard, furtive and cunning. Wings brushed against her skin and all around was evil, dark and threatening but she ignored the pleas to remain and gradually merged back into the lifeless form that stretched out on the earth in the forest glade. Fully conscious, she remained lying on the ground, her eyes closed, unwilling to break the spell of pure enchantment. She had reached the ultimate plane in meditation which left her depleted but completely calm; at peace but strangely alert.

She had chosen to remain an earthly creature in order to bring enlightenment to the masses and although the rest of her kind frowned upon the line her work had taken, it was indisputable that her sphere of influence had reached further than any esoteric system. If she had chosen to live as a human then she would have to face up to those human responsibilities

251

that become part of daily living. On two occasions she had mistakenly married for protection; this time she would marry because it was *right* - but not yet.

Charlotte found Alex sitting alone in the garden, out of sight of the house in the stone arbour. The hurt he felt was evident from the expression in his eyes and judging from the number of cigarette stubs on the paving, he had smoked continuously since her sudden disappearance. She had not realised that she had been missing for some hours.

"I'm sorry, that was an incredibly stupid and selfish attitude to take. Your proposal came as a bit of a shock, that's all."

His manner was cool and withdrawn. "I don't see why. Perfectly normal people get married every day because they care about each other."

"Alex, we are not *normal* people."

"Oh, shut up," he answered crossly. "I obviously misread the signs. I thought you cared enough about me. With all the changes that are going on around us, I just felt it was a good idea to make a clean sweep of everything."

Charlotte resented being liked to a re-decorating pro-gramme but bit her tongue. The male ego was an extremely delicate flower, and Alex's ego had taken a severe battering. A veteran of countless affairs, he had taken the precipitous step of proposing marriage only to have been rebuffed by the headlong flight of the object of his desire. It was a bitter pill and Charlotte, not the most tactful of people at the best of times, found it difficult to deal with.

Taking his face gently between her hands, she lowered her her voice to a caressing, hypnotic whisper - it was an unfair advantage but what the hell!

"Darling, I love you very much." Using the word for the first time came surprisingly easy. "But my track record in marriage cannot be said to be exemplary. Can't we stay as we are for the time being? Sell your flat as you suggested and then the four of us can have a week in London and look for

252

one to share. I *do* think it's a good idea but the prospect of marriage takes a bit of getting used to."

Melting a little, Alex pulled her towards him, holding her tightly against his chest. "I love you, Charlotte and I'm bloody terrified you'll just slip away from me. I thought if you were my wife, I would feel more secure but that's not really true, is it?"

She shook her head and with a seductive laugh suggested, "How about sealing a non-aggression pact upstairs, thereby declaring this union a permanent one?" She kissed him in a demanding manner, nibbling his bottom lip and exploring his tongue with her own. She rarely made the first overtures so it never failed to excite him; sweeping her off her feet, he carried her hungrily into the house.

Connaught Manor was an old country house that some years before had been converted into a hugely successful conference centre. Twice a year there was a Grand Ball, one for the local hunt and the second a charity fixture which was always well attended by the elite of the county. Tonight was the occasion of the Grand Charity Ball and the opulent ballroom was transformed back to its former grandeur. Beautifully gowned women basked in the flattering gleam of the chandeliers, bare shoulders and jewels glowing under the soft lights. The tables, set for individual parties paying for exorbitantly priced tickets, were decorated with elaborate floral arrangements and candles.

There was no doubt that the three most attractive men in the room were all at one table. Serge Butler, Alexander Martin and Paul Kerrick drew some predatory glances as the lady guests plotted manoeuvres for later in the evening. Paul had escorted Anna and they had been joined for the evening by the Bransons and the Morris's.

An excellent dinner had been served and the dancing had been in progress for some hours. Some of the older couples began drifting away; having spent an obligatory sum

253

on the charity auction they departed before boisterous youth took over. Both Alex and Serge were astounded at the antics of some of the younger county set. One girl had already been carried shoulder high across the ballroom, one broken shoulder strap revealing a soft, immature breast and hair from a once elegant hair-do, now in tatters about her shoulders. Another had been pitched forward into the floral arrangement whilst riding on the shoulders of her partner, plump buttocks in mauve French knickers displayed for all to see. The dance band were having difficulty at times, in making themselves heard above the din.

"Don't forget, my dear Alex, that the upper classes invented debauchery," murmured Paul, as amid the yells and cat-calls, Alex was pulled to his feet to dance with a delicious seventeen year old beauty.

"What do you think to my idea of selling the two London flats and buying one between us?" Serge asked Charlotte, as he lounged well fed and content with a large cigar. Eleanor had been whisked away some time before by an old school friend who needed to catch up with the gossip.

"I'm all for it."

"It will make Alex a lot happier," began Serge.

Charlotte laughed and patted his hand. "Intrigue doesn't suit you, my darling. Don't worry, we've had a little chat and everything has been taken care of."

"Really ..." Serge brightened but was interrupted as another teenage nymphet claimed him as a partner.

All evening Charlotte had been aware of the tight lines around Paul's eyes but until now she had no opportunity to speak to him privately. "It is bad?"

"I'll live," he replied, letting the mask drop for a moment.

"There's a summer house in the garden ..."

"And there's a different type of laying on of hands going on out there." He tried to joke but the mask of pretence had slipped and he could not control the spasm of pain that racked his body.

"Look, there's a small bedroom off the cloakroom, go up and I'll join you in a moment."

Unable to catch Alex's eye, Charlotte ran upstairs, holding up the hem of her black evening gown, her sandled feet barely touching the carpet. The heavy gilt mirror on the landing reflected a pleasing image. The only relief for the black gown were her bare shoulders and the pearl collar that Alex had given her for Christmas. Amongst the kaleidoscope of colour the simple black gown had set her apart.

Paul lay on the bed with his eyes closed. As the door closed, he raised his head, the pain now raw and exposed. Each movement like a red hot knife thrust.

"Take your shirt off."

"What if ....?"

"Paul, for goodness sake. If anyone comes in, they'll think we're making out and leave!" replied Charlotte crisply.

No sooner had he removed his shirt and seated himself on the bedroom stool, than Charlotte's cool hands began to move over his bare skin. For a while he allowed her to work in silence, studying in the mirror the well known frown of concentration on her forehead.

"It appears that Alex has become a permanent fixture."

"You could say that, yes, I hope so."

"It should have been me, Charlotte!"

"Paul, it was you who sent me away, remember."

"I didn't want to, you know that. I had to do what was best for both of us although I've never stopped loving you for one moment."

"I know," she whispered softly, her lips gently brushing his bare shoulder.

Gently at first, her barely perceivable touch was more like a whisper over his flat stomach, hip bones and around his waist. Almost immediately the tension began to subside, as the caressing hands drew the pain from his body. The pain was replaced by an unfamiliar tingling sensation that was reminiscent of desire. Almost like an amputee still believing

255

the limb is still there, he thought to himself. Gradually, the pressure of her expert touch grew firmer until her fingers were probing the muscles, releasing him from the knotted, twisted agony that had gripped him for so long.

"How's that?" she asked finally.

"Better."

She waited while he slipped into his shirt, carefully studying his face and when she was satisfied that no pain remained, she turned to leave. As she got to the door, he called her name softly and as she turned, he held out his hand with the little and fourth fingers raised, the thumb covering the folded index and third fingers.

"Blessed Be," he intoned in the traditional manner.

"Blessed Be," she answered and smiled in return.

As she turned back to the door, she was confronted by Alex, with a look of manic fury burning in his eyes. The state of Paul's undress and Charlotte's flushed face were all he needed to confirm his worst suspicions. The thought flashed through his mind that they had obviously been so engrossed in their clandestine activities that neither of them had been aware of him entering the room.

"What the hell's going on here?" he growled.

Her eyes were wide with genuine surprise as she answered in truth, "I was easing Paul's pain."

"And what was he easing for you?" he snapped.

For a second there was no answer as surprise gave way to rage. Without warning Charlotte swung her fist in a super-human punch that connected with his jaw, almost removing his head from his shoulders. In blind fury, she would have struck him again, only this time Kerrick caught her arms, holding firmly a spitting, writhing wildcat.

"Charlotte!" He shook her roughly before turning to her lover. "Alex, I'm not in a position to ease anything for any-one."

"Paul, No!" Her voice a keening wail and tears glistened beneath her lashes.

256

"It's all right love." Paul cradled her head against his bare chest. "Alex, you've heard about my hunting accident and my injured spine but what we've not told you, is that I was also castrated through some complications with the fall. I'm not capable of having sexual intercourse with anyone."

Charlotte's tears were flowing freely. Grief for Paul and the agony it must have caused him in revealing a secret that had been concealed from everyone. Pity for herself over Alex's betrayal - by his lack of trust.

Realising his terrible mistake, Alex would have welcomed the ground swallowing him as he saw the full implications of his jealousy. Mortified, he reached for Charlotte's hand but she pulled away from him, in both anger and hurt.

It was Paul who ended the silence. "Charlotte, go downstairs and wait for us. I think it's time Alex and I had a talk."

Dumbly she nodded, ignoring Alex's eyes silently pleading for some sign of forgiveness. Without a backward glance, she walked out of the door, closing it quietly behind her. Not once since she had struck him had she even looked in his direction. She would consider his action a monumental act of betrayal but at least now he understood the reasoning behind her inexplicable friendship for Paul Kerrick.

The drive home had been a silent nightmare and Alex was convinced that everything that had existed between them was over. Serge's shrewd eyes had shown concern and surprise at Charlotte's disappearance but he had said nothing as his friend bade him a hasty goodnight. Now she sat staring into the dying embers of the fire as though in another world. The black gown accentuated her remoteness and she might as well have been the subject of a painting for all Alex could reach her. His jaw still ached from her blow and he found it difficult to reconcile himself to the exhibition of demoniac fury that had been such a contrast to her normal self control.

"Look, I've apologised to Paul and he's accepted it."

"He's too much of a gentleman not to." These were the first words she'd uttered but they fell like ice.

257

Alex ignored her goading. "That's fine but I don't live with *HIM*. I want *YOU* to believe that I'm sorry. It was bloody stupid, unfair and totally out of order. I don't know whether I had too much to drink or what happened, but I made an idiot of myself and I'm sorry."

For the first time she turned her cold green eyes to meet his. "Do you know what it must have meant to a man like Paul to have to admit that he's a gelding, just to pay for your stupidity?"

"Yes, I think I do," he answered humbly.

She nodded. "You have a remarkable change of attitude. Do you feel that now you know Paul is less of a man than you first thought, that you have the advantage?"

"As wrong as it may be. Yes, I do," he replied heatedly. "I've never been able to understand why you weren't still lovers. You're alike in every way, you come from the same backgrounds, have the same thinking and humour. There was always something that didn't fit and I always felt that he was laughing at me. Anyway it doesn't matter now, Paul's told me everything."

"Everything?" I hope not, she thought hurriedly.

"I think so. Look, Charlotte, I don't want to come between you and Paul. You're old friends and no-one has the right to break it up. He's told me how much he needs you. He even said that if it wasn't for you, he'd be unable to work and live the way he does, that he'd be in a wheelchair."

"A slight exaggeration perhaps, but certainly the pain would be unbearable and he *would* become more and more dependent on drugs."

"But why did you both have to keep it secret?"

"Simply because it's not the done thing to discuss another man's masculinity, or lack of it. Besides, Paul has as much, if not more, pride than you."

Alex poured a large cognac for each of them. "Today, you told me for the first time that you loved me, even though you won't agree to marry me. It didn't really matter then but when I found you with Paul, bare-chested with his fly open, my first thought was, 'This is why not'. I didn't stop to think why you'd never married him, or why he'd permitted me to take you away. I was simply jealous."

"I thought you liked him."

"I do, but I've resented him from the first time we met. He's everything I'm not and I could never compete. I've told him that whenever he needs you, he *must* call. I'll make the same promise to you that I've made to him, that I'll never stand in the way again."

"You must also live with the fact Alex, that I'm not like ... other people. The longer we are together, the more you will see things that to you appear strange and inexplicable. Paul accepts that side of my nature but if you have any doubts about accepting me as I am and without question, then it would be best for both of us if we agree to part now."

"Is that what you want?" He felt a rising stab of panic.

"No. The point I'm trying to make is that you are capable of causing great hurt. You have your own ideas of what is normal and acceptable and if you subsequently discover that I don't conform to those ideas, will you be able to live with it?"

His strong arms encircled her shoulders as he pulled her roughly towards him. He was prepared to take her by force if necessary. "Sweetheart, I couldn't care less if you are Circe incarnate. Tonight was a touch of pure masculine jealousy, which I deeply regret and just to show there's no hard feelings, how about allowing me to indulge in a spot of pure masculine lust!"

Chapter Twenty One

Although the fight over Paul Kerrick had been a serious set-back in their volatile relationship, harmony had been quickly restored. It appeared that they had finally sorted out their differences and Alex accepted that she liked nothing better than a good fight to clear the air. He was determined, that *whatever* the future revealed, he would not allow himself to react in such a juvenile manner to things about which he knew nothing. He would also need all his wits to keep a tight rein on her headstrong nature.

He had just settled himself for a mornings' work when the telephone rang. It was Serge. Half an hour later, he found himself sitting at the bar of the Saracen's Head with a half pint glass of beer in front of him, listening to complaints against the police in unmarked cars, who waited in lay-bys and forest clearings, observing locals going about their daily activities.

Serge breezed in with smiles all round and seated himself at the bar, next to his friend. Already he was beginning to gain weight as a result of Mrs Lacey's excellent cooking. However, as he had remarked previously to Alex, he was more at home in Gwen's kitchen. All you had to do was eat to please her; cast-iron Mrs Lacy required homage after every meal.

"What's new with you?" greeted Alex.

Serge slowly sipped his beer. "Eleanor's pregnant," he finally announced with smug satisfaction, tempered with a perceivable nervousness and embarrassment.

"No wonder you wanted to meet here and not at the house," grinned Alex. "Gwen couldn't keep that quiet."

"Exactly. But the thing is, I don't know how it happened!"

"Christ, Serge - how old are you?"

"Don't get acid with me Alex. I mean, after all these years it takes a bit of getting used to, I can tell you. Eleanor was always told it was impossible because she'd had rheumatic fever or something when she was a kid and we've never bothered with any precautions. So you tell me how it happened."

Briefly Alex's thoughts turned back ten years to the time when he, too, had sat in a bar, listening to the announcement that he was to be a father. Life hadn't turned out that way. "How does Eleanor feel about it?" No sign of his own memories showed in his face.

"Bit uncertain, same as me."

"Well, here's to parenthood. Bet her folks are pleased, grandson, heir and all that."

"Haven't said anything. Eleanor wants to wait until it's been confirmed, just in case ..."

"Is there something wrong?"

"No, except that as neither of them expect a grandchild, we'd rather make sure it's not a false alarm. That would be down right cruel. But now, suddenly, it appears I've hit the jackpot."

"You always were a virile little sod," said Alex fondly, "Have another beer and don't worry."

"Where's her Highness today?"

Alex explained her visits to Kerrick and their conversation turned to other things as the bar began to fill with lunch-time drinkers. Men who worked on the land, and popped in for the company rather than the beer. Trade would never make Bob a fortune but he preferred the convivial atmosphere of the tiny flagstoned bar, with its open log fire to a 'typically English pub', designed to bring in tourists. His customers were predominantly those referred to in a recent government White Paper on

261

Rural England, as 'deprived' by the urban well-intentioned. Ashmarsh had stubbornly refused to conform to the townsman's concept of country living, a fact that had not passed unnoticed by the newspapers reporting on The Beast. It was *"out-dated, unfriendly and unco-operative with strangers ..."*

"Hello Brian, William. Drink?"

Alex had developed a liking for Brian Carradine. The quiet little man had to put up with a lot of good natured ribbing over his wife's gossiping tongue but it never ruffled his temper. He accepted the fact that Gwen was known as the 'town crier' and even laughed a little at her himself, when she referred to her 'position' at Hunter's Moon. When all was said and done, there was no kinder soul than Gwen Carradine when anyone was in genuine trouble. She would be the first to roll up her sleeves and help out, as everyone in the village knew.

When the two older men had their drinks, the little group retired to the alcove by the fire, out of Bob's way. William Peters was a fourth generation native of Ashmarsh and admitted to being over ninety years old. His walnut stained features resembled a Durer woodcut and arthritis made it difficult in getting about. Whenever health and weather permitted, Brian Carradine would bring him down to sit in the chimney corner of the 'Saracens' to talk and gossip with his old cronies.

"William, you must know quite a lot about the Manning family, having lived here all your life. Charlotte says they weren't particularly interesting but what's your opinion?"

Alex was now known enough for William's pride in his knowledge of local families to overcome his native reticence in gossiping with outsiders. "Weren't Manning then, of course," he answered. "Family name were Neville. Some say a branch of the old Neville's from Warwick, but I don't know if it's true. I can just remember Mrs Manning's great grandfather. Old he were in my time but my Dad told me, he were a lusty old bugger when he were younger. Wasn't a maid servant or farmer's daughter safe when he was about." The

262

old boy chuckled, enjoying himself. It wasn't often that youngsters like to listen to the old stories.

"Used to ride around the countryside on his big chestnut hunter and many's a young girl bin rolled in the ditch by old Neville. Then up he'd get on that horse of 'is and off, leave the girl to shift for herself as best she could. They say that the vicar warned him not to expect a place in consecrated ground, so Ol' Neville built hi'self that tomb up in the woods and thumbed his nose at the lot of 'em."

Brian coughed, embarrassed by the rattling skeleton of Charlotte's virile ancestor. "Tales get exaggerated as time goes on, William."

The old man laughed aloud, showing broken teeth. "More's bin left out than has ever bin told about him, Brian."

"What happened to him?" prompted Alex.

"Thrown from that damned horse of his, when he was over eighty. Some said the Devil struck him down for his arrogance but my Dad told me that the old sod was drunker than a fiddler's bitch and that's what killed him."

Serge was also enjoying the story. "Rest of the family must have been pretty tame in comparison."

"Don't you believe it boy." William, gratefully accepted a refill and continued with his tale. "He left two boys and a gel. The gel married into the Hamilton family, up at The Grange, your wife's lot. Docile enough by all accounts and the new husband wasn't about to let her brothers taint his family name so she weren't allowed to see much of 'em. George the elder of the two, inherited and tried to live up to the reputation of his Pappy but he hadn't got the stamina for it. Found in bed with some bloke's wife in London and the husband shot 'im, so poor old Stewart, who'd been sent to earn his living in India had to take over the family affairs."

"That would be Charlotte's grandfather?"

"That's right. He was about my age and a real gent. Never pass you by without a word. But folks around here thought he was a bit queer like. Had all these geegaws he'd brought home from the East and some of 'em were real scary. Not today, of course, see all sorts of foreign stuff but then it were enough to frit the living daylights out of yer when he told stories of the strange things he'd seen. Knew all about 'erbs and medicines and things, too."

Alex had been under the impression that Charlotte's family had been reserved county folk but William's illuminating saga shed a different light. "What was the next generation like?"

"Old Neville's blood were too thick to wash away and his character came out with a vengeance. This time there were two girls and two boys, and a fine looking bunch they were but you could see the strains of the old man from the day they were born.

"The eldest son, Anthony were a real bad lot. There were some scandal involving a couple 'o married women which was hushed up, so he joined the army and disappeared for a while. Course, there weren't the money around there'd been in Old Neville's day but that didn't stop Anthony none. He took up with some other married woman and this one shot *herself* rather than face the scandal of a divorce. Last we 'eard he took part in that commando raid at St Nazaire and was killed. Gwendoline, the elder daughter were a right handful. She married some Polish count and vanished when the Germans marched into Warsaw; don't know what happened to the other girl, Jennifer."

"That just left Charlotte's father?"

"Peter Neville had married some lass he'd found along with some ruins over in Wales," chuckled William. "Lovely, gentle woman she was, daughter takes after her for colouring. Everyone grieved when they died. You know, no-one would take their kiddy to a doctor if Peter Neville were home. Genius with healing he was, same as Mrs Manning is now. Very friendly with old Doc Howard, sit for hours in this very corner arguing about their 'erbs and potions but the Doc hadn't got his gift for science. Folk from the other villages tried to make summat out of it, you know, causing trouble about following the Old Ways but nobody outside knew for sure. Still they've all gone now," reflected the old man sadly.

Alex and Serge were still laughing over William's revelations when they arrived back at Hunter's Moon to find Charlotte had returned from Paul's earlier than expected.

"We've just been treated to a fascinating thesis on your family history," teased Serge. "Why don't you make them the subject of your next book. They're worth a literary fortune."

"They're really rather commonplace."

"Commonplace!" echoed Alex. "Not the way old William tells it. You never told me you were descended from a long line of witches and warlocks. The only one he couldn't account for was your Aunt Jennifer. What happened to her?"

"Jennifer? Oh, she was the family artist who contracted syphilis during her short but flamboyant lifetime and died in a Paris lunatic asylum."

"I don't believe you," Alex responded but he could tell from her manner that she wasn't joking. Her mind was pre-occupied and she wasn't about to waste time on frivolity, so he let the subject drop.

Serge, however, was too full of his own euphoria and with a yell, threw Charlotte back on the sofa. Pinning her down with his own body weight he began nibbling her ear and in a stage whisper murmured, "As the wife's now with child, I think it's time for me to take a mistress!"

"Oh God!" said Alex, going out to make the coffee and leaving Charlotte to fend for herself.

"How do you suggest we're all going to fit into this arrangement?" she queried, gasping for breath.

"I'll wait until I get you to the big City then it's pre-natal visits and literary luncheons for them, good straight raw sex for us." With a powerful but good natured shove, Charlotte sent him sprawling onto the floor.

"So much for the feudal baron routine," remarked Alex, sticking a coffee mug in his friend's hand.

"Perhaps I'd better stick to gentle seduction," shrugged

Serge gently biting Charlotte's knee. "Isn't there some way of telling whether it's a boy or girl with a wedding ring on a bit of string?"

"I don't do fortunes and that's for women."

"How about a wager and the winner pays for a celebratory dinner?"

"Good idea. I say a boy," said Serge getting in first.

"A girl," was Alex's choice.

"One of each," said Charlotte.

"The last time I had a bet with you I landed up married," replied Serge with an edge of suspicion.

"I was right wasn't I? And you didn't pay up."

"That's the point, I'm making," countered Serge, ignoring the second statement. "If it was *anyone* else's suggestion I wouldn't take a bit of notice but you ... Has Eleanor said anything?"

"Only that she thought she was expecting but you wanted to be sure before making the grand announcement to family."

"Twins! *Please* say you're joking."

Gwen Carradine was worried. Charlotte had been away for five days and under normal circumstances, Anna remained in the house to take care of any queries. However, she had not been seen during the whole of the previous day and on arriving that morning, Gwen discovered that her bed was still undisturbed. What made it even more unsettling was the fact that usually, if she had to go out, the telephone answering machine was switched on to take any messages but Gwen had done little else other than answer it.

"I don't know what to do," she told Brian, who had called at the house, knowing his wife was concerned. "I don't like to bother Mrs Manning, in case it's nothing."

The sensible little man thought for a moment. "You say she's never gone orf like this before, love? I mean, girls today have boyfriends and stay out at night. Mrs Manning

266

might have been told and if she hasn't, you'd just be getting the girl into trouble."

"But it's not like Anna to go off without saying *anything*. I think something's happened to her."

"Don't start letting your imagination run away with you, Gwen. She just gone orf somewhere."

"Brian. You call London for me, you know I don't like them 'phones and talking to strangers."

"Gwen, you're making a fool of yourself."

Gwen was adamant, the more she thought about it all, the more concerned she became until her only resolve was to get in touch with Charlotte Manning as quickly as possible. She was frightened she had delayed long enough as it was.

"*Please* Brian, they like you. She won't mind."

Brian gave a resigned sigh. Her concern was beginning to affect him; he knew and accepted his wife's shortcomings but it wasn't like Gwen either, to make a mountain out of a mole hill. "What's the number?"

"I don't know!"

After another half an hour's deliberation, Brian finally called The Grange and spoke to the Colonel, finding himself pouring out the whole story to the old military man. With his usual brisk efficiency, George Hamilton, took charge and assuring Brian that he had done the right thing, promised to get hold of Charlotte and tell her to call home. It was not until much later that afternoon that the Colonel managed to locate them and when Charlotte finally called Hunter's Moon, Gwen was in tears.

"Sorry to interfere in your affairs, Mrs Manning," apologised Brian humbly, "but Gwen here's got herself into a real state. There's still been no word from the young lady and that's two days now she's been gone."

Charlotte's mind worked swiftly. Why, she did not know but like Gwen, for some reason she felt the stirrings of unrest. They all knew Anna too well to believe she would go off without telling anyone of her plans.

267

"Brian, call Alan Morris, the Inspector who's been dealing with the other business. Give my name and they'll put you straight through to him. Tell him exactly what's happened and that we'll be leaving London in about an hour. We should be in Ashmarsh by eight at the latest. And Brian .. thank you"

"That's all right, Miss."

With a shaking hand Brian Carradine, dialled the number for Alan Morris and after a series of delays, he was eventually connected with the Incident Room. After giving him all the details as Charlotte had instructed, the little man took Gwen's hand in his own and sat down at the kitchen table to wait.

Within twenty.minutes, Alan Morris had joined them after looking through Anna's diary and with Gwen's help, searching her room, they could still find no reason for the girl's disappearance. Morris had stopped visiting Hunter's Moon while the house-to-house-enquiries were carried out in the area because, as he had explained to Alex, their friendship could jeopardise the outcome and he wanted no outside interference now that the new man had taken over the investigation.

Now he was back at Hunter's Moon with another case - the disappearance of Anna Fenton - when earlier that morning he had been planning to visit the household on a less personal, but no less important, matter.

Weeks of heavy rainfall had caused the steep cliff at the far end of the dis-used quarry to collapse, bringing down hundreds of tons of earth and part of the fencing which separated Charlotte's land from her neighbour's. Although the quarry was not his responsibility, the farmer investigated the subsidence which was threatening to carry away his boundary markers because he was anxious to protect his cattle. On closer inspection he discovered a human skull protruding out of a pocket of clay and immediately called the police.

Alan Morris paled slightly at the news of another body

on his patch but the fear had turned to merriment when the report came through that the remains were a little too old to be of interest to the police. The body had been lying there for a few hundred years and would become the province of science. When the debris and rubble had been cleared away, the clay was found to contain a burial pit containing some dozen or more skeletons.

By the time Charlotte and Alex arrived back in Ashmarsh, the house was full of people wanting to talk to her. Deep down, in her inner-most being, Charlotte knew Anna was dead but she was afraid to voice aloud her fears, thereby superstitiously suppressing the reality of her friend's fate. Inwardly she wanted to scream and rage but years of self discipline forced her to maintain icy calm while she listened to the details surrounding Anna's disappearance. Alex watched the fine lines around her eyes deepen as she concentrated her efforts on answering the questions put to her by the WPC.

Having heard that Anna's car had been located, Alan Morris had already left to organise a search of the woods, leaving Carole Marchant to talk with Charlotte. Uneasy and on her guard with Morris's new team-mate, Charlotte mechanically responded to her enquiries, giving no more than simple, straight-forward answers to the careful probing. The interview was interrupted by sounds of more people entering the main hallway and Charlotte breathed a sigh of relief as she went out to investigate.

The man taking charge of the archaeological excavation, Professor Jonathon Boyd had chosen that moment to arrive with his assistant, having spent all day on site; both men more concerned with 900 year old dead than the disappearance of a secretary. Boyd wanted Charlotte's assurances that no-one else would be involved in the excavations which would ensure him untold fame in his chosen field - and possibly a knighthood. This was history in the making.

Amongst the bedlam of raised voices Gwen and Brian

269

bustled around the kitchen making coffee and sandwiches, glad of something to do to take their minds off the awful fear that Anna might come to harm. Serge and Eleanor had driven straight to Hunter's Moon rather than wait for any news to arrive at The Grange and tried to help Alex placate the rising annoyance of WPC Marchant. Paul was waiting in the study as Charlotte came in with the Professor, arguing the toss over Charlotte's insistence that as soon as the scientific process had been completed, the bodies of the Iceni were to be re-interred near the circle in an hermetically sealed container.

The archaeologists were barely able to suppress their excitement since the burial pit was one of the most remarkable finds in ancient British history. Preliminary investigations had already unearthed a quantity of identifiable artifacts and weaponry which suggested that the site was indeed associated with the last great battle between Iceni and Roman. The word was out and competition fierce.

As a result, Professor Boyd was quite happy to agree to relinquish a collection of discoloured bones once they'd undergone scientific examination by his laboratory, on the understanding that he could carry off any prize that was discovered during the excavation. Two museums were already offering prime exhibition space for the collection and judging from the items already unearthed, his name would be linked to the most fabulous discovery in ancient British archaeology to date. Both Charlotte and Paul realised that Antedios's gold torc alone would justify Boyd's generosity in handing back the bones.

Despite persistent requests from the Professor, Charlotte refused to allow them to extend the excavation to within the area of the stone circle and insisted that the metal cage remain in place until the dig was over. She gave the reason that her parent's remains were interred in the circle which was reluctantly accepted by the archaeologist, especially on being given as a gift, a copy of Peter Neville's notes on his own excavations

270

and a valuable first edition of his book on stone circles.

"But your parents aren't buried here," remarked Paul quietly as the Professor left. "Their bodies were never found."

"I know that and you know that, but they won't bother to check. If they start digging around they're sure to discover who is buried there"

"Antedios?"

"No, I think they'll find him amongst the others. He was probably killed before he could get away. The circle is the burial place of Boudica's daughters whom Antedios poisoned so that they wouldn't be Roman victims all over again. The Romans must have caught up with him and his party just after the girls were buried. That's why he's still here, he didn't have time to make any alternative preparations. Once the remains are re-interred, we'll re-consectrate the circle and then they'll rest in hallowed ground again. We owe him that."

"That's assuming he *is* amongst the dead. Perhaps this impromptu discovery of the burial pit will neutralise his power," suggested Paul hopefully.

"It might have done in the beginning but since the first deaths he's been drawing power from his victims, that's why he appears so much larger now. No, Antedios will not rest until he has the Black One's head on a charger and I'm the only one who can give it to him."

Chapter Twenty Two

"If I see anymore of these, I'm going to resign" P. C. Derek Thompkins told Morris, as he tried to stop the bile rising in his throat.

Alan Morris rubbed his chin thoughtfully, but he could not rid himself of the apprehension of breaking the news to Charlotte Manning that Anna Fenton was dead. "Don't be too hasty, boy," he muttered, his hand on the Constable's shoulder. "This one has all the earmarks of a copycat killing. It's different from the rest."

"Don't see how" retorted the young P.C.

"Because this is the only instance where the victim lost her knickers! If I'm not mistaken, this is a rape case that went sour and then dummied up to resemble the others."

Morris went back to where the mutilated body of Anna lay partially hidden in the undergrowth. He kept out of the forensic team's way but his shrewd eyes missed nothing. The corpse, which was once an attractive young girl, lay on its back with the legs parted obscenely. Clothing had been cut away in a frenzy and the torso viciously lacerated but the scene lacked the grisly disembowelment usually connected with The Beast. Her face was untouched, as though the killer was reluctant to mar the flawless complexion; the expression was almost peaceful, suggesting that the girl was unconscious or already dead when the rape and mutilations were carried out.

Anna's death was different in other aspects, insofar that there were plenty of footprints in the ground. There were hardly any signs of a struggle, which suggested she may have known her assailant and even been lured unsuspectingly to the remote spot in the forest. It was difficult for Alan Morris to remain dispassionate in this case; he had known her as a pretty, laughing redhead and now she was a bloody, mutilated corpse.

He had reacted swiftly to Brian Carradine's call, knowing that Charlotte Manning was no alarmist and so it was just after eight in the evening when a patrol car found Anna's car in a fire-access in the woods. The search was delayed when a hoax call came through informing them of the finding of another body and it was not until late the following morning that the search party found Anna in a forest glade, some distance from the road.

Charlotte had spent the night prowling about like a caged cat, waiting for some news from the police. She deliberately withheld her own astral searching, almost too afraid of what she might find. She knew through instinct what the answer would be but she waited with the others for Alan Morris to reappear. Though her outward expression was composed, her insides seethed like a cauldron. Finally, in the early hours she had curled up in the protective curve of Alex's arm and allowed him to comfort her.

One look at Morris's face and Gwen burst into tears. Once Charlotte had taken her friend's disappearance as a serious matter, Gwen cursed herself for not doing something sooner. No matter how much Alex tried to assure her, the housekeeper blamed herself for anything that might have happened to the girl.

Alex steadied Charlotte as he mouthed the question no-one else wanted to ask. "She's dead isn't she?"

"'Fraid so."

"Was it a car accident?"

Alan Morris was not usually a man to take liberties but

before answering he sat himself down and motioned for Gwen to pour the coffee she had prepared. His actions spoke louder than any report. The watching pairs of eyes bored into him and a lump formed in his throat.

Alex sat Charlotte down and stood behind her chair, steadying her shoulders in a firm grip. "What happened?" Charlotte's voice was clipped and tight.

"It's my guess that your little girl was raped and then stabbed. Obviously we'll need to wait for the autopsy report to confirm it but my guess is that's what happened."

"But there's more than that," Alex prompted, feeling Charlotte's tension transmitting signals under the pressure of his fingers.

"The killer tried to make it look like the work of The Beast. Her body had been mutilated, probably with the same knife he used to kill her. She'd been dragged to a clearing and hidden in the undergrowth where he'd raped her, however, there were very little signs of a struggle where the murder actually took place. This is all unofficial as yet ...." he trailed off.

"And no one's seen anything or come forward?" asked Gwen.

"To be honest, we don't know which way to turn. There was a hoax call about a body found in the woods and that's what delayed us finding Anna. I think it was the man who killed her. We haven't got around to assigning the investigations and that's why I wanted to tell you myself. I may not be dealing with Anna's murder because I'm too close and I didn't want you to hear it from a stranger."

"Thank you Alan, we appreciate your concern."

"Thanks. No doubt I'll be speaking to you again shortly, but in the meantime, if there is anything, give me a call."

"Thanks Alan," Alex showed him out and returned to find Charlotte had vanished and Gwen could not tell him where she was.

In the shade of an oak, Charlotte crouched with her back

to the bole, listening to the bird song. Wild and thrilling, the music from the feathered throats rose and fell on the breeze, heralding the season of rebirth and warmth. She *knew* who was responsible for Anna's death; as sure as though she had personally witnessed the attack and violation of her friend but whilst she had the power at her fingertips to deal with the offender, something held her back. A vague, uncomfortable stirring demanded a more earthly form of justice.

Perhaps a subconscious message told her that Anna wanted it this way, rather than have her killer blasted into eternity, his guilt unchallenged. Also, to avenge Anna's death in such a manner would be a violation of her own code of ethics and one she had adhered to unswervingly for centuries. To jeopardise her own credo purely for personal revenge would serve no valid purpose.

To cut through methodical police procedure, evidence, forensic examination and a trial was tedious but necessary. But the gods never ignore a sincere petitioner. It was later the following day that her prayers were answered. The SIO had accepted the preliminary SOCO evidence that this latest death was not connected with The Beast, leaving Alan Morris free to investigate the murder of Anna Fenton despite his involvement with Hunter's Moon.

In truth, Morris was also relieved. As a policeman it offended his sensibilities that a killer who had stalked the countryside under a cloak of darkness in the past months would never be brought to book. He and Charlotte Manning were the only two people who accepted that the murderer an entire police force was searching for was inhuman, and that the mystery of the killings would never be solved. He had dreaded the day when he would present his findings to his superiors, but now the responsibility was no longer his and he could apply himself to finding the bastard who tried to emulate The Beast's grisly technique. In the meantime, he trusted Charlotte to sort out the psychic mess according to her own lights.

His relief however, was still tinged with misgivings. He too had a strong presentiment where the finger would point. Subtle enquires proved that John Sinclair was not in the country when Anna met her death and was in fact in France. He had booked a package tour to Paris and had taken a flight from Heathrow, two days before the girl died. Morris, however, who hated investigations that turned up one of his own men, still harboured a suspicion over the reaction Sinclair had taken against the occupants of Hunter's Moon. Before he issued instructions for passenger lists on the ferries and flights to and from France to be checked, he wanted something more to go on than mere gut reaction.

Charlotte found him waiting for her when she returned with Rev. Branson from Alicia Howard's funeral. The grand old lady had finally been laid to rest beside the husband she had loved so much in life, and had faithfully remained devoted to in death. There had been no children of the marriage and with the few bequests to friends and neighbours, the old lady had left her entire estate in a trust fund to be managed by Archie Branson and Charlotte, for the benefit of the people of Ashmarsh. Her husband's books, her own personal effects and jewellery she had left to Charlotte.

"You've been surrounded by death, love," muttered Morris familiarly but with sympathy. He had a great deal of respect for this strong, intelligent woman.

"A man's dying is more the survivor's affair than his own," she quoted with a weak smile.

"If you don't feel up to it, I can come back later."

"Ask your questions. Please stay," she added as Archie Branson made to leave. "I have something to ask of the Inspector when he's finished, and I would like you to remain."

Morris was intrigued. He knew Charlotte mistrusted the clergy and although she looked on Branson as a friend, he was still puzzled. "Gwen has finally remembered that Anna took a telephone call early on Wednesday morning and she

276

said that Anna was a little bit shaken by it. Surprised. Even a little bit angry. But she thinks it was a personal call by the way she lowered her voice so's not to be overheard. Apart from one short call telling me to 'phone my publisher, I hadn't spoken to her at all," Charlotte frowned.

"Well, apart from that call and the hoax, we have a complete dead end. Did she mention anyone she might have met up with when she stayed over in London?" Charlotte's face was impassive but her sharp green eyes bore into his. "It crossed my mind too, but he's in Paris on a package tour."

A sharp hiss escaped between her teeth. Her solution was a long shot, but she would still like to try. After all, Morris himself had originally suggested supernatural phenomena without any prompting from her. Perhaps he would be open to her unorthodox methods of criminal investigation and it wasn't *impossible* for Sinclair to have slipped back on the same day, killed Anna and re-joined his tour.

"This is why I wanted Archie to stay. Alan, would you be prepared to sit in on a seance where we ask Anna *herself* who the killer is?"

"Christ!" breathed the detective in disbelief.

"I know it wouldn't be admissible as evidence," continued Charlotte quickly, "but if you had the answers you could perhaps frighten the murderer into revealing himself. If Archie is willing to act as an independent witness - and he doesn't believe in clairvoyance I hasten to add - we could find out from Anna."

"Look, this is taking things a bit far."

"No further than suspecting a psychic manifestation has been on the rampage."

Morris looked embarrassed at Archie Branson's surprised face. "Would it work?" he asked hastily in order to avoid any further discussion.

"I don't know unless I try," she answered innocently.

Morris was doubtful but at the same time fascinated. "What would you want me to do?" he asked cautiously.

277

"Nothing. The dead don't always come up with the expected and they don't always perform on cue. That's why they're useless in laboratory experiments, some form of astral perverseness I suspect. I just want you to listen. Paul will help and if there is anything you want to know, write it down and pass the message to him."

"I'm game," said Morris, "What about you Rev?"

Archie was dubious. "If it's really important, of course. Who else will be here?" he asked, not wishing his parishioners to get wind of their Vicar engaging in occult practices. He also recalled being dowsed with water during a previous demonstration.

"Besides ourselves and Paul, there will be Alex and Serge."

"Okay by me."

"Yes, of course."

Alex was more than annoyed when he heard of Charlotte's plans for the evening but on her insistence he called Serge, requesting his presence. He and Eleanor were both at The Grange but Charlotte felt that in her present condition, Eleanor should not be exposed to any effects from the psychic ether. Without question, Paul confirmed that he would help.

Taking only a light supper and a bath, she wore a tight fitting black leotard which covered her from throat to ankle while the sitting room was prepared for her experiment. The fire was piled with logs, so that the flames lit the room by casting a weird flickering shadow-play on the walls, and the scent of sandalwood from a Tibetan incense burner, quickly pervaded the room.

In a corner, furthest away from the fire, she had arranged a plain buffet with drinks for the men; her preparations were only just complete when Paul Kerrick arrived. He barely responded to Alex's greeting, his face drawn with concern and anger as he took Charlotte's hands between his own. He was about to speak but a secret look passed between them and he remained silent. Serge arrived next, curiosity outweighing the trepidation as they waited for Alan Morris and Rev. Branson to make up the number. After a few moments of preliminary chatter and when everyone had a drink, Charlotte explained what she was about to do and gave them their explicit instructions.

"I will go into a trance and attempt to contact Anna. I will remain horizontal on the sofa in front of the fire throughout and no matter what happens, do *NOT* under any circumstances attempt to wake me once I've gone under. I don't know what form, if any, the materialisation will take but you needn't be frightened of it." Alex made an exasperated noise in his throat but she ignored him.

"The point of the exercise is to obtain the name of Anna's killer. You have been asked here because I trust you all and to prove that there is no trickery, I want you to examine the sofa, cushions, anything you like to satisfy yourselves that there are no hidden props." She stood in front of Alan Morris with her arms above her head. "Just to satisfy yourself that there are no hidden devices." The leotard was so tight that any concealment would have been obvious but Alan Morris expertly conducted a body search as requested.

While the others examined the sofa, Charlotte poured herself a fruit juice. Paul had no doubt in her powers and joined her by the table as she began to light the candles.

"I don't want you to do it," he urged in a undertone. "They don't know it but this is necromancy, not a normal seance!"

"I have no choice now. Trust me Paul, I know what I'm doing."

"What are you two whispering about?" Alex asked.

"Do you realise how dangerous this is?" Paul challenged him.

"Paul!"

"This isn't a little old ladies' table rapping session. This is necromancy. She's damned well going to try to raise the dead!"

Charlotte walked away from them and joined the others by the fire. "You can smoke, drink, eat and talk quietly amongst yourselves while I go under, it won't disturb me in the slightest. But once I've gone under don't cause any sudden noises or movements. Paul will communicate any questions to me."

Having made perfectly sure everyone understood what was about to happen, she stretched flat on the sofa cushions, with a cushion under her head. The firelight cast deep shadows on her face, even throwing tiny shadows from her lashes onto her cheek, reminding Alex of the stone effigy on the tomb in Ashmarsh church. With closed eyes, she began to relax and her breathing grew shallower until finally there was hardly any rise and fall of her chest. Some fifteen minutes had passed and the company were beginning to feel a little embarrassed over the ridiculousness of the situation. All except Paul, who watched her like a hawk, never taking his eyes from her still form, not even when a remark was addressed to him.

"Perhaps nothing will happen," said Alex hopefully.

"Shhh! Something already has."

The flames from the fire had died down and in the darkness of the room, now illuminated by candle light, they saw a fine luminous vapour trailing from her mouth and nostrils. Like mist rising from the river bank, the vapour began to drift upwards, drawing its energy from the recumbent figure. The mass became denser and tinged with a greenish light, until it hovered some three feet above Charlotte's head.

For a time it hung motionless in the air, a thin column of green vaporous smoke, until finally a shape began to form inside. The contours rounded and became firmer, the deep eye sockets were cast in shadow, giving the face a mask-like appearance. Serge felt a gasp burst from him involuntarily as he suppressed a shudder. It wasn't the form of the remembered flesh and blood Anna; this image was far more terrible than any of them had expected.

The fine features of the girl were now completely recognisable but the greenish hue of her face served to remind them that the figure before them had been dead for several days. The curly red hair, deep blue eyes and fresh complexion were no longer evident but no-one doubted that they were looking into the face of Death. In contrast to the heavy incense, there was the astringent smell of damp earth and rotting wood.

"You called me." The voice was certainly Anna's but it was muffled and slightly distorted, like a bad tape recording. "You want to know how I died and who I name as my killer?" The phraseology was strangely formal and stilted, totally unlike the bubbling voice of the living Anna.

Paul responded. "We ask you to name those responsible for your death and tell us how you came to die."

The expression on the face showed intense sadness and as the voice responded, the words became less formal. "I was stupid and did not listen to the advice given by my friends. If I had listened to them, I would have not departed this life just as it had begun in the service of The Goddess. The one you seek is John Sinclair. He persuaded me to meet him in the woods while Charlotte was away. In my heart I knew it to be foolish but I still loved him. Tell Charlotte I am sorry."

"She can hear you," answered Paul.

"I left my car and he drove to a remote part of the wood. I began to be frightened when he began admonishing me for my association with the followers of the devil. He was becoming hysterical. I finally realised that he was unable to control his rage and tried to get out of the car, but he pulled me back, hitting my head against the car door. When I recovered, I found myself lying on the grass and realised that he....." the voice trailed of in a sob.

"Go on," Paul voice was firm but coaxing.

"He'd raped me while I was unconscious." The voice was firmer again. "I called him the most contemptible of men and told him that I did not betray my own beliefs as easily as he seemed to be able to betray his own. I was still dizzy from the blow and everything went dark again. Then he stabbed me - when I was helpless."

As the apparition spoke, dark stains appeared against the vaporous fabric of the shroud. More and more appeared and the voice took on a hoarse choking sound. "I was already dead when he mutilated my body but my spirit recoiled in anger at what he had done, and that is why I was unable to leave immediately." The face was now contorted with grief and not one of them remained unmoved by the experience.

Morris quickly scribbled a note which he passed to Paul. "Do you know what happened to the knife?"

"He pushed it into a rabbit hole near to my body, almost an arms length inside the burrow."

"That's why we didn't find it," muttered Morris to himself and scribbled another note.

"Do you know that Sinclair was supposed to be in France when you died?"

There was a silence until the voice responded with uncharacteristic forcefulness. "John Sinclair is my murderer and I want revenge!"

"Inspector Morris is listening to you and he promises you justice."

The voice emitted a coarse laugh. "Your justice! Have you not discovered that there is a higher power to dispense justice?"

The voice laughed again and the image began to fade as mist will disperse when caught by the wind, leaving a heavy oppressed atmosphere in the room. Charlotte lay with her head turned to one side, one arm dangling over the cushions. Her eyes were open but there was no sign of movement. Alex sprung to shake her but Paul restrained him. Quickly taking her pulse and listening to her breathing, he shook his head.

"She won't come out of this much before midday tomorrow. Take her upstairs and put her to bed. I don't think any of you realise what a tremendous strain this has been. In fact it was downright, bloody dangerous for her to attempt it."

"What exactly have we seen?" asked Serge nervously. His usual calm had been ruffled but he would not have been excluded from the experience for the world.

"You've just seen a psychic demonstration by one of the most fantastic minds in the civilised world," Kerrick answered thoughtfully.

Chapter Twenty Three

Alan Morris played his hand carefully in allowing John Sinclair to return to duty before pouncing, simply because there was no plausible reason to question him over the crime. Using the excuse of the detective's previous involvement, he informally asked him to listen to a recording which he hoped might throw a light on why Anna had been killed. Unwittingly Sinclair sat down with Morris and Carole Marchant under the vague impression that he was listening to a hoax telephone confession. The WPC believed the tape had been sent by a local spiritualist and was both amused and sceptical about the experiment. Within moments, however, Sinclair turned ashen as the distorted but unmistakable voice of Anna Fenton echoed around the interview room.

With the words supposedly from Anna's own mouth taken down on a portable tape recorder during the seance, Morris confronted his former colleague with her accusation and to his immense surprise and relief, the girl's ex-lover wasted no time in admitting his guilt. At first Sinclair was remorseful but as he answered Morris's probing, his manner became more and more belligerent, and threatening. He was charged and remanded in custody, much to the satisfaction of Alan Morris and Carole Marchant, both of whom had been forced to listen to the ranting and the tears for over three hours.

Sinclair had apparently convinced himself that Anna was an innocent in the clutches of evil and his feelings swung from a passionate loathing to that of knight errant. One moment he saw her as the girl he loved possessed by demons and on the other hand she appeared to him as Lilith. During their last meeting he had contrived to persuade her to redeem herself and return to the Church, but his love had swiftly evaporated on her angry defence of her employer. The knife had flashed and the sinner was slain.

Fortunately for Morris, WPC Marchant and another officer had also obtained a recorded confession that the obsessed Sinclair had killed Alison and Gail before an intense interview with his solicitor prevented any further indiscretions. There were whispers of an insanity plea but the fact that he had booked his Paris trip, caught the next flight back and then rejoined the party a day later, smacked too much of pre-meditation. It would be some time before he actually came to trial and since there was reason enough to believe that he would jump bail or even commit suicide if given the opportunity, Morris was taking no chances. Nevertheless the court appearance when Sinclair should be committed for trial, produced a few more surprises that even the Inspector hadn't foreseen.

Alan Morris sat in the kitchen at Hunter's Moon, the local newspaper open on the table announcing 'Beast Unfit To Plead'. There was stunned disbelief all round. "I was speechless when his brief claimed that he was The Ashmarsh Beast and his insanity had manifested itself as a message from God to cleanse the world of heathen practices. That apparently explains why his victims died near the stone circle."

"What about Emily Trasker?" responded Alex sarcastically.

"We haven't got around to specifics," answered Morris hollowly. "The bugger actually sat and smiled at me and I can't do anything about it. He's no more insane than I am but it offers a solution to The Beast, so everyone's keen to accept his confession. I doubt if they will accept that he's unfit to plead but I'm not putting any money on it."

"Damn it all, Alan, even the Ripper couldn't get away with

285

being unfit to plead, how did Sinclair manage it?"

Morris shrugged. "Beats me. What I objected to most of all was the inferrence that he had a justifiable reason since Anna was employed here as Charlotte's secretary. They went into great detail about your occult connections as if this were justification enough for his actions. These buggers," he tapped the newspaper, "lapped up every word."

"Don't worry Alan, I've weathered worse storms. Perhaps it is time to appeal to a Higher Law."

The response brought no reaction from Morris but Alex glanced at her sharply. He was remembering something that had been said on his first visit to Ashmarsh. Then he had dismissed it as affected nonsense - now he wasn't so sure.

Later that day, Charlotte and Paul Kerrick strolled through the woods and stopped at a gateway leading through to neighbouring meadowland. "So what are you going to do about Antedios? You can't expect him to understand the intricacies of the 20th century legal system, and once he knows nothing is going to happen to Sinclair, he'll be on the rampage again."

"There are two choices," she answered. "On one hand we have a spirit which has proven itself to be honourable and loyal but can only be controlled in this instance by total annihilation. On the other we have flesh which has betrayed both its religious principle and the law it was supposed to uphold. The flesh can be destroyed but still has the opportunity to work out its own *karma* in its next incarnation."

Paul leant on the gate with a grass clamped between his teeth. "And you're still reluctant to destroy Antedios?"

"Wouldn't you be? Paul, I want you to put the question to those who were present on the night when we first contacted Antedios, but you must ensure they understand that we are not talking about personal vengeance. If the Sinclair problem remains unsolved, Antedios will remain earthbound and dangerous. It can be sorted but the decision must be unanimous."

286

"Can't Antedios carry out his own execution?"

"I thought of that but his powers are obviously limited to the immediate area of his burial place, or I'm sure he would have found a way. Is your vision clear over this?"

"As clear as the roebuck in the thicket," her companion muttered ruefully.

Anna's body had been released for burial and her family had requested that she be interred in Ashmarsh churchyard, amongst the people she loved. The sun shone briefly between the showers and as the coffin was lowered into the grave, a passing breeze shook the overhanging birch trees, sending a cascade of raindrops onto the lid. Although Anna had been born a Catholic, her parents asked Archie Branson to conduct the service, touched by the whole village paying their respects to their daughter. The floral tributes lay either side of the cobbled pathway, glistening with crystal droplets from the showers. Every home had sent flowers, from the tiny hand-picked posy to the elaborate wreath from Charlotte's publisher.

The interior of the church was Charlotte's personal tribute to her murdered friend. The local florist had been working for two days to arrange the mass of white blooms. Contrasting sharply against the whiteness of the blossoms were splashes of scarlet - like blood. The effect was a little theatrical but Charlotte appeared to have developed a taste for the dramatic and Alex dare not interfere. Likewise the rooms at Hunter's Moon where the funeral breakfast was being held, were also a mass of white and scarlet flowers. Gwen Carradine had ignored Charlotte's request to bring in outside caterers. She hated funerals, particularly of folk she knew, and she made her excuse that she would do this one last task for young Anna.

Since Mr and Mrs Fenton had no knowledge of Anna's defection to the pagan faith, the Rev. Branson read from *The Book of Ruth*; an analogy that was not lost on the non-

Christian congregation. Archie guessed rather than knew that Anna had chosen the Old Ways and did not want to offend her memory amongst the villagers or her family. Like Solomon, he chose wisely. Although deeply touched by Charlotte's suggestion that her friend be laid to rest in the Neville mausoleum, the Fenton's preferred the site of the old churchyard for their daughter's final resting place.

After the mourners had left, Alex and Charlotte faced each other across the sitting room in silence. Because of the lengthy meetings with the television company, Alex was spending days away from home and it seemed to him that Charlotte was becoming more and more introverted as time passed. He was reluctant to plead domestic problems so early in his new career, especially as the pilot show had provoked such a positive response from the viewing public, but he would have gladly sacrificed it all just to have everything back the way it was. He hoped that now the funeral was over, she would snap out of the blackness that was consuming her from within.

Finally, she pushed one of the cats aside and got to her feet. Walking over to the windows, she stared out into the night for a few moments before speaking. "I'm meeting with the coven tonight, do you wish to come?"

"Not tonight," he responded. "And I don't think you should go. You're letting this whole business get out of hand. You don't even know if Sinclair will get off on an insanity plea but you're acting as if it were a foregone conclusion. There's nothing you can do."

The eyes that turned on him were cold and slightly mocking. "Do *you* really believe he's The Ashmarsh Beast?"

"Damn it, he's confessed!"

"And the police have accepted it because they haven't got a clue who the real killer is. You *know* who's responsible Alex, you just prefer to ignore it!"

He got up to put more logs on the fire. "Look Charlotte, enough's enough! You can go along to keen and wail or

288

whatever it is you do in a coven, when one of your own dies, but get it over with and forget it. You're powerless against the law. I appreciate that some pretty unpleasant accusations have been aimed at you in the press but it will blow over. Let's get on with living ..." But he was talking to an empty room.

For the first time in months, a candle burned in the narrow window of the mausoleum. The same people were present with the addition of a surprising sixth person - Michael Hughes. The boy's eyes were wide with wonder as he gazed around the Sanctuary, taking in the details of the ancient lamps and the exquisite inlay of the magic circle. His rapt expression was one in keeping with what one would expect from an acolyte confronting the magnificence of Deity for the first time.

Charlotte noticed immediately that the usual stang cut from the ash tree had been replaced by one of blackthorn and without anyone speaking she learned the decision of the coven members as to the fate of John Sinclair. Again her eyes turned back to the boy as Paul divined the reason for her concern.

"Since Michael's release from prison he's been initiated into the Craft," explained Paul. "As you know, we don't normally accept anyone until their eighteenth birthday but we felt these were exceptional circumstances."

Charlotte nodded. "But is it a good idea for someone so young to be expected to experience the repercussions of destructive magic before they understand the full implications of becoming a witch?"

Not yet versed in coven etiquette, Michael answered before his mother could prevent him. "I've lost Gail and been accused of her murder. I've been locked in prison and told I'd never be freed. I've been questioned and bullied for hours on end by social workers, police and psychiatrists and I never talked. On top of that, the person responsible walks free!"

289

"We're not here to take care of the matter for personal motives - which in truth, we *all* have. We are here to raise the power to prevent any more deaths in retribution for the desecration of the circle. Remember that. And if any of you are unable to participate in this ceremony without rancour or bitterness, then you must leave now!" No-one moved in response to her words.

"So mote it be!"

Six people clad in black robes with the cowl pulled well over their faces, stood inside the circle. None of them looked on the ritual as being a frivolous undertaking; all other avenues had been explored and there was nothing else left that could be used in its place. Each member knew the risk he or she was taking in using the rite of cursing, because the depths of emotion plumbed during the ritual would no doubt upset the equilibrium of the coven for some time to come. Each was aware that once the negative aspect of magic has been brought to the fore, it would be extremely difficult to suppress and control it again. Nevertheless they were willing to take that risk in order to release Antedios from his earthly bond.

The next few weeks were the most painfully frustrating Alex had ever spent. He was almost convinced at times that Charlotte was on the verge of madness. Her normal rationality had vanished; she was transformed into a remote automaton which functioned, made the right noises and spent a lot of her time absorbed in an intense brooding silence. He desperately tried to interest her in his work, and although the reviews were even more positive than predicted, he had a morbid fear that his whole world was about to crumble.

The powerful barrier she had erected between them was insurmountable and he could find no way to reach her. If he turned to her in the night, her whole body stiffened with rejection and after one abortive attempt at stimulating desire, he made no further attempt to touch her. In the

darkness she lay with her eyes open, staring into the blackness and when she thought he was asleep, she prowled
through the house on soundless feet. He felt as though he
was part of some profound primitive mystery of which he
was incapable of solving the riddle. His body and mind ached
for her but he remained an outsider. There was, however, no
question of him leaving her. He would look on her present
behaviour as an illness, and if it were to prove terminal, he
would stay with her until the end.

He was almost afraid to leave her alone and had asked
that either Eleanor or Serge remain at Hunter's Moon once
Gwen had left for the day. On the odd occasion when he
was away overnight Paul had volunteered to stay, although
he often commented that she would snap out of it when the
time was right; that Alex should carry on with his own affairs
and not worry. The dark circles under her eyes and the
tightly drawn flesh over the cheek bones would only vanish
when she had fought the inner conflict that was consuming
her. Paul, it seemed, knew her strength only too well to be
concerned.

Throughout her own career, Charlotte had relied solely on
her powerful memory and her phenomenal thirst for giving
and receiving knowledge. Until Alexander Martin had walked
into her life, she had never felt it necessary to resort to the
manipulative power of magical illusion that had lain dormant
for so long. The intensity of feeling she had for him sharpened her senses but it had also been responsible for her lack
of single mindedness in the channelling of her psychic
powers. She had allowed John Sinclair's negative and malevolent attitude to slip amongst them undetected; she had not
been attuned to the inner misery that had culminated in Anna's
death.

The appearance of Anna's spirit had been a product of
illusion and not necromancy, as Paul had feared; the
simulacrum used to manifest the cadaver of her dead friend
came from her own mind - not beyond the grave. She had

291

already detected the truth by visiting the scene of the crime and letting the impressions in the forest clearing speak for themselves. The discovery of the whereabouts of the murder weapon was academic; by seeking out impressions left on the inanimate object, it was easy for her to discover its hiding place.

Nevertheless the grisly thought form had produced the desired affect on the watchers and none of them doubted her, not even Paul, who was no stranger to occult phenomena. Anything less dramatic and theatrical would not have produced the same results and while her earthly form remained in a self-induced trance, her spirit was travelling out across the astral in pursuit of the departed murderer. Although the demonstration of psychic materialisation was not exactly fraudulent, it had not been entirely honest either.

The real test of her strength, however, would take every ounce of energy she could summon from the core of the earth itself. This time there would be no illusion or theatricals; this would be a demonstration of ancient magic from one whose power extended back across the centuries to the beginning of time. From the new moon up to the full, her magical powers would wax strong along with the cycle of the lunar body. If she allowed Alex to make love to her now, the emotional effects of orgasm would deplete her psychic strength which was generating an immense store of electro-magnetic energy. The only chance she had of resisting him was to remain behind her protective barrier.

She was also anxious to avoid the scornful and often angry exchanges resulting from any attempt at explaining that the practice of magic necessitated a mastery of everything - evil as well as good, cruelty as well as mercy, pain as well as pleasure. Since Alex had difficulty in reconciling himself to the fact that in order to master all things, the true magus carried the unshakable conviction that everything has its place in the order of magical lore and the universe; Martin was still unshakable in his own theory that all magic was fraudulent and, at times, perverted.

292

As an Adept of such ancient mystical belief, Charlotte had been schooled in the esoteric teaching that the universe, and everything in it, was the One, or Godhead, made manifest. And since man himself was the universe in miniature, by pursuing a path of spiritual expansion, he had the capability of attaining the highest pinnacle of knowledge; to reach out over the entire world and subjugate it to his will.

This then, was *her* reasoning behind her insistence in preserving the life-force that still burned in the Iceni. Although Antedios had developed his impressive shamanistic powers nine hundred years earlier, he had been trapped in a primitive time-warp which had prevented him from undergoing the natural process of death and re-birth.

Those strange, mystical qualities that set such beings apart from the rest of the human race, should have the opportunity to return with their message of divine wisdom; and if it were a question of whether to sacrifice the immense spiritual potential of Antedios for the life of John Sinclair, there was no hesitation in her answer. Sinclair would have the chance to work out his *karma* in his own way, but if Antedios were to perish, he would be lost forever.

Charlotte experienced the penetrating astral cold as she waited for Antedios for the last time in the moonlit clearing. The full moon was two days away and it was time to send him on his journey of death and re-birth. His form moved through the trees towards her but this time the haughty demeanour was replaced by thinly disguised fear - almost as if he sensed the final trial he was about to undertake. He stood facing her, a great bear of a man, whose limbs trembled with awe and uncertainty of the moment. This man, whose courage had remained steadfast in the face of the Roman legions; who had remained trapped as an earth-bound spirit to protect the daughters of Boudica, now balked at the uncertainty of his own release.

"It is time for you to begin your journey," she said softly.

His ancient eyes widened with apprehension of the unknown path his feet were to follow. "I am afraid, Lady."

"You have nothing to fear Antedios. It will be but a short time before your feet touch the earth again. Your trials as an earth-bound spirit have gained you nothing but honour."

"You would not deceive me, Lady? The Black One will die?"

"The sentence has been passed, his life is forfeit. On the night of the full moon he will die and you are free. My people will take up your burden of tending the dead."

The lined face of the Iceni turned upward to face the stars. There was wonderment and longing, and yet still a trace of humbleness in his demeanour. "Then I will bid you farewell and carry with me the wonder of your power."

For the first time Charlotte stretched out her hands, which the Iceni grasped firmly in his own, seeming anxious to delay the moment of parting. Falling to his knees before her, Antedios gazed up into the face of the one who offered him peace. He felt her inner strength pour into his own depleted spirit-form and in that moment of brief astral contact, his great courage returned. Getting to his feet and stepping two paces backwards, Antedios bowed deeply in what appeared to be some form of ritual salute before his image began to fade.

"We will meet again Antedios. When the time is right our paths will cross again," responded Charlotte but her voice echoed in the emptiness of the forest clearing.

Chapter Twenty Four

Suddenly Alex felt the scales fall away from his eyes and as he faced Paul Kerrick across the book-lined study, he felt his anger mount apace with the fear and frustration. "Charlotte's going to kill Sinclair, isn't she?"

"Rather a melodramatic accusation isn't it?" responded the vet coolly, his impassive face betraying nothing.

"I don't think so. For weeks now she sits staring at the wall or disappears into the woods alone. She hardly eats or sleeps, and I can't get near her. I thought that Anna's funeral had unbalanced her mind but Charlotte's too strong for that. But *you* knew that and you said nothing! Then I realised what a damn fool I'd been. It wasn't after the funeral she changed, it was after that last coven meeting where you obviously decided that you couldn't leave Sinclair to the law. This is some form of purification ritual as the run-up to the pagan notion of retribution, isn't it."

"And how do you suggest Charlotte is going to carry out this act of vengeance? For months your scepticism had belittled all we believe and now you confront me with an accusation of possessing magical powers that you've previously denied us. You need to be extremely careful my dear Alex, before you accuse someone of plotting murder."

As always, they had him at a disadvantage. Alex could feel his own hysteria mounting while Paul remained cool and aloof, almost indifferent to his suffering. The dark eyes glittered angrily and Alex understood that the vet would be an extremely dangerous enemy if he thought for a moment that Charlotte was threatened.   He had come to ask for support in convincing Charlotte she needed medical help but he now realised that appeal would be pointless.

"You're nothing but a bunch of freaks!   Setting yourselves up as judge and jury because ..."

"Because *WHAT*, Alex?   Because the legal processes in which you have such faith will refuse to exact a just and rightful penalty for the murder of one of our own people and   the child of another?   Because the council for the defence will try to destroy Charlotte's reputation in court in order to justify his client's actions?   It might be the law, but in my book, that's not justice."

"Charlotte's not worried about it?"

"Isn't she?   In the past the attacks have been by religious fanatics and   whereas   they've been widely quoted in the tabloids, no real harm has been done.   This time we're talking   about   a man claiming the credit for, God knows how many murders, because he plans to undermine Charlotte's professional reputation in court. Do you realise what will result from that sort of sensationalism?   It's not just a question of a few bookshops refusing to sell her books, you're talking about her life's work being destroyed. I don't know about you Alex but *I'll* not stand by and let that happen!"

"So you've put a curse on him?"   Alex's voice still carried a hint of mockery that Paul found impossible to ignore.

"How could we possibly do that?   We've listened to your biting irony, endured your derision and smiled benignly at your dismissal of our explanations.   We've suffered your taunts and tolerated your lack of spiritual development.   Why have we suddenly been accredited with such ability?"

Knowing himself to be manoeuvred into a corner, Alex felt his self control snap.   Leaping to his feet, he faced his rival across the desk.   Once again, it was the lover who had shown himself to be treacherous and doubting, while the friend remained steadfast and loyal. The realisation only served to fuel his anger and clenching his fists, he forced himself to control his desire to smash that handsome, glacial mask that regarded him so impassively.

"It would give you a great deal of satisfaction if I moved out, wouldn't it, Paul? But what if I went to the police and told them what I know?" he added lamely.

Paul features dissolved into laughter. "Alex, you're the biggest bloody fool I've ever met. Sit down."

Deflated the journalist sank back into the chair, taking with a trembling hand the cigarette Paul offered him . "Paul, I don't know what to do. I'd walk fire for her if I thought it would help but I can't take any more of this rejection. Can you imagine what it's like lying next to a woman who drives you crazy and not being able to touch her?" he asked without thinking. "Sorry. That was thoughtless."

Kerrick's facial muscles softened. "Charlotte isn't going to kill *anyone*. Besides, the fate of Sinclair was decided by the group unanimously; one person alone cannot assume that burden. It's in the hand of Deity now."

"But Sinclair *is* going to die?"

Paul shrugged. "You've actually seen the Iceni and his handiwork. If he's not appeased, then the killings will continue."

Alex blew a stream of smoke towards the ceiling. "But the Iceni, according to Charlotte, is already dead."

"He's in ... limbo. Death is merely an interruption, a brief interposition before the soul continues on its course of spiritual development. Our friend needs to be put back on the Path."

"So how will Sinclair die?" Alex persisted.

"The maxim of any occultist is To Know, To Dare, To Will and To Keep Silent. But I think I can say that Anna's killer will die by his own hand. You've seen enough since you've lived at Hunter's Moon, not to doubt the existence of magic. Go to Charlotte. She needs your guardianship although you

297

might find that hard to believe in the light of what's happened. Trust her and try to understand, because without that trust, you have no place in each other's lives."

She wasn't at home when he arrived but surprisingly enough a copy of Lewis's novel, *The Monk,* lay unopened on the hall table. Then he remembered the contractors had been hired to clear the protective fencing away from the stone circle and he guessed that would be where he would find her. Approaching through the woods, he could hear the sounds from the burial pit excavation but it was far enough away from the circle not to intrude on their privacy.

Charlotte was sitting on a fallen oak tree outside the circle and although she must have heard his approach, she made no effort to turn. Finally he lit two cigarettes and passed one over her shoulder.

"It's a long time since we've come out here."

"Things seem to get in the way," she responded but the sharp edge of rejection was no longer there.

Taking advantage of the almost imperceptible softening, Alex pushed home his cause. "I've let you down again, haven't I?"

"You're still here."

"The question is, do you still want me here? I'm trapped in a quagmire of something I don't understand and that frightens me. I don't want to be an outsider, Charlotte. I don't want to be shut out of the greater part of your life - because that's what has happened."

"Do you believe in God?"

He hesitated before answering. "Not in the Christian concept of the omnipresent being sitting in judgement on man's foibles. But I do believe in a Universal Creator. Something rather than someone."

"Then why can't your indefinable 'something' be the same as mine? The only difference between you and I, is that I have been a seeker for a long time and have reached my goal.

298

We all have the divine spark, Alex. It takes very little to step onto the Path."

Charlotte stubbed out the cigarette, carefully putting the remainder in her pocket. In silence they walked towards the circle where grass had already been clipped by her neighbour's sheep. The ground surrounding the stones was badly scarred where the workmen had torn the metal posts from the earth, exposing the rich dark loam beneath the surface.

Like the earth their relationship was badly scarred but those ragged wounds could be healed. The antagonism between them had already evaporated and the peace of the woodland seemed far removed from the nights of fear, frustration and lonliness. For the first time in weeks, he put his arm around her shoulders in a gesture of friendship rather than love; he would wait for her to be ready.

The spring woods were full of bird song and as the late afternoon sunlight reached down through the trees, Alex spotted something bright at the centre of the circle. There in the short grass, in the exact centre of the ancient stones, lay a heavy gold torc. Charlotte's eyes followed his and for a moment they stared at the twisted gold skeins glinting in the sun's rays, recognising it as the ornament worn by the Iceni whenever he appeared.

Alex stepped forward and picked it up, marvelling at the intricate workmanship that had gone into producing such an exquisite badge of office. Teasingly he placed it around her neck, amused at the incongruous effect of an ancient Briton's handicraft against the black designer knitwear of the 20th century. Despite the humour, they both realised the significance of the torc being left inside the stone circle.

There was no sign of mud or clay in the deep carvings which suggested that it had not been discovered by the excavators. Neither would a professional like Jonathon Boyd leave such a priceless artifact lying on the ground. It was improbable that a thief had dropped it, since the sheer weight of the torc would have drawn attention to its loss. The fact that it had

299

been carefully placed in the exact centre of the circle, sug-gested that the gesture was deliberate. Had the Iceni left a final message in this offering?

"Is it all over?" Alex asked cautiously.

Charlotte brushed her dark hair away from her eyes and squinted into the dying rays of the sun. The fiery orb had turned the ancient woodland into a surrealist landscape of blood with darker shadows cast by the trees reaching out across the forest floor. The effect of orange light through dappled leaves cast her features in bronze as she listened to the emptiness and silence caused by the Iceni's departure.

"Yes. It is finished. Antedios has finally begun his journey home to his Queen."

John Sinclair lay back on the cot in his cell and allowed the final surge of adrenalin to flow through his body. After lasting a five hour interrogation he knew he'd fooled the psychiatrist with his feigned descent into madness. His solicitor had pleaded with him not to confess to being The Ashmarsh Beast but Sinclair had been adamant. He knew Alan Morris well enough to realise that the case against him for the murder of Anna Fenton would be sewn so tightly that no barrister was going get him off.

His guilt-ridden conscience had also triggered the spon-taneous need to 'witness' and with the admission of killing the two girls, without a doubt, he would be in for a life stretch. It wasn't the fear of incarceration that worried him, it was the punishment metered out by fellow prisoners to sex offenders and child-murderers that he dreaded. Added to the fact that he was a policeman, his future behind bars was extremely bleak.

Years in the force had shown him just how eager senior officers were to close an investigation, especially one that had no prime suspects, and by offering them a serial killer he would guarantee his safety in a secure prison wing. While Morris wouldn't be convinced, any objections he raised would be swiftly quashed by his superiors. His biggest difficulty was convincing the medical team that he wasn't responsible for his actions.

He had been fearful of the consequences of those actions - a fear that was spiritual rather than temporal. Nevertheless, even that apprehension evaporated after a private visit from the Rev. Samuel Tyrrwhitt. Sinclair had expected censor but instead the minister was euphoric that a member of his own flock had struck a blow for the Lord in striking at Charlotte Manning and her evil teachings. There was nothing the Lord loved more than a crusader and Sinclair was more than willing to embroider his reputation with the blessing of the gullible Tyrrwhitt.

Although his psychiatric examiner was less generous, even he failed to shake Sinclair's resolve. When asked how he had managed to commit the murders without leaving footprints in the snow or muddy ground, he merely replied that God had guided him. "He's either the most fiendish killer since Jack the Ripper, or he's a bloody sight cleverer than the whole lot of us," complained his psychiatrist to a colleague during their lunch break. "And *I* can't bloody well tell which it is."

Having worked as Morris's Sergeant during the earlier investigations, Sinclair had no trouble in describing the grisly murder scenes and station gossip had provided enough detail for him to *ad lib* his way through the murders at the barn, even though he had not been privy to those particular en-quiries. Morris protested furiously against the plea but was over-ruled by the Grimme Reaper - John Sinclair was given credit for all the murders! Politics had won, not the judicial system.

As the prison grew quiet around him, Sinclair reached for his bible. Try as he might, his mind would not focus on the words. In private he needed to turn to his faith for comfort and try to find some form of justification for his crimes but he was finding it more and more difficult to concentrate. His earlier excitement drained away, leaving him depleted

301

and depressed. He began pacing the cell and as guilt broke over him like a wave, he leaned against the painted brick wall and began to cry.

As the sobs receded he became aware of a tinkling, whispering sound that seemed to come from the far corner of the cell. Tiny pinpricks of light danced before his eyes and as he stared in fascination, the shimmering particles grouped together to produce a tangible shape of two young girls, barely more than children. They appeared unaware of his watching eyes and suddenly he was transported into a sunlit glade as the girls danced away some distance ahead of him. Clad in thin diaphanous robes which did little to conceal the swelling of adolescent breasts, they glided gracefully between tall neolithic monuments that grew out of the ground like savage teeth.

The girls playfully chased each other between the standing stones oblivious to the monster that watched them from the undergrowth. The inner circle was still illuminated by sunlight filtering through the trees; outside the stones, dark shadows began to creep stealthily forward. Sinclair wanted to cry out and warn them but his voice was stifled in his throat. Watching from gloom he saw the shadows reach the edge of the circle as the girls became aware of the danger. Girlish faces transformed by terror to hideous masks of nightmare.

Sinclair turned to grapple with the monster and the sight confronting him turned his own blood to ice. The huge menacing creature was nothing more than a hideous caricature of himself, grinning savagely at the prospect of the brutal slaying and mutilation that was to come. Frantically he battered against the mass that was trying to engulf him but the *doppleganger* brushed him casually aside and lumbered forward into the circle ...

The rattling of keys in the cell door brought him to his senses and the realisation that he was screaming and battering the walls with his fists, which were now broken and bleeding. Two prison officers surveyed the bloodied walls and the hysterical man who now lay on the cot sobbing and babbling wildly.

"It was just a nightmare, son," muttered the elder of the two but he indicated that his colleague should not delay in calling for the doctor.

If Dr Preston and his colleagues hoped that Sinclair would break under the strain, they were doomed to disappointment. Heavily sedated, he tried to find his salvation in love and allowed his thoughts to drift over his brief affair with Anna, recalling to mind the sweet smell of her perfume and the laughter in her voice. The bright hospital ward was less threatening to him than the solitary prison cell, even if the staff were watching his every move.

Anna's face hovered inches from his own and he felt himself smile at her memory. He remembered that first morning in the woods when he'd met her and had been unable to forget the beautiful creamy skin and teasing blue eyes, framed by luxuriant red hair. He remembered that first night they'd spent together under Charlotte Manning's roof. There was no doubt in his mind that he'd loved her but what he could not forgive was her unswerving loyalty to the arch-purveyor of evil, whose books polluted naive and receptive minds.

On several occasions he'd tried to explain how, under the innocent guise of mystery writing, Charlotte Manning extended her influence in the global satanic conspiracy to overthrow decent spiritual values. The deepening scowl on his face was noticed by the staff nurse as Sinclair recalled how Anna had laughed in his face and ridiculed his claims. The more he tried to reason with her, the angrier she became and was more than a match for his arguments; it was then that he realised just how strong the hold the Manning woman had on her. In desperation he had even gone so far as to drive her to the evangelical church and begging her unsuccessfully to pray with him, had tried to drag her inside. She had retaliated by slapping his face.

The light over the night desk gave Sinclair something on

which to focus. He had hoped that the sedative would have given him the sleep he so desperately needed but so far it had evaded him. Suddenly there was a popping noise as the bulb went out and his eyes became slowly accustomed to the darkness and the dim light from the corridor. Then he caught the sound of rustling garments accompanied by a high pitched tinkling sound, similar to that which has preceded his dream from the night before.

The smell of damp earth and decay reached his nostrils causing an involuntary shudder for all men, waking or sleeping, recognise the stench of the grave. The swirl of tiny lights reappeared, then condensed into a swirl of mist by the window as a form began to grow, silhouetted against the night sky. Outside he could see the moon hanging low in the heavens as the chilling light streamed in through the reinforced glass.

Slowly the simulacrum that Charlotte Manning had conjured up for her bogus seance, manifested itself at the bedside. The green tinge to the features distorted the beauty of the memory that had been in his thoughts all afternoon. Hollow-eyed, the cadaver leaned forward and as the mouth opened in a kiss, vipers dropped out of the yawning jaws and eye sockets. The bloodied wounds that had appeared so dramatically on the shroud during the seance, were now gaping holes of decomposing flesh. The entire hospital ward erupted with screams.

The following night Dr. Charles Preston walked with his colleague across the car park. The rain lashed across the concrete as high winds tossed the branches of the yew trees lining the drive. He'd given Sinclair a sedative large enough to comatose an elephant in the hope that the man would allow the hospital to pass the night in relative calm.

"At least he can't do himself any damage while he's in the rubber room," sympathised his colleague.

"I wouldn't be so sure," replied the older man. "By all the laws of chemistry he shouldn't have been able to get out of the bed last night but he was up and smashing into the windows like a thing possessed. Whatever it is that's ailing him, it isn't responding to modern medicine."

His colleague studied him across the roof of the car. "Guilty conscience?"

"Lawson won't have it and he's the psychiatrist. My job only requires me to keep the buggers fit and healthy - physically. Their sordid minds I leave to Lawson to pick over."

"But you must have an opinion."

"Wouldn't matter if I did but I'll tell you this much, whatever is bothering our friend is a damn sight more effective than medicine or his love of God. And whatever it is, I hope it gets him. He might try to feign madness to get out of standing trial but that counterfeit madness will eventually consume him entirely. May the Lord have mercy on his soul."

As the tail lights of Preston's car disappeared through the thick yew trees, his colleague stopped and shivered. "Well, he's picked a good night for it!" he muttered.

The dark clouds were racing across the sky in abandoned fury - one moment the night was black as pitch, the next illuminated by the brilliant full moon. The young doctor shivered again as he unlocked his car in the deep shadow cast by the yews. He wanted to be at home in front of a blazing fire not standing here in the rain-swept grounds of a Victorian asylum, watching the menacing clouds form into the shapes of strange creatures, as they hurled themselves across the face of the moon.

John Sinclair sat hunched in the corner of the room, his head resting on the bandages that now covered both arms from hand to shoulder. The grisly grave-form had drawn him towards the window until, in sheer desperation, he had tried to destroy the fiendish shape that mocked him from the glass. No matter how hard he tried to conjure up the real image of Anna, this disgusting nightmare intruded on his senses, waking and sleeping.

"I thought it was time for us to talk, my friend," a deep

voice echoed around the small room and in the corner, barely discernible by the dim ceiling-light, Sinclair could make out the form of a man.

"Who are you?" he asked, not really caring who this nocturnal visitor might be. If it was someone against whom he could pit his wits, then the phantoms could be kept at bay.

There was a deep, throaty chuckle. "You mean you don't recognise me. And you've been doing my bidding for all this time?"

The prisoner peered into the gloom. He could barely make out the figure of a large, muscular man reclining against the padded wall until with a sudden shock, he realised his visitor was entirely naked. Hurriedly he got to his feet. He'd heard of sexual assaults on inmates and he wanted to be ready to fend off any attack. Almost as though the stranger was reading his thoughts, another chuckle echoed in the confined space as he stepped into the direct beam of the overhead lighting.

Sinclair almost gagged with revulsion. The glistening skin, reflected light and shadow as his gaze travelled along the hard, knotted muscles of the powerful creature before him. Black hair curled over the broad chest and down the flat stomach, into the groin which was shrouded in shadow. In the darkness the hair seemed to extend over the thighs but Sinclair could not be sure if his imagination was playing tricks in revealing a cloven hoof.

For some reason he dare not look into the man's face for fear of what he might see. "It's time to honour your pact, John."

Sharply his head jerked up to confront the angular features that composed a darkly handsome countenance, a finely curved mouth and finely chiselled nose. The eyes, yellow like a cat's and mocking, were intelligent under the close fitting helmet made from enormous ram's horns. A pungent musky odour permeated the cell and John Sinclair realised he had finally come face to face with the Devil.

"I made no pact with you! I put my faith in Jesus."

The apparition howled with laughter that shook the foundations of the building. "You made the pact the day you watched from the shadows and planned the murder of the two young girls. Did you enjoy the warmth of their blood on your hands, John? Were all my disciples as malleable as you."

"I'm not your disciple," replied the prisoner, hysteria beginning to rise in his voice. "I'm a disciple of Jesus!"

"Obviously Christianity has taken a turn for the better," responded the demon amiably. "Nevertheless, you re-affirmed your pact when you killed the beautiful, innocent Anna. Did you enjoy her, John? That lovely creamy skin. Such a delectable creature and so faithful and pure ..."

"She was your servant," interrupted Sinclair with passion. "That was why she had to die."

"Oh, that she were!" chuckled the visitor. "But also, no. You got it wrong John, my friend. Your Anna was no disciple of Lucifer, no Devil's handmaiden but I can't possibly let you make such sacrifices for nothing. We have no choice other than to welcome you into the fold, so are you ready?"

"Ready for what?" Sinclair pushed back against the wall. He could sense a change in the demon's attitude and his fear began to grow. He held out the bible at arm's length as if to keep the creature at bay. "I put my faith in God. I am his servant, not yours."

The demon plucked the bible from the outstretched hands and deftly flicked through the pages. "In that case, John, I think you'll find that you've been made redundant! I don't think you'll find a lot of forgiveness in the old boy since you've blamed him for all your misdemeanours, and a few others besides. Ah, here we are! *Thou shalt not take the name of the Lord thy God in vain; for the Lord will not hold him guiltless that taketh his name in vain.*'"

With the ease of a child destroying a comic book, the demon tore the bible into tiny pieces and scattered them

307

about the room. The flimsy fragments whirled around as the finely manicured hand reached out and seized Sinclair's bandaged arm in a vice like grip. Before the terrified man knew what was happening, he was rising up through the air, blasting through timber and slate under the impetus of the rapid aerial ascent. Higher and higher the demon flew above the roof of the hospital wing, until Sinclair's face was blinded by wind and icy rain.

The dark storm clouds overhead parted briefly to reveal the sharp brilliance of the full moon. Looking into the cold face of the lunar disc, Sinclair saw another face that filled him with even more terror. A face so full of contempt and loathing that it terrified him even more than the awful creature that still held him firmly in its grasp. Suddenly he screamed as the demon released his hold, and he fell spiralling down toward the cobbled courtyard in the centre of the hospital complex.

In the seconds before his body hit the ground, John Sinclair knew he had indeed come face to face with the Devil - his own conscience. Hundreds of pages, torn from the bible and fanned by the wind, swirled in the air above until caught by the driving rain, they fell to the ground.

A wet fragment settled on the broken face of the corpse, the lettering clearly readable in the moonlight -

"Thou shalt not kill."